DARK DAYS IN DIXIE

JAMES LEE

PublishAmerica
Baltimore

First printing

ISBN: 1-4137-3540-1
PUBLISHED BY PUBLISHAMERICA, LLLP
www.publishamerica.com
Baltimore

Printed in the United States of America

To my beloved, Ammie

To write a novel is to embark on a voyage over uncharted waters with no compass or map—only an idea and your imagination to move your fingers from one key to the next. It can be a lonely journey unless one is blessed with family, friends, and associates who share your enthusiasm and support you if only with an unsolicited "How's the book going?" or "I can't wait to read it." Simple words, but powerful motivation, like bread to a starving man. I am blessed with many such supporters, and they have contributed to the completion of this novel in many ways. Listed below are only a few.

To Patty, who critically edited my first work: thanks for challenging my creative processes.

To Aunt Vicki and Uncle Richard, who have gratuitously labored through original drafts: the finished product reads better for your input.

To Robin, who lends her professional experience to the editorial process: I might not have finished this work without your encouragement.

To my fishing buddy and fellow writer, Mike, who has followed this journey with interest and who suffered with me through every rejection letter: thanks for being a dear friend.

To the Friday night dinner group: your optimism motivated me on many occasions.

And, lastly, to my wife and my best friend, Ammie: without you, none of this would matter.

PROLOGUE

May 2, 1963. The tension was only slightly mitigated by the exhilaration of the mission. As the two pickups rolled to a stop, both drivers sighed with relief. Negotiating the pitted road in darkness had made a few minutes seem like hours. They were close to their destination, and for the next quarter-of-a-mile, success would depend on stealth and a little luck. A barking dog, the explosive wingbeat of flushing quail, or the crack of a broken twig could spell disaster. Anonymous completion of their task would be the only acceptable measure of success—anything less would bring the federal government to their doorsteps and add fuel to a raging wildfire of public disdain and indignation.

The young leader had been careful in the selection of the raiding party. Each man had been chosen for his allegiance to their cause and dedication to their way of life—one that was fading as the outside world became more aware and more punitive toward its champions.

They moved deliberately, holding close to the underbrush and pines lining the narrow passageway. The timbers they carried were slick and awkward to manage. The pallid glow from a window became visible, and their pace slowed even more. One of them fell, his ankle twisting when the edge of a rut gave way beneath his heavy frame. He wanted to cry out but understood the cost. The others moved forward, committed to finishing the task with or without him.

Thirty yards from where the road opened into the yard, the leader halted. Changing course, the remaining men followed him into the bush, where every step had to be measured else surprise could be lost. Reaching a small break in the underbrush, where deer and livestock had rested to escape the afternoon sun, they lowered their burden to the ground and began the task of assembly without benefit of hammer or nail—only baling wire.

7

"Sally, come in here. I've got a surprise for you. We got another letter from your brother. Tell your aunt to come in here, too," he announced from his worn, overstuffed chair. "Bring me my bifocals."

"Okay, Uncle Aaron," answered the excited fourteen-year-old. "Aunt Lizzie, where are you?"

"In the root cellar. Whatcha need, child?"

A dull light flickered between the cracks in the floor planks.

"Uncle Aaron wants you to come up. We got a letter from Bubby!"

"Coming. I need to put out the candles."

Within a few minutes, the three of them were gathered in the living room. Elizabeth Collins sat on the tattered sofa while Sally took a position on the floor—her knees tucked under her chin. With little fanfare, Aaron began reading another epistle from the first member of the extended Collins family to attend college. As the words were lifted from the page, each of them smiled, pride radiating from their faces.

"Read it again, Uncle Aaron," Sally pleaded.

"Tell you what, you go help your aunt finish up what she's doing while I check on the mules. I'll read it again when we're finished."

"Goodie!" exclaimed the youngster as she leaped to her feet, pulling her aunt up from the couch.

Aaron walked to the corner behind the door, retrieved a kerosene lantern, and strolled out on the porch. Raising the wick, he struck a match and lowered the globe. He paused on the steps and inhaled. The aroma of honeysuckle and the chirping of crickets reinforced the contentment he felt. Making his way toward the barn, the beads of perspiration went unnoticed as his skin responded to the ever-present humidity of South Alabama.

"There he is," whispered the young leader, standing in the shadows of the pine forest.

"Do we take him now?" came a nasal response filled with Alabama redneck.

"Not yet. I want them all in one place."

"I still don't feel right about this. You sure he went on that march on Birmingham last month?" challenged one of the others. "I been knowing Aaron Collins all of my life and ain't never seen him act like no uppity nigger."

"We already been ova this! Enough of this mealy-mouth nonsense," announced the leader in a voice filled with emotion and louder than intended.

The lantern abruptly stopped moving by a massive oak tree. Aaron called out, "Somebody out there?"

The five men froze. A few seconds passed, and the lantern began moving again.

Upon his return, Aaron closed and bolted the door before extinguishing the flame of the lantern—something he would normally have done before entering the house. Although he'd convinced himself the breeze through the pines had played tricks with his hearing, he remained uneasy.

"Read it again, Uncle Aaron!" chirped Sally as she sprang through the kitchen door, her aunt close behind her. "Please."

Her enthusiasm was contagious, and all thoughts of the phantom voice became a distant consideration. Retrieving his glasses, he seated himself as before. Elizabeth and Sally took their places as he began to read again.

The only warning was a barely audible *Swshhh* followed by a dull glow that silhouetted the windowpanes on the wall opposite the door. Two detonations rocked the house as the front windows imploded. Like miniature meteorites, shards of glass chased the buckshot across the room. Elizabeth was seated in the direct path of the force.

Aaron leaped to his feet; his eyes flashed to his wife. Dozens of red droplets blanketed her exposed skin. Her eyes snapped shut; her expression projected pain; a guttural utterance preceded her head dropping into her hands.

Sally, whose position on the floor had saved her from the projectiles, screamed and lurched toward her aunt. Grabbing at her wrists, she jerked Elizabeth's hands from her face, now masked in blood. Her eyelids were tight slits—rivulets of crimson flowed from each.

Terror flooded Sally's young face. Her voice trembled and she cried out, "Please don't be dead! Please don't be dead!"

"Aaron Collins, come out here!" a voice bellowed from the yard.

Aaron heard the words, but his mind wasn't listening. Helping his poor Lizzie was all he could think about.

"Hey, nigger! You best get your black ass out here before we burn you out!" another voice commanded.

As the worst soaked in, he softly touched his wife's hair, turned, and sighed. Tears filled his eyes as he trudged toward the door. He paused as a thought crossed his mind.

"Sally, can you help your aunt to the root cellar?"

She continued mumbling, "Please don't be dead. Please don't be dead."

Hoping to buy a few seconds, he yelled, "I'm coming out! Just a minute, I'm coming out!"

"Don't you be bringing no gun with you, or we'll shoot you down on the spot," the leader threatened.

Gently touching his niece's shoulder, he whispered, "Sally, can you hear me?"

Her eyes were glazed, and a sobbing voice continued the chant, "Please don't be dead."

Cradling her limp body in his arms, Aaron carried her to the trapdoor leading to the root cellar. After securing her below, he returned for his wife, who was leaning quietly against the back of the sofa.

"Lizzie, can you move?"

"Aaron, I can't see. Everything's black," she whimpered. "Just let me rest here for a minute."

Tears continued to flow over Aaron's cheeks as he looked into the mangled face, once the most beautiful he had ever seen. Eyes that had sparkled with life were only sunken depressions in a mass of blood.

"That'll be just fine, my sweet, sweet Lizzie. You just rest here for awhile, and everything's gonna be just fine."

Resolved, Aaron reached over the door, retrieving the shotgun he had only used to kill rabbits and squirrels to supplement their meager table. He felt the metallic click as both barrels were readied for firing. Holding the weapon behind one of his legs, he stepped onto the porch.

The brilliance of the flaming cross forced his eyes to blink. Straining, he could vaguely distinguish five silhouettes positioned beside the symbol of racial hatred.

"Aaron Collins, you've violated the laws of the South, and you must pay," announced the figure holding a straw torch. The voice, although muffled by the sheet, sounded familiar.

"Who are you? What've I done? I've not broken any laws," Aaron responded, assessing the strength of his adversaries.

"Our negras don't have no right to participate in protest marches," the leader shouted, pointing the flaming straw toward his quarry.

"Protest marches? I've never marched in anything. All I've ever done is work this land for the Pendletons and raise my family here in my home," he declared. Defiance filled his voice.

"We ain't gonna stand here all night arguing with some lying negra," proclaimed the leader. "Let's get on with it, boys!"

In one rapid motion, Aaron swung the shotgun to the front, firing both barrels. The leader's right leg was thrust backward, throwing him to the ground.

"Shit!" he screeched. "The son of a bitch shot me! Kill him! Kill him now!"

Aaron leapt from the porch and began running for the forest, praying they would follow. Glancing over his shoulders, he saw his pursuers lumbering over the ground, their sheets flowing behind them. He heard the discharge of a carbine and sensed the heat of the projectile as it flashed over his shoulder. His heart pounded as adrenaline filled his legs with power and speed he had never before possessed.

Two more shots were erratically fired into the darkness as his pursuers began to falter—each gasping for air—each fearing the mission was lost.

The one who had stumbled before the raid began watched the scene unfold from a distance. Hobbling between the pines, he estimated the intersection of a tangential course. Breathing heavily, attempting to ignore each painful step, he watched as his prey began to slow his pace. The stalker smiled.

"I lost them!" Aaron cried out.

As his body slowed, his mind began to churn. Reaching into his pocket, he retrieved two more shells, fumbling with the shotgun. His hands trembled as one shell slid into a chamber, the other falling to the ground.

"I've...I've got to go back for Lizzie and Sally," he gasped, his chest heaving for much needed air.

He heard a shot in the distance and his heart pounded harder. "Oh, my God, they've shot her!"

Another blast echoed through the pine boughs and his muscles tensed, nausea swept over him. "Sally? Oh, Lord, please help me. I've got to—"

Before he could finish, he felt a sharp pain in the back of his neck, and, then, nothing.

His head throbbed and his throat burned when he regained consciousness. Aaron struggled to free his arms and hands from their tight bindings. Opening his eyes, he looked down on the men still clad in sheets. Even in his confused state, he noticed two of his attackers supporting a third, whose covering displayed a distinct reddish stain. Turning his head, he could see the house, and his eyes began desperately searching for any sign of his beloved wife and niece. Looking upward, he could vaguely make out the shadowy branches of the large oak tree beneath which he and his family had shared Sunday picnics from the time he was a small boy.

"He looks alert enough now," proclaimed the wounded one. "Kick that barrel, and let's watch the sucker dance."

Aaron felt his body drop, his neck muscles constricting in a futile effort to support his weight. In a matter of seconds, he was dead. His last thought was, *Lizzie.*

With the body swaying in the breeze, one of the Klansmen asked, "What about the woman? And I thought there was suppose to be a young nigger girl? We looked everywhere: the attic, root cellar, barn—everywhere we could think of. You want us to burn 'em out?"

"Hell no! That's my property, you idiot. You say his wife's in on the couch, and there's no sign of the girl?" scowled the leader, pain radiating from his knee.

"Yeah, I think the woman's blind. Her face looks like someone took an ice pick to her."

"Well, get me inside and we'll finish this thing. Get this bloody sheet off me and get me that negra's shotgun."

CHAPTER 1

FIRST IMPRESSIONS

I never liked W.C. Fields, which is to say, I didn't like the character he portrayed—a stereotype blowhard, the clever gibe, always drinking or joking about it. He reminded me of a blown up penguin in a wrinkled suit. Perhaps it was the likeness, both in appearance and demeanor, but from the beginning, I didn't like Judge Raleigh A. Pendleton either.

"Mules ain't stubborn, like some folks say," the judge proclaimed, whiskey in hand. "They're just a genetic accident—a strong enough body but lacking the brains to be of much use. Just like the negra. He ain't all bad—just not far enough up the evolutionary chain to carry the burden of freedom them Yankees imposed on him."

My first meeting with the judge was in February of 1996. The chosen venue was the bar in Ruth's Chris Steakhouse in Mobile. A mutual business associate, Leander H. Rutherford, had arranged the meeting. Leander had often boasted, during the two years I had known him, he was in the inner circle of the movers and shakers of the Alabama political establishment, without whom nothing of financial importance could be accomplished in the state George Wallace had ruled.

This particular location had been chosen for its reputation as the watering hole for the politically powerful. For three decades, since Mrs. Fertel expanded her epicurean empire from its humble beginnings in New Orleans to numerous locations around the world, this bar in Mobile had allegedly welcomed such notables as Governor Wallace, Senator Edward Kennedy, several Democratic presidential hopefuls, and the infamous Governor Edwin

Edwards of Louisiana, to name only a few. You might have noticed none of the listed is, or ever was, a member of the Grand Old Party, although a few Republicans have probably frequented this Democratic den just to piss off the good ol' boys.

"Now, Mista Mitchell, Leander here tells me you're expanding your trash business into Alabama through the purchase of the Jefferson Construction Company here in Mobile," proclaimed the judge while sipping straight sour-mash whiskey. A flushed face and swollen eyelids suggested the judge and Jack Daniel's were more than casual acquaintances.

"That's correct, Judge. Leander searched out Mr. Jefferson's company, which holds a couple of landfill permits, and I hope to expand that part of the company's business," I replied.

"Me and Leander's been friends for years, and any friend of Leander Rutherford's a friend of mine."

Rutherford, also of the swollen eyelids, smiled triumphantly as if the judge had knighted him. "Mighty nice of you to say so, Judge. Jack and me've formed kind of a partnership for his new venture. He provides the money, and I supply the sweat, and you know from past experience, I ain't never been afraid of hard work."

"Truer words never been spoken, I assure you, Mista Mitchell," added the judge while motioning to the waitress for another drink.

As I reflect on that initial conversation and the copious accolades exchanged between these two old men of the South, I have often wondered how much time they had spent rehearsing the dialogue for my benefit. The evening was filled with affirmations that Leander was indeed a member in-good-standing of the party, and the judge could be counted on for support. You see, I hadn't yet closed on the Jefferson Construction deal, and Leander was pulling out all stops to convince me that South Alabama was the place to do business. While I was not naïve to the ways of dealing by that time in my career, I remain embarrassed that I was drawn into the web of a system I was incapable of understanding. It was a life-changing experience, and I've regretted it ever since.

CHAPTER 2

LEANDER

The oldest of seven children, Leander Rutherford had been born during the Depression on a small farm in northern Mobile County. Unlike his parents and their parents before them, he had yearned for a life more invigorating than the drudgery of toiling the soil from dawn until dusk. A demanding father had created within him a healthy work ethic, but Leander's most notable characteristic was a gregarious nature, bordering on hypertensive. His enthusiasm was often contagious, even to those most suspicious of his intentions. He never met a stranger, but his exaggerated personality often set people aback.

After graduating from high school, he attempted to join the Navy to escape the expected role of working on the farm for the joint benefit of his siblings and parents. Flat feet frustrated his efforts to enlist, however, and for the first time in his life, he ignored the demands of his father, taking, instead, a construction job in Mobile as post-war America and the returning GIs created an acute shortage of housing.

His free time was spent hanging around the pool halls, bars, and barbershops, listening to the old timers talk of Alabama politics, Klan activity, and how fortunes had been made and lost by enterprising young men who learned to work within the system. Such conversations lit a fire in him, and he became obsessed with claiming his place in Alabama folklore.

By the time he was forty, he had started Rutherford Construction Company and gained a reputation within the city and county political structure as a man who could be counted on for payoffs, kickbacks, and other forms of illegal, although totally acceptable, practices within the system.

Emerging political hopefuls and established incumbents could always rely on Leander for contributions in return for fat road construction projects or favorable rulings relative to the questionable business practices he employed. For fifteen years, the sun shined brightly on Leander.

By 1988, Rutherford Construction had grown to become one of the largest construction companies in South Alabama, and Leander's ego had swollen to enormous heights. Cheating the taxman had become an art form. Padding construction costs to payoff city and county officials were a way of life. When the full effects of Reagan's Tax Reform Act of 1986 were felt across the country, Leander found himself up to his neck in debt and with a construction business failing at a meteoric pace.

Not to be deterred, Leander increased his borrowings and stowed the proceeds in numbered bank accounts in the Cayman Islands and Switzerland. Too late, his lenders realized they were collateralized with inflated assets as the bank examiners began to question the validity of the loans made to Rutherford Construction. Leander, true to his nature, placed the company in bankruptcy and retired to his homestead, letting the chips fall as they may.

Some of his creditors were mortally wounded, and the name Rutherford fashioned a new definition of business dishonesty in and around Mobile. But also true to the Alabama political system, his exploits and misdoings became almost legendary, and he continued to enjoy a certain amount of guarded respect within the party.

His standing with the political power brokers became his primary focus in life, and within three years, most of the money he had stashed had been contributed to senators, judges, gubernatorial candidates, and anyone else who would massage his ego. As the money dwindled, so did the number of telephone calls he received. Invitations to fundraisers and clandestine meetings to discuss political strategy for the upcoming elections became only fond memories of days gone by.

By the end of 1992, Leander was broke, starved for political affection, and over half-a-million dollars in tax liens had been filed against anything he owned, including his beloved homestead. The need to eat forced him back into the business world. The only unattached asset he possessed was his incredible line of bullshit, and he began beating the bushes for any business deal he could put together and sell.

March 16, 1998. "Jack!" exclaimed Leander when I answered his call. "I've found the dam'dest opportunity of my lifetime. We'll make millions."

Since closing on the Jefferson Construction deal over two years earlier, this wasn't the first time I had heard words such as these from my business associate. It had taken me only a few months to speculate that Leander H. Rutherford's middle initial probably stood for hyperbole. Every conversation was filled with exclamations such as "incredible," "extraordinary," "fifty million big ones," and so forth. While I was at first charmed by his enthusiasm, time and repetition were taking a toll, and his fantasies were becoming a frustration for me.

"What do you have, Leander?" I inquired with an imperceptible sigh.

"I don't want go into too much detail over the phone, but you need to come ova here and see for yourself."

Likewise, this was not the first time he had inferred that telephone conversations were not secure, and important matters should be discussed only in person.

"My schedule's pretty full for the next few weeks, Leander. Just give me an overall picture of the deal."

Undaunted, he charged on. "This's too huge to take any chances on, Jack. You need to get ova here soon as possible. Our window of opportunity could close at any minute, but I can say this much—I was at the bar last night and one of the city councilmen was loaded." Leander's voice then changed to a whisper, and I imagined him lowering his head, cutting his eyes side-to-side, alert for an imaginary eavesdropper. "They're getting' ready to lower the boom on Allied Aluminum for that mess they left out on the island. He said the cleanup could cost ova a hundred million, and with the right support downtown, we could get a big piece of the contract."

Now, let me translate what that means. In the late forties, an aluminum smelter had been built adjacent to Mobile Bay on a small deltaic piece of ground. At that time, the technology employed in the smelting process was environmentally unfriendly, but it would be decades before Green Peace, the Sierra Club or other such organization would raise any level of public interest in the decline of the snail darter populations in estuarial ecosystems, such as Mobile Bay.

Allied Aluminum had been the last owner of the smelter, and, when it became apparent the environmental cleanup expense would far exceed any profits derived from continued operations, the plant had been dismantled and the site abandoned. This occurred in 1981. In true Southern fashion, it was rumored that a deal had been cut with one, or a group, of the power brokers, and Allied simply walked away, leaving no trespassing signs, locked gates, and a cratered landscape unfit for any life form existing on the planet. It had long been anticipated there would be a public outcry for retribution, but to date, nothing of note has been done to correct the problem.

The second innuendo of Leander's cloak-and-dagger pronouncement was someone at city hall could be counted on for political support in our favor, for the right price.

"Leander, we've been through this before," I responded. "I've never paid a bribe in my life, and I don't intend to start now."

"Now, who said anything about a bribe? Hell, Jack, why're you always the Boy Scout? Always looking for the worst in every situation. You don't know how things gets done down here. It's a way of life, and you can either get with the program or get left in the dust."

"The dust is fine with me," I countered. "To a more immediate matter, the last quarterly statements for Delta Disposal and Jefferson Construction look like hell. What's going on down there?"

"That last construction job, ova at Harveyville, didn't turn out as good as we thought, and—"

"I thought we agreed if the construction company couldn't carry its weight, we'd either sell it or close the doors. I thought we were on the same page when I bought Jefferson."

"But, Jack, there's a lot more opportunity in the construction business down here than you realize. I've got three bids going out tomorrow on some really sweet projects that'll make us millionaires."

"Leander, I've been looking at the books for the last two years. We continue to make good money in the landfill business and then give it all back to the construction company. If you're so damned enamored with construction, why don't you make me an offer, and I'll sell you Jefferson. I'm in the waste disposal business, and I'm tired of subsidizing an activity I care nothing about. I'll be over there next month, and I want to come to some resolution on this matter."

"Billy!" Rutherford shouted from his desk. "Get in here."

"Coming, boss." The nasal twang was typical redneck.

Billy Cudjoe slithered in, dressed in stained overalls, tee shirt, a green John Deere cap, and steel-toed boots. Except for the cap, everything he wore appeared to be three sizes too big for his skeletal frame.

"What's up?" he asked before spitting into a Pepsi can—ever present when he was confined within a roof and manmade flooring.

18

"I need to talk to you about something important."

"That Harveyville road job was rough," he offered casually, exposing the tar triangles separating each of his lower teeth. He dripped into the can again.

"Yeah," replied Leander. "That damn county inspector screwed me good on that deal."

"Ain't it the truth. That greenhorn had his level stuck up my ass every day 'til we finished up. No way I could thin the base. That old road'll last twenty-five years if it lasts a week. Have you told Mista Jack we didn't come out so good on that deal?"

"Didn't get a chance. He saw the numbers and called me. He wasn't real happy, but we'll get them next two Washington County jobs, and the judge promised we'd be covered on those deals by one of his boys. Water under the bridge, but that's not why I called you in here. How're we coming on Miss Vivian's patio? I saw her last night, and she wants to have a barbecue a week from Sunday. I need that concrete poured damn quick like. I've invited the judge and some of his important friends ova."

"I can get the forms in place by tomorrow afternoon and have the pour made Friday morning, but where we gonna charge the materials off to? We ain't got no active concrete projects working right now."

"Code it to Harveyville. Hell, we're so far ova budget, another couple of thousand or so won't make no difference."

"What about Mista Jack? Thought you said he was already pissed off."

"He'll never know. I'll just tell him it was a late bill from the curbing contractor if he says anything, and Kenny damn sure won't make a big deal out of it. I got to get," he announced while putting on his suit coat. "I told Miss Vivian I'd take her to the bar for lunch. Get someone ova to her place an get them forms laid."

"You be back later?"

"Maybe about four. Hoping for a long lunch," he replied with a wink.

A matronly woman in her mid-fifties tapped on the door. "Mista Leander, Kenny wanted you to sign these checks. He had to go over to the bonding company."

Leander acknowledged Rosie Johnson, the newest addition to the office staff.

"What're they for?" he asked, reaching for a pen.

"Mostly payroll and a couple of small invoices."

Leander scribbled his name several times.

"Rosie, if anyone comes looking for me, tell them I'm out estimating a job. If my wife calls, tell her I may be out late at an important political meeting."

Rosie nodded and waddled back to the reception area.

Leander shook his head. "I don't know why in the hell I hired such an ugly, old woman for the front desk. Gives me cold chills ever time I see her."

"As I recall, you didn't hire her, boss. Miss Vivian done it just before she retired."

CHAPTER 3
FROM SIMPLE BEGINNINGS

For one hundred and twelve years, not a single Republican had occupied the governor's mansion. The Democratic Party's control over state politics seemed boundless until Republican underdog, Guy Hunt, took advantage of disharmony within the ranks and broke the string in the 1986 election, riding the wave of conservative popularity championed by Ronald Reagan and confirmed by his landslide victory over former Vice President Walter Mondale in 1984.

The leadership of the party was in disarray and embarrassed. The spoils of victory turned state government upside-down as Republican appointees began running the good ol' boys out of Montgomery. Political chaos continued as the old-line pundits argued Reagan's popularity would slide and the pendulum would swing back their way. The new blood challenged that belief and the party remained split throughout the 1990 campaign. Governor Hunt claimed an unprecedented second term, and the state political landscape slipped even further to the right, disheartening even those most entrenched within the Democratic ranks.

The hard-liners regrouped, deciding to take another tact. Instead of sitting on the sidelines for another four years, they turned their attention to reclaiming the mansion in a more ingenious manner. They began collecting the evidence—some real and some prospective—and it worked. During the summer of 1993, the governor left office after conviction of ethics violations. When the lieutenant governor, James E. Folsom, Jr., one of theirs, was sworn in, the Democrats rejoiced. They were back in business.

Confident the son of popular two-term governor "Big Jim" Folsom would have little trouble dispensing with anyone the Republics would sacrifice in the '94 election, particularly after upstart Bill Clinton had defeated the Republican incumbent in '92, the unthinkable occurred. Without warning, ex-Democratic governor Fob James changed parties and stole back the mansion for the Republicans, leaving the boys out of power again, and swearing revenge.

Shaken but resolute, the machine searched for a chink in the turncoat's armor, but they had a problem: he had been one of their own and dragging his skeletons through the streets of Montgomery might turn over rocks they'd rather not disturb. Prudence won out and the backrooms begin to fill as the party elite hunkered down to weather another four-year storm. Out of their deliberations, a decision was made to do something they had seldom done in the past.

Except during George Wallace's three terms in Montgomery, the party's control had rested in the hands of the power brokers, a small group—attorneys, bankers, businessmen, judges, landowners, and lobbyists—whose will could make or ruin a candidate's political future. The party machinery had seldom handpicked an aspirant—whether for a local or statewide election—waiting, instead, for the hopefuls to bludgeon one another to death in the primary. The survivor, then broke and bleeding, would come crawling on hands-and-knees for the support necessary to win the general election. As a result, the machine didn't really care whose name ended up on the ballot, only that they wielded control over whoever it was.

For weeks the power brokers debated the possibilities. They would groom someone, perhaps an unlikely—someone not generally regarded a party man—and throw their weight behind him from the get-go. For the first time in many years, the Republicans would face a united party with an undefeatable candidate on the ticket.

Dozens of names were considered. The lieutenant governor was a party man, but the second-in-command often carried a stigma and his own bag of political garbage. The politically obscure, but someone with name recognition—former athletes, country singers, and the like were debated. After weeks of deliberation and arm-twisting, Lawrence T. Rifle, Birmingham businessman and former state auditor, drew the long straw. The lieutenant governor and any other challenger would have to either wait his turn or grind it out without the machine's support. While the plan had merit, as with all plans, unexpected events sometimes create the need for adjustment. Such was the circumstance Lawrence Rifle faced that morning in the spring of 1998.

"Good morning, Mista Governor-to-be," acknowledged Probate Judge Raleigh Pendleton. "What can I do for you this fine Monday morning?"

"How're things down there in Washington County?" responded Rifle.

"Not bad. Not bad at all. How's the investment business up your way? That mutual fund you put my retirement money in last year's doing pretty good. 'Course, some of them oil stocks we've been buying are still wallowing around a bit. You've always been a better politician than investment man."

Rifle laughed politely. "I know, Raleigh, but I needed a break from the limelight."

"Damn those Republicans anyway. Now, how's the campaign going? You got a substantial lead ova the rest of the field according to my precinct captains. I think I can hold my county together for you."

"That's why I'm calling. We're doing pretty well in most of the rural counties, but I need some help in Mobile, Birmingham, Huntsville, and Tuscaloosa. I'm a little short on money and need more television exposure. We're getting ready to run a smear campaign against State Senator Laughlin and we need to focus on the more populated areas. Him being from Tuscaloosa, Baptist, and all, we've got to mitigate his draw with the religious vote and the conservative elements in the party. He's always claimed he's for affirmative action, but his voting record in the senate says he's not. We've got to reach the black population and get them out to the polls."

"How can I help?"

"I'm making a request to all the insiders in the party. We need to raise another five million over the next two months. You have several industrial plants located down your way, and I want you to put the bite on them for some more help. You could hit up the local attorneys, too."

"What do I have to offer? Most of the lobbyists from the industrial corridor have been pretty generous already. They'll want to know what's in it for them," queried the judge, knowing the game was on.

"Depends on how much you can raise."

"What would half a million do?"

"Half a million, huh," the candidate thought aloud. "When I'm elected, I'm gonna appoint a new director of the state environmental board. He'll be sympathetic with any problems of that nature your constituents might be facing."

"How about any tax incentives?"

"Raleigh, you know better than I do that tax reform's contrary to the platform and would be counter-productive to your own interests down there. Tax cuts are what the Republicans are all about."

"We're in bad need of some state road improvements down here. I got some contractors in my pocket I could squeeze if there was some more road money coming our way. Could be worth a hundred, maybe two-hundred-thousand."

"I think that could be arranged, Judge."

"I have one little favor on a personal level. You're going to be appointing lots of new people and my nephew's a bright young engineer—graduated from Auburn four years ago. I'd like to see his career pushed along. He needs a good position up there in Montgomery. He's an up and comer in the party, has a pretty new wife with a baby on the way. Could I count on you for some help there?"

"Anything's possible for my old friends, Raleigh. The party always needs new blood, and we always take care of our own. You just do your part and leave the rest to me."

"You got a deal, Mista Rifle. I'll raise that five hundred thousand, and maybe a little more. Naturally, me and the missus will be up on the podium when you're sworn in?"

"Of course you will, old friend. Everything's possible when the money shows up."

Raleigh sat back in his desk chair and stared out the window. His mind was racing, preparing for the task at hand. His thoughts were interrupted when the intercom buzzed.

"Leander Rutherford's on the phone."

"Did he say what he wanted, Bonnie Jean?"

"No, Uncle Raleigh. He said it was important and would only take a minute."

A minute of Leander's bullshit's about all I can take, he thought.

"Okay, put him through."

"How're you and Mrs. Pendleton, Judge?" greeted Leander.

"She' a little croupy this morning, but otherwise, her same mean ol' self. What can I do for you today? I'm on kind of a short rope."

"I know you're busy, so I'll make it quick. My business partner, Jack Mitchell, you remember him, nice looking man, kinda—"

"Leander, I remember Mista Mitchell. I'm not senile quite yet," Raleigh croaked.

"Yeah, I was sure you would. Anyway, he's making noises about closing down Jefferson Construction."

24

"So?"

"Well, the money I sent you for that Harveyville road job you helped me with came out of the construction company, and—"

"Leander, where you calling from?"

"Oh, don't worry, Judge, I'm on a pay phone. There's nobody listening in on my end."

"Good. You got to always be careful when you call me."

"I think that's all ova with, but I'd never put you in an awkward situation, Judge."

"Good boy. Now, what's this about your partner and all?"

"Well, Jefferson Construction ain't looked so good on the books for the past couple of years, and he either wants to sell it or shut it down."

"Where you going with all this, Leander?"

"Well, I thought you might be interested in keeping the money moving your way, and there's no way I'll be able to hide the withdrawals if I don't have any construction activities available. Mista Mitchell pays close attention to the landfill side of the business."

"What can I do about it? Sounds like you can't control your partner."

"Well, I had a thought. There might be something you could do that could make him a little more inclined to see where the construction company might be more important than he thinks."

"I'm listening."

CHAPTER 4
JUST A MORNING AT HOME

Having been raised in a small rural community in north Texas, only a nameless dot on a map where two farm-to-market roads intersect, I've always been an early riser. The sound of a rooster crowing at first light permanently programmed my mind. I've seldom remained prone past 5:30, and today was no exception. A request from my youngest sent me to the back of our three-car garage and to the workbench to tune up the go-cart I had built for him a year earlier. I was confident I could have him back up and running before breakfast.

My father had owned the only gas station and garage in the area. My younger brother and I had pulled many transmissions and overhauled dozens of engines, both large and small, by the time we completed high school. I had built my own go-cart at the age of twelve, using the rust-frozen engine from an old lawnmower I retrieved from a ditch. I rebuilt the engine from scratch, fabricating some of the obsolete parts needed for ignition. It was a beauty and served my brother and myself for many years.

As graduation from high school approached, my father asked where I was going to college. I replied, "I'm not. I'm going to stay here and work with you."

"The hell you are. Your mom and I've been saving ever since you and your brother were born. We never had the opportunity to do any different, but you're not going to be stuck here for the rest of your lives like we've been."

And that was that. I attended Texas Tech, received a degree in Business Administration, and played the corporate game with a major environmental company for a few years. "Environmental company" is a nice term for the trash business.

I guess my independent upbringing made working for someone else intolerable. In 1977, at the age of twenty-eight, I borrowed all the money I could, bought two used container trucks, and started hauling trash from construction sites as the Houston population continued to sprawl across the landscape, converting once agricultural and timber land into thriving bedroom communities.

Over the years, as financial success provided more money and opportunity than I had ever expected, my avocational interests were drawn back to my roots. I relaxed by tinkering with mechanical devices rather than watching the boob tube or chasing a small white pellet around a manicured pasture.

At 7:00, with the small engine purring like a Siamese, I walked down the hallway, knocking on three separate doors and singing, "It is morning, it is morning, in my heart," a rather ill-tuned remembrance from the week-long church camp I had attended when I was ten. I recall how annoying the pastor's off-pitch twang had sounded over the loudspeaker. While I pride myself on a rather melodic voice and the ability to carry a tune, I often yodel, just to make the experience even more grating for my beloved children.

"Go away," my oldest, Jackson Christian Mitchell, Jr., yelled.

"Dad, you're sick," Katie, my middle and only girl, called out.

"I like it, Daddy, sing it again," snickered nine-year-old, Michael—my pride and joy.

Leaping into the hallway, he escorted me to my bedroom, where we began our morning ritual of him snuggling under my covers and watching cartoons, while I showered for the day.

"Jackson, would you pass me the jelly?" I requested, sitting down at the kitchen table.

"It's closer to Katie," he offered without looking up from his cereal. "Besides, I'm busy right now."

"Other than chewing, what are you busy doing?"

"Thinking."

"Thinking, huh. About what?"

"Stuff."

"What kind of stuff?"

"Dad, would you get off my case? I've got things on my mind. Why can't I just sit here and eat my cereal and think about stuff? You're really a bitch sometimes."

"A bitch? Well, while you're thinking about stuff, would you pass me the jelly so I, too, can think about stuff while I eat breakfast? As a matter of fact, I'm thinking about some stuff right now. I'm wondering how you're getting to school this morning without the car keys this old bitch is getting ready to take from you if you don't pass me the jelly in about two seconds!"

For the first time that morning, my oldest glanced up. I maintained eye contact and a firm expression; although, I was laughing inside.

"Jeez, Dad. Why are you always on my ass?" he blurted while reaching for the jar of Smuckers immediately in front of him.

"You have a pet? A donkey? Where do you keep him? I presume you're talking about an animal; otherwise, I'd consider your response vulgar and disrespectful, particularly in front of your sister and brother."

Katie and Michael both giggled, causing Jack's eyes to cut sharply in their direction.

"Don't give me the evil eye," laughed Katie while making a crucifix with her forefingers.

"Oooooh, that's scary, Jackie," Michael joined in, placing a napkin over his eyes. "Make him stop, Daddy! Please make him stop. I'll have bad dreams."

At this point, Jackson had no place to go. The younger ones had diluted the situation, and he was feeling a bit foolish. Jackson isn't a bad-spirited kid, and he loves his younger siblings. He's simply going through that difficult time I refer to as "turning sixteen and getting a driver's license." Coolness is king; hostility is normal, yet there is a loving child hiding somewhere in the recesses of a testosterone-driven mind.

"Okay, that's enough from you two," I whispered. "Jackie, I have to go to Mobile Thursday morning. I'll be gone until Friday evening, but I'll be back before your game. Mrs. Larson will be staying with you guys, and I'm depending on you to help her keep things in order. Okay?"

"What about Mom?" Michael asked. "Why can't we stay with her while you're gone?"

I hesitated for a few seconds, chewing my lip and hoping they wouldn't notice. My wife and I had divorced three years earlier after eighteen years of matrimonial combat. While I had my faults, the courts had determined the children's interests would be better served under my parental direction—a decision I fought hard to win and believed to be correct.

"I asked your mother if she could keep you, but she said she didn't get enough notice, and she's studying for an important exam. You know how

28

hard she studies, but I'm sure she'll check on you since she knows I'll be out of town."

"She's always studying, always busy. I hope I'm never too busy for my children when I'm a mother," responded Katie.

"Kathryn, that's really not fair. Our divorce has been hard on all of us, particularly your mother, and she's trying to put her life back together. Let's give her a little time. It's only been a couple of years and—"

"My ass, she—" Jack uttered.

"Now, there you go talking about that donkey again," I interrupted, raising an eyebrow. "How about we go to San Antonio when I get back? We can go to Jackie's game Friday night and leave early on Saturday. We haven't gone there in a long time."

"Neat," offered Katie. "Can I take Ginger with me?"

"Sure, the more the merrier. How about you, Jackson? You want to take a friend?"

"I don't know. I'd really rather stay here. I…I…"

"Jackie has a girlfriend," announced Michael with a mischievous smile.

"I do not, you little creep."

"You do too. I saw you kiss her in your truck yesterday afternoon."

Jackson's face turned slightly pink, and he stared contemptuously at his little brother.

"He's doing it again, Daddy. Make him stop! Make him stop!"

"Okay, okay. That's enough, Mikey. Who's your friend, Jack?" I inquired.

"Mary Sue Baker," answered Katie without hesitation.

"Your friend, Mary Sue?" I asked, looking in my daughter's direction.

"The same," she responded.

"Is that right, Jackie? Isn't she a little young for you?"

"She's a freshman, just like Katie. She's almost sixteen. I think she was held back a year when she was little. Anyway, I like talking to her. She's cool."

"She's an awfully cute little girl. Would you like to ask her to go with us? We could have a boy room and a girl room at the hotel."

Jackson's face flushed a little brighter. "I don't know…I…I might feel a little funny."

"You could take your donkey," added Michael.

"Very funny, Bozo. Hey, Dad, could I take my truck? We could follow you and Katie and blabbermouth."

Michael pulled at the corners of his mouth, stuck out his tongue, and crossed his eyes. I watched with amusement as the two of them exchanged unspoken jabs.

"I don't know about that. There'd be plenty of room in the Suburban, and her parents might not feel comfortable—"

"Please, Dad. I can have her ask her parents. I don't think they'll mind. Her father's kind of a hard-ass, but her mother seems pretty cool. You could call her and tell her everything'll be okay. Please."

"All right. Have her talk to her parents and tell me what they say when I get home this evening. If they're okay with it, I'll call them. If everything feels right, you can take your truck, on one condition."

"What's that?"

"If you ever talk about that damn donkey again in front of me, your brother, or sister, I'm going to kick yours. Deal?"

"Deal," he surrendered.

CHAPTER 5
THE SETUP

The area referred to as the industrial corridor resides in the southernmost part of Washington County adjacent to the Mobile River. For centuries the river meandered quietly through the stands of timber, slowing to an almost stagnant condition before emptying quietly into Mobile Bay. In the early thirties, one of Raleigh Pendleton's ancestors had visualized the value water access would provide for the timber industry, an important part of the Pendleton land holdings in the county. The initial dredging of the river had been completed during one of the seven terms of Judge Erwin J. (Bull) Pendleton, Raleigh's grandfather and the second in a succession of four Pendletons who have run Washington County politics for almost a century. Bull had been instrumental in obtaining the federal money needed to fund the project and its economic impact on the county had made the Pendleton name legendary in the area.

While pine timber has continued to be a mainstay in the economic fabric of the county, the industrial facilities along the corridor have continued to expand to include pulp mills, chemical companies, processing facilities, and other businesses dependent on cheap transportation of goods and materials. This cluster of industrial neighbors now collectively represent the county's largest employers, leading taxpayers, and are the beneficiaries of a friendly political environment—a protected reality which amplifies the sitting probate judge's already substantial power base.

With his cane in hand, Raleigh limped around his office while waiting for his secretary to place the next call to one of the companies along the corridor.

While his first run at these businesses had been met with solid resistance, he had decided to take a different tact—the embellishment of an idea Leander had planted during their last conversation.

Six weeks had passed since Lawrence Rifle had made his first request for money. Raleigh had made the rounds of usual contributors, but his efforts had yielded meager results. Up to now, he had been able to pacify the party's chosen candidate with promises and lies, but he knew it would be only a matter of time before the pressure would be applied with greater force. His reputation within the party was at stake. He had to raise money, and time was working against him.

Although no one else was in the room, Raleigh mumbled aloud, "I got to admit, even though old Leander's full of crap most the time, this idea of his does offer some options I hadn't considered. I'll pitch it and see if it flies."

"Uncle Raleigh, Mr. Bitterman's on the phone," announced Bonnie Jean Moseley, Raleigh's niece and receptionist for the summer.

"Thank you, sweetie," he replied as he rounded his desk. "Make sure I'm not interrupted during this call, if you please."

"Hello, Bobby, you old polecat. How you been?" he blustered.

"Been doing real good, Judge, considering the cutbacks we've had to make here at the plant," responded Bobby Bitterman, plant manager of General Paper Company's pulp facility. Bobby was a local boy who had started with the company directly out of high school, gone to college at night, earned a college degree in forestry, and worked his way up the ladder to the highest position in the plant. The entire process had taken almost twenty years, and he was well regarded in the community as a local Christian boy who had done well.

"Them damn Republicans have made life hard for all us folks here in Alabama," Raleigh replied. "Where you been? I ain't seen you lately."

"I guess the last time we talked was last month when you wanted another contribution to Mr. Rifle for his run for governor. Sorry I couldn't help, Judge, but the home office has put me on a real tight budget these days, and I just couldn't sell it. I hope you received the hundred dollars I sent you."

"Sure did and it was mighty appreciated. Hey, Bobby, I completely understand about the company and all, and so does Mr. Rifle. You've always been a good party man, and sometimes the timing just ain't right. That's not why I'm calling. Me and some of the boys are getting together for some poker Thursday night ova at the lodge. Thought you might want to join us."

Bobby sat in silence, remembering the last time he had gone to the lodge with the judge.

"Bobby, you still there?" prompted the judge while sipping from the bottle of sour mash he always kept in his desk drawer.

"I don't know, Judge. The last time you had them ladies over there, and I got in a pack of trouble with Myrtle."

"Oh, this won't be nothing like that. The last time was that damn fool Leander Rutherford's doing, and I already told him I didn't want none of that kind of trash ova there this time. This'll just be the boys, some whiskey, a little politics, and cards—penny-ante type stuff. We'd sure like to have you join us."

"Well, if you're sure there won't be no hanky-panky, I suppose I could come around for a little while. Myrtle and the kids have gone up to Birmingham for a few days. What time you going start?"

"We'll be gathering at about six. Most the boys can't get there any earlier, but you can come as early as you like. Me and Johnny will be going ova early to set up the bar and all."

"Okay. I'll be there around five-thirty. We have a shift change at four, and I always like to make sure things are going all right before I leave for the day. Thanks for thinking about me, Judge. I've missed seeing you boys. I was afraid you were mad at me about the contribution and all."

"Nonsense, Bobby. We'll be looking for you, and be sure to bring a little extra cash. I'm a pretty damn good stud player."

He hung up the phone and smiled.

"Like I've always said, there's more than one way to skin a polecat." Pushing the intercom button, he issued another command. "Bonnie Jean, go on and put a call into Harvey Painter ova at Republic Chemical."

CHAPTER 6

JANE

It was almost nine o'clock, and the Catfish Kettle was preparing to close for the evening. Viola Wilson bustled about, refilling the salt-and-pepper-shakers while eyeing the young girl huddled in the back booth. She watched as the child wiped her eyes with the back of her hand. After the last table was set up for the next day's business, Viola shuffled toward the back of the dining room.

"Do you need anything else, my dear?" she asked in a scratchy voice, puffing on an unfiltered Camel.

"No, ma'am. I'm just waiting for someone," the young girl answered with a dialect suggesting she wasn't a local.

"Are they coming pretty soon? We close at nine, and I'm gonna have to ask you leave as soon as I close out the register."

"They should be here any minute. Could I wait outside?"

Tired eyes and streaks of dried tears suggested the child was not telling the whole truth. Viola looked at the stained and dusty backpack resting beneath the table and was convinced the girl was either a runaway or in some other kind of trouble.

"Where you from, dear?"

"Birmingham," lied the young black girl.

"You run away from home, didn't you?"

"No, ma'am. I came in on the bus this afternoon. My daddy was supposed to pick me up. We must have gotten our days mixed up. After I waited for awhile, I called him, and he said he'd be right over," she lied again.

"Where does your daddy live?"

34

"Some little town around here."

"What's your name?"

"Jane," the child replied honestly.

"What you gonna do if he don't show up? It'll be real dark outside when I lock up and turn out the lights."

Again, tears began to form in the child's eyes. Viola looked into the youngster's face and decided what she had to do.

"You go on and sit here for awhile. He'll show up pretty soon, and I don't mind waiting a little longer. Let me get you a piece of coconut cream pie. We only got one piece left, and it'll go bad by morning. I'll be right back."

"Thank you, ma'am," Jane offered. Her lower lip quivered.

Viola went to the kitchen, picked up the phone, and dialed a number listed inside the vinyl jacket covering the phone book.

"Sheriff's office," the dull voice answered.

CHAPTER 7
A PLEASANT INTERRUPTION

The week had been a blur. By 10:15 on Thursday morning, I had gotten the children off to school, made the drive to Houston Intercontinental, and was seated in an aisle seat in the exit row of Continental flight 1427, a non-stop to Mobile. While first class was well within my reach financially, I could never justify the cost for a wider seat, slightly quicker service, and a drink before take-off. At a little over six feet in height, the extra room would have been convenient, but I had found the exit row, when available, to be adequate.

After retrieving the most recent copy of Delta Disposal's financial statements from my briefcase, I settled in to refresh my memory of the concerns I had noted a few days earlier and prepared my mind for a day-and-a-half with Leander. While I generally enjoyed the people I had met in Alabama—those outside the social and political circles of my business associate—I had grown to resent my time there. Listening to the never-ending speculation, political gossip, and promises of grandiose achievements had become tiresome, at best. In short, two and a half years of mediocre performance had lessened my enthusiasm for my investment in South Alabama.

Lost in thought, I was startled back to the moment by the presence of a slender black man standing in the aisle above me. He possessed a genuine smile, was clad in a gray tropical wool suit, and was politely motioning to the window seat from which my legs were denying him access.

"You looked as if you were busy. I apologize for the interruption, but the stewardess just announced we wouldn't take off until everyone was seated. I think she was referring to me," he said in a voice well educated and professionally honed. His appearance and demeanor reminded me of Denzel Washington as the *Washington Post* reporter, Gray Grantham, in *The Pelican Brief.*

"No need to apologize. How are you this morning?" I responded, unbuckling my seat belt and standing.

"I'm fine, thanks, and you?" he replied.

I've made an art form out of avoiding idle chitchat with fellow passengers over the many hours I've spent in airplanes. Seldom have I been drawn into a conversation with a stranger for longer than three minutes. After a brief "How are you today?" or "Going out or coming home?" I've busied myself with a file folder, buried my face in a book, or opened my laptop and furiously typed away while ignoring any interruption. Such was the beginning of this trip, but an intriguing comment from my fellow traveler caught my attention and I never regained the initiative. We had been in the air for about ten minutes when my concentration was broken again.

"You look like you have a problem."

"I beg your pardon?" I responded, looking toward the friendly face by the window.

"I don't mean to be impertinent, but I've been watching you for several minutes and couldn't help but notice your exasperation. I guess it's something I do as a result of my work. I'm a people watcher. Sometimes the manner in which they carry themselves or the way they fidget with a newspaper or, in your case, that file you're working on, tells more about them than anything they might say," announced the stranger.

Normally, I would have made some polite statement of dismissal, but the directness and accuracy of this fellow traveler caught me off guard.

"Actually, you're right—guilty as charged. What do you do that provides such unique insight?"

"I'm a lawyer, a prosecutor to be more specific. Body language is a very reliable source of information. Over the years I've spent in the courtroom, physical actions and reactions have led me to the real truth on several occasions."

"You work in Houston?" I asked, resting the folder in my lap.

"No, Alabama. I'm with the U.S. Attorney's office in Mobile."

"Mobile, huh. That's where my company is, or I should say, one of my companies. I'm in the solid waste business."

"Solid waste? You mean you're a trash man," he said with a wink.

"Yeah," I acknowledged without taking offense. "It's a pretty good business. The world couldn't function without the trash man."

"Pretty political, isn't it?"

"Yeah, that's the down-side. Everyone wants their trash picked up, and everyone likes to bitch about where it goes."

"Ever have any problems with political pressure, bribes, and so forth?" he asked.

"Should I have my attorney present for this conversation?" I quipped. "Yeah, I've been asked for everything from a new television to a bag full of used bills. I just say no and occasionally get hassled by some local politician. They normally back off when I suggest the authorities might like to join us in the conversation. That's usually the end of it."

"Why don't you call the authorities?" he asked with a more serious tenor in his voice.

"I talked to an FBI agent once in Oklahoma—I used to own a company there. He told me until the crime was committed, there was little they could do. It's like, if someone threatens to kill you, not much is done until you're already dead. I guess I just don't trust the legal system very much, and my way seems to work."

"Solicitation of a bribe for political favors is damn sure a crime, but it's often hard to prove. Bribes usually aren't solicited in writing," he conceded. "Ever been shaken down in Alabama? I guess I should say, has anyone ever tried to shake you down?"

I could sense a little higher level of interest from my travelling companion. "Sure, three or four times a year since we've been operating there."

"Sounds like you've been around the block a few times, Mr....eh..."

"Mitchell. Jack Mitchell," I announced, extending my hand.

"Lawton Tremont," he replied with a smile. "Glad to meet you. You got a card?"

He reached into his shirt pocket and retrieved an ordinary looking business card bearing the emblem of the Justice Department. I reciprocated by handing him one of mine.

By the time the plane landed, Lawton Tremont and I were only another conversation or two away from becoming friends. I knew his wife's name and that he had two children: a son in his second year at the University of Alabama, and a fifteen-year-old daughter, who was in some kind of trouble at home. He shared with me a detailed history of his childhood, which was typical of many Southern blacks born in the early fifties—personal tragedies, racial bias, limited opportunities, and plenty of hard work.

The turning point in Lawton Tremont's life had been the recognition that he had been blessed with fast legs and native intelligence. These talents had provided a college education at Grambling State University, where he had been a third-team All-American his senior year. One year as a reserve with the Redskins had afforded him enough money for law school at Georgetown. His name and reputation on the gridiron had helped land a job clerking for a respected federal judge, and, ultimately, an appointment to the U.S. Attorney's office in Washington.

"Jack, sometime when you're in town, give me a call and we'll have lunch, a drink, or something," he offered as we gathered our effects from the overhead bins.

"Thanks, and that same invitation is open the next time you're in Houston."

As we said our good-byes at the departure lounge, I reflected on how much I had enjoyed the trip that morning. The diversion had kept my mind distracted from the remainder of the journey and the frustration of Leander.

CHAPTER 8

A DIVERSION

As planned, Leander met me at the curb in front of the Mobile airport. Characteristically, he was puffing on a Winston and leaning on the fender of his sedan, which was parked in a no-parking zone. Leander didn't concern himself with laws meant for others.

"How the hell are you, Jack? How was your flight? Have I got some good news for you! We may be getting the biggest job you've ever seen ova at the State Docks. I just got a call from the engineer and he said the job is ours if we can get it bonded. We'll probably make a couple of million on this deal."

He was beaming as he wrestled my flatboard from my hand and placed it in a trunk filled with crumpled clothing items, a filled garment bag, three cartons of cigarettes, and a large gift box from Macy's.

"How big's the bond?"

"No big deal, Jack, only two-and-a-half million."

"Two-point-five million! Leander, have you lost your mind? The last time I looked, our bonding capacity was slightly more five hundred thousand. How the hell do you expect to come up with the collateral to secure the balance?"

The visit had started out worse than I had expected.

"I've already taken care of that, Jack, my boy. You don't expect me to sit around and let the biggest deal we've ever had just go by the wayside. I know how to get things done down here, and it's all set. We'll have to pay an extra couple of points for the bond, but we can do it, and it's real simple. We put up the landfills as the primary collateral, and they'll accept your personal guarantee as the secondary. They've seen your balance sheet, and I don't mind telling you, they was real impressed."

He tossed the expended cigarette butt to the curb and lit another one.

"Leander, you have lost your mind. There's not a respectable underwriter in the country who would accept a landfill as security on a bond. It's an environmental risk they wouldn't take. You can bet your sweet ass if anything went wrong and the bond were called, they'd come straight to me for the money. So let's get real straight on this right now: we're not putting up the landfills for security, I'm not signing any personal guarantees, and as I've told you twenty times, I don't like construction. We're going to sell Jefferson and focus on Delta Disposal."

In his normal fashion when challenged, Leander reacted as if I had said nothing at all.

"Let's get in the car, Jack. I have something I want you to see."

We drove out of the airport entrance and turned east on Airport Boulevard, toward downtown. Leander turned on the radio, opened his window, and pulled another Winston from his pocket. Under normal circumstances, I would have been offended by such behavior, but the discussion at the curb had emotionally drained me, and I was content to ride in conversational silence, while Bonnie Rait belted out, "Let's give 'em something to talk about."

Half an hour later, we arrived at the area referred to as the State Docks— the heart of the port of Mobile and a significant contributor to the local and state economy.

Halting the car by a small building and without saying a word, Leander placed the transmission in park and exited the Oldsmobile. A few minutes later, he emerged from the small building waving two red squares of cardboard above his head. He was beaming.

"Leander, what's this all about?" I inquired, not attempting to hide my frustration.

"Jack, my boy, this is what being on the inside's all about. Take this here security pass and attach it to your lapel. I'm going to show you the biggest damn pile of money you ever seen."

We drove around the State Docks while Leander pointed out the various points of interest. While it was an informative tour, my patience was shot. Finally, we pulled up to a remote area that was mostly undeveloped.

"There it is, Jack, better than gold," he announced as we exited the car beside a massive pile of chalky material.

"What is it?" I asked, immediately noticing the unmistakable odor of hydrocarbons.

"Gasoline and diesel saturated soil, tons of it. They've started reclaiming the area where they used to store all the fuel to service the barges and ships coming in and out of the port. They have a whole slough of underground storage tanks that's been leaking for forty-some years. The EPA came in and tested the area and found all the surrounding dirt soaked with residue. They been put under a federal order to clean it up, and this pile's just the beginning. They don't know exactly how much there is, but it's huge."

"I know leaking fuel tanks are a problem all over the country, but what does this have to do with us?"

"We're gonna get to take it in ova at our landfill on the north side of town. We'll get at least twenty bucks a ton. Figure it out for yourself. There's at least a million tons. That's twenty million dollars!"

"Leander, this stuff has to be classified as industrial waste, and we're not permitted to take that kind of material. How would we get around that little problem?"

"That's where my contacts come in. I already had a meeting with some of the big boys in Montgomery, and all we got to do is get our permit amended and it's all ours. This deal's worth a fortune."

"A permit modification could take eighteen months or more, and we might not be able to get one at all. I doubt the EPA will just let them stockpile this stuff by the bay while we go through the process. Hell, it's polluting the air and the underlying dirt right now," I argued.

"You still don't get it, do you, Jack? That's what being a power broker's all about. Me and my friends know how to shortcut things, cut through the red tape. We're meeting with someone ova at the bar in about half an hour, and you can hear the details for yourself," crowed Leander. "This gentleman was the governor's right hand man for twenty-five years. Still goes to see him every week. He's the key to this whole deal. He knows where all the skeletons been buried, so to speak."

"The governor...Fob James?"

"Hell no. Governor Wallace—the man. When someone refers to 'the Governor' around here, there's only one person they's referring to—George Wallace."

"What'll it cost us? You know how I feel about kickbacks and—"

"Jack, this here's the cleanest deal I ever come up with. We're going hire us a lobbyist. That's what this gentleman we're meeting with is. He's a lobbyist, registered with the state, all legal and proper like. He's a big hitter, Jack, probably the biggest, and he's already agreed to represent us. He knows how to work through the system without stepping on anyone's toes, but he also knows when to flex his muscles. He has lots of old friends beholding to him. He thinks he can have us permitted in two to three months."

"How much?"

"What do you mean?"

"How much do we have to pay him to represent us, Leander?"

"Not as much as you might think, but I'll let you and him talk about that. You just think all I worry about is the construction jobs. That ain't so, Jack. The construction business is faster and easier to get done and that's why I been putting in so much time on it. I know the real money's in the waste business, but I just been waiting for the right opportunity, and here it is. We're gonna make a bundle on this deal, Jack, and once we're in with the big boys, the sky's the limit."

CHAPTER 9
A FRESH FACE

It was approximately 1:30 when we walked through the outside entrance to the bar. A quick scan of the room suggested the luncheon crowd had dispersed. There were two barflies barely maintaining equilibrium on bar stools, and one thirty-something bleached blonde, sipping a parachute drink and sitting alone at one of the vacant tables. To my disappointment, she immediately arose from the lounge chair and began to swagger in our direction. *All we need to complete this boondoggle is a prostitute hitting on us while I listen to some has-been politico attempt to impress me with his importance,* I thought as she approached.

While I had been around Leander more times than I cared to remember, and never ceased to be amazed with his behavior, what happened next took me by complete surprise.

"Hi there, Leander baby," she announced, wrapping her arms around his neck and placing her lips solidly on his. Even more to my amazement, he reciprocated just as tastelessly, grabbing each cheek of her generous buttocks and pulling her pelvis into his. After what seemed like an eternity of guttural moaning, she removed one arm from his neck, placing her hand between legs.

"Has the big boy missed Miss Vivian?"

The discomfort of the moment suggested I should either: make an about face, exit the establishment, and immediately fly back to where sane people live, or join the two inebriated gentlemen at the bar.

"Sort of an interesting situation you find yourself in, right, Mr. Mitchell?"

At the corner table, behind the still open door, sat a stately looking gentleman, his sinewy hand clamped around a highball glass. A white linen suit and black and white wingtips, suggested he had just stepped out of the pages of *The Great Gatsby.*

"I'm afraid you have the advantage, sir," I offered after regaining my composure.

He chuckled.

"This kind of behavior's not particularly unusual in here. There's sort of an unwritten rule that the gentlemen of the South don't allow the wives to frequent certain establishments, except on weekends. Every important city in Dixie has such a place—a rather unique tradition, don't you think? It probably dates back pre-Civil War, when it was accepted that the landowners bed down with their prettier young slaves. Back in those days, it wasn't unusual for young black males to be included, but bi-sexuality finally made its way to the closet as our society became inbred with Northern morality. The odd thing is the divorce rate down here, among the more gentile members of our society, is far below the national norm. Our lady folk seem to overlook our transgressions, and even an occasional tryst by a married woman of aristocratic upbringing is ignored, if her lapses are not too often or too public. Have a seat and we'll allow Leander and Miss Vivian a few moments of euphoria. I'm Findley Ross, my friends call me Fin."

I listened to this historical discourse with interest, and while I didn't agree with the principles described, I did appreciate his candor and comfortable manner. Several things about my new acquaintance were unique, but the one that most struck me was the missing Southern drawl.

"Good to meet you, Mr. Ross. Leander told me of your past positions with the party. I understand you are close to Governor Wallace."

"Fin, please, and I hope it's acceptable if I call you Jack."

"Of course," I conceded. While I was still wary of anyone introduced by Leander, I liked Findley Ross from the beginning.

"Yes, the governor and I've been friends for most of our lives. I served him in all three of his administrations and was heavily involved in his presidential election campaign. I understand your company has a rather significant opportunity down at the State Docks."

"You probably know more about it than I do," I confessed. "I have environmental interests in two other states and can assure you, modifying a permit would take much longer to accomplish than Leander suggests it can be done here."

"Oh, I don't know, Jack. You might be surprised what can be done in anywhere if you know the right people. What you, or I probably should say, what Leander is wanting to do is a bit aggressive, but not impossible."

"Forgive me for cutting straight to the chase, Fin, but tell me how you work. What I mean by that is, what do you do and—"

He cut me off. "How much do I cost?"

"Yeah, to be blunt, what will your services cost me?"

"You know, Jack, you and I are going to get along just fine. I've lived my entire life in Alabama. Everyone down here wants to go through a bunch of meaningless bullshit before getting down to business. Unlike most of my colleagues, I don't, and I've probably made some enemies along the way. That's one of the reasons the governor and I got along so well. He thought small talk was a waste of time. If something needed to get done, he got on with it. If something needed to be said, he said it and damn the consequences. I guess I grew into the same type of person. If some jackass came into my office and started all that patronizing bullshit, I'd cut him off, and cut straight to the chase, as you put it. As to your question, I get two thousand a month as a retainer, and I keep track of my time. If it requires more than anticipated, I tell you in advance, and we work out the difference. If we're successful, I get a half-a-percent of the revenue generated. It's that simple."

"What's your game plan? How do you expect to shorten the permit modification process?"

"Fair question and I'll tell you my initial thoughts, but projects like this have a life of their own, and our strategy could change as things progress. I'll first talk to one of the environmental department heads, a fine young man I've known for quite some time. He'll give me the lay of the land up in Montgomery."

"What do you mean by 'lay of the land?'"

"The general attitude of the permitting department, how far behind they are in permit applications, and so forth. From that information, I should be able to determine where the resistance may come, if any. Most of the people up there have a price and—"

"Fin, before you go any further, I don't do kickbacks. I don't want to seem impertinent, but we all have our little quirks and that's one of mine."

"Good. Neither do I. How do you think I've lasted up there so long? Not everyone involved in Alabama politics is dirty. Now, I reckon there are different degrees of dirty, but I've made all my connections by doing favors for people—getting jobs for relatives, making legitimate contributions to campaigns, and so forth. I started one of the first PACs in the state, and it's still in business and has never been investigated. I simply don't screw with anything that's illegal," Fin replied.

"I didn't mean to jump to conclusions, and I hope you haven't taken offense," I offered.

"No offense taken, Jack."

"Just as a matter of curiosity, Fin, you said you've always lived in Alabama, correct?"

"Born and bred."

"You don't seem to carry the accent like most of the natives. I was just curious."

He laughed. "I'll take that as a compliment, Jack. That exaggerated drawl is about half real and half for show. It's some kind of cultural thing. Don't get me wrong, there are plenty of Alabama rednecks that can't help themselves. They just slur away like their predecessors have for generations. But most of the boys you come in contact with use it to disarm their prey. When you deal with anyone who's educated or held any position of power, and that syrupy shit starts, be on your guard. They consider you an outsider ready for the slaughterhouse."

"Fin, you seem like a straight-up guy, which is refreshing considering how I met you. How the hell did you get hooked up with Leander over there?"

We both looked to the center of the room where Leander and Miss Vivian were giggling and whispering like two sixteen-year-olds in study hall.

"I have a better question, Jack. You seem to be a straight-up guy yourself. How the hell did you?"

CHAPTER 10
PRIMING THE WELL

Raleigh exited his white Cadillac sedan and proceeded to the entrance of Celia's Café, one of the few decent places to eat in this sparsely populated part of the state. Already seated in the corner booth at the far end of the single dining room was Harvey Painter, political liaison for Republic Chemical Company.

"Sorry I had to switch our meeting from tonight to a late lunch. I had an emergency hearing come up and, well, you know, duty calls," lied Raleigh as a greeting and self-serving apology. "I think what I need to talk to you about is mighty important to Washington County industry and Republic, in particular."

"Happy to do it, Judge. What can I do for you?"

"Before we get into all that, how about a little warmer upper before we eat?"

"Does Celia have a liquor license?"

"No, but we're in my county and can do about anything you want, within reason of course, so long as you're with me," bragged Pendleton as he motioned to the only waitress in the dining room. "Minnie, would you go back to the kitchen and bring Mista Painter and me a couple of coffee mugs of sour-mash and ice."

"Sure, Judge. You gentlemen ready to order?" responded the aging waitress.

"Let us enjoy our drinks and talk a few minutes, Minnie, and then we'll order up some hot links and ribs. They fresh today?"

"Miss Celia's been smoking 'em since midnight," she answered proudly.

"Well, that's fine. Now, you run along and fetch us them drinks. And Minnie, don't seat nobody too close to us unless you have to. We got some things to talk about."

"What's on your mind, Judge?" asked Harvey after the waitress was dispatched.

"Money, Harvey, dirty old stinking money. Looks like we got a damn good chance to regain the governor's mansion this year, and we're needing some more money to make sure our boy gets out of the primary."

"Judge, Republic has already contributed heavily to Mr. Rifle's PAC, and we gave a bunch to the state senator's war chest as well, to say nothing of what we had to give to the Republicans. You know we have to stay in the middle of the road in these state elections. We have too much invested down here to get caught on the wrong side of the winning team. Naturally, our loyalty is with Mr. Rifle—served our company well as secretary of state— but we have to be pragmatists."

Before the judge could respond, Minnie arrived with the drinks.

"Thank you, my dear. Why don't you fix us up with a mess of barbecue, beans, tater salad, and rolls? Bring them ova here in twenty minutes or so. We might have one more drink before we eat. That okay with you, Harvey?"

"Sure. I'd like the spicy sauce on mine, ma'am."

When Minnie was out of earshot, the judge continued. "I know how careful you boys have to be and we understand, but the fact remains that the party needs the money and you have a vested interest in the outcome of this election."

"How so, Judge?" Harvey asked while sipping from the coffee cup.

"You got yourselves a pretty big problem with them settling ponds ova by the river, and the current head of the state environmental department ain't inclined to cut you no slack. My boys tell me it could cost you twenty to twenty-five million and the cleanup order's got a pretty short fuse on it. As I understand it, more than half of the work has be completed before the end of the year or they'll fine you a thousand a day until you get caught up."

"We're well aware of our problem, and we've appropriated the funds in our budget to meet the order's requirements."

"There's been so much publicity about your contaminating the river for so many years and all, you're for sure going to have to clean it up, but what I'm talking about is timing. What would it do for your bottom line if that cleanup expense could be spread out ova a longer period of time, say five years or more?"

"Well, it would make this year look a damn sight better, but—"

"That can happen, Harvey. Now, I play the stock market a bit and I own some of your stock. I read the annual reports, press releases and such, and I know you boys ain't having a bang-up year. Those stock analysts'll murder you when you release them numbers. Now, just imagine how good the home office would feel about your operation ova by the river if you could give them ten to fifteen million back to the bottom line this year? You boys would be heroes, and that can happen."

"Okay, you got my attention, Judge. Now give me some details."

"Well, I talked personally with some of the boys up in Montgomery the other day, and we talked about your problems. I then talked to Mr. Rifle, and he assured me, when he's elected, the first thing he'll do is replace the head of the environmental department with someone, let's say, a bit more reasonable. You boys will just file an appeal with the department, and he'll see to it that the time for completing the cleanup is set out a long time. Hell, he might even request a new engineering study that cuts the cost in half or better. This is your time to shine, Harvey, and if you want us to, we'll make sure your boss knows who orchestrated this deal for you boys. You might even find yourself back in the home office in Illinois."

Minnie arrived at the table with fresh drinks which, for Harvey Painter, was a welcome respite from the judge's bullying.

"Why don't you go ahead and bring us that food now, Minnie. I'm gettin' hungrier than a vegetarian at a chili cookoff," croaked the judge. "What do you say, Harvey? We got a deal or not?"

"How much, Judge? We haven't talked about money yet."

"Not much, Harvey. Let's say fifty."

"Fifty? Fifty thousand! If I went to my boss for that kind of money, he'd send me off to rehab. Shit, that's more than we've done collectively and well beyond the legal guidelines. There's no way I could even ask. You're being unreasonable, Judge, and if I'd known that was the kind of money we were talking about, I wouldn't have wasted my time driving over here."

"Simmer down now, Harvey. Don't blow a gasket. There's more than one way to skin a polecat. It don't have to come in the way of a political contribution. As a matter of fact, we wouldn't want it that way. You have a capital improvement budget for the plant, don't you?"

"Sure, but I don't see how—"

The judge interrupted. "Now, I have a good friend down in Mobile that has a fine little construction company. They've even done a little work in your plant from time to time. All you have to do is find a little job that needs doing anyway, and make sure my friend gets the work. He'll have a crew in there lickity-split, and they'll be out of there in no time. Just make sure there's an extra fifty thousand of profit in the job. Republic gets to put it on their balance sheet as an asset and depreciate it ova time. You won't have to take an expense hit; you'll get the tax benefit; the party'll get its fifty thousand, and you can call the home office with the good news. Everyone wins."

"How do you know this Mobile guy can be trusted?"

"Oh, he can be trusted. He had a little trouble a few years back, and I kept him out of the pokey. I know, and he knows I know, where his little skeleton is hid. He can be trusted all right."

While Minnie served the barbecue, nothing of importance was discussed. After she moved to another table, the judge tucked a paper napkin under his collar and bit into a piece of smoked sausage. Deep in thought, Harvey sat in silence. Finally he spoke.

"How do you fix the existing order? The new governor won't take office until after the first of the year. We close our books at the end of December. The timing's all wrong."

The judge gnawed mercilessly on a rib bone and shook his head. While his demeanor was one of concern, inside he was gloating. *I got'cha, Yankee boy. You've taken the bait, and now all I got to do is set the hook.*

"I got to hand it to you, Harvey, you're one bright young feller. If all the folks at Republic was half as smart as you, you boys would own the whole damn industrial corridor. But I'm a pretty smart sum'bitch myself, and I thought of that little problem, too. I called the state Attorney General this morning—a good party man—and told him our problem. We talked about it a bit, and he came up with the answer. You have your legal boys file an appeal of the cleanup order. It don't matter what points of law they raise, just do it quick like. He'll have it reviewed, and they'll find some merit in your brief. Then, he'll set the order aside pending further legal review. It won't get looked at again until Governor Rifle's sworn in and that'll be that. What do you say, Harvey? We got us a deal?"

"I'll have to talk to my boss, but I may be able to sell it."

"Good! That's great, Harvey. Just don't take too long because time's against us and this needs to be done quick like." *I guess old Leander's idea had some merit after all.*

CHAPTER 11

COMPLICATION

The phone behind the bar rang and was promptly picked up by the bartender. "Leander, it's for you," he shouted across the still quiet room.

Leander looked up from the table where he and Miss Vivian were still knotted in a state of rapture.

"Thanks, Tom. Can I take it up front?" Standing, he placed his hand on one of her saline-injected breasts, and whispered, "Daddy'll be right back. This here's probably the important call I've been expecting."

"Hello," he rasped into the receiver, trying to swallow the lust still present in his throat.

"Leander, is everything ready on your end?" asked the judge.

"I'm all set. All I got to do is call Billy and tell him when and where. He's been sitting on go all day. When do you want us out at the lodge?"

"Be out there by six, and don't be late. I got this deal worked out to the last detail, and I don't want anything screwing up my timing. Speaking of timing, that Jack Mitchell coming into town today wasn't very convenient. Why didn't you stall him?"

"I got that under control," Leander bragged. "I got Miss Vivian here at the bar with us, and we been smooching around and such. I'm telling Jack I need to take care of her tonight."

"How're you gonna get rid of her then?"

"We just finished pouring a new patio at her house and I got her a pretty nightgown ova at Macy's. She'll do whatever I tell her to do."

"And Mista Mitchell won't be a problem?"

"Got that covered, too. I had Findley Ross come down and babysit him tonight."

"I didn't know you and Fin was that close. He's a pretty big hitter up in Montgomery."

Leander was tempted to lie by claiming he and Findley had been good friends forever, but he knew the judge would check out his story. When it didn't pan out, there would be hell to pay. Raleigh Pendleton didn't tolerate misrepresentation from subordinates.

"I really don't know Mr. Ross very well at all," he painfully confessed. "I called my old attorney up in Montgomery and asked for the best lobbyist in the state. Turns out he and Mr. Ross went to school together and he arranged a telephone introduction."

"Leander, what do you have going on that would interest Findley Ross?" Raleigh demanded. "He ain't the kind of man who just comes down there to Mobile on a whim, I don't care how good of friends he and your lawyer is. You holding out something on me, Mista Rutherford?"

"No, Judge, I ain't holding out on you. I just hadn't had an opportunity to talk to you about it yet, you being so busy raising money for the party and all. I got a landfill deal cooking ova at the State Docks, and it's gonna need some powerful help up in Montgomery to get done. I described the deal to Mr. Ross, and he agreed to come down and talk. It worked out good for our party tonight." Leander's emotions were turning from lust to uneasiness. He was being reminded of the cost of doing business with the power brokers.

By four o'clock, Findley Ross and I had consummated a business deal that would hopefully generate generous profits for both of us; although, we agreed the task at hand was probably a long shot. Except for his brief absence to take a phone call, Leander had spent the entire time molesting, and being molested by, Miss Vivian. Shortly after his return from the telephone, he had escorted his mistress out the door with a promise that he would pick me up at my hotel at eight o'clock the next morning. While it had gone unspoken, Fin and I assumed he and his lady would be distracted by conjugal bliss for the balance of the night.

After an early dinner with Fin, he dropped me off at the Holiday Inn where I settled in for the night, relieved to be absent the company of Leander. A call home included the arbitration of a turf battle over the computer between Michael and Jackson, a report from the babysitter that she couldn't find the cat, and confirmation by Katie that my ex-wife hadn't bothered to check in during my absence. After saying goodnight to everyone, I replaced the receiver, cursed my ex-wife, pulled up the covers, and reflected on meeting

Lawton Tremont on the plane and my conversation with Findley Ross. All in all it had been a long day, and I was asleep by nine-thirty.

CHAPTER 12
THE LODGE

Confident Harvey Painter and his boss would be unable to ignore his scheme to add a substantial amount to the reelection fund, the judge drove to his house to change for an evening with the boys and his guest of honor, Bobby Bitterman. Johnny Docker picked him up a little after 4:00, and they arrived at the lodge by 4:30 in Johnny's new Dodge pickup—one of the perks provided to a loyal clerk who was well qualified for any depth of activity: immoral, physical, or illegal.

The bear-like subordinate began to unload the ice chests, bottles of booze, cases of beer, barbecue, and other assorted items for the night's gathering. Raleigh entered the lodge to insure that the preparations made the day before were properly in place. An expensive camera and case swung slowly about his neck as he limped around the main room, his oaken cane steadying every other step.

The Brotherhood Lodge was a three-room, t-shaped structure located on timberland owned by the Pendleton family since shortly after the turn of the century. The site had been chosen for its remoteness and proximity to the Mobile River, which created the northern border of the farm and separated Washington County with the southwestern border of adjoining Clarke County. Jurisdictional boundaries, three locked gates, and a long unimproved road rendered the area almost impenetrable to legal access by any authority other than the Washington County sheriffs—a succession of flunkies who had always been controlled by the probate judge's office.

The original lodge had been a single room log cabin built in 1921 during the second term of Judge Dwayne Pendleton, the first of the family to hold public office in Washington County. During those early years, the lodge had hosted hunts, political fundraisers, and had been correctly rumored to be the official meeting place for the local Klan chapter.

Dwayne had successfully championed the growth of the Klan in this rural area and his recruiting achievements and racial brutality had received much attention within the Klan hierarchy. In 1937, he was on the verge of taking the reigns as the grand dragon of Alabama when an untimely quarrel with a local black minister left the judge dead and the minister hanging from a river oak in front of his burning church.

Bull Pendleton's succession to his father's position brought increased activities to the lodge and expanded wealth to his family. As the Depression lingered, forcing landowners to relinquish ownership of family farms, most of the land adjoining Pendleton properties was gathered up; some through normal purchase agreements, but most by foreclosures conducted under orders issued from the judge's office. The foreclosed farms were auctioned, usually without the statutory notice, at sheriff's sales conducted by Bull's political subordinate. The purchaser was always a nominee who would hold the land for a few months and then sell it to the newly created Pendleton Timber Company.

By the end of the war, and with increased housing demand created by the boys coming home, the timber company had become one of the largest landowners in the county and its mill, outside of Chatom, was one of the most active in the state. Throughout this period of growth, the original farm had been left untouched, and the lodge had continued to be the focal point of political power and racial hatred.

Toward the end of the third term of Judge Ambrose Pendleton, Bull's son and Raleigh's father, the FBI had taken a particular interest in the lodge as the civil rights movement gained momentum in the early sixties. Fearing evidence of past misdoings might be discovered, Ambrose burned the lodge and all of its contents, bulldozed the underlying and surrounding ground, and placed fresh dirt and pine straw over the entire area.

The remains of decomposed bodies unearthed by the excavation—all victims of rapes, hangings, and even more grotesque mutilations—were moved to shallow graves along the bank of the Mobile River. Even with Ambrose's prudence, confirmation of decades of serial murders would have been discovered but for an act of God. Two weeks before federal authorities obtained a warrant to search the site of the Brotherhood Lodge and its surroundings, a massive flood rushed down the river, undercutting the banks adjoining the Pendleton property, and washing away the buried remains. Even into the mid-eighties, an occasional human bone or skull would be found by a fisherman, hunter, or a game ranger, but the effects of time had erased any connection between the bones and their origin.

When Raleigh's time came, fond childhood memories of the stories told by his grandfather, and more vivid recollections of lodge activities and raids in which he had participated as he grew into manhood, created an unbridled desire to rebuild the lodge and revive its legacy. Hoping to accomplish his dream without drawing unnecessary attention to the project, he purchased an old, yet serviceable, gasoline-powered band saw with which unfinished green boards could be cut from the timber surrounding the original location. A black sharecropper who had farmed a parcel of Pendleton land for years was hired to build a small barn in which to store the freshly cut planks, and then, construct the new lodge as the pine cured. It took over two years for the sharecropper and his nephew to hand cut every tree, slice the planks with the saw, and erect the frame. But the judge had been content to wait and even enjoyed an occasional Saturday afternoon helping nail the rough pieces together.

For the first five years after its completion, the structure was as rustic as its predecessor: plank floors set on sunken timbers, unfinished walls with no insulation, no plumbing or electricity, a hand-made wooden table with a bench on either side, and a few uncomfortable folding chairs placed around the walls. The only major deviation was its relative size—almost twice as big as the original.

Raleigh would have been content to leave the lodge as it was for the rest of his days, but he had been in Montgomery one day in 1986 and Governor Wallace asked if he could someday come to the lodge for a fundraiser. Fearing the governor might consider him backward and unworthy of a place of importance in the party structure, Raleigh hired Rutherford Construction to bring in a crew and finish out the cabin in a manner more suitable for a gubernatorial visit.

When the structural work was completed, two small bedrooms had been placed on either side of the rectangle, forming the shape of a cross if viewed from above—a subtle feature that amused Raleigh. The wooden floors were sealed and finished; electrical lines were brought in from over two miles away; central heat and air conditioning was installed; insulation was placed behind finished paneling; a well was drilled, plumbing installed, and electrical kitchen appliances replaced the wood burning oven and stove top.

Naturally, the judge paid Leander only eighty-percent of what had been agreed upon, promising he would never forget the favor, and suggesting Leander was well on his way toward joining the ranks of the party elite. Although the financial loss Leander's company suffered contributed to its ultimate demise, the judge's offering was perfectly acceptable to the political wannabe. Ironically, Governor Wallace never made that trip and never laid eyes on the modernized structure.

CHAPTER 13
SURPRISE, SURPRISE

Johnny waved to Bobby as the lumberman pulled through the first of the three gates leading to the lodge. Johnny was holding a can of Busch in one hand and a lever-action carbine in the other. A lemon-size chew disfigured his face, adding to his already menacing appearance. As intimidating as this setting would have been to an innocent passerby, it was a totally normal welcome for an invitee to a lodge function.

Bobby gunned his pickup down the rough road, looking at his watch as he passed by acres of southern white pine. It was 6:30, and he was an hour late.

"I sure hope the judge didn't give up on me," he uttered as he approached three parked vehicles.

Exiting his truck, he heard the screen door slam. Raleigh shuffled off the porch, a glass of sour mash in hand.

"Bobby! Where you been, you old polecat? We was beginning to get worried about you."

"Sorry, Judge. Got a call from my boss just as I was leaving. Couldn't get him off the phone for over half an hour. I hope you boys went on ahead and got started without me."

Raleigh smiled broadly and placed his arm around the younger man's shoulders.

"Sure is good to see you, Bobby. Glad you could make it out. Come on inside and we'll get you something to drink. I'm afraid you got a little catching up to do."

They entered the lodge where three men were sitting at a wooden card table. One of the trio stood and rushed over to greet them.

"Bobby Bitterman, if you ain't a sight for sore eyes," exclaimed Jim Bob Davis, the under-sheriff from adjoining Clarke County. "I ain't seen you since we run into each other down on the river fishing that day. What was it, ova a year ago?"

"How you been, Jim Bob? It has been a while. I didn't know you were aiming to be here tonight."

"Didn't know myself until about two hours ago."

"Ben Jackson was gonna be our fifth player, but one of his youngsters fell off a swing and he had to run her ova to the clinic at Chatom to have her checked out. Said he might join us later if everything worked out all right," lied the judge. "Jim Bob was good enough to fill in for him at the last minute."

In reality, Jim Bob was an up and comer in the Klan and the party, and had been a willing and important participant in the evening's activities. He was only a couple of years away from taking the reins as the Clarke County Sheriff when his boss retired at the end of his current term.

"Let me introduce you to the other two old boys ova here," offered the judge as he turned his attention to the card table. "This odd-looking, pudgy feller's Leander Rutherford. Leander owns a fine little construction company down in Mobile, and this scrawny boy here's his head superintendent, Billy Cudjoe."

Leander stood and extended his hand.

"Actually, me and Bobby met the last time he was here at the lodge," Leander offered.

"Well then, you know he's the head duck ova at the General Paper pulp mill. Bobby's kind of a local hero in these parts. Started at the mill when he was seventeen and now he's the top knocker. Now, let's get you something to drink and get down to the dirty business of gambling," the judge suggested, briskly rubbing his palms together.

The door opened, and Johnny Docker filled the doorway.

"You get all the gates locked up?" asked the judge.

"Yes, sir. We're all tucked in," replied the clerk with a wink intended only for his superior.

"Good boy. Now, why don't you make yourself and our good friend Bobby a drink? What'll it be, Bobby, some Jack and coke or what?"

"I have to work tomorrow, Judge. Better just make it a beer."

The game went on for about two hours, and Bobby won every major pot. As planned, numerous winning hands were folded in favor of the pulp mill manager. Also as planned, every time Bobby's beer bottle approached empty, Johnny produced a fresh one, gently laced with Ecstasy.

"Damn, I'm getting a little woozy," Bobby commented after taking a long draw from the Busch bottle and raking in the biggest pot of the evening.

"Bobby, you're the luckiest sum'bitch I ever seen," commented Leander with a faked slur.

"Why don't we rest a minute and have a bite to eat. I have a little surprise for your viewing enjoyment," Raleigh announced. "Everyone, make yourself a plate, and I'll put the tape in the VCR. Let's move ova here by the TV, boys. You're gonna like this."

Everyone settled in front of the big screen as the judge dimmed the overhead light. The screen blinked a couple of times and a fuzzy scene began to focus as gray images came into view. Two women, one black and one white, entered a cheap hotel room, took off their clothing, and began to touch one another in places where they shouldn't.

"Damn, look at that nigger's tits," Billy blurted out. "Why're they wasting that sweet nigger pussy on another woman?"

"Hang on, Cudjoe, it gets better," the judge announced.

Soon a balding man entered the fray, and the three naked bodies responded to every contorted position the director of the porn flick could imagine. Fifteen minutes later, the screen faded as each of the actors fell lifelessly on the bed.

"Damn, that was good, Judge. You got any more?" mumbled Jim Bob with a generous hunk of brisket in his mouth.

"Yeah, I got one more that's really special. Put that other one in there, Johnny."

As the second presentation began, Bobby blinked his eyes several times. The combination of alcohol and drugs were becoming synergistic. He still possessed enough sobriety, however, to gaze at the screen as a young black girl, no older than twelve, was methodically undressed by an older black man. The picture quality was much better than the first—color and sound adding a more erotic dimension.

"Oh, Daddy, what are you doing?" the young girl moaned as her body swayed back and forth.

Every man in the room ceased eating and stared numbly while the young girl was raped in front of their eyes.

"Hot damn, Judge, that was the durn'dest thing I ever saw," Leander said as the production ended. "Where'd you get it?"

"It was confiscated in a raid on a methamphetamine cooker a couple of months ago ova by Tibbie. The sheriff thought I might enjoy it."

The next five minutes were filled with obscene comments from the men as they critiqued each of the carnal offerings. When the judge felt the time was right, he stood, leaned over the couch, and placed his arm around Bobby's shoulders.

"Bobby, come outside with me. I got something I want to show you."

He attempted to stand but lost his equilibrium and fell back into the sofa.

"Damn, I guess I had a little more to drink than I thought," he mumbled. "Give me a second to gain my bearings."

"Johnny, help Bobby up and let's go outside so we can get some air. That's all you need, boy. You just need to move around a bit and get some air," urged the judge.

After a few minutes of stumbling through the forest, Bobby, Johnny and Raleigh found themselves standing beside the old barn where the rusting band saw still resided.

"You feeling any better, boy?" the judge asked. Johnny released his grip and stepped back.

Still wobbly, but able to stand, Bobby replied, "Yeah, Judge. All I needed was some fresh air, like you said."

"Johnny, why don't you get on back up to the lodge while Bobby and I talk a minute."

As the massive frame of the clerk disappeared into the darkness, the judge reached inside the barn door and flipped a light switch. A faint glow illuminated the ground outside the entry. Again placing his arm around the younger man, he led him into the barn.

As his eyes adjusted to the light, Bobby stopped and stared—his expression confirmed his feelings. In front of him on a makeshift pallet was a young black girl, partially clad in a flimsy nightgown. Her eyes were dilated, and she was shivering.

"This here's a little surprise for you, Bobby. Pure virgin and ready to go."

He swallowed laboriously and felt himself becoming aroused.

"Damn, Judge, where'd she come from?"

"That's not important, my boy. What's important is, what are you gonna do about it?"

As if in a trance, Bobby began to unbuckle his belt.

"I'll just leave the two of you alone and let you all become better acquainted," the judge announced, retreating from the barn with a knowing smile.

As the drug did its work, Bobby quickly stripped his clothes and fell down beside the child. In his stupor, he failed to notice Johnny lurking in a dark corner and holding the expensive camera the judge had worn around his neck when they arrived.

CHAPTER 14
LEANDER'S INITIATION

When the judge reentered the lodge, the other conspirators were still eating barbecue, drinking, and laughing.

"Is he screwing her yet?" inquired Jim Bob, with a grin on his face.

"I believe the two lovebirds are romantically involved as we speak."

"Do we get to fuck her when he gets through?" blurted Billy.

"Sort of an indelicate way of putting it, Cudjoe, but, yeah, you can have a tryst. You'll have to use a rubber. We don't want no one's semen, except his, in her vagina. Leander, would you make me a little glass of Jack and ice? I ain't had hardly a drink all night. The work's been done and I feel like celebrating a little."

Fifteen minutes later, the door opened and Johnny entered the lodge, carrying Bobby's half- naked body over his shoulder.

"He passed out," Johnny announced.

"Before or after?" the judge inquired with a hint of concern in his voice.

"After."

"And the pictures, did you get the pictures?" pressed Raleigh.

"Yeah, I got plenty and the special ones you wanted."

"Is the girl okay?"

"She's fine. The drug ain't worn off yet, so she's pretty fucked up, but she's fine."

"Okay, then. Put Bobby in one of the bedrooms and you boys figure out who's next. I'm going to pass tonight, but you boys help yourselves," the judge announced. "Sorry, Johnny, but you have to be last."

For the next couple of hours, Jim Bob, Leander, and Billy took turns walking down to the barn and back, while Raleigh and Johnny played gin rummy and drank. When the participants had satisfied themselves, the judge nodded to Johnny who walked briskly out the door. Fifteen minutes later, he returned.

"She dead?" asked Jim Bob casually.

Johnny nodded.

"Dead!" Leander squealed, jumping up from a leather recliner. "What do you mean, 'dead?'"

"We mean dead, as in deceased, no longer living, gone to meet her maker," announced Raleigh.

"Judge, we never talked about nothing like this. Dead! I can't believe it!"

"Well, you better start believing it because it's damn sure true," added Johnny. "I wrapped her in a big piece of plastic, like you ordered, Judge, and she's laying outside by Leander's car."

"Good work, Johnny." The judge's tone was as if his clerk had washed his Cadillac.

"By my car? This can't be true. What're we gonna do with the body? Oh, my God!" Leander babbled.

"Leander, you need to get a hold of yourself. You and Billy are going take the body ova to one of your landfills in the morning, early like, and bury her. I assume one of you can run a dozer."

Unfazed by the revelation, Billy nodded.

"Judge, we can't. Why can't we just bury her here, out there in the woods? We could—"

"Leander, me and you need to go outside and visit," Raleigh ordered. "You boys excuse us for a minute and make yourselves at home. Come on outside with me."

Leander nodded and followed.

"Leander, what's gotten into you? You didn't think we'd just let that little lady go on about her business, did you? She might go straight to the NAACP, and we'd have a powerful big mess on our hands. She's just a negra bitch from up north, up by Birmingham. You've always wanted to get in with the big boys, and if you do your part on this thing, I'm gonna tell Mr. Rifle what an important role you played in raising the money he's needing, and you'll be on your way. Now, I about got you that contract ova at Republic Chemical, and you'll make a nice piece of change out of that deal even after me and the party takes our cut. And if everything goes as planned, you'll get another big job ova at Bobby's plant. Now, are you in or out?"

Leander stood in silence for several seconds.

Pulling a cigarette from his pocket and lighting it, he finally replied, "Yes, sir, I'm in. You promise the big boys up in Montgomery'll realize that I'm becoming one of the power brokers down here? Someday, I want to be the kingpin of Mobile County. If you can help me, you know you'll always have an important ally down there."

After an appropriate period of silence, the judge answered, "Leander, we've had you picked out for some time to become the party chief down there when Johnson Alexander either dies or retires. You just need to keep doing as you're told, an' everything'll work out like it's supposed to."

"I sure appreciate them words, Judge," Leander responded, taking a deep breath. "By the way, who was the girl?"

"Just a runaway, we think. Jim Bob picked her up at a café ova at Grove Hill the other night. I'd told him I was looking for somebody like her for a special project, and she fell right into our lap. Now, let's get back inside. You and Billy's got some work to do."

CHAPTER 15

ANOTHER DAY, ANOTHER DRAMA

I awakened early the next morning with mixed emotions. A good night's sleep had prepared me for what I assumed would be another frustrating day of listening to Leander's embroidered contrivances. On the positive side, I realized I would only have to deal with him for a few hours before climbing back on an airplane and escaping to a more rational world, four hundred miles away. As I sat in the hotel coffee shop, I read the paper, checked in with the babysitter and waited.

Forty-five minutes after our agreed rendezvous, Leander lumbered through the door. He had the appearance of a street person. Clad in the same suit, tie, and shirt he had worn the day before, his movement and facial appearance reminded me of Willie Loman at the end of a particularly difficult day.

"Leander, you look like shit!" I greeted. "Did you and Miss Vivian do a little mud wrestling last night?"

Not only were his clothes disheveled, his pants were soiled from the knees to his cuffs. His shoes were caked with mud and there was a small grease smudge on his brow.

"Hot damn, Jack, that woman damn near killed me. She's a sex devil and cain't be satisfied. I never did make it home. I slept at the south side landfill for a couple of hours. I'd forgotten Billy and I was doing an inspection this morning in case the state people showed up. I been out there until about half an hour ago. I need some coffee before we get going."

"Don't you think you're getting a little old for that kind of behavior? Yesterday, Fin offered up some remarkable history concerning adultery in the south, but judging by your appearance this morning, you may have set a new standard. Mrs. Rutherford doesn't care if you go cavorting around until all hours of the morning?"

"We been married a long time, Jack. She knows where her bread's buttered, and besides, she didn't expect me last night with you being in town and all."

"So I was your cover, huh?"

"You and Fin. I called her from out on the hill this morning, so she could hear Billy running the dozer. She thinks we were out there spiffing things up for you."

"How thoughtful."

Fortified with black coffee and a fresh change of clothes retrieved from his trunk, we drove to the strip center office suite that bore the names Jefferson Construction and Delta Disposal. Leander H. Rutherford—Managing Partner was set out below in disproportionately larger letters.

I greeted the receptionist as we entered and observed Billy Cudjoe napping in one of four vinyl chairs. Leander kicked one of Billy's muddy work boots.

"Don't you have anything better to do this morning?" barked Leander as he passed his subordinate.

"I didn't get much sleep last night, boss," he offered while pushing the Skoal cud to one corner of his inner lip and spitting in an empty Pepsi can. "How you doing, Mista Jack?"

"I'm fine, Billy. Leander tells me the two of you were at the south landfill early this morning touching things up. Are you having operator trouble out there? I thought everything was to be ship-shape before the operators leave in the evening."

"Yes, sir, it's supposed to be, but Freddie's been having some personal problems with his old lady and his performance ain't been up to par. I been pitching in until he gets his head back on straight. He's a good hand, and I don't want him to lose his job."

"Very noble of you, Billy. What happened on the Harveyville job? We lost quite a bit of money over there."

Before Billy could respond, Leander interrupted. "Billy, you better get going up to Republic Chemical. We may be getting that new job up there, and you need to get up there and meet the plant engineer. Jack, come on in here and let's discuss what you and Fin talked about last night."

I wanted to press Billy further but decided not to make a scene. "You take care now, Billy, and let's make sure we come out better on this new job at the chemical plant."

"Don't worry about a thing, Mista Jack. I got this deal under control."

"Did you and Fin come up with a game plan for the permit modification?" Leander asked as he painfully seated himself behind his desk.

Taking a chair opposite him, I replied, "Yeah, Fin's going to talk to some people up in Montgomery over the next few days. He suggested we have someone go around to our neighbors and try to create some goodwill. He thinks it should be someone local. Any ideas?"

"Now, let me think. There's this old boy I been knowing for quite a few years that used to do some legwork for the last mayor. Name's Byron Teters. He's a good man, and I think he lives ova on the north side. I haven't seen him in quite a spell, but he might be our boy. Let me make a few calls and see if he has any enemies on that side of town." Leander scratched his unshaven chin. "There's this nigger boy that used to work the north side precincts in local elections. You know, picking up old folks and carrying them to the polling locations, but someone told me he might be a boozer. Why don't you go into the conference room and make your calls while I do some checking?"

While being dismissed by Leander was offensive to me, I was grateful to escape his presence for a few minutes.

As I walked toward the door, the receptionist squealed from her desk, "Judge Pendleton's on the phone for you, Mista Leander."

Within an hour, I had finished my daily calls to my managers in Texas and Louisiana. I could still hear fragments of conversation coming from Leander's office, so I busied myself with the most recent financial statements and again reviewed my notes on the last quarter's performance. A quiet knock at the open door broke my concentration, and I looked up to see Kenny Quincy shifting from one foot to the other.

"Hello, Kenny. I didn't think you'd be here today. Leander indicated you'd been ill."

Kenny was the bookkeeper for both companies, and while I had occasionally talked to him on the phone, I knew very little about him.

"Hi, Mr. Mitchell. I've had a summer cold for the past few days, but nothing serious. You have a good trip over?"

While I am not as astute at reading body language as my new acquaintance, Lawton Tremont, I could sense Kenny was uncomfortable and had something of importance on his mind.

"Come on in, Kenny, and take a load off. I'd be much obliged if you'd call me Jack. I'm not a very formal guy. Besides, every time someone calls me Mr. Mitchell I look around to see if my father's here, and he died twenty years ago," I offered, trying to lighten the moment.

"Oh, I'm sorry about your father, I...I didn't know."

I tried another tact. "I've been reviewing your work for the past, let's see, how long have you been with us, Kenny? I should know, but my memory gets shorter the older I get."

"I've been here almost two years," he announced, still standing and looking over his shoulder in the direction of Leander's office.

"Time gets away, doesn't it?"

"Mr. Mitchell, I—"

"Jack."

"Oh yeah, I'm sorry. Mr. Jack, I need to talk to you sometime." His eyes flashed back down the hall.

"Well, here I am, Kenny. Shoot. You know, I don't believe we've ever had a face-to-face conversation in the two years you've been here. The more I think about it, you've rarely been in the office when I've been in town."

"Yes, sir. That's part of what I wanted to talk to you about, but I can't talk now, and...eh...I can't talk to you here. I'll call you over in Houston in the next few days."

Before I could respond, I heard Leander's door upon. Kenny turned and moved briskly out the door.

CHAPTER 16

TROUBLED HEARTS

When Lawton finished his final disposition for the day, he quickly excused himself from the plush conference room of the most prestigious law firm in Mobile and rushed out. Without waiting for the elevator door to open, he retrieved his cell phone and placed one of several calls he would make over the next few minutes.

"Any news yet, baby?" He held his breath, hoping for a positive response. This was his fourth call to this number that day.

"No, nothing," answered his wife, Barbara, with a broken delivery. She was obviously crying.

"Have you talked to all of her friends?"

"Everyone I can think of. I tried to call the principal of her school, but he and his family are out of town. Lawton, tell me she's okay. Where would she have gone? I'm scared to death." She began to weep again.

"Hang in there, baby. I'm through for the day and will be home in a few minutes. I'm calling the police again."

"I already did that about an hour ago and got the same answer. They're doing everything they can. They're not taking this seriously. Why, Lawton, why'd she leave? Why'd I have to argue with her? This is all my fault. If only I'd—"

"Barbara, nothing is your fault, and I'm sure she's just over at some friend's house cooling off. She'll probably call any minute and want to come home. Now, you quit blaming yourself and hang on until I get there. I'll be home in twenty minutes."

He prayed his words would be true. As he entered his car, he dialed a familiar number.

"FBI. Special Agent Carleton speaking."

"Fred, this is Lawton."

"Hey, man, how's it hanging? You gonna get that inspector over at the county commissioner's office?"

"They're sweating. Listen, Fred, I need your help."

"You got it. What's up?"

"My daughter's missing."

"What do you mean 'missing?' How long she been gone?"

"About forty-eight hours. She and my wife got into an argument Wednesday, and she left the house sometime after 6 P.M. When she didn't show up, we started calling friends and neighbors, but no one had seen her. I called the police and got the usual runaround, twenty-four hours and all that. Barbara keeps calling them, but nothing seems to be happening. Is there anything you could do?"

"How about relatives? Anybody close?"

"No. Barbara's mother lives outside of Memphis, but we haven't called her yet. We didn't want to worry her. She's almost eighty."

"Probably a good decision, but that's a call I'd make if you don't hear from her pretty soon. Let me see. I'll call the sheriff's office. I have a buddy over there and that'll at least get them cranking on it. I'll need a picture, social, names of close friends. You know the drill. Any boyfriends?"

"Not that we know of. She's barely fifteen and pretty, but we haven't noticed any boys hanging around. No one in particular, I mean."

"You might want to call some of her girlfriends and ask. They'll know and, well, these kids are growing up a lot faster these days, Lawton. If she has a boy, he'd be my first choice."

"Good idea. We hadn't thought of that. I appreciate your help. Please keep me posted. You got all my numbers?"

"Sure and try not to worry any more than you have to. We'll find her. I'll send someone over to the house to get the picture."

"You're a good friend, Fred. If I can ever—"

"Hey, what are friends for? Lord knows you've helped me out before. Keep your chin up, pal. We'll find her."

CHAPTER 17
RAISING THE STAKES

Raleigh sat back in his desk chair and reflected on the previous evening's activities. A couple of aspirin had mellowed the banging in his temples that had pulled him out of bed at six o'clock that morning. Two fingers of sour mash had put him well on his way to recovery.

"I believe I'll let old Bobby stew about his transgressions for a day or two before I spring the trap," he gloated, and then he laughed. "I can't wait to see his expression when he sees himself all wrapped up with that pretty little negra girl."

His moment of revelry was interrupted by the intercom. "Uncle Raleigh, Mr. Lawrence Rifle is on the phone."

"Thank you, Bonnie Jean. Would you mind bringing me a fresh cup of coffee?" he responded and picked up the blinking line.

"Judge, I'm just taking a poll of all the party leaders on where everyone stands. How's it going down there?"

"Pretty much on schedule. I got two hundred thousand committed so far from the industrial canal, and—"

"How much do you have in hand?" Rifle interrupted. "We're looking at a primary in less than three months, and we have bills to pay."

"Well, let me think. I believe we've collected about seventy-five so far, and I got several deals working. We'll get the five hundred I promised. You can rest assured on that."

"Raleigh, we need to up the ante a bit. This television campaign's going to cost more than we thought, and Senator Laughlin's gaining some momentum. I need you to raise your goal by another quarter of a million."

"Two hundred and fifty thousand? Damn, Lawrence, that's a bunch of cash. What's in it for me? I mean, that's a powerful lot of work on damn short notice."

"The truth is, you're running about a month behind the other party leaders already. No one has asked for anything more than what was already discussed. Are you in charge down there, or do I need to be talking to someone else?"

"No need to get testy, Lawrence. We're a poor county down here, and I don't have access to the money some of the other leaders have. It just takes more effort down here, that's all." Years of dealing with candidates had taught Raleigh restraint in saying what he wanted to say. "I just might need a little more powder in my pouch to get the job done."

"I might have an opportunity to appoint a new judge to the state supreme court if Judge Gordon's health keeps failing. Would you be interested?"

"That's a mighty nice gesture, but I'm pretty set up down here. I was thinking about something I could offer to some of my more affluent constituents."

"Most of the important appointments are already set. I'll need to think about that," Rifle countered.

"Then, you think about that, and in the meantime, think about a little bigger piece of the highway budget and some more money for education. We sure enough could use some improvements in our schools. Like I said, we're a poor county down here."

"I think both could be arranged. Now, I need for you to get all the money you've got in hand headed this way. Use the normal channels. My brother Charles will contact you with the details. I know I can always count on you, Raleigh, just as you know you'll always be able to count on me. Have a good day."

"You, too, Lawrence, and don't worry, I'll get it done."

After replacing the handset, he reached in a desk drawer and retrieved a fresh pint of Jack Daniel's. What had started out as a day of celebration had turned into a morning of self-doubt.

"Another quarter million, damn. Maybe I'd better go on and talk with Bobby a little quicker than I expected," he muttered, placing the bottle to his lips.

CHAPTER 18

THE MILK RUN

As the last rays of sunset flickered over the light chop of the harbor, schools of mullet stirred the surface while hungry shadows cruised beneath them. In the distance, the Miami skyline had begun the evening transformation from rectangles of marble, brick, and glass to faceless monoliths jutting up from the flatness of the surrounding area. The tranquil setting was lost on the owner of Santos Exporting Company as he paced the bulkhead in front of his warehouse.

Grinding the end of a Cuban cigar, he scrutinized his gold Rolex repeatedly. "The bastard should've been here three hours ago," he cursed, launching the expensive butt into the water. "I should've fired him the first time he was late."

Unusually tall, considering his Cuban lineage, Roberto Santos had used his imposing physical appearance and street savvy learned in the Cuban ghetto district to murder, extort, and bully his way to becoming the largest cocaine distributor in the southeast. The importing business he operated as a front and money laundering mechanism was active and profitable in its own right, which had kept the drug enforcement agencies only mildly interested in his activities. The Colombians regarded his operation as an integral part of their distribution system into the interior of the United States—the result of a brilliant, yet simple, delivery scheme he had devised and sold to his South American partners five years earlier.

"Hey, big brother," yelled a familiar voice from the closest of four loading bays. "You're wanted on the phone. Anna says it's Charlie, and he sounds pretty messed up."

"Damn him! I'm either going to fire him or kill him."

"I don't think you'll need to kill him, Bertie. He's doing a pretty good job of that by himself. He fights with the elephants, man, and it's bad," offered Julio Santos, Roberto's baby brother.

The two of them walked out of the dispatcher's office, and the rage Roberto felt was obvious.

"That sorry bastard! Why have I put up with his shit for so long?"

"Because he saved your ass up in Florida state prison, that's why," offered Julio, trying to calm his older sibling and boss. "This isn't the first time, and it won't be the last."

"But now we have to delay the run for another day. I'll have to call all our customers. Bernardo's threatened to leave us before. We're not the only supplier available to him, you know."

"Are you going to get him out of jail…Charlie, I mean?" queried the smaller Cuban-American.

"Not right away. He needs to get sober. If I get him out now, he'll go right back on the booze."

"We need to find something less responsible for Charlie to do. Putting him out on the road with over a million in coke, and then carrying all that cash. We've been lucky he hasn't been busted or run with the money before now."

"He may be a drunk, but he's very loyal to me. He would never—"

"You just said the magic words. He's a drunk. I don't think Charlie would ever screw you if he had a clear head, big brother, but someday, he'll get out of control out on the road, and there's no guessing what could happen. Why don't you let me make the run this time? I've done it before," offered Julio. "First, I hit Lauderdale, then Tampa, Orlando—"

Roberto cut him off. "You're a good kid, and I love you very much. That's why you can't make it. Besides, you've only done it a couple of times with me, and that was over two years ago. You take care of our legitimate businesses. No reason to put you in harm's way when we can hire others to do the dirty work. I don't want to lose you like I did Miguel Angel and Tomas," he said, crossing himself. He gave Julio an affectionate slap on the cheek. "I better call Bernardo and try to set it up for tomorrow. Rico made the run last week. I'll get him ready to go tomorrow. Go inside and get us a Corona."

Julio shrugged and walked up the stairs leading to the office.

CHAPTER 19
POLECAT SKINNIN'

The intermittent flashes of sunlight, broken by the shadows of standing pines along the roadway, forced his eyes to blink as his pickup raced north along state highway 43. Bobby glanced at his watch and calculated the time necessary to reach Celia's by 6:30. His foot pressed harder against the accelerator pedal. He didn't want to be late.

He had been both confused and apprehensive after the call he had received from the judge the day before. Myrtle had not been pleased when he told her he wouldn't be home when she and the girls returned from Birmingham that evening. A made-up story about an emergency meeting at the plant had not appeased her, as he had hoped, but the judge was so insistent.

Raleigh had arrived at his favorite backwoods establishment forty-five minutes early. He wanted the most intimate table and time to enjoy a cup of sour mash. He had been disappointed when he entered—only scattered tables were occupied by patrons. His concern faded, however, as additional diners began to gather. By the time Bobby walked through the door, there was a steady buzz of activity flowing throughout the single dining room.

"How are you doing, Bobby, you horny old polecat," Raleigh greeted in a voice gauged to be just loud enough to create some measure of embarrassment for his dinner companion.

Bobby's shoulders slumped as he uncomfortably glanced about.

"Evening, Judge," he almost whispered, slipping into a chrome and red vinyl chair.

"We had us a grand old time the other night," the judge announced. "Just like the good old days, wasn't it?"

"Well...eh...that wasn't exactly a normal evening for me," Bobby offered with an embarrassed grin. "To tell the truth, I've felt plumb guilty ever since. I haven't ever acted like that before. I guess I had too much to drink before we ate. How'd I get home?"

"Johnny loaded you in your pickup and drove it to your house. I followed up in his. I didn't think we'd ever figure out which key was the right one. There must be twenty or more on your key ring. Nothing to feel embarrassed about though. I've had my share of needing help in my time." The judge winked knowingly at the younger man. "Can I have Minnie bring you a little something to clear the road dust out of your throat? I'm having a little sour mash myself."

"No thanks, Judge. I don't need to go home and have Myrtle smell alcohol on my breath. She thinks I'm meeting with some people over at the plant."

"Mrs. Bitterman must be something else to live with. Actually, that's part of what I needed to talk to you about."

"What do you mean, Judge?" replied Bobby, fidgeting in his chair.

"Why don't we order something to eat, and we can talk while we're waiting? Don't want to keep you away from your family any longer than necessary."

Bobby nodded as the judge summoned Minnie with his empty cup.

After their orders had been taken and his cup replenished, Raleigh leaned over the table, peering from side to side.

"I'm afraid I got some terrible news."

"News? What news?" the lumberman replied, louder than he would have liked.

"Shhhh, Bobby. Keep your voice down. We don't want no one paying any attention to us right now." Again, Raleigh looked about and took a deep breath. "Jim Bob did a damn fool thing the other night and we have to do something about it. It was partly my fault. Me and Johnny went out early to take some pictures with a new camera Lottie gave me for our anniversary—thirty-nine years with the same woman. Anyway, Jim Bob saw it sitting on the kitchen counter, and when me and you went out to the barn, he grabbed the camera and snuck out behind us. To make a long story short, he took some pretty dicey pictures of you and that negra girl."

"Oh my God!" whispered Bobby.

The judge sat in silence for several minutes. Minnie arrived at the table with two steaming Friday Night Specials: chicken-fried steak, mashed potatoes and gravy, fried green tomatoes, and pan-fried cornbread.

"Thanks, Minnie, that looks mighty good. Bring me a glass of sweet tea."

Bobby ignored the waitress and continued starring out the window overlooking the parking lot. When she departed, the judge continued.

"Now, I know how you feel—sort of like being violated. The real bad news is that someone else has seen the pictures. In fact, someone else has all of them but one."

Raleigh slipped an envelope across the table.

Bobby sighed and asked, "What's this?"

"Open it up and see for yourself."

Deliberately, he opened the envelope and withdrew a photograph—a quick glance and he slapped it face down on the table.

"Oh my God!"

Raleigh nervously looked around the room. An older couple, sitting at the nearest table, was looking their way.

"Bobby," the judge whispered, "you're going to have to get control of yourself. There's people starting to look at us, and we don't need no busybody getting interested in what we're talking about. Now, why don't you eat a bite or two and act normal like?"

"Eat a bite! Are you kidding? I'd throw up right here at the table. Oh, my Lord, what am I going to do?"

The judge paused, taking another bite of cholesterol.

"Bobby, there's a way out of this mess. I think we can make a deal."

"What deal? Where are the other pictures? How many are there?" he spit back.

"Just settle down and listen," the judged pleaded. "Here's the story. Jim Bob had a friend ova in Clarke County develop the pictures—there's fourteen. Anyway, he put them in his desk at the sheriff's office figuring he'd call you in a day or two and prick you around a little. Then, of course, he'd give them to you and you could destroy them or whatever you like."

"What the hell would I want with something like that? I'm gonna kill Jim Bob!"

"Now, you ain't aiming to kill nobody. He's your friend and was just having a little fun. Things just got a little out of hand."

"What do you mean?"

"Harley Logginfield, the County Sheriff ova in Clarke County, he was looking around the office for something—some paper clips or something—and he looked in the drawer and saw the pictures in a folder. I guess he thought it might be some evidence from some case Jim Bob was working on.

When Jim Bob came back from lunch, Harley called him in and asked what the pictures were all about and why you were mounted up on that negra girl."

"He recognized me? How? I don't even know him."

"That, I can't tell you, but he did, and he got pretty direct with Jim Bob."

"Oh, shit! Are they gonna arrest me? Myrtle will—"

"Nobody's getting arrested, but there's a catch. Harley's not running for re-election when his term's up, and he's getting ready to retire. You don't know Harley—I've been knowing' him for years—and I can tell you there's not a meaner son-of-a-bitch in south Alabama than Harley Logginfield. Harley pressed Jim Bob some more and threatened to fire him if he didn't tell the whole story. The boy didn't have no choice. He told him everything. Told him who was there, where we were—everything."

Bobby sat quietly, allowing the revelations to wallow in his brain. Swallowing hard, he asked, "What's the sheriff going to do?"

"Nothing, if he gets two hundred thousand dollars," Raleigh replied.

"Two hundred thousand! I don't have that kind of money. Oh my God! What am I—"

"You don't have to come up with all that money. Me and Jim Bob and Leander have talked, and we're all pitching in fifty thousand apiece. Fact is, I've already paid mine—kind of a down payment. Jim Bob's putting a second mortgage on his farm, and Leander's pulling his part out of his company down in Mobile."

Bobby pondered what he had just heard. "That's nice of you boys, Judge. Problem is, I don't think I can come up with my part. I have a few thousand in savings, but my house already has a second on it from when Myrtle's mother got sick. I don't know how—"

"As for it being nice of us and all, we're in this thing together. Sure, you're the only one he has pictures of, but we take care of our own, and we all feel just terrible about how things turned out, especially Jim Bob. I have an idea about how you could come up with your share. You boys ova at the pulp mill have to bring in construction folks for repairs, plant improvements, and such sometimes, don't you?"

"Yeah, but—"

"Well, me and Leander was talking and thought if you had some project ova there that his company could handle, he could come in and do the work quick like, and he'd take your part out of the profits. Your name would never show up. Of course, Leander would have to put a little fluff in the bid to make sure he covered the costs and your fifty as well."

"I don't know, Judge. Like I told you before, the company's had a tough couple of years. What did the sheriff say he'd do if we didn't pay up?"

"He said the first thing would be to send a few to Myrtle, and then he'd start trying to figure out who the negra girl is."

"Won't he check into her anyway?" Bobby asked. His brow furrowed.

"For two hundred thousand, Harvey wouldn't look for his own mother. While he claims to be a liberal, he's as big a racist as there is in Alabama. He don't give a damn about some negra girl."

"Judge, I can't give you an answer tonight. I have to go into the office in the morning and see what capital projects we have approved. I just hate all this, but maybe you're right. Your plan for my part could work if I can find some spare money in my budget."

"Fair enough, Bobby. I'm sure sorry to put you in such a position, but like I said, it just got a little out of hand, but we're all in this together."

Amazing how quick the bible beaters forget about all that do unto others nonsense when their peters get caught in a ringer, thought Raleigh as he made his way home over the dark county road leading to Chatom.

CHAPTER 20

PROBLEMS IN MIAMI

"That sorry son-of-a-bitch just threatened me!" bellowed Roberto, throwing the half-empty Corona bottle through the nearest loading bay.

Julio, who was standing on the wharf, jumped to the side as the exploding bottle left a trail of foam, liquid, and glass shards, the larger pieces skidding over the bulkhead.

"Bertie, you trying to kill your baby brother?" retorted the youngest Santos with a laugh.

"No, but I'd gladly kill Bernardo Carrera Rojas if that slimy Puerto Rican were here right now," Roberto answered as he stomped outside. "He said if his delivery wasn't made by midnight, he'd change suppliers and his cousin Ramos would do the same. He even suggested he might start supplying his cousin and some of our other customers."

"You know he can't do that. The Colombians don't know him, and it would take him years to gain their trust for the quantities we handle. Sure, he might be able to buy from someone else here in Miami, but he'd be paying twice what we pay. He could never compete with us," offered Julio.

"You're right, little brother, but it could start a price war, maybe even a real war, and no one would win. We'd only lose money."

Roberto sat down on the stairway and unsheathed a cigar.

"Is the truck ready?" Julio asked.

"Yeah, but that's not the problem. I called Rico, and his old lady said he was laid up in bed with the virus. I talked to him, and he sounded like shit. Had to run to the crapper while we were on the phone."

"Bertie, you're going to have to let me make the run tonight. If you don't want to lose Bernardo's business and take a chance on a war, I'm your only choice. Besides, a road trip would do me some good. I haven't been out of this warehouse for six months."

"Like I said before, Julio, I want to keep you out of the mainstream of the business. You have a clean record, and I don't want to risk you getting busted."

"We've been making the run for over five years now and never had any problems. Even if someone was watching us, a truck going out of the warehouse, even late, is normal. For heavens sake, I've been driving a truck since I was fourteen," Julio pleaded.

"No, I don't feel good about it. What about Manuel? He used to make the run when we first started."

"Bertie, he's the only brother we have left, and he's been out of the joint barely six months. Another felony bust, and he'd probably spend the rest of his life locked up," Julio argued. "The last four years he served took something out of him, Bertie. He isn't his same old self. I don't think he'd make it very long if he had to go back. I'd rather risk a war than put Manny in that position."

"Yeah, he's in pretty bad shape. He gets his work done but, I don't know, something's missing," agreed the older Santos. "I could make it, I guess. It's been awhile, and maybe it would give me a chance to straighten that fucking Bernardo out."

"That's the dumbest idea you've ever had. All our ties with the Colombians are with you, not me, not Manny. If you got hit, we'd be out of business overnight. Besides, I've seen your temper in action. A face-to-face with Bernardo could end real bad. You're going to have to face it, I'm the only logical choice."

Roberto sat quietly and contemplated his options. Without speaking, he arose and walked into the warehouse. Shortly, he returned carrying a .44 magnum revolver.

CHAPTER 21
QUINCY'S DILEMMA

Leander sat behind his desk, perusing a list of special items Miss Vivian needed to pick up for the backyard party she was hosting on her new patio Friday night. Initially, he had been reluctant to buy the collapsible awning and matching lawn furniture she wanted, but a particularly fulfilling evening the previous week had weakened his resolve. The awning had cost fifteen hundred dollars and had been coded to a small fencing and landscaping job Jefferson Construction had just completed for one of Leander's political friends.

The fact that the project had lost money, before bearing the burden of Miss Vivian's decorating tastes, had seemed irrelevant as he reflected on how delicately she had placed her lips over his foreskin just after making the request. "Commissioner Terrance said he might drop by, and he's a mighty powerful man in the party," he had rationalized when he agreed to the most expensive chaise lounges and chairs in the store—another two-thousand-dollar coding manipulation.

Leander looked up from his yellow pad. The shuffling of feet and a muted cough from his open door had broken his concentration. Sighing, he placed his pen on his desk.

"What do you want, Kenny? I'm real busy this morning."

"Sorry to interrupt, but the bonding company wants a construction update on the job at Republic Chemical."

"We ain't started that job yet."

"Well, they apparently sent an inspector out there yesterday, and he reported just that." Quincy shuffled his feet again—his normal reaction when in the presence of a bully.

"Why would they send an inspector up there?"

"I have to send them a progress report every two weeks, and the one I sent in Monday said we were twenty-percent complete."

"Where'd you come up with that?" Leander growled.

"I guess I assumed we were that far along because you told me to make up a draw request to Republic last week and to say we were twenty-percent complete. I sent it to Mr. Painter in like you told me and got a check the day I filled out the bonding company report, so it all made sense. I figured Republic wouldn't have paid if the work hadn't been done."

"You don't get paid to think, Quincy. You get paid to do as you're told. Why didn't you talk to me or Billy?"

"Well, sir, you haven't been available much lately, and I tried for two days to reach Billy at the site trailer number he gave me, but it was out of order. I haven't seen Billy in over a week," answered the bookkeeper defensively. "The bonding company gets real skittish if those reports are late. Remember, they threatened to call the bond on the Harveyville job because you kept delaying the reports."

"I don't need to sit here and listen to no smart mouth from you, Quincy. Remember, I'm the only son-of-a-bitch in four states who'd hire you after your felonious activities ova in Mississippi."

"I know that, Mr. Leander, and I'm much obliged that you gave me a chance," he responded, staring at the floor.

"Get on back into your office and don't send nothing to that bonding company again without talking to me."

"Yes, sir," mumbled the young bookkeeper as he turned toward the door.

"Wait a minute. Your interrupting made me forget. I need thirty thousand dollars. There should be plenty of money in the construction account right now, and I got some things that need to be paid for. Make out one check for twenty-five and another for the balance."

"Where do you want them coded?" Quincy asked in a flat voice.

"Let's see, make up an invoice from R and P for the twenty-five. Here's an invoice form." Leander reached into his briefcase and produced a printed purchase order and billing form bearing the letterhead R&P Products Company. "Make sure the purchase order matches the bill, and make it look all proper and all."

Kenny nodded. "What project should I code it to?"

"I'll let you know that later."

"It's a lot easier if I know which project so I can make the materials list match the type of job it's coded to."

"Shit, do I have to do everything around here?" cursed Leander. "Okay, code it to the Republic job. No, wait a minute. Open up a new job account for General Paper Company ova on the industrial canal."

"Do we have a job over there?"

"Not yet, but we will, and make the materials look like general stuff—some small tools, sheet rock, and so on."

"How about the other check?"

Leander handed him another set of forms bearing the name L&V Materials, Inc.

"Put the five thousand on this one and code it to the councilman's landscaping job."

"But we're way over budget all ready."

"Like I said, Quincy, you don't get paid for thinking. Just do it."

As the young accountant retreated from the room, Leander arose from his desk and closed the door. Picking up the phone, he dialed a number he had memorized years earlier.

"Hello, Judge. I got some good news for you," he announced excitedly.

"Leander, you know I always like good news."

"R&P just sold twenty-five thousand worth of materials. The check'll be in the mail today."

As Kenny drove his '86 Chevy pickup down Interstate 65 toward the cheap apartment he had occupied since moving to Mobile, his emotional state deteriorated with every mile. A foolish act, three years earlier, had forced him to return to the state of his birth to find work, but just being here had made him callused toward life. Although he had desperately needed the job when he had petitioned his parole officer to allow him to leave Mississippi to take a position in Alabama, he was disappointed when the petition had been approved. Opting to remain subject to Mississippi law, he had forgone the opportunity to transfer his reporting obligations to the Alabama parole system. The two-hundred-mile drive to Jackson every month had become a welcome respite from the verbal abuse administered daily by his employer. Kenny had grown to hate Leander, Jefferson Construction, and every day he was forced to labor in an environment where he was treated with disrespect.

The only positive aspect of his move to Mobile was the separation by miles from the woman whose extravagant spending habits had forced him to embezzle from his Jackson employer to keep her satisfied. But for the illegitimate manner in which his former employer had handled his tax issues, and the federal government's desire to prosecute the malfeasance, Kenny would have likely ended up the guest of the Mississippi correctional system for several years. His willingness to help with the complexities of the creative accounting implemented to cheat the IRS had netted him a suspended sentence for felony embezzlement with five years' probation.

I'm in the same kind of deal I was in over in Jackson. Rutherford is robbing the company blind, and he's forcing me to be an accomplice. He'll eventually get caught, and with my record, he'll blame the whole thing on me and I'll get burned. I have to get out of this mess, he thought as he pulled into a convenience store for gasoline and a six-pack of Budweiser.

When he arrived in the parking lot of his apartment building, he surveyed the surroundings for anyone lurking in the shadows. His domain was located in a part of town where safe passage to his doorway could require the use of a tire tool or other blunt instrument. Observing nothing suggesting immediate danger, he quickly opened the door and dashed toward the building. He left his truck unlocked, hoping to save a window should a neighbor or a passerby desire entry.

After warming the remaining three pieces of last night's pizza, he settled in front of the nineteen-inch TV screen and popped the top on his first of six cans. The Braves game was nothing more than a meaningless distraction as his mind continued to consider his dilemma.

I should've talked to Mr. Mitchell when he was over here. He seems like a fair enough guy, even though Leander says he's straight as an arrow and would fire me on the spot if he knew about Mississippi.

He popped another top and placed the last bite of pizza in his mouth. *I wonder what the connection is between Leander and that old judge up in Chatom? I know that's who he called the minute I walked out of his office today. Somehow, I have to figure something out.*

By 10:00, all the beer had been consumed, and Kenny lay in a death-like sleep on the vinyl couch, just as he did every night. As the local news played on the cheap television, he missed the picture and report of a missing girl who was the fifteen-year-old daughter of a lawyer assigned to the southern district of the U.S. Attorney's office in Mobile.

CHAPTER 22

DESPERATION SETTING IN

Raleigh and his clerk had just cleared the last locked gate leading to the lodge. It was three-fifteen in the afternoon, and a fundraiser was scheduled to start at six. As was customary, the judge and his aide had driven out early to prepare for the activities.

"Johnny, go on ahead and start unloading the refreshments. I need to walk around a bit and stretch my leg. My knee's been acting up all day," he announced as the pickup came to a stop.

While the clerk began the task of removing a large cooler, several bags of groceries, and two cases of liquor, Raleigh hobbled down the gravel path toward the old barn. Johnny watched his employer for a few seconds, thinking he had been unusually quiet on their way out to the old farm— uncharacteristic of the usually buoyant behavior of the man for whom he had worked since he was a teenager. Something was wrong.

"That damn Lawrence Rifle did everything but threaten me this morning when my seventy-five thousand didn't show up," he said aloud as he limped by the rusting band saw. "That arrogant son-of-a-bitch don't understand how hard it is to raise quick money down here. Hell, I haven't had but a little ova a month to work on the fundraising, and he thinks I'm just stalling to raise the ante when he's elected. Thank goodness Leander came through with that twenty-five grand yesterday. At least I was able to tell Mista Rifle that the first installment was really on its way."

As he turned into the barn, his eyes were drawn to the dirt floor where the young black girl had been repeatedly assaulted six days earlier. He absently scratched his cane across the bare earth as if to cleanse the death scene of any overlooked evidence.

"Reminds me, I need to call that Bobby in the morning. He's had plenty of time to figure out a project for Leander to go to work on."

"Judge!" he heard from the direction of the lodge. "Judge, you got a call up here. It's Sheriff Crawford. Says he's returning your call."

Raleigh ambled back out into the sunlight.

"Make sure he's coming out this evening, and if he is, I'll wait and talk to him then. See if he can come out a little early, say about five or so."

Raleigh waited by the corner of the barn for a reply. Removing his seersucker suit jacket and loosening his collar, he casually leaned against the rusting saw and was reminded of the sharecropper and his nephew who had labored for over two years rebuilding his masterpiece.

I wonder what ever happened to that negra boy after we hung old Aaron Collins and I shot the woman? That was the only hanging I ever regretted. I sure hated it when I heard we hung the wrong negra. That old man was a good worker—good farmer, too—always paid us our fair share. He and that boy sure cut a bunch of wood on this old saw.

Sheriff Virgil Crawford drove the Jeep Cherokee through the first of the three gates. He glanced at Johnny, poised by a fence post. Crawford slowed the county vehicle and, with a tip of his straw Stetson hat, acknowledged the younger man. Without speaking, he proceeded down the rough dirt road.

Virgil was a native of Washington County. He had never crossed the county line until he was drafted and spent eight months of a thirteen-month tour in Vietnam. A sniper's bullet had left him with a Purple Heart, a shattered left elbow, and a ticket home. Like many of his fellow countrymen, who had served their country with honor, he found life back in Chatom filled with despair. An occasional odd job was the only work he could find. Too proud to apply for welfare, for three years he lived a paltry existence on the small disability check he received from the Army and the few dollars he could manage doing manual labor normally reserved for members of the black community.

In 1972, at the age of twenty-eight, he was invited to a Baptist church social by the elderly lady whose rose garden he weeded occasionally. For the first time since departing for Vietnam, good fortune smiled on him.

While standing in the corner of the newly constructed Pendleton Recreation Building, he caught the attention of a rather homely young lady seated at the table of honor. At the age of thirty, Mary Belle Pirtle was considered an aging spinster who would likely spend the rest of her days unwed and without flower. Her only attribute was her lineage and the land she would inherit from her aging mother, Lottie Pendleton's cousin.

Virgil shifted from foot to foot uncomfortably as he watched the woman point in his direction and whisper in the judge's ear. Within a few minutes, Raleigh made his way to Virgil, asking him to join the group at the Pendleton table. Three months later, Virgil and Mary Belle were standing at the altar of the Antioch Baptist Church.

Financially fortified with the salary he enjoyed as a new deputy in the sheriff's office, a position arranged by the appreciative judge, Virgil and Mary Belle moved into their new home after returning from a short honeymoon at Gulf Shores, east of Mobile. Although not particularly proud of his less than beautiful bride, Virgil relished his newfound respectability as a member of the county law enforcement agency and a relative, by marriage, of the powerful probate judge.

Eleven years and three children later, fortune again smiled on Virgil. While watching *Cool Hand Luke* with his wife at the Roxy Theatre in Chatom, the county sheriff suffered a massive heart attack and died before the usher could call the community's only ambulance. With Raleigh's bullying, the city council appointed Virgil acting-sheriff until a special election could be held to elect a new one. He was the unanimous winner of the election since he was the only candidate filing for the position. All other potential candidates had recognized the futility of bucking the Pendleton money and political machine when a picture appeared in the local weekly showing Raleigh standing behind Virgil as he signed the filing form in the court clerk's office. From that day forward, he easily won every re-election campaign, and Raleigh controlled the sheriff's office just as his predecessors had for almost a century.

"What's up, Judge?" Virgil asked after radioing his office and advising he was out of service.

Cane in hand, Raleigh lumbered over the porch to greet the first arrival.

"The boys enjoyed those naughty movies you provided the other day," he announced. "Come on inside and take a load off. My knee's been acting up, and I can't stand on it too long."

"Sorry to hear it, Raleigh."

"Everyone has his burdens, but it seems like I got more than my share right now," the judge lamented, leading the sheriff across the porch and into the lodge. "Help yourself to a drink."

"Thanks, I believe I will. Now, what can I do for you? Your message sounded a little urgent."

"How many prisoners you holding down at the county jail?"

Virgil sipped his drink and removed the Stetson, revealing a shock of brown hair. He scratched his head thoughtfully.

"Let's see, I believe we have four, no three. That nigger boy made bail this morning."

"How many you think you have out on bail waiting for trial?"

"Geez, I don't know. Probably five or six. Why?"

Raleigh paused, counting in his head. "I expect that's about right. I looked at my calendar before I came out and five or six sounds right. Virgil, I need a favor."

"I'll do anything I can."

"Any of the ones in custody in there for non-violent crimes? Bad checks, drunks, petty theft?"

"Let's see. One of them is in for a DUI, his third. He's waiting for his lawyer to make bail. One for shoplifting ova in Tibbie. The other one's in for armed robbery and battery. He stuck up a gas station and beat up the attendant a couple of weeks ago. You remember, you arraigned him and the words you used were something like, 'I'll make sure your black ass spends at least ten years at hard labor.'"

Raleigh laughed. "Yeah, I remember him. Had a smart mouth. I remanded him without bail, huh? Well, he won't work. What about the other two? They have any money?"

"I think the shoplifter's just a street kid from Mobile, so I doubt he has any. The DUI is, hell, you know him, Judge. He's one of the Harrington boys from ova by Vinegar Bend. His daddy has a big bunch of land and I think he owns a couple of small banks around. I believe he owns the bank down in Citronelle."

"Jesse Harrington's boy, huh," Raleigh said thoughtfully. "That might be worth something."

Virgil stood and walked to the refrigerator. "You need any ice, Judge?"

Raleigh nodded, still deep in thought.

"What's this all about, anyway?"

Raleigh turned his tumbler up and swallowed the last of the sour mash. "Bring me that bottle of Jack and I'll tell you."

The judge started from the beginning and his first call for money from Lawrence Rifle.

"You see, now that he's raised the ante, I got to scrape the bottom of the barrel to make my pledge. I've still got a couple of big deals cooking ova at the industrial canal, but I'm running out of places to look, and I'm about three hundred thousand short if everything I got working comes through."

"So you're gonna shake down Jesse Harrington for a reduced plea? Don't you think that's a little dangerous? He's a pretty crusty old fart and could create a bunch of trouble for you," cautioned Virgil.

"I know it ain't perfect, but I'm getting a little desperate," acknowledged Raleigh in a rare verbal expression of weakness.

"Damn, I hate to see you take a chance like that, Raleigh. Maybe you should sleep on that one for a day or two. By the way, who's coming out here tonight?"

"All the local attorneys. I'm gonna put the bite on them. They won't be able to come up with more than a thousand or so apiece, but every little bit helps. I am gonna put a pretty big bite on one of them that has a big civil case in front of me next week—an insurance deal. If he'll play ball, I aim to rule big for his plaintiff, and he can show his appreciation by ponying up a piece of his contingency. Could be worth twenty grand or more into the kitty."

"That sounds safer than taking on Jessie. Is there anything I can do to help?"

"Can't think of anything right now, but I'll keep you in mind. You're a good friend, Virgil," replied Raleigh. "I'll get this business done here tonight and then get back to a project I'm working on ova on the canal in the morning. If I don't get this money raised, it could do serious damage to a lifetime spent gathering up favors from the big boys up north."

CHAPTER 23

CONFESSIONS

Kenny Quincy's auburn tee shirt stuck to his back as he drove west on Interstate 10. Although the sun was just peeping up over the eastern horizon, open windows and moving air were no match for the morning mugginess of southeast Texas in late May. The air conditioner on the old pickup he was driving had long since gone the way of the radio, which didn't work either.

It was 10:30 in the morning, and I had just finished a telephone conversation with my operations manager in Louisiana when my secretary buzzed over the intercom, "Mr. Quincy's here to see you."

When Kenny had called, two days earlier, asking if he could come to Houston and talk, I had offered to buy him a ticket on Continental, but he declined, declaring he had relatives he wanted to see while he was in town. While I didn't believe his reason for shunning the offer, I didn't insist, concerned it would challenge his self-esteem. I would soon find out the real reason.

"Hello, Kenny. Have a seat. I just need to make a note," I said as he entered my office.

Although he wore a freshly pressed dress shirt, I noticed the streaks of dried sweat across his forehead and beneath his sideburns. Out of the corner of my eye, I watched him trudge across the carpet and slouch into one of the two chairs in front of my desk. He carried a cheap black briefcase. His freckled face and the manner in which he carried his smallish frame portrayed a combination of fatigue and defeat.

"Can I offer you anything? Coffee, a Coke? One of the girls brought in some donuts this morning. Have you eaten breakfast?"

"No, thanks," he muttered.

"You sure? You look tired. Did you drive all night?"

"Yes, sir."

"That's a long haul, all the way from Mobile. Must be, what? Five or six hundred miles by car?"

"I actually started from Jackson, Mississippi yesterday evening."

"Jackson? Why Jackson? You have family there?"

"I do, kind of, but that's not why."

For the next twenty minutes, Kenny Quincy recited a detailed history of his life for the past seven years, including his felony conviction for embezzlement in Mississippi. If he left out anything of importance, I'm fairly certain it was an oversight. Listening to the confession was somewhat uncomfortable for me, but it was pure hell for Kenny. On two different occasions he broke down and cried like a guilt-ridden third-grader admitting to stealing the teacher's favorite pen.

"So I guess you'll fire me now," he conceded as he finished his story.

"Why would I fire you? Have you stolen from me or my company?" I asked.

"Mista Leander told me you'd fire me for sure if you ever found out about my past."

I thought about those words for several seconds.

"Kenny, everyone makes mistakes of one kind or another. I have a friend who had to spend three years in a federal prison for fraud, and he's still my friend. As a matter of fact, I talked to him yesterday. He's back at work and his life is looking up. I even loaned his wife a little money while he was gone to help her get through some rough times, and he paid me back. I made some mistakes when I was younger, nothing criminal, but I sure made some decisions I regretted. It took a lot of courage for you to come to me with this, and I respect you for it."

Kenny sighed and tears again formed in his eyes.

"But you haven't told me everything, have you?" I inquired.

He lowered his eyes and shook his head.

"Something's going on over in Mobile that shouldn't be?" I guessed.

He nodded.

"Kenny, why don't you get a Coke or something while I go to the head. It looks like this conversation might go on for quite a bit longer."

We both returned to my office at about the same time. I carried a cup of coffee—Kenny, a Coke and three donuts—one half-consumed.

"Before we go on, I have a question. I require every administrative employee in my company to be bonded—a fidelity bond. How on earth did you get a bond?"

"I don't know anything about a fidelity bond."

"Don't you pay the bills?"

"Yes, sir, but I've never paid a bill for a bond for anyone in Mobile," he responded with conviction.

I pushed the button on the speakerphone. "Kelly, would you bring me the bond file for Mobile?"

Thirty seconds of silence passed before my secretary laid a blue folder on my desk. I flipped it open, and there were six bound packets, each containing four or five pages. I thumbed through the stack and pulled one out.

"Here it is. In fact, it was renewed just a month ago. Kenneth Allen Quincy, social security number, 455-55-9385. That's you, isn't it?"

"Yes sir, but…is it an original or a copy?"

"It appears to be an original. It has a raised seal." I flipped a couple of pages. "Here's the application. The ink's blue. Is this your signature?"

"The signature's close, but I didn't sign this." He rubbed his finger over the seal on the certificate and then held it up to the light. "This isn't a corporate seal. It's a notary seal, and the name of the notary is…I can barely make it out. It looks like, Viv, Vivian Thompson. Vivian Thompson, our last receptionist."

"Miss Vivian?"

"Yeah. Is there a bond in there for Mista Leander?"

"I'm sure there is. Yes, here it is. I wonder—"

"Mista Jack, I'd bet my parole that both of these bonds are fakes, forgeries. Mista Leander's no more bondable than I am."

CHAPTER 24

STILL MISSING

"Lawton, you got a minute?" asked Charles Shumaker, head of the Mobile office of the U.S. Attorney.

Lawton looked up from the file he'd been trying to work on all morning, with little success. "Sure, Charlie, come on in. Have a seat." He closed the file and sat back in his chair.

"I don't guess there's any new word about Janie?"

Lawton shook his head and sighed.

"Why don't you take some vacation or leave? This job's stressful enough without the added burden you and Barbara are dealing with. How's she holding up?"

"She has her good moments, and then some bad ones—mostly bad. She keeps blaming herself for Janie running off. Can't get passed it. I keep trying to tell her Janie's always been stubborn and headstrong, something she inherited from her father. But so far, she won't let go of the guilt she feels."

"Like I said, why don't you take some leave? You look five years older than you did a week ago."

"Thanks. At least I don't look as old as I feel. I appreciate the offer and your concern, Charlie, but if I just sat at home, I'd go crazy. Besides, I offered to stay around the house, and Barbara wouldn't hear of it. She feels like if I'm working there's a better chance of someone finding her. Her mother's staying at the house with her, and I check in every couple of hours or so."

"Lawton, there's not much you can do here to help find her. You have all the authorities working on it and—"

"I know, Charlie, but if I'm here working, I feel like maybe if something bad happened, if someone…well, if I'm working on trying to put some bad guy where he needs to be, maybe I'm indirectly making a contribution to the system and maybe the system will find her. I don't know, Charlie, I'm not making any sense, but I'd rather be here than just sitting on my hands."

"I could order you to go home, you know."

"I know you could, but I sure hope you won't. If you see me doing something stupid or fucking up somehow, let me know and I'll leave voluntarily. Until then, I'd sure like to hang around." Lawton's eyes burned as he spoke, but the tears didn't come. Seven nights of crying seemed to have depleted the reservoir.

"Okay, but if anything breaks or Barbara needs you, drop what you're doing and get the hell home. Deal?"

As Charlie walked out of his office, the phone rang.

"Lawton Tremont," he answered.

"Lawton, I just got your call. What's up?" asked Fred Carleton.

"Fred, thanks for calling back. I don't guess you have anything?"

"Sorry, Lawton, nothing yet, but I'm on it. How's Barbara doing?"

"Not well. Fred, there's a possibility she was on her way to Tuscaloosa the night she disappeared."

"How so?"

"As I've told you, we checked with Aaron a couple of days after she left. We waited because he was in the middle of finals, and we didn't want to distract him."

"I remember, and he hadn't heard from her," added Fred.

"That's right, but he called last night and said he was deleting old messages from his cell phone and there was one from Janie. He didn't know why it hadn't shown up before, but luckily it was still in the memory."

"Go on."

"Well, it's not conclusive, but I had him recite it back to me, word for word, and it's possible she was heading up to the university to cool off."

"Tell me what it…she said."

"She said she and her mother had a fight, and she needed to get away for a little while. She asked if he knew how much a bus to Tuscaloosa would cost."

"That's it?"

"Yeah. Oh, she went off on her mother a little bit and hung up. I haven't told Barbara about it yet, and I told Aaron not to say anything. Until we know more, Barbara doesn't need to hear what Janie said about her."

"Lawton, this is really good news. The honest truth is we haven't found any kind of lead. We followed up on the list of her friends you gave us and came up with nothing. Now, we at least have something to work on. Did she have any money? I mean, why would she be concerned about the cost of a bus ticket?"

"Janie was…isn't exactly thrifty. She gets a weekly allowance and occasionally earns extra money babysitting, but she spends it about as fast as it hits her billfold. I doubt she had the price of a ticket to Tuscaloosa."

"Is there any money missing? From your wallet, Barbara's purse, a cookie jar?"

"I don't think so. We don't usually keep cash around the house. Probably should, but we don't. There wasn't any missing from my wallet, and Barbara always uses credit cards. Probably never has over fifteen bucks in her purse. I haven't asked her, but she would have probably mentioned it before now. It's about all we've talked about for the last week."

"I can imagine. Well, we can start from there and see where it leads us. Now that we know this, maybe we should check back with any of her friends who have cars. You don't think she would consider hitchhiking, do you?"

"I wouldn't think so, but like I've said before, she's stubborn and headstrong—"

"Just like her father. Let me get working on this angle, and I'll let you know when anything turns up."

"Thanks again, Fred. You're a damn good friend."

"If the situation were reversed, wouldn't you do it for me?"

"Of course."

"Well, there you go. Hang in there. We'll find her, and my gut tells me this is going to all be nothing but a bad dream."

"Thanks, pal."

As the line clicked, Lawton considered how patronizing Fred's last statement had been. He knew as well as anyone that the likelihood of a positive recovery decreased exponentially with time. It had been over seven days and time was working against them, and Jane.

CHAPTER 25

HEAT'S RISING

"Uncle Raleigh, Mr. Bitterman's on the phone," announced his niece while placing a cup of coffee on his desk.

"Thank you, sweetie," he responded. "Could you close the door as you're leaving?"

Bonnie Mae did as requested while the judge eyed the blinking button. *I wonder if him calling me is good or bad? I guess I'll know soon enough.*

"Morning, Bobby. Good to hear from you so soon."

"Maybe not, Judge. I don't have any good news."

"Oh?"

"I've spent the last two days doing nothing but working through the budget looking for something your man could do to take care of our...eh...problem. I don't have a nickel left in the capital budget for the year."

The judge signed deeply as the reality of the words sunk in. "Bobby, surely you got something ova there in that big old plant that needs fixing."

"Judge, I've walked the entire facility at least four times, looking for problem areas. I found a couple and I called the home office and asked if I could send in a special requisition, but I got turned down flat. In fact, they told me I might have to cut back on production and layoff some more people before year's end if paper prices don't improve. I'm only running two shifts as it is. I'm sure sorry, Judge. I feel terrible."

The line was silent for several uncomfortable seconds. The desk drawer was opened and the ever-present bottle of Jack Daniel's was extracted.

After a large gulp, Raleigh asked, "Bobby, what happens ova there if you have an emergency?"

"What do you mean? What kind of an emergency?"

"I mean, like, if one of the production lines goes down and you can't keep the production going. Something like that."

"Well, we have a maintenance department who would get right on the problem and fix it."

"What if it couldn't be fixed by them? I mean, what if it required buying a new piece of equipment or something?"

"Depending on how important the equipment was to the line, I'd call the home office and they'd authorize me to order it in. Where you going with this, Judge?"

"Oh, nowhere. I was just wondering. What's the most important part of your production operation?

"That's kind of a hard one. The pulp kettles, I guess. Everything starts there. Judge, I don't understand what—"

"Bobby, it's a damn shame we got you in this situation, but we're in it up to our necks, and I need to give it some thought. You keep thinking about it, too, and don't forget, Harley Logginfield threatened to send some of the pictures to Myrtle if he didn't get his money."

Bobby started to reply and then realized no one was on the other end. He replaced the receiver and sat behind his desk for a few seconds before he began to cry.

"That son-of-a-bitch!" Raleigh swore after hanging up the phone. "He ain't gonna get off that easy. I'm gonna get that fifty thousand if it's the last thing I ever do."

Taking another sip from the bottle, he began to relax. The idea that had begun formulating in his mind at the end of the conversation was starting to sound better and better. After a few more minutes of thought, he smiled and touched the intercom button. "Bonnie Mae, would you get Leander Rutherford on the phone for me?"

"Okay," his niece replied, "but you're due in court in five minutes."

"After you call Mista Rutherford, call Johnny and tell him to send everybody home and to reset the docket for tomorrow."

A minute passed and Bonnie Mae broke the silence of his office. "He's on the line, Uncle—"

Raleigh grabbed the receiver from the cradle. "Leander, go to a public phone and call me back, quick like."

Without waiting for a reply, he hung up.

CHAPTER 26

UNANNOUNCED

Kenny and I walked out of the lobby of the airport at 10:15 Wednesday morning. We were accompanied by two young men dressed in almost identical navy blue suits, starched white shirts, and striped ties—one maroon and blue, the other navy and white. Both carried black leather briefcases. They could have had "I'm gay" stamped on their foreheads and not been any more conspicuous in the casual atmosphere of Mobile.

After hearing the rest of the story Kenny had driven to Mobile to confess, I had made a call to the accounting firm I paid thousands of dollars per year, demanding immediate attention. Actually, the partner in charge of my account was very sympathetic and cooperative and made my traveling companions available with little fanfare.

I had convinced Kenny that an airplane ticket with his name on it would never be used as proof he had left the states of Alabama or Mississippi without the permission of his parole officer, as he had feared when he had declined my earlier offer to fly him to Houston. Apparently, Kenny had decided I wasn't the fire-breathing dragon Leander had described in order to rein in control over the felonious accountant. As for his car, I told him I would provide sufficient funds for a better automobile should his allegations of wrong-doing be confirmed by the young men we had brought with us—sort of a reward for blowing the whistle before the losses got out of control. I only hoped we hadn't already reached that point.

After driving my rental car to the office, and numerous failed attempts to persuade the twins not to call me Mr. Mitchell, we arrived and were greeted by the welcome news that Leander was out for the rest of the day. I was prepared for a confrontation, but his absence would give us more latitude to perform the task at hand.

"He said he had an important meeting with Judge Pendleton up in Chatom and wouldn't be back until tomorrow at the earliest," announced Lollie Masters, the prettier receptionist Leander had hired to better suit his appearance requirements. He had fired the ugly one the previous Tuesday— the day Kenny had left Mobile for Mississippi and then Houston.

"That's fine, Lollie. I'm Jack Mitchell, and I own this business. We're happy to have you aboard," I announced as a way of introduction. "We know our way around. We'll be working in the conference room and in Kenny's office."

"I don't know you gentlemen, and I think I should call someone," she declared, blocking the door to the back of the office suite.

"Ma'am, I'm Kenny Quincy, and I work here in the office, right down there. I'm the accountant for the company, and I'll be writing your paychecks," offered Kenny as an introduction and a veiled threat as to her vulnerability. "I can assure you Mr. Mitchell is exactly who and what he says he is. Mr. Rutherford works for him."

"But Mr. Leander told me he was the boss."

"That's true, Lollie, but everyone has a boss, and I'm his. Mine is my wife," I offered jokingly, although I almost choked on the words.

With Lollie satisfied with our credentials, we proceeded to work through the myriad transactions Kenny had documented before coming to Houston. The youngsters checked and double-checked all of Kenny's work. At the end of the day, they had confirmed the following: more than fifteen thousand dollars of work done on Miss Vivian's home had been improperly coded to six different jobs; over one hundred and twenty-two thousand had been paid to R&P Products Company of Chatom, Alabama; approximately thirty-eight thousand had been paid to L&V Materials, Inc.; and there was almost sixty thousand of invoices containing various irregularities, yet to be confirmed.

A quick check with the secretary of state's office found no record of any corporate filing for either of the two suspicious companies. A telephone call to the number on the R&P invoice revealed the number was not in service. All in all, while there were more confirmations to be made, I was totally convinced that all of Kenny's suspicions were true, and there was probably more to be uncovered. I needed to take quick and decisive action.

My first call was to my attorney, Josh McTiernan. We had been fraternity brothers in college and good friends ever since. When my business interests had grown to the point where legal issues became a regular occurrence, I had placed Josh on retainer. He had been my counselor and trusted advisor ever since.

"Josh, it seems my business in Mobile has been looted by my partner," I declared after we dispensed with quick personal exchanges.

"How bad, Jack?" he inquired with no hint of surprise.

"A quick and dirty number is between two hundred and two-fifty."

"Holy shit! Can the company take a lick like that?"

"We can survive it, but it hurts. I may have to put some more capital into the company."

"What do you want me to do?"

"First, look at the employment contract we have with Leander. I know it provides him with the opportunity to earn out a third of the equity in the company. Obviously, I don't intend to stay in business with a thief, so tell me my options. Second, does the company have any liability? I think some of the money could've gone to illegal contributions, kickbacks, that sort of thing. Third—"

"Hold on. Why do you think there could be kickbacks and such?"

"He's all hung up with being one of the big power brokers in Alabama. Down here, that often means political connections and paying people off. He's in bed with this judge in the county north of here, and almost half of the money's made its way up there. I don't know much about this judge yet, other than I met him before I bought the business and didn't like him much. I intend to check him out further."

"Okay, go on."

"Let's see. Find out what you can about how many criminal laws he may have broken, based on what I've told you. I know you aren't an Alabama lawyer, but the criminal laws can't be that different from Texas."

"Is that all?"

"All I can think of at this moment, but I'm sure there'll be more. Call it a starter list."

"I'm on it, Jack. How can I reach you?"

I gave him all my numbers.

"Oh, one last thing. Should I call the FBI or someone?" I asked.

"Bad idea, Jackson. I need to see where you and the company stand regarding legal liability. I know you were in the dark about all of this until now, but you're an outsider on his turf, and I want to have a clear picture of your legal standing."

"The FBI's federal, not local. How could his being from here influence them?" I argued.

"They operate on somebody's turf every day, and they have to get along. Sure, based on what you've told me, you're the good guy here, but until I know what your potential liability is, let's leave the authorities out of this. Right now, I don't know where the jurisdictional issues reside. Okay?"

"Okay, but it sucks."

My next call was to Montgomery. I had only talked to Fin Ross once since meeting him in the bar, but I thought he could be a possible source of information on one subject.

"Fin, this is Jack Mitchell."

"Good to hear from you, Jack, but I'm afraid I don't have much more to report than I did when we talked the other day. Things might move a little slower down here than they do over in Texas."

"That's not why I'm calling. When we first met, you said we'd get along just fine because we both cut straight to the chase. I realize we haven't known each other very long, but I have a situation down here, and I need some information about someone you might know about. Is that covered under your retainer agreement?"

"No. No, but it's covered by respect and friendship. If you want information about someone I'd rather not talk about, I'll tell you so, and that'll be that. On the other hand, if the information isn't potentially compromising to me, I'll tell you anything I can."

"Fair enough. Do you know a guy in Washington County named Pendleton? Judge Raleigh Pendleton?"

Fin laughed. "Raleigh? He's just an old Alabama polecat, but not someone to trifle with. What's your connection with the judge?"

"Well, I don't have one, but our mutual friend Leander does. It appears Leander and this Pendleton guy have some sort of business relationship or, more likely, a front. Money has been going out of my company to Chatom at a fairly rapid rate. I hope I can trust you with this information, Fin. We haven't gotten to the bottom of it yet, but the facts are pretty reliable."

"This is just between you and me until you say different, Jack. I have an idea of what it could be about, but I'd need to make a couple of calls and still might not be able to confirm anything."

"What's your theory?"

"Well, I'm just speculating, of course, but Robert Laughlin, one of our state senators, is putting up a pretty respectable fight against Lawrence Rifle

104

for the Democratic nomination for governor. Rifle's a part of the old Wallace machinery and, word has it, he's been out shaking the bushes for money. I've had a pretty respectable amount of money flow into my PAC for Mr. Rifle's benefit. Raleigh's an old line Democrat and is probably the biggest fish in his county. Could be that Rifle's been hitting him up for constituent support, and Raleigh's running his traps. I don't think we've received anything from the judge, but there are lots of ways of getting money into a campaign. Some legal, and some not so legal. Based on past experience, the judge would probably prefer the latter."

"I see. So you suspect the money going out of here could be ending up in this Rifle fellow's war chest?"

"Could be but let me do some checking. I do have to have your word on something."

"What's that?"

"I don't give two shits about Raleigh Pendleton or Leander Rutherford. If you find they've been up to no good, that's okay with me, but if I help you and your investigation leads you to Lawrence Rifle, you have to agree not to pursue him."

"Why, Fin?"

"Jack, I'm a part of the old Wallace political machine, too, and Rifle's our candidate. We've spent a shit load of money grooming this guy, and we're committed to getting the governor's mansion back under Democratic control. I can't help you derail this election, and I doubt you'll find anyone else who can get you the information you want on the judge, other than me. I don't want to play hardball, but this election is too important to the state. Besides, you don't have a fight with Mr. Rifle, do you?"

"No, I don't see how I do. I want Leander, and I'm only interested in the judge if he's a party to the embezzlement that's been going on in my company. I can agree to your terms. Mr. Rifle's safe from me, as if that's really a big deal—being safe from one of the slaughtered sheep you told me about when we met."

Fin laughed lightly. "Good deal. I hope you get him, and I'll help you if I can."

"Fin, I appreciate your willingness to help. I'd be obliged if you can make your calls quickly. As you can imagine, I need to move on this as soon as possible."

"I'll start when we hang up. What are you going to do about old Leander?"

"Kill him."

CHAPTER 27

TRAVELLING NORTH

The rhythm of Carlos Santana filled the cab of the rented truck. Julio Santos tapped the dashboard with his right hand—his left occupied with the business of steering the vehicle. He mumbled his way through the words he didn't know, belting out the lyrics he remembered. The milk run had gone smoothly, although he was almost seven hours behind schedule. Only two days and four drops separated him from Atlanta and a flight back to Miami. His mood was bright, but he wanted to make up time. He had wrestled with the thought of increasing the pedal pressure on the accelerator, but common sense had won out.

Seven wrapped packages of white powder and over nine hundred thousand dollars rested behind a false panel in back. The cargo area was half-filled with crates of imported costume jewelry, hand-painted Mexican pottery, woven wool rugs, and machine-carved marble chess sets. Delivering the legitimate cargo would be his last stop before removing and discarding the false panel, securing the money in the empty suitcases, and returning the one-way rental to the Texaco station close to the airport. Roberto had always felt a yellow rental truck was less likely to be stopped than a company-owned vehicle and easier to deal with legally should a mule be caught. For over five years, he had been right.

When the discomfort in his bladder finally overcame his desire to keep driving, Julio exited Interstate 10 for a rest stop between Pensacola and Mobile, his next drop point. Pulling into the parking space closest to the cinder-block restrooms, he observed a beaten up '89 Ford Taurus with its hood up and steam belching from the radiator. He jumped from the panel truck and moved gingerly toward the door displaying the silhouette of a man.

His body shuddered as the clear liquid flowed into the latrine. Still mumbling the tune from the radio, he projected the stream in circles around the pink cake of disinfectant resting on a rubber screen.

Feeling much better, he exited the building and looked at his watch. *Four-thirty. I'd better check in with Roberto,* he thought. Extracting the cell phone from the clip on his belt, he dialed the number of Santos Importing Company.

"Anna, how's my girlfriend this afternoon?" he greeted.

"Thank goodness, it's you, Julio," was her response. "Roberto's been pacing the bulkhead for the last thirty minutes."

"My big brother worries too much."

"He loves you, Julio. He didn't want you to make the run."

"I know. He thinks of me more like the son than the brother. I love him, too, but he worries too much. Put him on."

Latino music played over the line as Julio watched a woman pacing in the parking lot behind the smoking Taurus.

"Julio, where the hell have you been?" Roberto demanded. "You should have called in by four o'clock. It's a quarter-to-five. You're supposed to call in every eight hours."

"Take it easy, Bertie. I was making good time and didn't have any reception on my cell phone until just a few miles back," he lied.

"Where are you?"

"About forty-five minutes out from Mobile. Everything's gone like clockwork since I talked to you this morning. Roserio wanted an extra kilo when I made his drop, but I told him the amounts were fixed when I left Miami and it would short someone on down the line. He wasn't happy, but he understood. He wants to increase his weekly allotment by one extra from now on. Says his business is booming."

"You made a good decision. Shooter Pinkston has already called me. He asked for a double this trip, and I told him no. I guess the beaches are starting to fill up. You've had no problems?"

"Everything's cool."

"Have you stayed on the major highways like we discussed?"

"Yes, Bertie. I'm not an idiot. And I haven't been on the road at night, except the night I left. Bertie, if you don't want to have to go through this again, you're going to have to replace Charlie. He's a mess."

"I know. I'm working on it. You going to Shooter's place before you check into a motel?"

"Yeah, but I'd like to drive on up to Montgomery this evening. I could make up some of the time I lost when the alternator went out yesterday."

"No way, Julio. No driving at night, and I mean it. You understand, Julio?" Roberto's delivery became louder with every word.

"Okay, okay. I just thought it would be better if we didn't make our customers on the end of the run wait."

"I've talked to all of them, and everyone's okay. Just follow the route and get your ass back here safely."

"Okay. I better get going. I'll call in at about nine tonight. I want to get to bed early, so I can get an early start in the morning."

"Just be careful and don't drive any faster than—"

"Bertie, you're becoming a bore," laughed Julio. "You take care, and I'll call at nine."

Julio walked toward the truck and again noticed the young woman behind the smoking vehicle. Straining his eyes, he could see she was crying while looking up and down the interstate.

"You okay, miss?" he asked from the corner of the truck.

She turned quickly, startled by the unexpected voice.

"I'm sorry, I didn't mean to frighten you," he offered, walking slowly toward her. "Are you in trouble? It looks like your car's had it."

Although her appearance was disheveled, he could see she was younger than he originally thought. He could also see she was very pretty.

"Can I help you? Give you a ride?"

"Who are you?" she responded, her eyes darting.

"Miss, I'm no threat to you. I'm actually on a very tight schedule, but you looked so…eh…upset. I thought maybe you were in trouble. Never mind. I hope your day gets better." He turned and walked toward the truck.

"Wait!" she almost screamed. "Wait, I'm sorry. I do need help."

CHAPTER 28
A GENIUS PLAN

Leander pulled his new white Mercury sedan, compliments of L&V Materials, Inc., through the first of the three gates. In his usual position stood Johnny, carbine in hand.

"How's it hanging, Johnny?" Leander said, stopping the car.

"Where's Billy?" the clerk asked.

"I told him to stay ova at Republic and I'd handle this meeting by myself. That job's going real good, and I want to get it finished quick like."

Johnny looked curiously at the man he considered a buffoon.

"Better get on up to the lodge. I think the judge has something he wants to discuss with you before Bobby gets here."

"He said he wanted me here early. You take care now," Leander offered as the engine screamed. He looked sheepishly toward Johnny as he placed the transmission back in drive.

"What a dumb-ass," Johnny mouthed under his breath.

"Leander! Come on inside," the judge yelled from the recliner where he was resting his bum knee.

Checking his shirt pocket for a fresh pack of Winstons, Leander ambled up the stairs.

"How you doing, Judge?"

"Not worth a shit. This damn knee of mine hurts more and more every day that goes by. Excuse me for not getting up, but I need to keep my leg elevated as much as I can. Pour yourself a drink, but don't drink too much until we get this Bitterman business done."

"Thanks, Judge. I think I'll just have one short one," replied Leander, moving toward the kitchen area. "Can I get you anything?"

"No, I got all I need right here." Raleigh lifted up a pint bottle about one-third consumed. "Leander, I called Harvey ova at Republic this afternoon and asked him if he could manage an advance on the job you're doing ova there. He said the plant engineer had just left his office and was threatening to kick you off the job. Said you were a week behind schedule and the whole damn job shouldn't have took ova two. What the hell's going on ova there?"

"Well, Billy did say something last week about some problems he was having with some suppliers that plant engineer made us use. He's pretty sure the Republic man must be getting a little back under the table," Leander lied, hoping the judge wouldn't follow up on his accusation.

"I don't give a damn what the problem is, get it fixed. You understand? I got Lawrence Rifle calling me damn near every day, and he's busting my chops for money. I thought if I could get a little advance from Harvey, I could send it up north and take a little heat off. That ain't gonna happen because you're running so far behind. Republic probably won't give up another nickel until the job's finished, so get the son-of-a-bitch finished!"

"That's why I'm here alone this afternoon. I left Billy up there, so he could run roughshod ova the workers and get some production out. We'll get it finished and be out of there in no time flat," Leander proclaimed and then swallowed over half of his drink in one gulp.

Raleigh eyed him suspiciously. "Do you think Billy Cudjoe's worth a shit? Every job he's handled that I know about's been fucked up and didn't make any money."

"Billy's a top hand, Judge. He's had a couple of bad breaks on a job or two, but when the chips are down, Billy's the man I want on the ground. Hell, he's been with me ova twenty-five years."

"You better be right, because I got this plan I told you about for getting the money out of General Paper, and I'm assuming he'll be your man on the ground, as you put it."

"He's my man alright. We can count on old Billy to do a fine job ova there this weekend," Leander blustered while walking back to the kitchen for another drink.

"I told you to go light on that stuff until the deal's been made with Bobby," Raleigh said. "I don't need to have no drunk construction man babbling like an idiot while we finish shaking him down. Leander, you've been very helpful with certain things ova the years we've been knowing one another, but your performance of late hasn't been up to par. Maybe you should spend a little more time at the office and a little less with your head stuck up Miss Vivian's butt."

Before Leander could reply, they both heard a blast from Johnny's horn—the signal announcing the arrival of the guest of honor. Raleigh pulled down on the handle on the side of the recliner, lowering his swollen knee. He picked up his cane.

"Bobby, that you, you old polecat?" Raleigh yelled as he limped onto the front porch.

Bobby exited his pickup while Johnny drove past and parked behind the barn. He would not be a participant in this meeting. While Johnny had proven his loyalty on numerous occasions, the judge subscribed to the concept that everyone was on a "need to know" basis when certain acts were being contemplated.

The first fifteen minutes of the meeting had been filled with the usual banter when Southern boys get together. The judge had reassumed his position in the recliner, Leander dangled from a barstool with a glass of tap water in front of him, and Bobby sat on the sofa, fidgeting with the can of Busch he hadn't sipped.

"Bobby, me and Leander's been talking about your problem coming up with your share of the two hundred thousand Harley Logginfield's demanding. We think there could be a way out of this trap," Raleigh began.

Bobby sat a little more erect. "Oh?"

"Well, you actually came up with the guts of the idea, and I got to hand it to you, it's a genius plan."

"I don't remember coming up with any plan. Everything I've tried has been shot down by the home office," Bobby replied.

"You didn't actually come up with the plan, but you sure enough put the idea in my head. Now listen up and don't get all riled until you hear me out."

Bobby threw his head backward, allowing half the contents of the can to flow into his mouth.

"You said the pulp kettles were probably the most important part of your production operation. Right?"

Bobby nodded, his brow furrowed.

"Well, this coming Sunday night, actually Monday morning, there's going to be a fire in one of them kettles, maybe two of them, depending on what you think. Leander tells me there's three of them ova there. Is that right?"

111

"Yeah, but—"

"Now, just hear me out. We figure, depending on the seriousness of the fire, the repair or replacement cost could be ova a million dollars. Right?"

Bobby nodded again and chugged the remainder of the can. Beads of sweat were popping out on his forehead.

"The company would have to fix it, wouldn't it?"

Bobby said nothing.

"So now we got that emergency situation you was talking about the other day and because of the importance of getting the plant back on production as fast as possible, you could just give the job to Jefferson Construction without fiddling with the bidding process. A million is plenty enough money to hide your fifty thousand, and Leander's promised he'll be damn fair on his profit in the deal. Ain't that right, Leander?"

Leander nodded enthusiastically while handing Bobby another beer.

Bobby sat silently for over a minute. The judge placed the pint to his lips and took a generous pull. Leander gratefully poured scotch over the ice in his glass—his part in the meeting being successfully completed. Now it was up to Bobby.

"I can't be a part of anything like this, Judge. This just ain't right. I guess I'll have to go to Myrtle and fess up."

Raleigh projected an icy stare. "Bobby, I wanted to save you from what I'm getting ready to show you, but your damn self-righteous attitude's left me no choice."

Reaching to the floor, Raleigh produced a manila envelope and handed it to the younger man.

"What's this?"

"Open it up and see for yourself," the judge ordered.

Bobby stared directly into Raleigh's eyes while his fingers extracted a photograph. Raleigh never blinked. Looking down at the picture briefly, Bobby tossed it onto the coffee table.

"I told you I didn't want to see any of those pictures that damn fool Jim Bob took."

"No, you need to look closely at this one. Go on, look at it again."

Bobby again fingered the photograph.

"That your belt around that pretty negra girl's neck?" Raleigh asked.

"Yeah, but...I never put any...where's the girl now?" Bobby asked, closing his eyes.

"Bobby, what we never wanted you to know—cause you're a good Christian boy—we never wanted you to know you killed her."

"I did not! I couldn't do anything like that."

"We know you didn't mean to. I'm sure things just got out of hand. But when Johnny went in to get you after you passed out, she was dead, and your belt was around her neck. Hell, Jim Bob watched the whole thing and never did see anything that looked like you was trying to hurt her. I guess she was such a little thing. You probably didn't pull very hard, but all I know is, she was dead."

The judge sat back in the recliner and waited.

Several minutes passed. Bobby slouched in the sofa and stared at the floor. After what he judged to be an appropriate amount of time, Raleigh spoke again.

"So you see, Bobby, we can't let Harley pursue this mess. He's got the same picture I showed you, and he knows the girl's dead, too. He'd have hell coming up with a body, but in my court, it would be a toss up on whether any of us would walk out of there free or not. Hell, we might even get an ambitious federal prosecutor who'd go for murder against all of us, particularly you. This deal's more serious than your old lady kicking the shit out of you. Harley's demanding that fifty thousand—even talking about interest. Me and Jim Bob and Leander's tapped out. It's your call, Bobby, and we have to know now."

CHAPTER 29
THE GOOD SAMARITAN

"So you're a dancer in Lauderdale, Tina?" Julio asked while the panel truck headed for the causeway leading to Mobile. "But you were raised in Alabama, in what? Citro something?"

"Yeah, Citronelle. My stepfather works in a plant over on the industrial canal. My mom and dad got divorced when I was twelve, and she ended up marrying this jerk. The sick son-of-a-bitch used to walk in on me every time I took a bath. I couldn't walk by him without him pinching me on the butt. One day, right after my seventeenth birthday, he forced me into the garage and started licking me on the neck and humping me against a wall. I kneed the motherfucker good where it hurts. He knocked the shit out of me, but I got away from him, packed my bags, and hit the road."

"Did you tell your mother about him messing with you?"

"Once, but she was drunk half the time and trying to keep him from kicking the shit out of her the rest. Talking to her didn't help, so I left. This'll be my first trip back in four years, and I would never have come back if my real father wasn't lying in that fucking nursing home dying. Hey, you mind if I smoke?"

"Not at all. I'll join you," Julio replied. "Like I told you at the rest stop, I'll need to drop you somewhere for about an hour while I deliver some of these trinkets in the back. You have any place in mind? I don't know anything about Mobile, other than where my delivery is."

"Yeah, there's a bar down by the docks. I worked there for a couple of months until I got enough money to move on down the coast. The owner was real nice to me. I'll just hang out there until you finish your business."

"It should only take about an hour."

"Don't hurry on my account. I just want to get to Citronelle in time to see my dad before he dies."

Julio dropped Tina at the Blue Oyster Bar and Grill. He felt a little guilty leaving her in such a seedy part of town but convinced himself that anyone messing with Tina Tucker might get more than they bargained for.

With the drop completed and another fifty thousand behind the false panel, Julio made an early call to Roberto, listened to all the standard warnings and reminders, and headed back to the Blue Oyster. He didn't mention anything about Tina to his brother.

After retrieving his passenger, he proceeded north of Mobile on state highway 43, the first single lane road he'd been on since leaving Miami. When the truck passed the sign indicating they were only ten miles from their destination, Julio looked at his watch and glanced at the sun fading behind the low clouds on the horizon. *I should make it back to Mobile just before dark.*

As the rural houses along the highway began to cluster into small neighborhoods, he glanced at Tina, who had been particularly quiet for the past ten minutes. Small droplets transporting black specks inched downward over her cheeks.

"You okay?" Julio asked softly.

Tina sighed and then sniffed like a lumberjack with a sinus infection. "Yeah, I'm great. Motherfucker, why'd I come back here?" She sighed again, wiping her nose with the back of her hand. Lighting a cigarette, she took a long drag. "You got any booze in here? I need a drink before I do this thing."

"No, I don't carry liquor. Is there a package store nearby?" asked Julio, feeling sorry for this young girl who had grown up much too fast.

"There's not one here, but there's a place just over the county line."

"How far?" Julio asked, again looking at his watch.

"Only a few miles, but you've done enough. You said you don't like to drive at night, so why don't you just—"

"I don't mind another few miles," he offered. "It's not like werewolves are out there."

"You might be surprised in this part of the state. If you don't mind, a drink would sure make me feel better when I see him. Mom said he looks pretty bad."

As they drove through town, she looked at the Shining Hope nursing home, tightly closed her eyes, and lit another cigarette. Six miles later, flashing neon signaled their destination. Neither of them had noticed the broken pole, which a week earlier had supported a sign that read, "Entering Washington County." Neither of them saw the gray Jeep Cherokee sitting in a grove of trees immediately across the highway from the roadhouse.

With a pint of vodka in hand, Tina stepped up into the cab and uncapped the bottle. The bubbles rising upward reminded Julio of a miniature water dispenser as air replaced the liquid being sucked from the container.

Tina shook her head and announced, "There. I'll feel better in a minute. You can take me back now. Julio, you're a great guy."

Julio smiled and felt good about himself. "I know," he said with a wink, flipping on the lights and pulling onto the highway.

Deputy Lester Holmboe, the greenest addition to Virgil Crawford's nine man force, hit the siren and the bubble-lights on his cruiser a mere five seconds after the van pulled onto the roadway. Knowing the Mobile County line was only a mile away, he knew he must act fast or lose a ticket to one of his counterparts to the south. Lester liked to issue tickets.

"Mista, could you step out of the truck?" Lester said politely, the Alabama slang almost sticking to his tongue.

Shit! thought Julio, reaching for the door handle. *Keep your cool, Julio. This is no big deal.*

"What's the problem, officer?" Julio asked when his feet reached the pavement.

"Broken tail light," Lester announced.

"You're shitting me!" blurted Julio, instinctively walking to the rear of the truck.

"Don't take another step or I'll blow your ass off!"

Julio turned and was staring at the working end of a Smith & Wesson .45 caliber revolver. He threw up his hands. "Sorry sir, I was just going—"

"Shut your mouth and lay down on the ground, hands above your head and legs spread. Now move!"

Julio paused for just an instant, dropped to his knees, and then to his stomach. *What the hell's going on here?*

Tina watched the scene with disbelief. Panicking, she reached into her purse, extracting the open bottle and a small bag containing a few stems and the seeds from her last marijuana purchase. She pushed the bottle and the baggie under the seat as far as she could reach.

"Miss, you'd best get out of the truck, too. And go on and bring out that bottle you just bought with you."

"What bottle?" she responded without looking back.

"The one you just bought from Dirty Dickson ova at the roadhouse. I watched the whole thing, even saw you pop the top and have a little taste. Open containers is against the law in Alabama."

Remembering the outstanding warrant for failure to appear at a solicitation hearing two years earlier, Tina jumped to the pavement with her purse, and started running south as fast as her twenty-one-year-old legs would carry here. She screamed when she heard the discharge from the revolver, but her legs kept moving until she crossed the county line.

Lester was in a rage. A suspect had escaped, and there was nothing he could do about it. He walked over to Julio, who was craning his neck upward, attempting to see if this lunatic had actually shot the girl. Lester placed a knee in Julio's back, roughly grabbed one arm and secured it with handcuffs. The other arm was shackled harshly, and the young officer arose and walked to his car. Looking back, he watched Julio squirming as the metal cut into his wrists. Fearing this subject might also attempt to run, Lester returned to the truck.

The kick to the side of his head was swift and vicious. Everything went black for Julio Santos.

"Shit! I broke my toe," squealed Lester, hopping on one leg until falling to the pavement. For the next five minutes, both captor and captive lay beside the roadway—one unconscious, the other massaging a throbbing appendage.

With one boot removed, Lester hobbled to the truck and shined his flashlight into the cab, searching for the evidence he knew was there. Observing nothing but a road map and a pack of cigarettes laying on the seat, he limped to the passenger's side and opened the door. Leaning over, he projected the beam under the seat and saw the reflection of a piece of plastic.

"What have we here?" he said aloud, pulling the baggie from its hastily chosen hiding place. "Holy shit! My first drug bust!"

CHAPTER 30

A LEAD, THEN REALITY

Lawton put down the file he had been trying to close out for the past week. The progress had been painfully slow, his powers of concentration dulled far beyond ineffective. At the beginning of the nightmare, Barbara's calls had come almost hourly, but as he looked at his watch, he realized the workday was about over and she hadn't called all day. Once-athletic hands massaged his face and then found their way to a chronically stiff neck, aching from the tension of hours sequestered at his desk and compounded by a gnawing feeling of dread.

When the telephone interrupted his lethargy, he slowly reached for it, expecting the quivering voice of his wife. "Lawton Tremont."

"Lawton, this is Fred. We may have a break in your daughter's disappearance."

"Thank God," Lawton exclaimed. "Have you found her?"

"I wish it was that good, but no. We think she may have been in Grove Hill the night she ran away. We're pretty sure she's a runaway at this point, and that's good news."

"Where's Grove Hill? I'm not familiar with it."

"It's the county seat of Clarke County, about seventy miles north of Mobile. It's a small town, probably around two thousand residents—mostly rural. It's a bus stop for the Greyhound puddle jumper that runs up Highway 43."

"Why would she have gone there?"

"She apparently only had enough money to get her that far. We talked to a ticket agent at the main bus terminal here in Mobile, and he remembered her from the picture Barbara gave us. He remembered that she asked about Tuscaloosa, and when he told her the fare, she seemed disappointed and walked away, but she picked up a map and a fare schedule. A few minutes later, she bought a ticket to Grove Hill."

"Why the hell didn't he stop her? Jesus Christ, any idiot would have known something wasn't right."

"He didn't sell it to her. Another agent relieved him before she returned to the counter to buy the ticket. We were lucky both of them were able to put the whole thing together," Fred explained.

Lawton sighed deeply. "What else do we know?"

"Nothing else yet. I just got this about fifteen minutes ago. I have an agent heading up there to see what he can find out. With a little luck, we'll find someone who remembers seeing her, and we can follow up on that. You know the drill, Lawton. We take it one lead at a time."

There was silence for a few seconds while Lawton's mind assimilated the information.

"Why the hell would she get on a bus she knew wouldn't get her all the way to where she wanted to go? That doesn't make any sense."

"She's your only girl, right?"

"Yeah."

"Well, I've raised three, and I can tell you when those hormones start kicking in, logic goes straight to the toilet. Kitty and I were just lucky to get ours out of high school without them being pregnant, in jail, or—"

"A runaway," Lawton finished the sentence.

"Yeah, I guess that's one of the possibilities. You just need to hang in there and let us do our work. With a little luck, we'll find her, and we'll all be laughing about this the day when she graduates from college."

"Thanks, again, Fred. I'd better call Barbara with the news."

Lawton sat quietly, his eyes closed and his head leaning against the back of his desk chair. He was preparing himself for the call to his wife and trying to guess how she would receive the information. Contrary to Fred's optimistic outlook on the situation, Lawton knew the chances of a favorable outcome were not good. He felt Barbara had already given up hope. The ringing of his phone interrupted his stupor.

I had stared at the business card for twenty minutes, pondering the wisdom of making the call. I had picked up the receiver half-a-dozen times, before returning it to the cradle without touching the keypad. While Josh had often profiled me as one of the most deliberate people he'd ever known, and I respected his opinion relative to any liability my company might have, my instincts were telling me my new acquaintance from the airplane could be trusted. Besides, I really didn't know anyone in a better position to properly assess my situation. After wrestling with the variables, calculated thought gave way to intuition, and I dialed the number.

"Lawton Tremont."

"Lawton, this is Jack Mitchell," I announced.

There was an uncomfortable pause on the other end of the line.

"Remember, we met on the plane from Houston to Mobile. I'm the trash man," I offered, feeling a bit awkward.

"Jack, of course, I remember. Sorry, I went blank there for a second. It's been one of those days," he recovered, but not very effectively.

"Maybe I caught you at a bad time. You could call me back when it's more convenient," I countered, hoping he would accept the offer.

"No. No, I'm sorry. I had something on my mind when you called, and I hadn't reconnected with the world yet. How're you doing, Jack?"

"I've been better," I answered honestly. "You remember our conversation on the plane about political problems and kickbacks?"

"Yeah, I remember. You got a problem with some politician?"

I could sense he was more alert and interested. "I may. My lawyer advised me a few minutes ago that I shouldn't talk to the authorities about this, but he's a corporate lawyer and I believe what I may be dealing with falls more in your area of expertise. I'm in town and thought I might buy you a drink. You got time?"

"Today? This evening? I don't know, Jack. I've got a little situation…eh…hang on a minute."

I was put on hold.

The phone reconnected. "Jack. Yeah, I can have that drink. Where do you want to meet?"

"Your office is downtown, right? How about the bar in the…eh…what's the nice hotel downtown?"

"The River View?" he guessed.

"Yeah, that's the one. I've only stayed there a couple of times, but I remember the bar was nice and pretty quiet."

"That works for me. When can you get there?" Lawton asked.

"Will five-thirty work? I need to drop some people off at a motel out by my office."

"Five-thirty's fine."

Lawton and I arrived in the lobby of the hotel at the same time. While he was nicely dressed, as he had been in the airplane, something was different about him. As we walked to the bar, we exchanged pleasantries and it hit me—he looked much older than I remembered.

I sipped Dewar's and water while he slugged down half of his Tangueray and tonic in one gulp. He seemed to need it.

"What's your little problem, Jack?"

"First, I guess I need to understand the rules you work under," I proclaimed too cheerfully. "I don't have all the information I will have, but I'm pretty sure one of my employees has stolen, or embezzled, a rather large sum of money."

"If you're worried about whether you can speak freely to me, it sounds like you're a victim, in which case, I'd be your advocate," he replied, now only sipping his drink.

"Well, it could be a little more complicated than that. No matter what, I'm certainly the victim here, but my company could have been the instrument of further illegal acts. Normally, I wouldn't be concerned about this because I require all of my key people to be fidelity bonded. In this case, I have the bonds, but they appear to be forgeries, so I don't have an underwriter to fall back on."

"Damn, this is getting interesting. My kind of case. Go on and don't worry about anything you tell me. I told you I'm a people watcher, and your body language tells me you're exactly who and what you say you are," he responded. His tone seemed genuine.

For the next thirty minutes, I told him my story, beginning with my first meeting with Leander and Raleigh three years earlier. I told him everything I knew, except the part about Kenny's earlier misdeeds in Mississippi. No need to create unnecessary legal problems for the young accountant, I decided. He interrupted me only once, and that was to confirm the name, Findley Ross, a name familiar to him. After I finished, he sat quietly for several minutes. I ordered another round of drinks.

"Jack, it's clear to me that Leander Rutherford, possibly this Miss Vivian, and Kenny Quincy face serious legal liability, both civil and criminal."

"Kenny?" I couldn't conceal my surprise. "He's the one who blew the whistle. He's one of the good guys as far as I'm concerned. This could've gone on a lot longer and another couple a hundred thousand if he hadn't stood up."

"Sure, but why did it take him two years and a quarter-of-a-million dollars to come forward? The way you explained it, he wrote all the checks, made the fictitious journal entries, did all the false coding. He's an accomplice and was obviously aware he was doing something illegal, but he did it just the same," Lawton explained.

"Well, there's something I left out. Sorry." I went on to tell Lawton the Kenny Quincy story.

"In my mind, your explanation only further condemns him. He not only participated in the embezzlement, he did it for personal gain."

"Lawton, I really don't think Kenny got any of the money."

"I don't mean that. He got to keep his job. That was his incentive. Have you considered why he came to see you and expose everything?"

"I guess his conscience. I really hadn't thought about that," I admitted.

"It sounds like things were starting to get sloppy, which is usually how embezzlers get caught. The longer they go and the more they steal, they reach a point where they think their schemes are bulletproof. Then they get sloppy. With Mr. Quincy's background, he probably recognized the shoe would eventually fall, and he wanted out of the way. But, we can consider that later. The more intriguing possibility is that this Raleigh Pendleton could be breaking about a dozen different laws all at once, even if the money isn't going toward illegal political contributions."

"Why is that more intriguing?" I asked, with no idea of where this was heading.

"Unless we can prove the postal or banking systems were used or abused in this embezzlement scheme, it doesn't come under my jurisdiction. It's a local issue. The potential of the judge's activities, however, could easily turn into a RICO case. The possible improper campaign contributions are in violation of federal law. If Lawrence Rifle is accepting illegal contributions, same deal. And the list of possibilities go on and on. All of those are directly within my jurisdiction."

"What about my company? Does it have any liability?"

"Technically, yes. Practically, no," he answered, appearing unconcerned with the question.

"Lawton, could you offer a little less provocative answer?"

"Okay. Technically, a corporation is an intangible entity and operates at the direction or lack of direction from its board and officers. If an officer or board member breaks a law, using the corporation as an instrument, the company is potentially liable, as are its other officers and board members.

Realistically, from a prosecutor's standpoint, the only time I'd go after the corporation would be to pressure the officers and directors into cooperating. You sound pretty willing to cooperate. In fact, I see a little vengeance in your body language, and when this thing blows up on these guys, I can't see the authorities coming after you or your company. Hell, you'd be the star witness for the prosecution, and your records would be imperative to a conviction. I wouldn't spend any time worrying about your situation other than getting the money back and prosecuting the suckers."

"Well, I'm glad I didn't take my attorney's advice. Thanks for listening and for your counsel, Lawton."

"Happy to be of service. You ready to turn this over to the enforcement guys? I think you have enough."

"You mean the FBI?" I gasped. I unsuccessfully tried to hide my surprise. "I don't know. I need to sleep on that. I'd like to tie down some loose ends before making that decision."

"Jack, I strongly suggest that you and I go over to the Federal Building, preferably right now, but no later than in the morning, and visit with a friend of mine at the Bureau. With what you already have, I think we could get a couple of wiretaps approved by a federal judge and we might get lucky."

"Why couldn't you just do it? I mean, why would we have to get the FBI involved?" I was almost pleading—overwhelmed with the speed things were proceeding.

"Jack, I operate in a system. It's cumbersome at times, but all in all, it works. The Bureau is investigation and enforcement, and we're prosecution—like *Law and Order* on television. It would be unusual for us to open an investigative file without first bringing in our counterpart. Besides, the guy I would take you to is dependable. He'd handle the deal professionally. He's working on the most important case of my life right now, and I have complete trust in him and his abilities." Lawton tone seemed to change as the last few words were spoken, but I had no way of knowing why.

"Wow, I don't know, Lawton. I'm in uncharted waters right now. I really need to sleep on it, and probably should call my attorney."

"I wouldn't take too long. I assume you want to get this Leander guy out of the way as soon as possible."

"Tomorrow."

"If you do, you think he isn't going to start covering his tracks? You think he won't call the judge the minute you throw him out? If you really want to get them, you'll take my advice, play along for a while, and nail all the suckers. If you fire Rutherford and then sit on this, Mr. Quincy should be looking for a safe place to hide. You might even consider some security for yourself and your family."

"Jesus, I hadn't considered…you don't think　"

"If this thing's as twisted as it could be, there are some pretty big players out there who'd like to see this problem never surface."

"You mean the judge?"

"The judge, Lawrence Rifle, Findley Ross, and the whole damn Democratic machine in Alabama."

CHAPTER 31
A RESTLESS NIGHT

For the eighth time since midnight, he glanced at the alarm clock on the nightstand. If he had slept at all, it was only for a few minutes at a time. Any respite from the self-loathing had been brief and unfulfilling. He had sobbed into his pillow several times as he relived the horrific events of the past ten days. The loud snoring from the lady of the house was only a minor irritation as he suffered through a night of living hell.

Resigning himself to the fact that needed rest would be unachievable, he slipped from beneath the covers, hoping not to disturb Myrtle and face her reliably insufferable morning disposition. Successful in this maneuver, he trudged down the hall toward the kitchen. He sat at the chrome dinette and waited for the coffee to brew. Through the lace curtain, a pale aura could be seen on the eastern horizon. It was 5:30, and Bobby Bitterman was a miserable man.

"Oh, God, will this ever end? How could I have been so stupid? A dead girl and it was my fault. Oh, my God," he whispered into his palms.

Feelings of dejection were interrupted as hissing from the coffee maker signaled the last drops of water flowing through the heating coils. After filling a blue ceramic cup embossed with the words, "Twenty-Five Years of Service," and the logo of his employer, he returned to the table, unconsciously blowing over the steaming liquid. His mind continued to grind.

An adulterer, murderer, and, now, an arsonist. How could things have gotten so far out of hand? And now we're going to blow up the pulp kettles to pay off that no good sheriff.

Violet clouds and a light mist hovered over the harbor, reflecting the earliest rays of morning sunlight. Roberto paced the bulkhead, occasionally staring at the cell phone in his left hand. The right fidgeted with a Monte Cristo de Habana with a long ash.

He had awakened at 4:00 that morning. Paranoid by nature, a sense of dread had pulled him from his bed and placed him at the warehouse several hours earlier than normal. A ten-milligram Xanax had only slightly relieved the tension in his back and neck. Strong coffee had partially counteracted the soothing effects of the prescription drug provided gratuitously by his Colombian partners. His baby brother was three days out on the road and the uneasiness he had felt when Julio had driven through the gate had mounted each day.

"Julio, why haven't you called?" he screamed out over the lapping water. The only reply was the screeching of two gulls, fighting in mid-air over a wiggling mullet.

"You said you were leaving Mobile early. You promised to call when you first woke up. You'll never make the run again, I can promise you that." His tone was less menacing than before, but the frustration continued to rise. "If anything happens to that boy, Charlie, I'm going to string your drunken ass up on a pole."

Tossing the cigar into the water, he retreated to the warehouse to again check the answering machine. The red message indicator continued to glow steadily, indicating no one had attempted to call. He sat down on a crate and placed his fourth call to the same number.

"This is Julio. I can't take your call right now, but if you'll—"

He clicked the off button. He had already left two messages.

Raleigh had wrestled with sleep and arrived at his office before 7:00 A.M. The message from Lawrence Rifle, left with his wife the evening before, had unnerved him. Reaching into a desk drawer, he retrieved the day's court docket file and the bottle of sour mash. He fumbled with both, trying to decide which he would open first.

By 8:30, the liquor had calmed his nerves and the day, both physically and metaphorically, looked a little brighter than when he had arrived. His phone rang several times before he realized Bonnie Mae was late for work. Annoyed with the distraction, he stabbed at the blinking button.

"Judge Pendleton," he barked.

"Good morning, Raleigh. You answering your own phone these days?"

The judge sat up in his chair and he grabbed the receiver. "Good morning, Governor Rifle. You're calling bright and early. I got your message last night, but it was late and I was waiting to call after you had your morning coffee. The missus said you wanted to discuss something important." Nervousness filled his voice as he placed the bottle to his lips.

"Sorry for the early call, but I wanted to reach you before you went into the courtroom. Raleigh, I'm calling to…eh…sort of apologize for all the pressure I've been putting on you over the past couple of months. I guess the strain of the campaign and the surge Senator Laughlin has made lately has…well …caused me to be a little impatient and demanding, particularly with my good old friends like you," Rifle responded.

Raleigh was silent for a few seconds, trying to digest the possibilities of this uncharacteristically humble overture. "No need for apologies, Lawrence. I've been through these political wars all my life and everyone's got a limit. Under the circumstances, I think you've handled yourself very professional like. I have some good news to report on our activities down here. I should be sending you a pile of money in just a few days and—"

"That's what I'm calling about, Judge," Rifle interrupted. "We took a tally yesterday and some of the boys have done much better than we expected. Right now it looks like we shouldn't be needing any more money for quite awhile, and maybe not at all."

"You mean, you don't want no more money sent up from down here?" Raleigh's head was spinning. He had never heard of a politician turning down money.

"Yeah, that's pretty much what I'm saying."

"But I've only sent up about fifty thousand so far, and I got a whole bunch more working. Lawrence, I told you every time we've talked, I'll raise my share. You figuring you can't count on me?"

"Not at all, Judge. We've just done better than expected in some of the larger, more prosperous counties, and I know you deal with limited resources down there. You've been a good party man all your life, and there's no need to burn up a bunch of favors with your constituents unnecessarily. In fact, things have gone so well, I'm sending back the money you've already sent in."

"Sending it back?"

"Yeah. We're not going to need it and you can put it in a war chest for another day, another fight."

"But…but, what about the road money, and…and the environmental help you promised? I've made commitments, Lawrence." Raleigh was now in an emotional tailspin. Steady breathing was becoming difficult.

"Don't worry yourself about that. I made a promise to you, and I always keep my promises. Raleigh, maybe you should slow down a bit. You've been in the middle of Alabama politics all your life, and your dependability has never been a question. Maybe you and your missus should have some time to yourselves. Travel, go see your grandkids, enjoy life. You've earned it."

"I don't understand any of this, Lawrence. You sound like you're putting me out to pasture. I still got a few good kicks left, and I spend all the time I want to with my wife and those ungrateful offspring of mine. Lawrence, I aim to have to talk with some of the other party leaders about this. This here's a potentially embarrassing situation for me and us party folks down here."

"Judge, you're taking this all wrong. You're a good man and an old friend. I'm just giving you some advice, for old time's sake. I'm afraid I better get going. I have a press conference in a half-hour, and I need to review my notes. You take care, Raleigh."

"Wait a minute. What about the inauguration? Will me and the misses still be up on the platform?"

"I have an election to win first. Good bye, Raleigh."

Raleigh slammed the receiver into the cradle, sucked in a mouthful of Jack Daniel's, and collapsed back into his chair. He sat for several minutes without saying a word, but his mind was in full gear.

Rising, he limped to the wall that displayed the portraits of the three Pendletons who had previously occupied this office. He stared into the dead eyes of each of his predecessors. Turning, he took a deep breath, and proclaimed toward the window overlooking Main Street, "You ain't putting Raleigh Pendleton out to pasture, Mista Rifle. I was running things down here while you were still popping pimples and pounding your pud. You don't want no money from me? I aim to gather up every damn dollar I got committed and a bunch more, and watch you gag when I deliver it to the party secretary. You're screwing with the wrong judge, and you can bet your sweet ass there'll be Pendletons sitting on the platform come inauguration day. "

Lawrence Rifle hung up the phone and turned to the visitor sitting across his desk. He shook his head.

"Was that what you wanted?"

"You did very well, Lawrence," replied Findley Ross. "We may've just avoided a train wreck. This Jack Mitchell's a straight shooter. If dirty money ended up in your campaign, I believe he'll blow the lid off the deal. You'd be embroiled in a federal investigation right in the middle of the general election. I don't need to tell you what the outcome would be. No, you had to do what you just did, and we want you to keep your distance from Raleigh Pendleton."

"But Fin, you know he won't take this lying down. I could hear it in his voice. No telling who he'll call. He's a dangerous old fart."

"At this point, I really don't care. All I know is, we've been grooming you for this election for over four years, and we're not going to let this redneck judge destroy your political career and frustrate our efforts. We don't intend to spend another four years with a damn Republican in the mansion. Our machinery's gotten rusty as hell over the years, and you're the man we've picked to bring unity back into the party."

"What about Senator Laughlin? You sure he's about ready to throw in the towel? He's put up one helluva fight."

"Yeah, the youngster's done a lot better than we thought he would. He'll withdraw next week, and it'll be smooth sailing until the general in November. Of course, we had to promise he'd be our man after your terms are over."

"What about Tom Walker? I thought he was next in line."

"Tom's got a philandering problem. We had to pay off two hookers last year to keep him out of the tabloids. I'm afraid secretary of state's as far as Tom will go. He'll get himself in some trouble sometime over the next four years and we won't bail him out next time."

"But what if he doesn't? He's held two state-wide offices and has a pretty good following."

"Oh, he'll get in trouble all right—either on his own or with a little help."

After my meeting with Lawton, I made a quick call to Josh, asking him to draft a document for me. I didn't mention my meeting downtown. I spent the remainder of the evening in my hotel room choking down a small pepperoni pizza and considering the revelations of the past two days. I desperately wanted to walk into the office the next morning and physically toss Leander Rutherford out the front door, after breaking his fingers—something I would have considered in my earlier years. I wrestled with the possibilities well into the early morning hours before falling into a fitful sleep, fully dressed, on top of the covers.

The alarm went off at 6:00 A.M., but rang for several minutes while I showered. I had awakened at 5:20. My first call was to the room occupied by

129

Kenny, who confessed to having watched television almost all night long. The second was to the twins who were already dressed in business suits and reviewing their notes from the previous day. Gathering everyone up, I took the young auditors to the airport for an early flight back to Houston and dropped Kenny at his apartment for a change of clothes. I gave him fifty dollars for breakfast and a taxi to the office.

Proceeding south on Interstate 65, I placed another call to Josh. He'd always been an early riser, and I was confident he'd be in his office.

"Josh, this is Jack."

"What's up, pal? You get any sleep?"

"Not much. I have a confession to make. I didn't totally take your advice."

"Should that surprise me? What have you done? Should I find a bail bondsman?"

I proceeded to tell him about my conversations with Lawton. He interrupted a couple of times to clarify things—a common practice of his. He was silent for a few seconds after I finished my story.

"So this Lawton Tremont thinks you have enough for wiretaps, huh? Jack, you're getting into issues well outside my area of expertise. I can't advise you legally on this, but let me ask you a question. Are you sure you trust this U.S. Attorney? You only met him on an airplane and now you're holding confessionals with him—not very typical of you. You're one of the most deliberate people I've ever known, even in college."

"Logically, I can't explain it, but in my gut, I think he's a good guy. He said he was in the middle of one of the most important investigations of his life, yet he took the time to hear my story, not knowing what it was all about. Now he's willing to go with me to the FBI."

"You think he'd be offended if you asked for immunity from any possible legal issues you or the company might face?"

"I don't know, but I could ask. I've given this a lot of thought, Josh, and he makes one very good point that's more important to me than anything else."

"What's that?"

"I don't want to put the kids in jeopardy."

"You act like these guys are Mafia, Jack. Don't you think you're being a little paranoid?"

"Maybe, but I'm beginning to feel like Alabama politics could be just as perverted as organized crime, and Findley Ross didn't leave any doubt in my mind that Raleigh Pendleton is a dangerous man."

"Go with your instincts and keep me informed. I'm going to check the Martindale-Hubbell. You're going to need an Alabama lawyer before this is over. I'm just not sure what kind."

"What do you mean by that?"

"Civil or criminal."

CHAPTER 32
WHEELS START TURNING

As they walked across the yard between the administrative office and the kettle room, spit hit the bare dirt, splashing the back of Leander's heel and pants' cuff. Billy was relieved his errant aim had gone unnoticed by both his employer and Bobby Bitterman. Bobby greeted each mill employee they encountered in a courteous manner. It was a routine event for the plant manager to escort strangers and VIPs through the facility, but never before had the motive for a tour been arson.

The noise of the boilers made conversation difficult, but the words being spoken were only a ruse to legitimize the façade. Billy was casing the building to determine the best location for the small device he would assemble after determining the concussion requirements.

After returning to his office, Bobby collapsed into his desk chair, staring through the window at the building they'd just visited. Neither Leander nor Billy could comprehend the despair he felt.

"What do you think, Billy? Can you do it?" Leander asked.

"Piece of cake," he responded, removing the empty aluminum can from his lips. "A small timing device behind the gas feed into the boiler, and boom, the first kettle's toast."

"What about any evidence?" Leander pressed.

"There's always a chance some hot-shot arson investigator could find something, but most likely the heat will cook everything into one mass of metal and wiring. Besides, even if arson is suspected, even proved, no one would have no reason to suspect us. They've had their share of labor problems ova here—layoffs and such. This ain't no big deal."

Leander turned his attention to the plant manager. "Good. How's that sound to you, Bobby boy?"

"Fine," he answered flatly, still staring out the window.

"Okay. It's set. Billy'll come in Sunday morning after the evening shift leaves and that'll be that. All you have to do, Bobby, is make sure the night watchman's nowhere near the kettle room, and give Billy a key. Sound good to you?"

Bobby didn't respond.

"Bobby, you listening? This's important. We aim to do this thing right, and you need to be clear on everything."

"No key," Bobby almost whispered.

"What do you mean, 'no key?' If this's going to look like an accident, there can't be no evidence of a break in. Billy has to have a key to get in."

Bobby turned his gaze to Leander. "There's a high spot in the perimeter fence out behind the kettle building. He can crawl under and leave the same way. We have a security panel on all the gates, and somebody entering a gate would be logged into the computer and the night watchman would receive a beeper call."

"That okay with you, Billy?"

Billy nodded.

Bobby stood and walked out of the room.

After checking with our new receptionist, Lollie, I began the drive to the office at 8:15. I was pleased to hear that Leander and Billy had a meeting at a paper company on the industrial canal and weren't expected in until after lunch. Famished from the unsatisfying pizza the night before, I stopped at the Copper Kitchen for about fifty grams of cholesterol and a cup of coffee. During those few moments of solitude and a country breakfast, I had made up my mind as to how I would handle Leander for the next few days, hopefully not weeks.

I arrived at the same time Kenny was stepping out of the taxi.

"Good morning, Kenny. How was Godzilla Meets the Japanese Boa?" I asked as we walked through the door.

"How was what?" he replied, obviously missing the point of what I thought was a humorous greeting.

"Nothing, just kidding. Let's go to your office."

Kenny shifted nervously from one foot to the other while I sipped from my styrofoam coffee cup and read the fax I had just retrieved from the machine in the conference room.

"Kenny, please sit down. You're making me as nervous as you are."

He obeyed.

"I want you to call a temp service and get someone out here to answer the phone today and all of next week. I'm going to send Miss Masters away for a little vacation."

"Why? She's only been here a couple of days."

"I don't want Leander to know I've been here. The only people who know are you and Lollie, and I trust you won't tell him. If she's not here, she can't tell. I want you to clean up anything we might have left in there yesterday. Make copies of anything the boys from Houston didn't get and mail them to me, but don't let Leander catch you. Right now, I want you to make another set of copies of all the checks that went to Chatom, the ones to Miss Vivian's construction work, and those to L&V Materials. I need to take copies with me. Leander must fill out expense accounts because I've seen the check references in the check register. Where are they kept?"

"You mean, you aren't going to fire him? Oh, shit!"

"Leander will have his day, but there are some things I need to do first. Now, what about those expense accounts? I didn't see them when the auditors were here."

"If there are any, he keeps them locked in his credenza. I don't think he fills them out though. I think he just gives me the total off his credit card invoices and I cut him a check."

"Great!" I exclaimed, my growing frustration showing. "Okay, look around and see what you can find. Now, I'm going to go out and make Lollie's day."

"But what do I tell Leander when he asks where she is and where'd the temp come from?"

"You just tell him I called in this morning and you answered the phone. When I asked where the receptionist was, you told me she'd called in sick, and I told you to get someone in here immediately. If he wants to take it up with me, he can, but he won't. You have any concerns we haven't discussed?"

"Only two," Kenny responded, looking down at his desk. "Will I have a job after you've gotten rid of Leander?"

"Yeah, Kenny, you'll still have a job unless I can sell the construction company," I replied, and then thought how my answer would only increase his insecurity. "And, even if I do, you can still work for the Delta. Don't worry about that. You've done me a great service, and you'll be taken care of. Okay? Now what was the other question?"

"What about a car? My truck's still in Houston."

"Go down to Enterprise and get a weekly rate on an economy car. We'll do something permanent in a few days. Look around at some car lots and get some prices. Now, get me those copies, please. I want to get out of here in case Leander comes in earlier than expected."

Thirty minutes later,, I was in my rental, driving down Government Boulevard for a meeting with Lawton and someone from the FBI. Lollie Masters had happily accepted the three-thousand-dollar check and signed the resignation letter Josh had faxed that morning. The document also contained a non-recourse note that provided she would have to pay the money back if she ever acknowledged to anyone that I had been in my office during her four days of employment. It further stated she would be paid an additional two thousand if and when Leander no longer worked for the company. We had said our good-byes and she scampered merrily out of the office. I was convinced Lollie would never betray our little secret.

I must admit that walking into a federal building with a briefcase full of evidence was one of the most unnerving things I've ever done. Fortunately, Lawton was able to calm my concerns in a simple greeting.

"Jack, I was sure you were one of the good guys and you just proved it. Most businessmen, put in your situation, never voluntarily come forward. They have to be dragged in by a Federal Marshal. If there were more like you, my job would be a helluva lot easier. Come on in my office and meet Fred Carleton."

I found Fred to be what I had generally expected from an appearance standpoint: short cropped hair, muscular frame—showing the first signs of an expanding waistline—a blue oxford shirt, and gray suit slacks. What I didn't expect was a friendly demeanor and a willingness to keep me as far from the investigation as possible, at least until sufficient evidence could be assembled for a grand jury.

Lawton had provided Fred with a fairly detailed explanation of the facts we had discussed the evening before. After they examined the checks, related purchase orders, and other documents I provided, Fred began to ask questions.

"Jack, my first objective here is to solidify at least one federal law violation; otherwise, we'll run into a jurisdictional problem. The hard evidence you have here would mostly fall under state law, and we won't be able to help much; although, we do know a few good guys in the Mobile

County prosecutor's office, and that could be helpful to you. The good news is, most of what I see here took place in Mobile County and not in Washington County. I'm sure the positives of that are obvious to you with Judge Pendleton basically running the show up there."

"What about the checks? If checks are used for the purpose of embezzlement, wouldn't that fall under the federal banking statutes?" I asked.

"Sure, but we have to prove the checks were instruments of embezzlement. Right now we suspect they are, but conjecture may not be good enough for a wiretap without hard proof or corroboration by a witness or accomplice," Lawton interjected.

"What about Kenny?" I offered.

"Lawton and I talked about him, but we don't think he should be brought in yet. We'll probably plead him out when the facts are all in place, but he's still an accomplice at this point, and we don't want to move on him too quickly."

Lawton tapped his desk with a pencil. "I guess you haven't heard anything from Findley Ross yet?"

"No, but I only talked to him yesterday afternoon."

We continued for another two hours, methodically working our way through every detail we had and didn't have. Finally, Fred turned to Lawton.

"What do you think? We got enough? You're the one who has to sell the wiretaps to the judge."

Before Lawton could answer, I asked, "Help me here. We have quite a bit of stuff. Why are you so concerned with all these jurisdictional issues just for the wiretap? If this thing runs all the way to Montgomery, isn't that the fact that we're trying to confirm?"

"I know that sounds logical, and it is, but the law isn't always that easy. If we get a wiretap on improper grounds, anything we learn could be thrown out of court," answered Lawton. "I want these suckers, but I don't want to give them a get-out-of-jail-free card on a technicality. Why don't I have some sandwiches sent in? I think we're close here, we just need to dig a little more."

"I'd be happy to spring for lunch at a nice restaurant," I offered.

Fred replied, "Thanks for the offer, Jack, but the last thing we need is for you to be seen by the wrong person talking to the FBI and the U.S. Attorney's office. Mobile's just a big little town."

I nodded and felt a little foolish for not thinking of that myself.

We were halfway through our sandwiches when Fred's cell phone buzzed. Looking at the caller ID, he said, "Excuse me for a minute. This could be important."

I thought I saw him wink subtly at Lawton. I was certain of it when Lawton dropped his pastrami on rye in his lap.

"Jack, could you excuse us for a couple of minutes?" Fred asked as he placed the phone back in his belt carrier.

Before I could answer, Lawton asked, "Is it about Janie?"

Fred nodded and smiled.

"Go on, Fred. Jack has kids, too."

"Okay. We found a waitress at a diner up in Grove Hill who recognized the picture. Janie was there the night she disappeared."

"What happened? Where'd she go?"

"The waitress apparently felt she could be in trouble and called the county sheriff's office. They dispatched a car and picked her up."

"Thank God. Where is she now?"

"We don't know yet. We've talked to the sheriff and seven of the deputies. None of them know anything about it. There are two more. One is on a driving vacation in the mountains with his family, and they haven't been able to reach him on his cell yet. The other one has two days off. They're looking for him."

"What about the waitress? Doesn't she know who picked her up?"

"We went back and talked to her. She didn't actually see the pickup. Whoever she talked to at the sheriff's office said someone would be there in half an hour or so. She was tired, so she left Janie on the bench in front of the diner and drove home."

"Drove home!" Lawton pounded the desk so hard his computer screen blinked and shut down. "Jesus Christ, are there no decent people in this whole fucking state? Why would anyone see a child in trouble and not stay with her until they knew she was safe?"

He dropped his head and tears began to fall on his sandwich wrapper. The room was very quiet for several seconds. He then sighed and stood up, pulling a handkerchief from his back pocket.

A moment later, his composure regained, he turned to me and said, "Sorry, Jack. I've had a bad couple of weeks, but I can't talk about it right now." He walked to the door, retrieved his suit coat from a hanger, and turned to Fred and me. "I need to go talk to Barbara. I don't know how she'll react to the news. Fred, please call me at home if they find the other deputies. Jack, I'm sorry to leave so suddenly, but I'll tell you about it when I can. As for the wiretaps, I'll be in Judge Avery's office this afternoon. We're a little thin, but I'll get the order. Talk to you later."

CHAPTER 33
FELL RIGHT INTO HIS LAP

Raleigh had just recessed the court for lunch. He was frustrated to be going through the motions of hearing an involved personal injury case, the outcome of which had already been negotiated. One of the local attorneys attending the fundraiser at the lodge the week before had agreed to a generous contribution if things went his way on the case being argued. Although his mind was preoccupied with his earlier conversation with Lawrence Rifle, Raleigh admitted to himself that the young defense attorney from Birmingham was putting on a pretty convincing, although futile, case.

"Uncle Raleigh, Mr. Rutherford's on the phone," came the familiar twang from Bonnie Mae.

"He say what he wants?"

"No, but he said it's important."

"Of course," Raleigh sighed. "I'll take it."

"Hey, Judge," greeted Leander. "We sure enough had us a productive meeting ova at the paper mill this morning. Billy said this'll be a piece of cake."

Raleigh closed his eyes. "That's fine, Leander. I always know I can count on you and Billy."

"All we got to do is slip under this fence, and—"

"Leander, you damn sure better be on a pay phone!"

"Course I am, Judge. I told you I am always careful when I call you. Anyway, Billy thinks there'll be no trouble at all taking out at least one of the kettles, maybe two."

There was a soft knock on the door.

"Hang on, Leander, there's someone at the door and I don't know where that flaky niece of mine is." Placing his hand over the mouthpiece, he bellowed, "Who is it?"

The door opened slowly and Virgil Crawford peeked inside. Seeing the phone in the judge's hand, he mouthed, "Sorry, Raleigh."

Raleigh motioned him in, pointed at the phone, and shook his head.

"Leander, you got anything else? The sheriff's here, and I need to get going."

"Well, I wanted to tell you how good that job ova at Republic's going. I went ova there myself and kicked them boys into shape. Me and that plant engineer's becoming good friends and I think—"

"That's good, Leander, real good. I have to go now. Thanks for calling."

As the receiver was being replaced, Raleigh could still hear, "Yeah, we're going to make ova two hundred, maybe three—"

"Sorry to come unannounced, Raleigh, but no one was out front, and I have something interesting over at the jail."

"Interesting, Virgil? I've already had a damn interesting day. What have you got?"

"We just made a for sure major drug bust," Virgil gloated.

"Get you another meth lab?"

"Oh no, much bigger than that."

"Spit it out, Sheriff. You got my attention."

Virgil detailed Lester's traffic stop the evening before, leaving out the part about one of the subjects escaping.

"Okay, so Lester's gung-ho as hell. He brings this Cuban into the station—he's been messed up a little. He books him in, fingerprints him and all, and puts him in that solitary cell we have in the back," Virgil explained.

"Solitary? Ova a couple of crumbs of marijuana? Good thing that Cuban boy wasn't running some coke or something. Lester might've shot him," chuckled Raleigh.

"Somebody already tell you about this?" A puzzled look passed over Virgil's face.

"What you talking about? Nobody's talked to me."

"That's exactly what this boy was doing. He had five kilos of pure cocaine and over nine hundred thousand dollars in a false wall in the back of his truck."

"Did you say nine hundred thousand dollars?"

"Yeah. Actually closer to nine five."

"Oh, sweet Jesus!"

Virgil relaxed in his chair, basking in the glory of the moment, and then he spoke. "I was getting ready to call the drug enforcement people down in Mobile, but—"

"Oh lord, Virgil, tell me you didn't."

"No, I decided I'd tell you first, but that's what I'm supposed to do on a deal like this," Virgil offered almost apologetically.

"Who all knows about this?"

"Well, me, you, Lester, of course. He's the one who found the dope. He was rummaging around in the back of the truck after the wrecker brought it in and noticed these screws that were worn down. Like I said, he's gung-ho as hell, so he got a screwdriver from his cruiser and there it was."

"There was someone on the desk when he brought the boy in, wasn't there?" Raleigh asked.

"Sure, Lonnie Pickford."

"Then he knows, too."

"Not about the cocaine and the money. He went off-duty at seven this morning, and Lester didn't find the stuff until about an hour ago. Where you going with this, Raleigh?"

"Call Lester right now and get his ass up here. You got your radio with you?"

"Don't need it. He's right outside. I thought I'd give him a little morale boost, him being young and all, and see if you'd mind telling him what a good job he did."

"Virgil, you're beautiful. Get that boy in here and let me shake his hand!"

Lester had only seen Raleigh in the courtroom and, occasionally, on the street or at the store. He had never actually talked to the probate judge of Washington County in person. The awe of this moment was almost overwhelming for him.

"Deputy Holmboe! Get in here and let me personally express the gratitude of the people of our county for your heroic work last night," gushed Raleigh as the young officer crept into the office.

"It was…it wasn't nothing, Judge Pendleton. Just…just doing my job," he stuttered.

"I'll say you did. Lester, I been watching you since you been on the job and I kept telling myself, 'That young man has big potential.' Yes, sir, I been saying that ever since Virgil hired you. Your testimonies in the courtroom have always been precise and, well, you're for sure the most professional acting enforcement officer we have, except for the sheriff, of course."

This was more that Lester could have ever imagined. He could feel the heat radiating from a cherry red face.

"Now, Lester, I know you worked all night long and ain't had any sleep yet, but we need to move that property you confiscated up here to my safe. The sheriff here's going to go down to his office and load it up, and I'd be much obliged if you'd be his armed escort for the transfer."

"I...I'd be honored to, sir." Lester threw out his chest and stood at attention.

Virgil looked at the judge with a puzzled look. *What the hell's he up to?* he thought but knew better than to ask any questions.

"By the way, Lester, did you write up any arrest and property reports on this fine work of yours?"

"Yes, sir. I wrote up the AR last night when I brought him in, but the sheriff and I just finished counting the money before we came over here. I can have the Property Log done up in no time flat," Lester announced.

Raleigh smiled. "You sure done good. Why don't you bring up that arrest report with the confiscated materials? I want to see it. I bet it's done perfect. Be sure and bring all the copies. I particularly want the one with your original signature. We might frame that one and put it in an important place in the courthouse, if you wouldn't mind."

"No, sir! I wouldn't mind at all. In fact, I'd be right proud to have it hanging in your courthouse."

Virgil walked out the door, followed by Lester and Raleigh. The judge had his arm resting over the shoulders of the young man.

"You told anybody about this yet?" he whispered into Lester's ear.

"No, sir. Like I said, me and the sheriff came here straight away after we put the money...eh...confiscated materials in the property room."

Raleigh turned the young officer to face him, their noses almost touching. "Lester, don't tell a soul about any of this. I can't tell you how important what I'm saying is. Don't even tell anyone ova at the sheriff's office. You married?"

Lester grinned, feeling embarrassed. "No, sir, but I got a girl. I'm living with my folks until I get enough saved up for a ring."

"That's a noble gesture, but I'm not surprised. Now, don't tell even your girlfriend, and I know you'll want to, but in time you'll be getting more publicity than ever in your life. Just keep all this to yourself until I tell you different. Okay?"

"Not a word to nobody, sir. You have my word."

"Tell you what. You know where my house is up north?"

"Yes, sir. I try to drive by every night at least a couple of times. You know, to make sure everything's in order."

"I knew you did. I've seen you, and I feel a whole lot safer knowing you're on patrol. Well, I have a little cabin ova on the other side of the lake, south of the main house. Why don't you—when you get through guarding the sheriff—why don't you go and stay in my lake cabin for a few days? After the job you've done, you deserve a little rest. If you'd like to take your lady friend, no one would ever know. Just tell her you're my man in the sheriff's office and I invited you out any time you want. I might even drop ova and say hello. I'd call before, of course. Wouldn't want to catch no one in an indelicate situation, if you know what I mean." Raleigh gave the young man a knowing wink.

"You sure? I mean, you really wouldn't mind?"

"Not at all, Lester. You've earned it. Just remember, keep all this property business to yourself."

CHAPTER 34
HOME AGAIN

With nothing more I could do in Mobile for the time being, I left the federal building and booked the next flight back to Houston. While waiting at the airport, I called Kenny to check on things at the office.

When the phone was answered, I heard an unfamiliar female voice. "Delta Disposal and Jefferson Construction. May I help you?"

"Mr. Jack, I'm sure glad you called in," Kenny breathed into the phone. I could sense his nervousness.

"Everything all right? Is Leander there?"

"No. He came in right after lunch, but he left about an hour ago. I think he was going over to Miss Vivian's."

"Naturally. Did he sense anything was wrong?"

"I don't think so. He was miffed about you telling me to hire the temp, but he didn't make a big deal about it. He said he and Billy were up at the canal, and we should be getting a new job up there next week. Wanted me to open a new account. Seemed to be in a pretty good mood."

"A new job, huh?"

"It could have something to do with the judge," Kenny offered.

"Why do you say that?"

"I'm just speculating, but he asked me when we paid the last invoice to R&P how much money we had in the construction account. I told him only five thousand, but we had some receivables out we should be collecting pretty soon. Truth is, there was over fifty thousand in that account, but I made a journal entry that moved most of it to the Delta account."

"Smart thinking, Kenny. Did he press you for money?"

"Yeah. He wanted an expense advance for three thousand. I didn't know what else to do, so I wrote it. Mr. Jack, what do I do if he tells me to write a big check?"

"First, when you get any checks in, don't deposit them immediately. Call me and tell me how much you've received. I'll tell you which ones to deposit, and we'll just try to keep the balances low enough that he won't be able to do much. If he asks for a small amount, say one or two thousand, go on and give it to him, make a record of the transaction, and call me as soon as you can. Kenny, I know I'm putting you in a bad situation, but you'll have to trust that I know what I'm doing. As long as you keep me informed of what's going on, I think everything'll turn out okay. I promise you, Leander's reign of terror will end soon."

"I sure hope so. By the way, I called about a small truck I saw in the paper."

"How much was it?"

"Only thirty-five hundred."

I thought back a few months earlier when I was looking for a used pickup for Jackson. Anything I saw for less than seven thousand was ready for the junk heap.

"Kenny, why don't you raise your sights a little higher. See if you can find one closer to ten."

"You sure? That's a lot money, and…eh…I should have come to you a lot earlier. I feel real bad. I just didn't think you'd—"

"I know, Kenny, but I'm glad you came forward when you did. Let's not worry about that now. That's all behind us." I resolved, at that moment, I would do everything in my power to keep Lawton and Fred from going after Kenny.

"You're a nice man, Mr. Jack."

"Thanks, Kenny. Oh, by the way, we may be having some telephone work done on the phones at the office. The phone company couldn't tell me when, but it could be over the weekend. I want to add a separate line for Delta and I told them it was an emergency. If they'll come out tomorrow, would you come down and let them in?"

"Sure, anything you want."

I arrived in Houston in time to drive to Mikey's school just before classes were dismissed for the day. Just as he was supposed to, Jackson pulled up at the loading area in the green Toyota pickup we had chosen for his first vehicle. He didn't notice my Suburban parked across the street. His complete attention was focused on Mary Sue Baker, who, if sitting any closer to him, would have been in his lap. I smiled, briefly remembering my first encounter with puppy love.

The doors of Sam Houston Elementary School flew open, and it appeared as if the inmates had finally stormed the gate of the prison. Dozens of screaming children rushed across the playground, some holding hands and skipping, others playing an impromptu game of tag, and the older ones, Mikey's age, walking with the aloofness afforded only to the sixth-graders. It was a sight I truly enjoyed and had seen too seldom during my years of pursuing my career.

Finally, I spotted Mikey, pulling his shirttail out in defiance of the tucked position required by the dress code. His three companions were doing the same. Two girls approached his group and it was apparent, at least to me, that the focus of their attention was my youngest. Parental pride often distorts one's view of reality.

I followed the kids home and pulled into the driveway behind them. My voyeurism had escaped their notice. Mikey jumped from the passenger's door, and, upon landing, saw my car.

"Daddy!" he shouted and ran as fast as his maturing legs would carry him to the driver's window. "You're home early. I thought you wouldn't be home until tomorrow."

I just looked at him and had to suppress the lump in my throat.

"I just couldn't stay away from you that long, big boy," I countered, exiting the car and pulling him tightly to me. "I'm sure glad to see you, son." I held him for an unusually long time.

"Hi, Pops," Jackson greeted as he and Mary Sue walked toward my vehicle.

"Hi, Jack. Hello, Mary Sue. What a pretty dress," I said, placing my hands on the cute young girl's shoulders. "You kids been good while I've been gone?"

"Aren't we always?" Jackson retorted.

"I don't know about that," I said with a wink. "Come here."

Jackson reluctantly edged toward me and I didn't disappoint him. I planted a kiss on his forehead, giving him a bear hug.

"Dad, don't do that," he whispered loud enough for Mary Sue to hear.

I responded by squeezing him harder and winking at Mary Sue, who was smiling.

"Where's Katie?" I asked after releasing my hold on him.

"She's at the game. Remember, I have a game tonight, and she and Mary Sue are cheering."

"That's right. I'd forgotten. You better go in and get changed. I'll throw on some jeans and a golf shirt. I'll need to pay Mrs. Larson and I have one call to make. Then, Mikey and I will drive over to the stadium in about half an hour."

After dispensing with the babysitter, I went to my room to change. Mikey made a bowl of Captain Crunch or some such sugar-injected concoction and went to the computer for a quick battle with the alien invaders. I sat on the bed, wondering if I should call or not. I finally did and received his voice mail. I decided to leave a brief message.

"Lawton, this is Jack. I didn't know what to say today when you left, so I didn't say anything. While I'm not sure what's going on, I can imagine, and I can't tell you how sorry I am. You and your family are in my thoughts. If there's anything I can do, anything at all, please call. Hang in there. I'll be praying for Janie."

CHAPTER 35
WHERE'S JULIO?

The Cessna 310 lifted off the runway at 11:30, Friday morning. The pilot, Tootie Gilbert, had over 12,000 hours of flight time, most of it spent flying tourist charters between south Florida and the many small strips of the Keys, the Bahamas, and further into the Caribbean.

One day, eight years earlier, a random customs search of his plane yielded six kilos of cocaine and Tootie five years in the Florida correction system, where he had met Roberto Santos. Having paid his debt to society, Tootie now had his own charter service and was the owner of the well-maintained twin-engine he was flying, courtesy of a soft loan from the man he had befriended in prison and who was one of his two passengers that morning. While Roberto had never felt completely safe in small aircraft, he trusted his old cellmate's piloting skills and found the Cessna to be a preferred alternative to the security procedures necessary with the commercial variety.

"Tootie, how long to Mobile?" Roberto asked over the headsets the three men were wearing.

"Just a minute, Roberto, I need to check in with Miami Center," Tootie replied, lifting his index finger.

Roberto and his middle brother, Manuel, listened as the pilot cleared departure control and switched frequencies for instructions to begin their journey northwest. The appropriate settings were made to the Loran and the autopilot engaged.

"There. Now I can talk for a few minutes," Tootie announced. "I filed a flight plan to arrive at McCarron Field at 1:45 Central. If we don't have to dodge too many of the thunderstorms building west of Pensacola when I checked the weather, we should arrive a few minutes early. Do you need a car when we get there, Roberto? I can have the FBO arrange it."

"No. I've already arranged transportation. Do we have to worry about customs in Mobile?"

"No. Our flight plan clearly states we're arriving from a U.S. departure point. Are we carrying anything I should know about?" Tootie inquired, remembering the day the drug dog had sniffed the cargo area in the nose of the Cessna 421 he had used only twice for illegal purposes.

"Nothing the drug enforcement people would care about. We do have a couple of revolvers in our luggage, but both are registered," Roberto lied, not wishing to distract his friend from the subtleties of safe flight.

"Good deal. Guns aren't a problem." Tootie's relief was apparent in his voice.

"Manny and I have a couple of things to talk about, and it would be better if you didn't listen. You mind us getting off the speaker?"

"Not at all. I have to monitor the air traffic guys, anyway. I picked up some sandwiches and cold drinks before we left. They're in the cooler behind you. Help yourselves. My flight attendant has the weekend off," chuckled the pilot.

"Thanks. We're off the radio now." Roberto turned to his brother and began speaking in Spanish.

"*Se hablo...Shooter Pinkston.*"

"What kind of guy is this Pinkston? And what kind of name is Shooter? He got a problem with guns?"

"No. He's a black guy. I've done business with him since the milk run started. He owns a pool hall he uses as his cover—called Shooter's. You want a sandwich or something?"

"*Si.*"

Robert turned and retrieved two sandwiches, a Corona, and a Pepsi. "*Cerveza?*"

"*Bueno.*"

Roberto knew the answer. His brother had been drinking more and more often since his last stay in the joint.

"Anyway, I talked to Julio Thursday night about six-thirty. He had just left Shooter's and planned to leave early this morning for Montgomery. He should've called at six or so, and he should've made his next delivery by nine-thirty or ten. He didn't do either."

"You think this Shooter might know something?"

"I don't know, but I think something's wrong. Julio knows how much I worry about him. He wouldn't leave me hanging like this. He had at least nine hundred and fifty thousand dollars with him and five kilos of stuff. With that kind of money, anything could've happened. We got to find out what and we got to get Julio."

"Any possibility this Shooter could have tried to score some big money and free coke?" Manuel asked, sipping on his beer.

"I doubt it, but I don't rule out anyone until we find Julio."

"I thought your Colombians were in town tomorrow. Who's meeting with them?"

"Me. Hopefully, we'll find Julio, and all of us will go back tonight or tomorrow. If not, you'll stay and I'll send Tootie back up here with some reinforcements."

"Where was his next drop?"

"Birmingham. I talked to our client, and he didn't show up there either. I also checked with Atlanta and nothing. The last known contact was in Mobile, so that's where we start."

"We'll find him. You worry too much, Roberto."

"That's what Julio says. That's what Miguel and Tomas always said before those fucking Puerto Ricans killed them," he responded, crossing himself as always when he thought or spoke of his two deceased brothers.

"Let's get some sleep. We have over two hours to go, and we could have a long night," offered Manny, attempting to calm the storm brewing in his older brother's mind.

The plane landed at 1:47, and the black Suburban was waiting in the parking lot, exactly as promised by another of Roberto's contacts, a local attorney who occasionally represented Santos Exporting's legal matters in Alabama. If things didn't go well during this trip, Roberto wanted his presence in Mobile to be as paper free as possible.

Dressed in flowing silk shirts, both for comfort and easier concealment of their weapons, Roberto and Manuel walked into Shooter's with the casualness of vacationers looking for a game. A couple of hustlers eyed them from a table in the back of the clean and well-appointed pool hall and bar, but no one else seemed to notice. Most of the clientele was made up of vacationing men, killing time while their wives added to the local economy, and young punks and pool hall junkies, killing time just for the sake of killing time. A huge black bartender polished a glass after tapping a button hidden beneath the counter.

As they approached the bar, the phone rang, and the bartender handed it to Roberto.

"It's for you," he growled.

Without flinching, Roberto took the receiver in hand, wishing Manny was still of the form that had once intimidated anyone with whom he came in contact.

"Yes?"

"Mr. Santos, what a surprise and an honor. You come all the way up here this fine day for some pool?" Shooter Pinkston said in a forced, cheerful voice.

"Hello, Shooter. No, I'm looking for my little brother. Where can we talk?"

"Upstairs in my office, but you'll have to leave the pieces you and your friend are carrying with Bugger. We have a no firearms policy here."

"Bugger?"

"That ugly son-of-a-bitch standing behind the bar. Just follow him over to the stairs and he'll return your property when we're through chatting. Would you mind putting him back on the line?"

Roberto, Manny, and Bugger entered the lavishly furnished room, which could best be described as deco-pimp. Shooter was seated behind a polished copper desk accentuated with two leopard-skin visitor chairs. He wore a white linen suit, no shirt, a heavy gold chain, and every finger displayed various sizes of diamond rings crusted in gold.

"It's been a long time," greeted Shooter. "Sit down, gentlemen. Sit down. Who's your friend, Mr. Santos?"

"My brother, Manuel. I need some information about my other brother, Julio. He was here Thursday night," Roberto said. "He was here, wasn't he?"

"Yeah, he was here. In fact, after you called and said your brother would be making the drop, I took it myself, instead of Bugger. Nice young man, unlike you." Shooter smiled, uncomfortably acknowledging a joke among dangerous friends.

Roberto could sense his unannounced visit had unnerved his customer, exactly as he had hoped. Now that he had achieved the desired effect, his demeanor became more amiable.

"Shooter, I need your help."

"Just name it, Roberto." Shooter relaxed slightly.

"Julio's missing, and I'm worried. Tell me what you talked about while he was here."

"Well, let me think. He was very pleasant, but he seemed a little anxious. I offered a beer or a drink, but he said someone was waiting for him."

"Someone waiting for him? Who?"

"It was a female. He'd picked someone up on the road, someone in trouble. I kidded him a little about trying to get some road pussy. He took it the way I intended, you know, just a joke, and said he'd left her in a rough place and didn't want to leave her there very long."

"Did he say where?"

"No, but he did say he was taking her home. Was going to drop her off at some nursing home where her old man was sick or something."

"Shit! I knew I shouldn't have let him make the run. He's too good. He'd pick up a mangy dog, if—" Realizing he was rambling, his emotions were showing weakness—something unwise in his business—he returned to the interrogation. "You sure he didn't mention exactly where he was taking her, or where he was picking her up?"

"No, Roberto, I don't think he did. Sorry, I should've asked more, I guess, but I had no way of knowing. I got the impression she was from up north of here. He said a couple of times he was taking her up. Up means north to me."

"How far north?"

"Didn't say, but he did say she was from Alabama, some little town. I assume north of Mobile, probably the northern part of the county. There aren't too many towns up there big enough to have a nursing home. Tell you what, we know the tough places around here—most of them customers of mine. Let me and Bugger do a little checking around. It'll take a little time unless we get lucky."

"What do you mean 'lucky?'"

"There are rough places all the way from the Florida state line to Bayou le Batre. I doubt he dropped her too far from here, but we don't know. He said she used to work wherever she was waiting."

"Julio said you wanted more goods."

"I sure do. I got more business than I got merchandise for."

"Tell you what, you help me find my little brother and you can have all the stuff you want at a helluva discount."

152

CHAPTER 36
PREPARATIONS

Billy Cudjoe had lived an isolated life since returning to Bayou La Batre in 1974. He had spent five years in the service of the US Army Corps of Engineers as a civil construction and demolition specialist. The job had been solicited as a political favor to an aging uncle who had served two terms as a county commissioner before being convicted for accepting kickbacks from asphalt contractors.

Only high school educated, Billy had learned his trade through the regimented process of following the manuals—probably an appropriate discipline for someone of modest talent and aptitude. Although his experience with the Corps was varied, he had only excelled at dealing with explosives—a skill of limited application.

As the Corps evolved into a more supervisory organization, using outside contractors for most of its activities, Billy's value diminished, and he was assigned to one of the Mississippi field offices. His worth became painfully apparent to his superiors and he was asked to resign. Billy was a hands-on guy with virtually no management skills. He always found himself at odds with the contractors performing the small jobs for which he was responsible. His normal response to any problem was to throw a fit and kick the workers off the job. Through his efforts, the Corps had found itself in more than half-a-dozen lawsuits, all of which it had lost.

Broke and angry at life, he returned to his home town and, for over a year, rummaged about the Alabama and Mississippi delta, searching for day construction jobs, occasionally going out on a shrimper just to keep food in his stomach. Unmarried and virtually destitute, he turned to drugs, specifically marijuana, to bridge the gap between reality and his inability to deal with it. His slovenly appearance and deep Southern drawl played well to disguise the mental capacity of a man stoned from morning until night.

In 1977, he went out on a job as a day helper on a pier renovation being managed by the Rutherford Construction Company. Its owner had the reputation of being uncommonly aggressive in his bidding and construction practices, and Billy, although anything but aggressive, fit the mold of Leander's construction philosophy—cheat every time you get a chance.

Billy recognized he could have a future with this man and made it his goal in life to always be close to his employer, succumbing subserviently to his every whim. Within six months, Leander considered Billy one of his best hands, and the relationship had withstood over twenty years, two bankruptcies of Rutherford controlled companies, three grand jury investigations for illegal payoffs, an on-going battle with the IRS, and numerous trysts with women of questionable character. It was the last part Billy had enjoyed the most, often preying on Leander's throwbacks, usually to no avail.

On this particular Saturday morning, Billy sat in his shack tinkering with the small timing device he had assembled using some wire, a windup alarm clock, a blasting cap, a small piece of dynamite, and other assorted materials lying about his cluttered dwelling. Normally struggling with a sense of personal inadequacy, he felt good about himself. He was needed. No one involved in the plan could perform this part—the most important part. Leander had begrudgingly provided three thousand dollars for the materials necessary to perform the job and nearly all of it still warmed the demolitionist's pocket. Padding an expense request was a trait he had learned well from his employer.

After several hours, a partially filled can of Skoal drip, and two one-hitters of a particularly powerful lid of pot he had purchased the evening before, he was satisfied with the miniature bomb. Scratching his oily hair, he stood up, put on his newest John Deere cap, and walked to a local bar for a couple of beers and some crayfish.

Slouching on a barstool, he spit his cud into a paper napkin and washed the remains from his teeth with a bottle of PBR. Initially, he had paid little attention to the new waitress who had brought him the beer and taken his order. His partially dilated eyes were not yet adjusted to the darker surroundings. He had noticed the rich aroma of her perfume, something uncommon for this familiar establishment.

When she brought the steaming plate of crayfish and a second beer, he looked at her shapely body, paying particular attention to erect nipples protruding beneath a hot pink tank top. He wanted to talk to this young woman.

"Where's Melva, young lady?" he asked with a grin, exposing his most unattractive physical feature.

"Who?" she replied, using a painted thumbnail to remove a spot of dried ketchup from the bar.

"Melva, the regular girl."

"Don't know her. I just started a couple of days ago. They said someone hadn't showed up that morning, so I was lucky, I guess. You need anything else?"

"Just a little lovin'," Billy cracked, smiling again.

The young woman winked, pinched his unshaven cheek, and strolled to a table where two other luncheon patrons were sitting. Billy stared at her butt— the lower cheeks partially exposed through the ragged edge of her cut-off jeans shorts.

"Hot damn, I'd sure like to have me a piece of that," he whispered, and continued to gawk until she finished scraping the remains of one plate onto another. As she walked toward the door leading to the kitchen, her sway was exaggerated by the four-inch spike heels she wore very comfortably. Billy almost fell from his stool, leaning as far as he could so as not to miss a single step.

"Man, oh man. I bet that little pussy could set a feller free."

While I'm normally up before 6:00, even on weekends, the phone sounded at 7:44 and I was still dead out. Mikey, the earliest riser of my threesome, knocked on the door. Cracking it slowly, he peeked into the room.

"Daddy, are you awake?"

I vaguely heard a noise, my mind still bathing in oblivion.

"Daddy, there's a man on the phone," he prodded a little louder.

"What? What time is it, son?"

"A little before eight. You want to talk to him?"

I sat up in bed, yawned, and rubbed my eyes. "Yeah, I better. Why are you up so early?"

"This isn't early for me. I'm playing a game. You want to play later?"

"You bet I do. I hope it's Pacman. I'm pretty good at that, you know."

Mikey laughed. "I don't think they even make that anymore, Daddy."

I reached for the phone and smiled at my youngest. I patted a spot beside me and he jumped on the bed.

"Jack, this is Lawton. Sorry to call so early, but I didn't have a choice."

"Not at all, Lawton. I'm normally up long before now. Guess I didn't get much sleep the night before last."

"Tell me about it," he lamented. "Okay, here's the deal. I got part of what we wanted. We can put a tap on your office phone, Leander's home phone, the judge's office, and his house."

"What about Rifle?"

"No go, but I wasn't surprised. We were probably lucky to get what we got. Maybe we'll pick up something on Pendleton's line that will lead us to Montgomery, but time will tell. The reason for the early call is, can we get into your office this weekend? We can do it from outside, but you have several lines, according to the phone company, and it would be better—"

"Already got it handled. Kenny's set up to let you into the office. He'll come in either today or tomorrow, which ever you like."

"Jack, you know we consider him a suspect. What did you tell him?"

"Nothing important. I just said I had ordered another line and the telephone company might want in over the weekend. That's all."

"And he bought it? They don't work on weekends."

"I guess he doesn't know that. He said he'd be happy to do anything he could to help. Lawton, I know technically he's a coconspirator, but I won't file any charges against him, not with what I know right now. I hope you guys go easy on him. I think he just got himself in a bad deal in Mississippi and an even worse one with Leander. I don't think he's a crook."

"We'll see how it goes. Right now, he's not number one on the hit parade."

"Good. How you going to get to the other phones?"

"We got a break there. The home lines are normal single line residences, and the judge's office is an old system. We can get all of them from the outside. All the hookups should be in place by noon today. Call Quincy and ask him to be there at 11:00. If you can, tell him to go run an errand or something while our guys work. It'll go faster if they don't have to do a theatrical performance."

"I can handle that. Lawton, did you get my message yesterday?" I asked in a more solemn tone.

"Yeah, I did, Jack. I wanted to call you back, but Barbara's not doing well at all. I had hoped the news you heard would give her some hope, but it was just the opposite. The next time you're in town we'll have a drink and I'll give you the details. The best advice I can give you is, give those kids of yours a kiss every time you get a chance. We take them for granted and we never know…" His voice trailed off.

A lump formed in my throat. I could feel his pain.

"Lawton, I don't know what to say, except I'll keep praying, and remember, if I can do anything, anything in the world, call me."

"Thanks, Jack. I know you're sincere and that means a lot to me. I'd better get the phone guys going."

"Right. Thanks for calling, and tell Barbara I'm sure looking forward to meeting her at a happier time."

"I will."

I sat in bed for several seconds, unaware of Mikey, still huddled up against me.

"Daddy, what's a coconspirator?"

"What?" His question caught me off guard.

"A coconspirator. You said someone was one of those."

I considered my answer carefully. "A coconspirator is someone who works with someone else to do something mean or bad. Here's an example, you and I could decide to be coconspirators this morning. You want to?"

"You want me to do something bad?" He wrinkled his forehead.

I laughed. "Well, not too mean. You know how Katie and Jackie like to sleep late on weekends?"

"Yeah?"

"Let's go in and jump on their beds and make them go to the Pancake House for breakfast."

"Great. Jackie will be so mad. I like being a coconspirator."

I hoped he never had to deal with a real one.

CHAPTER 37

EVERYONE'S FISHING

"I got another one, Dad!" yelled Jimbo from the other side of the pond.

Jim Bob lifted his head and squinted. "That's the biggest damn catfish I ever seen. How many you caught, boy?"

"Eight so far today. I caught six last night," sixteen-year-old James Robert Davis, Jr. answered.

"You still got plenty of nightcrawlers?"

Jimbo reached into the coffee can resting beside him. "Yes, sir. I got over a dozen."

"Okay. Just let me know if you need more and I'll send your mama into town," Jim Bob said, looking into the cooler and realizing he didn't have enough beer to last through the evening. "I better go on and send her in now. At the rate you're catching them channel cats, we'll need more bait before the day's over."

After finishing the dishes from the lunch she'd prepared an hour earlier, Geraldine Davis stepped out of the camper and walked to the foldable chaise lounge where her half-drunk husband was lying under a large river oak.

"Sissy's real sunburned. She wants to go home," she announced.

"Did you put some butter on her back?" Jim Bob replied without opening his eyes.

"Butter don't help sunburn. That's an old wives' tale. Besides, there's not much else for her to do out here but go swimming, and she sure can't do that anymore for a few days."

"Geraldine, I been working the night patrol for ova two months now, and I sure do need some peace and quiet. If we go home, sure as hell, the phone'll ring and the sheriff'll want me to come in and handle something he don't want to do. Until he retires, he aims to work my tail off, knowing I'll be his replacement and all. Why do you think I didn't bring my portable phone or radio? We'd already be packed up, and I'd be in my uniform fetching this and fetching that for Mr. Logginfield. Besides, look at Jimbo ova there. He's having the time of his life."

"What should I do about Sissy's back? It's red as a boiled crawfish."

"Tell you what. Jimbo's about to run out of worms. Why don't you run into town and pick up some of that green sunburn medicine, some coloring books and colors, maybe one or two of those girl's mystery books she likes, and some bait for Jimbo. I'll stay here and watch the kids and get the fire ready for the fish fry tonight. If you see anyone, don't say where we are. They might tell Harley, and he might send someone looking for me."

"Okay, but I think I'll take Sissy with me. She'd probably rather go to town than lay in there in that hot camper."

"Gerry, honey, while you're at it, would you mind picking me up a couple of cases of Budweiser? And we might need some more ice."

She sighed and shook her head.

Billy finished his second order of crayfish and was halfway through his fifth beer. His typical Saturday visit to the bar lasted about an hour and a half. It was now 2:30, and he'd been there almost three hours.

As time passed, his inhibitions waning with each bottle, every encounter with her became a little more vulgar than the last. She had taken every overture in stride. Rude behavior from potential johns was part of the profession she had been forced to choose.

"I'm thinking about going fishing tonight. You want to go with me?"

She continued clearing the dishes in front of him and smiled, shaking her head.

"Then show me your tits?" he quacked, expecting to be slapped as he had been so many times in the past.

To his astonishment, she glanced about and lifted her tank top to her neck, exposing the most symmetrically formed breasts he'd ever seen.

Billy's eyes widened, and he immediately felt the sensation of blood rushing to one of his lower appendages.

"Holy shit! Those are the most, most beautiful things I ever—"

Convinced this hillbilly wasn't an undercover anything, and having watched him flash the roll of hundreds every time he ordered a beer, she whispered while lowering her top, "You want to see more?"

159

After a dozen catnaps and a dozen exclamations from across the lake, Jim Bob sat up on the edge of the chaise and eyed the remaining beer in the cooler. His head was beginning to throb and he could think of nothing better to do than drink the last Budweiser. The sound of an engine approaching from across the pasture gave him reason for hope, and he returned to the position he had assumed for the past four hours. The vehicle stopped and he heard a familiar, yet, unwelcome voice.

"Hey, Jim Bob, the sheriff's been looking everywhere for you."

Without looking up, he retorted, "Frank, what the hell you doing out here?"

Frank Pooley was Harley Logginfield's nephew by marriage and had been sworn in as a deputy only nine months earlier.

"The FBI's been in the office questioning everyone on the force since yesterday."

"The FBI? What do they want?" Jim Bob inquired, only mildly interested.

"They're looking for some black girl that ran away from home about two weeks ago," Frank announced. "You're the only one they haven't talked to yet, and the sheriff's been raising cane with everyone to find you. Lucky for you, I ran into your wife and little girl in the drug store. She's sure a cute little thing."

Not yet absorbing the weight of the disclosure, Jim Bob adjusted the back of the lounger to a sitting position and leaned back, massaging the back of his neck with his free hand.

"What's so important about this nigger girl that makes the FBI get involved?" the future sheriff asked while yawning.

"Jim Bob, you know the sheriff don't like us using the 'n' word anymore."

Jim Bob spread his arms, palms up, and proclaimed, "Do I look like I'm on duty, Frank? I abide by all of Harley's rules while I'm on duty, but when I'm in the presence of nature, on my day off, I can use the 'n' word any time I like. Now, why are the Feds so interested in this nigger?"

Ignoring the rebuke, Frank answered, "The waitress over at the bus stop café at Grove Hill identified the girl they're looking for, and she said she called the office and was told someone would pick the girl up. And—"

For the first time since this unwelcome conversation had begun, Jim Bob was interested, very interested. "They talked to the waitress that called the station?"

"Yeah, and at first, Harley didn't think it could've been you because you've been on graveyard for the last two months and—"

160

"That's right. It couldn't have been me. What time did this all take place?"

"The waitress told the FBI about nine at night."

"Well, there you go. It couldn't have been me because I wasn't even on duty yet," Jim Bob exclaimed, breathing a sigh of relief.

"Yeah, but then Harley checked his notes, and he had brought you in early that night because Ronnie was coming down with that stomach virus. Anyway, you need to get into the station right away and get this whole mess straightened up."

Jim Bob's head was spinning. He'd been caught.

"Well, as soon as Geraldine gets back with the truck, we'll break camp and I'll come on in. Tell Harley I'll be in in the morning."

"That won't work, Jim Bob. I called in as soon as I talked to your missus. The sheriff told me to get out here and bring you in. Said he's tired of these FBI types hanging around his office and he wants to get this over with so we can get back to police work."

"Frank, just let me help my wife get all our shit together and I'll—"

"I found your wife over at the A & P after I talked to the sheriff, and she said she'd be happy to clean up the camp and meet you at home tonight. She said Jimbo over there could help her. Hi, Jimbo!" yelled Frank, waving to the youngster.

Jimbo raised his stringer of catfish for the young deputy to see.

"Damn, he's getting bigger every day. Some of the boys think he'll start on the varsity this fall. They think he'll play tight end, but I bet they make him a tackle."

"That bitch," Jim Bob whispered under his breath.

"Sorry, I didn't catch what you said."

"Never mind, let's go."

As he fixed his seat belt, Frank turned to Jim Bob and asked, "You never did say."

"Say what?"

"Did you pick the girl up?"

The phone was ringing when Jackson, Katie, Mikey, and I returned from our Saturday outing—early lunch at Applebee's, and the matinee showing of the newest James Bond thriller.

"Mitchell residence, Katie speaking," my middle one answered, hoping it would be Chuck Wilson, her first boyfriend.

The caller was a man, but not the one she hoped for.

"Hello, Katie. This is Lawton Tremont. Your dad has told me about you."

"Yes, sir," Katie responded, not knowing what she should say.

"I have a little girl about your same age. Her name is Jane. I hope someday we'll get to meet you and your brothers. Is your father home?"

"Yes, sir. Just a minute, please. Daddy, it's for you. Mr. Tremont."

"Hello, Lawton, I didn't expect to hear from you so soon. I hope it's good news about your daughter," I answered.

"I wish it were, Jack, but nothing new yet. I just wanted to let you know Kenny Quincy was prompt in getting us into your office, and the tap's in place there. We're also set and running at Leander's house, Vivian's, and the judge's office. We're having a technical problem with the judge's home phone, but I'm told it should be fixed in a few hours."

"Miss Vivian, huh? I hadn't thought about her," I replied, trying to remember if we had discussed her that morning.

"I did that as an afterthought."

"Probably a good idea. Leander spends as much time there as he does at home according to Kenny. This whole thing is, I don't know, surreal to me. If someone had told me a simple investment would have ended up in wiretaps and federal investigations when I bought Jefferson, I wouldn't have believed it. I sure hope this whole thing works. I have to tell you, Lawton, it's frightening to an old trash man from Texas."

Lawton laughed. "I'm sure it is, Jack. Just think of it like going fishing. We've heard some fish have been biting down here in Mobile, but we're not sure how big they are or what they're feeding on. All we know to do is put out some lines and see what bites. We never know what we might catch. Maybe nothing and maybe something we never expected."

CHAPTER 38
CLEANING THE JAIL

Dressed in casual weekend wear, Raleigh limped out on the veranda of his plantation-style mansion with a birch cane in one hand and a mint julep in the other. Viola Washington followed, carrying a sterling tray, a tall empty glass, and a frosty pitcher of light green liquid.

Viola was the third generation of Washington women to serve the Pendleton household as full time housekeeper and cook. Raleigh had grown up with Viola and had bragged for years that she undoubtedly made the best mint juleps in Alabama—a special recipe handed down by mouth from one generation of Washingtons to the next. He often admitted even he didn't know the secret ingredient that set her recipe apart from the rest. Having once entered her specialty at the state fair in Montgomery, he claimed her second place finish had been the work of an evil judge who'd taken a bribe in favor of a far less tasty concoction entered by a wealthy banker from Huntsville.

After easing into the oak porch swing that had withstood two hurricanes and four tornadoes over the past twenty years, he began to sway back and forth while configuring the final pieces of his most recent genius plan. After thirty minutes of concentrated thought and half of his second Viola special, he glanced up when a flash caught his eye. He watched the reflection of the mid-day sun bouncing off the bumper long before he could hear the engine of Virgil's Cherokee cruiser. Another vehicle with identical markings followed closely behind.

"Come on up here, Virgil. Hello, Lester, you old hero, you," he offered as a greeting as both men stepped out of their county vehicles.

Virgil, like Raleigh, was dressed casually, while Lester wore the starched and pleated uniform of the Washington County Sheriff's Department.

"Appreciate you boys driving out here this beautiful Saturday afternoon. How was your night at the cabin, Lester? You take your girl out there with you?"

Lester blushed and smiled. "Yes, sir. That lake house of yours is something else, Judge Pendleton. Me and Belinda sure appreciate you letting us stay out there last night. It was real swell. We cleaned it up real good when we left this morning."

"You didn't have to do that, son. We got negras that look after cleaning and such. You sure look good in that uniform, Lester. Slender, in shape, and all. Virgil, we once could see our belt buckles, remember?"

"It's been too many years for me, Judge," chuckled the sheriff, slapping his protruding belly.

"You on duty, Lester?"

"Not yet, sir. I go on in about two and a half hours. At 1600."

"That'd be four o'clock, wouldn't it? Never was very good with them military hours. If you weren't going on duty, I'd offer you one of Viola's mint juleps, but they pack a mighty powerful punch for something that tastes so good. How about you, Virgil? You can imbibe, can't you?"

"I never turn down one of Miss Viola's specials, Judge," he answered, filling a glass and sitting in the rocker opposite his host.

Lester stood quietly, hoping to appear as professional as the judge had told him he was the day before.

"Lester, you eaten anything?"

"Me and Belinda had breakfast this morning ova at the Copper Kitchen."

"You must be starving, what with all the good police work you been doing and all that extracurricular activity last night. Why don't you go inside and have Viola make you a sandwich or something? She just baked an apple pie with some fresh apples she bought at the A & P this morning. Go on in there and eat something while Virgil and I talk for a minute or two."

Realizing he'd been given an order, not an offer, Lester thanked Raleigh and walked into the house.

"How many inmates you got down at the jail, Virgil?"

"Three. I still got the Harrington kid. I guess Jesse's gonna make him sweat a few days before he bails him out. And there's the armed robber you remanded without bail, and Santos. We had a drunk Frank picked up ova by Choctaw Bluff yesterday, but I called in and had him released on my way out here. Why?"

"And Santos has been in the isolation room the whole time?"

"Yeah, just like you said yesterday."

"We haven't fed him anything, have we? No cigarettes?"

"No, just water like you told me, but he's getting pretty irritable. What's this all about, Raleigh?"

Ignoring the question, he poured another glass and topped off Virgil's. "I want you to go on back to town and clean the jail."

"Say what?"

"Not literally, Sheriff. I want you to release everyone but Santos, and I want them out of there by six o'clock tonight. I'll sign all the necessary orders Monday."

"What about Jesse Harrington's kid? He obviously wants the boy to learn a lesson."

"Call Jesse and tell him the boy's been real good and remorseful. Have one of your deputies drive the boy home. You'll probably make a few points with Jesse, which won't hurt you none come election time." Raleigh pulled two bills out of his pocket. "Give that nigger robber this forty dollars and tell him if he ever steps foot in my courtroom again, he'll go to prison for the rest of his life. Tell him I have an amnesty day once a year and he won the lottery. He won't argue."

"Raleigh, you feeling all right?"

"Virgil, I got a plan and I don't want you to be a part of it for the time being. I'll explain everything tomorrow and you'll understand. Just trust me and do what I say."

"Okay, Raleigh. If that's what you want, I'll do it. What about Santos?"

"Just leave him in solitary and make sure Lester's manning the jail tonight."

"He's scheduled for patrol. Henry's on the desk—"

Raleigh raised his hand and sighed. "Virgil, please just do it. It's important. Okay?"

"Okay, Judge, anything you say. If you have nothing else for me, I better get going. I got some work to do. You want me to go fetch Lester?"

"No, just let the boy finish his pie. I want to visit with him for a few minutes anyway."

As Virgil sped down the drive away from the Pendleton plantation, he removed his straw Stetson and scratched his head. *What the hell is Raleigh up to? This is the dam'dest set of orders he's ever given me.*

When he turned onto the county road leading toward Chatom, Virgil was engrossed in thought and took little notice of the panel truck parked on the narrow shoulder and the lineman perched near the top of the telephone pole.

CHAPTER 39

TAPS

Jim Bob rode in silence while Frank Pooley chattered away about the FBI and how he would have applied to the Academy if had he gone to college. Jim Bob stared ahead, wishing Frank would shut up and wondering whether the story he had told had satisfied his interrogators. He knew there were holes in it, but he felt Harley should have been supportive rather than demeaning him in front of the two agents.

Finally, they turned off the pavement and drove down the dirt road leading to his wooden frame farmhouse. Even to a casual observer, it was apparent the place was in bad need of repair. The white paint was peeling, the corners of the eaves were beginning to rot, and there were almost as many green shingles missing as were attached. Frank noticed, but Jim Bob did not. His gaze was focused on the camper, indicating his wife and children were home from the outing.

Stepping from the vehicle, he slammed the door without saying a word to the junior deputy. Frank shrugged his shoulders and backed out of the yard.

Entering the house, he shouted, "Geraldine!"

His wife walked into the living room, wiping her hands on the apron she always wore while tending to the endless duties of cleaning, cooking, washing clothes, and raising children.

"Where are the kids?" he barked, his head beginning to throb as the early evening hangover began to set in.

"Jimbo's taking a bath and Sissy's laying down in our bedroom. Her sunburn is really bad and she cried—"

The force of the blow to her chin was savage. Her eyes fluttered as her legs buckled. She tumbled back into an end table and then to the floor. A lamp crashed heavily beside her. She lay still for a few seconds. Her eyes blurred, and then refocused, as the pain began to permeate from her chin to the back of her jaw. Before she was fully cognizant of what had happened, he began the tirade.

"You sorry, selfish bitch. You couldn't wait to tell Frank Pooley where I was so you could bring your precious daughter and her fucking sunburn home. And after I told you not to tell no one where I was. I ought to beat your head in, you conniving whore. You were nothing but a fat, ugly orphan with no one and no hope for nothing when I took pity on you and married your ugly ass, gave you a home, respectability, and the thanks I get is you go put me in a helluva position." He charged toward her. "I think I'll just kill your selfish ass and be done with you."

"What'd I do, Jimmy? I didn't do anything. Frank said the sheriff might fire you if you didn't go in. I tried not to tell him, but he scared me. I thought I was helping you. I pleaded with him to let me come out and tell you, but he said he would tell the sheriff you were hiding from him. What should I have done, Jimmy? Tell me, what should I have done?" She began to cry uncontrollably, her bruised face lying in the crook of her arm.

"Daddy, what's wrong with Mommy?" Sissy cried out from the door leading to the hallway. "What's wrong with Mommy?"

The eight-year-old's body was thrust aside as Jimbo burst into the room, his hair still wet with shampoo and his muscular frame wrapped in a towel. He glanced at his mother on the floor and his eyes grew wild.

"I'll kill you if you ever touch her again!" he shouted. "If you want to hit someone, why don't you try me? I've watched you beat her and yell at her all my life, and this is the end of it. I swear to God, I'll kill you if you ever hit her again."

"What'd you say, boy?"

"You heard me. Now get your drunk ass out of here and leave us alone!" His fists were clinched, his face filled with resolve.

"Jimbo, honey," Geraldine said, her voice cracking as she lifted herself from the floor. "You apologize to your father. This is between us, and it was all my fault. I did something bad, and your daddy had every right to—"

"No man has the right hit to a woman," Jimbo retorted, still ready to fight.

Jim Bob looked around the room, shook his head, and stomped out the door.

As he drove his cruiser down the county road toward Tomkin's Corner, the gravity of the day and of the past few minutes began to build.

Jim Bob, you dumb son-of-a-bitch, how the hell did you get yourself into such a mess? Damn, I need a beer. My head's killing me.

He pulled into the convenience store and bought a six-pack. Quickly chugging one, he sat back in the SUV and began to settle down. He reached into his pocket, pulled out a quarter, and walked to the pay phone.

"Pendleton residence," answered Viola from the phone in the kitchen. The aroma of the two freshly baked pies filled the room.

"Viola, this is Deputy Davis from ova in Clarke County. Is the judge home?"

"Yes, sir, he's upstairs dressing to go out."

"Could you tell him this is an emergency and get him for me?"

He heard the receiver being placed on the counter top.

A couple of minutes later, he heard a click. "Viola, you can hang up now." Another click.

"Jim Bob?"

"It's me, Judge. We got a problem."

The deputy told the judge about his interview with the FBI. Raleigh listened without interrupting, continuing to put on his socks and shoes.

"Okay, let me get this straight," Raleigh began. "The FBI's looking for the negra girl you picked up ova at Grove Hill, and you're sure it's the same girl?"

"Yeah, they showed me a picture. It was her all right."

"And she's the daughter of a federal prosecutor down at Mobile? I thought she was a runaway from up north someplace—Birmingham, I thought you said."

"That's what she told me. How was I to know different?"

"I suppose you wouldn't. So you told them you went to pick her up, but she wouldn't come with you, so you gave her some money for a bus ride back home. It sure would've been better if you'd said she wasn't there when you got there."

"But she was."

"I know she was, Jim Bob, but they wouldn't have no way of knowing that. Now, they've got some more leads to follow up on—the bus driver, the ticket agent. This could get a little messy. Let me think."

"I'm sorry, Judge. Frank drug me into the station, and I couldn't think of anything—"

"Shut up! I need to think."

Raleigh sat on his bed, cursing to himself. *A damn U.S. Attorney's daughter. What kind of luck is that? Shit!* A soft clicking sound came over the receiver. It lasted about three seconds.

"You on a cell phone?" the judge asked.

"No, a pay phone ova at Tomkin's Corner. Why?"

"I heard some static on the line. Never mind."

The judge was silent again. Jim Bob reached into the paper sack and popped another beer.

"Okay, here's all we can do. They'll come back to talk to you after they can't find no other leads. You just stick to your story, no matter how hard they press you. And you can damn sure bet they'll press you. Remember how you drove by several times during the night to check on things and everything was all right."

"But, I—"

"You're not hearing me. You drove by several times during the night and she was okay. Then, before you went off duty, you made one last check and she was gone. You figured everything was okay, and you felt good about yourself for helping someone out. Ain't that right?"

Jim Bob was quiet for a few seconds and then a sense of relief flooded over him.

"Yeah, I did. Hell, anyone would've figured that. Anyone could've driven by and picked her up. Yeah, that's what happened."

"Good boy. Now, I got to go. I got a fundraiser in a little while and I got another call to make. Keep your head on and we'll all get out of this deal with our skins."

Raleigh replaced the receiver and shook his head. Reaching for a small black address book beside the bed, he looked up a number and dialed.

"Miss Vivian, is Leander ova there?"

"Hello, Judge. No. I saw him this afternoon, but he went home about three hours ago. I expect to see him later."

"Thank you, dear. You have a pleasant evening, you hear."

He dialed another number, putting on his gold Rolex while the phone rang.

"Hello."

"Leander, this is Raleigh."

"Hello, Judge. What a pleasant surprise. I was just thinkin' about you. That job ova at Republic is just about finished, and I think we're gonna come out on it real good. I bought that engineer we been having so much trouble with a new television set, one of them big-screen Sonys, and he was real appreciative. Yes, sir, we're gonna make a fortune—"

"Leander, I don't have time for all that foolishness right now. I talked to Harvey ova there yesterday, and he said he hoped we came out good enough to get—Hell, you got me doing it. That's not why I called. I got a deal working tonight, and if it works out, we won't be needing to do what we were planning tomorrow."

"You mean we won't be—"

"Yeah, but it's not for sure. Just get in touch with Billy and tell him not to do nothing unless he hears from you."

"Hell, Judge, I done gave him three thousand dollars to buy the—"

"Leander! You watch your mouth. You know I'm still worried about all them tax issues of yours, and I know you're on your home phone 'cause I called you. Now, watch what you say and don't worry about any money you gave Billy. If things go good tonight, there'll be plenty to cover expenses. Just get in touch with him and be careful what you say."

Leander hung up the phone and sat back in his recliner. After a few minutes of thought, he dialed the phone. He immediately got a recording saying the party he was calling was either unavailable or out of the calling area. He left a brief message. "Billy, don't do nothing tomorrow night without talking to me."

Satisfied he had completed his appointed task, he looked at his wife, who was knitting a sweater for one of the grandchildren. Staring back at the television, his thoughts returned to Miss Vivian and their rendezvous in two hours.

In three separate vans, long play recorders continued to wind while men made notes of three complete conversations, a partial one, and a voice message left on a cell phone. Notations were logged on pads, together with specific phrases and question marks. A small computer digitally identified the numbers of the unanswered calls and logged them into its hard drive.

CHAPTER 40
THE BAYOU

The black Suburban traveled west on Airport Boulevard. Its two occupants had just completed a day and a half of dead ends and the older one was frustrated.

"I should've never let him do it. How the hell do things get so screwed up?" Roberto stared through the windshield and sighed. "Okay, Manny, let's review what we know, or better yet, what we don't. We've checked every hospital we could find in the county, and he's not there. Tonight, get on the phone and start checking the surrounding counties. Even check over in Mississippi. Okay?"

"Got it," answered his middle brother, scratching on a notepad picked up at a convenience store.

"We checked, what, four nursing homes north of Mobile? The only lead we have there is that, what's his name?"

Manny flipped pages. "Yokum. Cecil Yokum. His daughter was supposed to visit him last Thursday night, but she didn't show up. Her name is, uh, here it is, Mary Yokum. That dude was in bad shape."

"See what you can find out about her. Probably a dead end, but you don't know. The sheriff's department and the Mobile police didn't have him, but I want you to check all the sheriff's offices in the surrounding counties. The highway patrol didn't have any record of a wreck anywhere in the state. I guess that's good. Dammit, Julio, where the fuck are you?"

As the vehicle drove through the security gate onto the tarmac outside the FBO, Tootie waved the rag he'd been using to check the fluid levels during his pre-flight inspection. Manny waved back, although the darkened windows shielded the gesture from anyone outside the vehicle. Roberto's cell phone rang.

"Santos."

"Roberto, Shooter here. We may have something on the girl."

Roberto closed his eyes, breathing a silent prayer. "What?"

"I have a customer down by the docks, a joint called the Blue Oyster, pretty sleazy. Anyway, Bugger talked to him, and there's this girl that used to work there, a barmaid—turned a few tricks on the side. She was in there the night Julio was here. Told my guy she was going up to Citronelle to see her old man who was dying of cancer or something. She was real nervous."

"Why?"

"Not sure. He thought maybe she was scared about her old man, and she has an outstanding here in Mobile for solicitation. She's been down in Florida for the past couple of years. Anyway, she was there an hour or so and the guy picked her up."

"Was it Julio?"

"Could've been. Bugger described your brother, and my customer said maybe."

"Hang on, Shooter." He cupped his hand over the mouthpiece. "Manuel, that guy up in the nursing home could be important. I'll explain in a minute. Go on, Shooter."

"Then, the girl came back about midnight. No shoes, her hair all messed up, and she was real upset."

"Why?" Roberto had a sick feeling in his stomach.

"She and the guy apparently got stopped by a cop up north. He didn't know exactly where. Here's the bad part. This cop was a real redneck type, and he hassled the driver—put him on the pavement with a gun."

"Shot him? Shot Julio?"

"Easy, Roberto. No, he didn't shoot him, and we're not even sure it's your brother. But he did take a shot at the girl when she jumped from the panel truck and ran."

"You said panel truck. That's what Julio was driving. It has to be him." Roberto's chest was heaving. "What else?"

"The best part is we may be able to find the girl. She wanted to crash there for a few days, but the owner's old lady always thought he was screwing her and he didn't want any grief. He called a friend who has a bar down at Bayou le Batre. She went down there."

"Is she there?"

"We haven't gotten that far yet. Bugger just came in with what I've told you. He's going down there this evening."

"Where's this bayou place? What's it called, Bayou le what?"

"Bayou le Batre. It's a small town down south of Mobile on the Gulf. It's a fishing place. You know, shrimp boats, seagulls, curio shops, that kind of shit."

"You got the girl's name?"

"Yeah. Tina Tucker. He doesn't think that's her real name, but that's what she goes by."

"Tell Bugger to wait at your place until Manuel gets there. I want Manny to go down there with him. This girl could lead us to Julio."

"Roberto, Bugger's capable of chasing this down by himself."

"I'm sure you're right, but the girl might need some persuading, and Bugger doesn't have near the motivation we have. I want Manuel to go," Roberto ordered.

"Whatever you say. Not to be, eh, indelicate, Roberto, but you mentioned some additional product."

"I'm leaving for Miami in a few minutes, but the plane'll be back with a couple of my boys in the morning. How much you want?"

"Maybe two k's?"

"I'll send four and the price for this shipment is half the usual. Thanks, Shooter. We needed a break, and this could be it. Tell Bugger to wait for Manny."

Walking toward the plane, Roberto told Manny every detail of the conversation he'd had with Shooter.

"So we think Julio was busted by some cop?" Manny asked.

"If it was Julio, it sounds that way. We've already checked all the authorities in Mobile County. Look at the map and start calling the surrounding counties. You can make some of the calls while you and Bugger drive down to this bayou place. Manuel, if you find that girl, don't kill her, but make her wish she were dead if she holds anything back. Got it?"

Billy Cudjoe slapped the match against his zipper, touching the flame to the bowl of the miniature pipe. A one hitter was all he needed to extend the euphoria for a couple more hours, until he picked her up.

His tongue had been thick with lust ever since she'd agreed to spend the night with him. All it would cost was a hundred dollars and an eighth of cocaine, which he'd purchased at the bar for another three hundred. A night in paradise for a total investment of four hundred twenty-five dollars, including the beer and barbecue he'd picked up on his way back to the shack. He'd even stopped by the barbershop for a shave and a trim, something he hadn't done since his uncle died in prison three years earlier.

A new shirt from a souvenir shop had been considered—a Don Ho with orange flowers, but he'd resisted the temptation. After all, she was just a whore. He had succumbed to a fresh bottle of Bay Rum from the drug store, however—she was the most beautiful whore he'd ever seen.

Twisting the lid from a bottle of PBR, he surveyed his one-room shack and was pleased. The mountain of trash, once occupying the corner by the old Frigidaire, was now floating in green plastic bags along the edge of the wharf. The bottom sheet on the single twin bed had been turned over, although he couldn't remember if he'd conducted that same operation since the last time it was washed. A clean sheet of butcher's paper covered the stained top of the dinette, and he'd even placed a small candle in a tumbler to anchor the table covering. Yes, everything was just about perfect for his evening of bliss.

She cleared out her last customer, picking up the seventy-five cent tip left for a twelve-dollar tab. She felt no contempt as they staggered through the front door. If things went as planned, she'd have enough money by morning to return to Fort Lauderdale where the tips were more appropriate and the johns less revolting.

Billy sauntered into the bar, his hair slicked back with an excessive quantity of hair tonic, the comb rows tightly following the contour of his scalp. The musk of last week's perspiration was only vaguely noticeable through the syrupy tang of Bay Rum, also generously applied.

"You ready to go, Tina baby?" he quacked with a wink and a pat to her sparsely covered buttocks.

"Give me a couple of minutes to gather my gear and freshen up a bit, Billy honey," she mocked, although her sarcasm was lost on him.

She went to the kitchen and picked up the sixty dollars due her. She had told the owner earlier that she wouldn't be back. His was a fluid business and transient help was the norm.

She visited the Lysol-treated bathroom, splashing her underarms with the cold water from the corroded facet and sponging her pubic area with a paper towel. She looked into the cracked mirror and brushed her auburn hair with her fingers, finally deciding on a tight ponytail secured with a rubber band.

174

Taking a deep breath, she gathered her belongings and whispered to herself, "Just do this guy. Don't think about how disgusting he is, just do him and get the hell back to Florida tomorrow. Don't think about him. Think about—a monkey." She smiled and then laughed out loud.

Manuel and Bugger walked toward the entrance to the bar just as the owner was locking the front door. Bugger, who normally delivered his product, tapped him on the shoulder. Startled, he jumped to one side, reaching for the revolver tucked under his belt.

"Dammit, Bugger! You scared the shit out of me."

Bugger only smiled. "You're locking up early for a Saturday night, Sammy."

"Real slow tonight."

"I understand you got a new girl working here. Somebody named Tina."

"Used to work here. She quit tonight. One of the reasons I closed early. If a crowd came in, I wouldn't have anyone to wait on them."

Manuel entered the conversation. "Have any idea where she went?"

Sammy looked at Bugger. "Who's he?"

"He's okay—friend of Shooter's. When did she leave, and where'd she go, Sammy? It's important."

"She left here about half an hour ago with a local, a regular named Billy. Don't know his last name. I think she was turning a trick with him. What a waste."

"What do you mean 'a waste?'" Manny asked.

"My clientele isn't exactly the cream of the crop, but this guy's as scummy as they get. This Tina Tucker's a real looker. Should be turning tricks in Vegas for a grand a pop. I'd a done her myself if she hadn't left so quick. I could've stabled her just for the blow."

"Why you think she likes the white powder?" Manny asked.

"Billy bought an eighth this afternoon. He never bought any before. He was coming on to her all afternoon, and she wasn't resisting. My guess is the coke's for her."

"Any idea where this Billy lives?" Bugger pressed.

"No. I don't think it's too far from here though. He's always on foot when he comes in, but I have no idea where that is. I don't even know if they went to his place."

"Where you think she's going from here? Did she say?" Bugger asked.

"Yeah. Said she was going back to Fort Lauderdale. Said she'd just come up here to see some family and was working her way back down the coast. I think she mentioned buying a bus ticket, if things worked out. Maybe Billy's paying her what she's worth, but I doubt it."

"Sammy, give us a description of this Tina," Manuel ordered.

"Like I said, a real looker. Five-four or so, brown hair, green eyes, I think, real shapely, like a coke bottle, but not too hippie. Dresses pretty much like what she is—lots of cleavage, high-heel shoes, too much makeup. At a glance, looks older than she is, but if you look up close, she's pretty young. Probably twenty or twenty-one."

Manny scratched on his note pad. He flipped the page and made another scratch, tearing the sheet from the spiral wire.

"If you hear from her, call me on that number. If you help us find her, it'll be worth your while."

"She in trouble with you boys?" Sammy asked, eyeing the piece of paper.

"We hope not," Manuel responded as he and Bugger turned to leave.

The first time was quick, very quick. The anticipation building in Billy all afternoon and evening erupted like a sixteen-year-old putting on a condom for his first time.

"You finished already, Billy baby?" cooed Tina as he rolled off of her, gasping like an emphysema victim. Without intending to, she had ruffled his masculinity.

"Shit, I'm just warming up. I screwed a young nigger girl a couple a weeks ago, and we fucked her to death."

Tina laughed hysterically. "Fucked her to death?"

Billy felt even more challenged. "You don't believe me? I even got a picture to prove it."

He leaped out of bed, went to a drawer, and returned. He flicked on a light and handed Tina the photograph Jim Bob had secretly given him as a souvenir.

"See, I told you so," he bragged.

Tina glanced at the photo of Jane Tremont lying naked on the mat of straw. She shivered.

"You gonna kill me, Billy?" she murmured, handing him the photo.

"No, I just wanted you to know how much I got in me." Billy paused, considering he might have divulged something he shouldn't. "Oh, that girl wasn't dead, just passed out, but we sure fucked her good."

"I'm impressed, Billy. You gonna fuck me good a little later. That first one was real satisfying, and you're so big. I mean, you're bigger than anyone I ever been with," she cooed, deciding she should be a little more careful with this repulsive little man.

Billy's muscles relaxed, and he unnecessarily sucked in his belly. "You just give me a few minutes, and we'll have us a fine old time. How about a beer?"

"Sure, and how about a little of that coke?"

Twenty minutes later, they were at it again, and, as promised, Billy's performance was longer, although no more satisfying for Tina than the first.

"Oh Lord, Billy. I never had a climax like that. You're a fucking machine, baby. I came three or four times. Can we do it again? I mean, are you worn out?"

"Shit no. I can go on like that all night," Billy boasted.

Tina shuddered at the thought.

"What you doing tomorrow, baby?" she asked. "Maybe I could stay here a few days. I won't charge you anything. You're too good, baby."

Billy's ego soared. "I can stay around, and we can screw all day long if you want. I got a little job to do over on the canal tomorrow night, but then I can take a few days off, and we can get us some more drugs and beer and just stay here and get messed up for a week."

"Oh, baby, that'd be great. A week with the biggest dick in Alabama." She wanted to laugh, but bit her lip. "I think I'll have a little more toot. Coke makes me real horny. Maybe you could go out in the morning and get a little more from Sammy."

"Sure, I can do that. Now, how about a little more fucking? He's getting mad again."

Hoping to put off the inevitable until the snort kicked in, she asked, "What kind of job you doing tomorrow night? Most folks don't work on Sundays."

Billy saw another opportunity to impress her.

"I got a little demolition work to do. Needs to be done when no one's around. Too dangerous you know."

"You mean explosives? You don't work with explosives?" She jeered, still buying time.

Billy stood and walked to the greenish-gray sink that was once white. He opened a cabinet door, retrieving the timing device and a red plastic tube marked "EXPLOSIVES."

"What does this look like?"

"I don't know, a clock, some wire, and a big cigar tube."

"This here's dynamite and a timing device—my own little creation. Now do you think I don't work with explosives?"

As the reality of what he was holding soaked in, she became panicky.

"Oh, Billy baby, I believe you now. Why don't you put that up? Let me take another little pop and you can tell me about it. This is all so, so exciting."

Billy replaced the bomb and opened another beer. Using a rusting razor blade, she lined up the powder on the butcher paper.

"This ain't no big deal, but you'll probably read about it in the papers. It'll for sure make the news."

CHAPTER 41
A VISITOR

Julio Santos lay on a stretched canvas cot, his overlapping hands served as a pillow. His olfactory system had long since become desensitized to the pungent odor of his own waste, decomposing in the bucket residing in one corner of the small cubical. Denied both food and tobacco for almost forty-eight hours, his stomach growled persistently, while the desire for cigarettes had subsided to a manageable longing a day earlier. His only human contact had been sets of eyes peering through the narrow slit in the metal door, and a brief glimpse of polished black boots when the water bottle was tossed through the one-way pet door.

The first hours of deprivation had confused him. *Solitary confinement for a broken taillight and an open bottle of booze?* He could make no sense of it. Anxiety as to whether the stash of money and drugs might be discovered had haunted him through that first night and the following morning, but no one had entered and begun the questioning that would surely follow such a find.

As Friday afternoon turned to evening, hunger and frustration became his dominant concerns, and for the first time, he began shouting into the open slit, but no one had acknowledged him. Not even a "Shut up!" had echoed through the narrow hallway leading to his place of confinement.

By Saturday morning, confusion and physical denial had turned to anger. He began screaming obscenities and threats, often reverting to his secondary language. The only response had been laughter and taunting from the other inmates, which had been squelched by a threatening redneck voice. He had thrown the folding chair repeatedly into the metal door, certain the loud crashing would eventually irritate the jailer into breaking the silence, but not a word or a warning was issued.

Although perspective of time was beginning to escape him, Saturday evening brought with it depression and feelings of self-pity. He had even silently cursed his brother Roberto for not having found and delivered him from the loneliness escalating to panic. As he lay on the board-like hardness of the cot, his mind was numb; it had given in to hopelessness and despair.

Lester Holmboe and Larry Rinker sat on opposite sides of the main desk of the sheriff's headquarters in Chatom. The powerful radio transmitter occasionally crackled from behind them. It was unusually quiet since there was only one inmate in custody, and he was sequestered in the small solitary cell at the rear of the building.

"King me," Larry demanded as he completed a double jump he'd been setting up for several plays. Larry was reasonably proficient at checkers while Lester was not. Assigned to patrol duty for the shift, Larry had returned to the station to answer nature's call, but he had stayed to entertain Lester for a few minutes.

As he contemplated a clever move to salvage a game hopelessly lost, the shrill ringing of the phone interrupted Lester's thoughts.

"Sheriff's office. Deputy Holmboe speaking."

"Uh, I'm William Pervis, an attorney in, uh, Montgomery. I've been hired to find the whereabouts of Julio Santos. We last heard he was in southern Alabama. Do you have him or do you have any information about him?" asked Manuel, trying his best to disguise his Cuban-American accent.

"Santos, huh? No, we don't have anyone by that name. In fact, we don't have anyone in custody at all right now," declared Lester. *This guy sounds like a Mexican.*

"You had any car accidents around there or had any yellow panel trucks picked up?" Manuel pressed. This was the fourth time he'd been through the drill and thought he was getting good at it.

"No, no panel trucks. What'd you say your name was?"

Manny clicked the off button and busily made notes of the conversation. Deputy Lester Holmboe was recorded phonetically in the note pad.

The flash of headlights through the front window signaled a car turning into the parking lot. Lester replaced the receiver and quickly lifted the checkerboard, concealing it in the wide drawer of the table supporting the radio. All thoughts of the call were erased from his mind.

Larry moved to one of the two gray metal desks facing the wall where prints of the current governor and George Wallace were displayed in cheap wooden frames. He began banging the keys of an old Smith-Corona. When the door opened, both men leaped to their feet.

"Evening, Judge Pendleton," Larry stuttered. He seldom had the opportunity to address the man of Washington County.

Raleigh looked in Larry's direction, straining to read the engraved nametag pinned above his left breast pocket.

"Evening, Deputy...eh... Rinker," he replied, eyeing the officer suspiciously.

Lester, who had been expecting the visit, was more at ease. "Hello, Judge. What an unexpected honor."

"Lester, you manning the fort tonight?" Raleigh commented while hobbling toward the central desk, balancing a cardboard box with one hand. "Viola did a mess of baking this afternoon, and I thought maybe you boys down here might like a little piece of the best damn pie you ever tasted. I tell you that old negra lady is one fine cook. Thought the inmates might enjoy a piece as well, but it seems mighty quiet in there." He motioned to the door leading to the holding cells.

"Nobody in there tonight, Judge," explained Lester. "Except for our special guest from Miami. Course he's been in isolation like you—"

"That's good. You boys've obviously been doing a bang-up job," Raleigh interrupted. "Crime prevention's a whole lot more effective than enforcement, and cheaper for the county."

Raleigh turned to Larry. "You on patrol tonight, Deputy?"

"Yeah, yes sir," he stammered. "Had to take a crap a while ago. I was catching up on a little paperwork."

"I passed a stranded automobile about fifteen miles back up County 413. It could've been Mrs. Terkle, the old retired junior high principal. I would've stopped, but I was on down the road before I recognized who it was. If you're through with your paperwork, you might run up there and see if she needs any assistance. I hate the thought of the elderly being stuck out in the dark. Some of 'em get scared. Old age, you know."

"I was just finishing up, Judge Pendleton. I'll get right on up there and help her out," Larry conceded, retrieving his official head cover from the coat rack behind the front door. "Good to see you again, Judge."

"You too, son. And you come on back later and have yourself a piece of Miss Viola's specialty."

"Thank you, Judge Pendleton. I will when I go off duty."

As the door closed, Raleigh reached into his khaki suit coat pocket. Retrieving an ordinary stainless table knife, he placed it on the desk beside the box.

"How's our special guest doing, Lester?"

"He was raising cane when I came on duty at 1600, throwing that metal folding chair against the door, cussing and all, but he settled down a couple of hours ago. He's been laying on his bunk real quiet like."

"Good. He's probably confused and scared by now. Nobody's talked to him? He ain't been told about the money and drugs you found, has he?"

"No, sir. Nobody's said a word to him. Don't you think it's time we charged him with something? Normally, we'd be getting him ready for an arraignment for drug—"

"All in good time, Lester. All in good time. I tell you what. I think I'll go back there and have a little conversation with our Mr. Santos. It's about time he understood the gravity of his situation. I figure he's just some mule for a big-time cocaine distributor. If he thinks we'll go easy on him, maybe we could end up finding out who the kingpin is."

"I thought that was what the drug enforcement people did. They got lots of contacts and know about how—"

"Lester, why would we want to give them all the glory? Hell, boy, this could be big news, maybe national. And you're the guy who made the bust, started the whole thing. Don't you think that pretty young girl of yours would like to see your picture on television? Hell, you might even be interviewed by that Geraldo feller."

"Yeah, I see what you're saying. No reason for us to not get some of the credit."

"Think what sort of message it'll send out to potential criminals. Don't come messing around in Washington County, Alabama. We don't tolerate no law breaking around here," Raleigh said. "Let's go on back there, and I'll see what this Mexican boy has to say for himself."

"I think he's Cuban," corrected Lester.

"Same difference. They're all spics to me. Now, I don't expect no problem with this boy, but I want you to wait down the hall in case he tries any funny stuff. Keep your gun handy. If I have any problem, I'll be yelling, and I expect you to come running. I'm putting my life in your hands, Lester. If anyone else was on duty here tonight, I wouldn't go back there."

Lester beamed. "Don't you worry, Judge. You can count on me."

182

Julio had nodded off, his mind mercifully providing a few minutes of respite from the emotional torment he'd been suffering. When the key was placed in the lock and the steel bar slid from the latch, Julio's eyes popped open.

Raleigh limped into the cubicle, grimacing at the foul odor.

"Good Lord! I've smelled outhouses that stunk less than this place. Deputy, why in the hell hasn't this prisoner's waste bucket been emptied? We don't treat no one like this in my county," Raleigh blustered.

"Judge, I thought—"

"Deputy Holmboe, get ova there and get that stinking bucket out of here."

Confused, Lester briskly moved to the corner and, holding his breath, did as instructed.

Julio watched the scene curiously, wondering who this older gentleman with the cane was.

"Deputy, empty that thing and assume your post," Raleigh ordered, placing the box containing the coconut cream pie on the floor.

Julio, who was now sitting on the side of the cot, sniffed the air, and the aroma was almost erotic. His saliva glands began to function in response to the smell of food.

Using his cane, Raleigh hooked one of the legs of the upended folding chair, uprighted it, and sat down. He was only eight feet from the prisoner.

"You hungry, boy?" Raleigh asked, reading the body language of the young Cuban-American.

Julio nodded calmly, not wishing to seem too anxious.

"I have a mighty fine coconut pie in this here box, and I thought I'd come down here and talk a little turkey with you. You understand what I mean?"

Julio glanced at the box. "No, I don't, sir. Who are you, anyway?"

"I'm the judge who'll arraign you Monday morning, and what I'm here to talk about is drugs and money. A whole bunch of it."

Julio sighed and his body slouched. They had found the stash.

"Don't know what you're talking about, Judge."

"Oh, I think you do. Now, I know you're just some delivery boy, and I don't have much interest in you. What I'm after is your boss, or whoever sent you here, distributing drugs to the unsuspecting children of Alabama."

Julio said nothing.

"Now, I'm prepared to deal. I give you my word, if you cooperate you'll never set foot in prison. If you don't, you'll be breaking rocks for the next twenty years. Every time you bend ova in the shower, some negra buck'll be sticking his dick up your ass. Now, you seem like a nice young man, probably never been in trouble with the law, and I can go real lenient on someone like you, but I want the big fish."

Having returned from the alley, where the contents of the bucket had been scattered, Lester strained to hear what was being said twenty-five feet away from him. He absently rubbed the barrel of his revolver with a handkerchief. *The judge is real good at interrogating. I bet he gets what he wants from this drug runner.*

Julio stared at the floor and continued his silence.

Raleigh also sat quietly, allowing his words, intended as much for Lester's ears as for his subject, to sink in. He finally decided this charade had gone on long enough.

"You want a bite to eat?" he offered, placing the pie on the closest corner of the cot and extracting a fork and the table knife he had exposed earlier in the main office.

Julio looked longingly at the pie. Though he would have preferred a steak or a juicy hamburger from the diner located a couple of blocks from the warehouse of Santos Exporting, anything, at this point, would be gratefully accepted. Straightening his back in anticipation, he looked at the judge.

Raleigh stood, grasped the table knife in his right hand and nonchalantly pulled the blade across the pad of his left. The small teeth dug into his flesh and blood immediately began to flow from the wound. Satisfied the bleeding was sufficient for his purposes, he smeared it over the front of his white linen shirt.

"Lester! Lester, help me!" he screamed, while Julio sat quietly, his expression portraying his confusion.

Lester sprung from the wall against which he'd been leaning, and rushed toward the solitary cell and the judge's frantic cry.

Fearing the older man might be having a seizure, Julio arose and took a step toward him.

As the footsteps came closer, Raleigh slathered his cheeks with his bleeding palm and tossed the knife to Julio, who reflexively caught it in mid-air. Raleigh stumbled backward out the door, bumping into Lester who was charging into the room. The deputy's eyes widened as he stared at the blood-covered shirt and face of his new mentor.

"He attacked me, Lester! He's trying to escape! Shoot him! Shoot him!"

Lester didn't hesitate. He pointed the revolver at Julio Santos and fired four times into his chest.

CHAPTER 42
WHERE'S EVERYONE?

The black Suburban had crawled through the dark streets and alleyways of Bayou le Batre for over three hours. Manuel and his new friend, Bugger, had smoked more than two packs of cigarettes while stopping every person crossing their path. Most of their interrogations had been brief, their subjects either intimidated or terrified by the mere presence of these two men—one, an Hispanic with a notepad, the other, black with the size and demeanor of The Hulk.

"What you think, Bugger?" asked Manny. "You think we should call it quits for the night and get some sleep?"

"It's pretty late, man, and there's damn few civilians out and about. We haven't seen anyone since those two kids riding their bikes, what, thirty minutes ago?" Bugger replied. "If she's a coke whore, and with this Billy character, they're probably screwing their brains out right now, and they won't be surfacing 'til tomorrow, if then."

"I think I should call Roberto and see what he wants us to do. The bar owner said this Billy comes in for lunch almost every Saturday and Sunday. Maybe we should be back down here in the morning. He might be hungrier than usual. Maybe we'll get lucky and the girl will be with him."

"Cool with me. You call your brother, and I'll check in with Shooter."

Raleigh sat in his study at home, pleased with the work he'd completed two hours earlier. His bandaged hand held a Jack Daniel's and water and his other rested on the telephone. Even though it was almost midnight, he contemplated the calls he needed to make. Before lifting the receiver, his phone rang.

"Judge Pendleton," he answered out of habit. The tape on the voice activated recorder started turning.

"Raleigh, you all right?" Virgil asked.

"Yeah, just a scratch," he responded. "Don't know why the lady ova at the clinic insisted on sewing up that little cut." In reality, Raleigh had insisted on the stitches, feeling it would read better in the newspapers if the wound sounded more serious than it was.

"Lester said that boy tried to kill you."

"Yeah, he was real violent. I guess I shouldn't have gone down there, but I thought I might be able to get some information out of him before we called in the drug enforcement boys. Virgil, where were you? We tried to find you after Lester shot that spic and all."

"Me and Mary Belle went down to Mobile to see the kids and their new baby. I thought it'd be a good time to go since there wasn't no one in the jail except Santos, like you wanted. Mary Belle's been raisin' cane to go down and see that new grandbaby for over a week. Sorry," offered Virgil, as if he'd done something wrong.

"How's the baby?"

"Doing just fine. She looks a lot like Mary Belle."

Raleigh grimaced. "Virgil, me and you need to talk. Can you drive out here in the morning?"

"Sure, before or after church?"

"Better be before. We can drive ova together after we talk. I don't think the missus is going tomorrow. Says she has the croup again."

"Sorry to hear that, Judge. What do we need to talk about?"

"We can discuss it in the morning, but it has to be done before the state or federal boys get involved in all this. By the way, I sent Lester and his girl back out to the lake house tonight. I gave him the next couple of days off and told him to stay there. I don't want him around where some reporter or someone can talk to him. If anyone asks about him until I've got him ready, tell 'em you gave him some time off—normal procedure after a shooting."

"Okay, Raleigh. What time you want me?"

"Say about eight-thirty."

Raleigh sipped his drink and pushed the phone button down with his finger. Lifting it, he called a number he'd retrieved from his address book.

"Hello," came the sleepy female voice on the other end of the line.

"Mrs. Rutherford, I'm terrible sorry to be calling so late. This is Judge Pendleton. Could I speak to Leander?"

The line was silent and he could hear shuffling. "Judge Pendleton, Leander isn't home yet. I thought he was with you."

Raleigh stumbled with his response. "Why, sure. I don't know what I was thinking about. We were getting together and I canceled this afternoon. The missus was feeling a little under the weather and I hated to leave her alone. I told Leander and...uh... the other boys to go on and do what we was doing without me. I had a little emergency and forgot all about what Leander was doing tonight. He's sure been a big help to me, what with the primary coming up and all. You go on back to sleep and forgive me for calling so late. Good night, Mrs. Rutherford."

"Leander, you son-of-a-bitch. Don't you ever go home?" Raleigh grumbled while flipping the pages of his address book.

The telephone rang several times before the syrupy voice of Vivian Thompson came over the recorder. "This is Vivian. If you're calling for you know who, he's with me and we're out or busy. We'll be available in just a little while and ..."

Raleigh listened to the remainder of the tasteless message and waited for the beep.

"Leander, you need to call me at home if you come in before midnight. I need to make sure you call Billy off on our deal tomorrow night. Call me in the morning early if, well, if we ain't talked before then."

Raleigh was perplexed. He thumbed the book again and found a number he didn't remember being there. W*hy'd I put Billy Cudjoe's mobile number in here?*

Pushing the buttons and squinting through his reading glasses, he waited. It rang one time and the automatic recording answered. He hung up.

One last call, he hoped.

"Sheriff's office."

"Is Deputy Davis there?" Raleigh asked, looking at his wristwatch.

"No, he ain't come on duty yet. He's not due in for another half-hour. You want me to take a message?"

"No, I'll call back."

Raleigh replenished his drink. Turning and lifting his aching knee, he leaned back against the arm of the leather sofa. His heavy eyelids burned while he thumbed through the latest issue of *Playboy*, hoping some masculine entertainment would keep him awake. It didn't and he found himself on the sofa in the study at 5:30 the following morning. When he arose, he didn't notice the subtle dampness in his crotch where the filled tumbler of Jack Daniel's had landed as it slipped from his bandaged hand six hours earlier.

187

A rooster crowing in the distance signaled the dawn of a new day. Two life-hardened souls lay naked in the single bed. One was content, lost in a drug and alcohol induced state, while the other was not. The cocaine had kept Tina's mind alert and calculating throughout the night, but the last scrapings of the razor blade had yielded more shavings of butcher's paper than the powdery substance her body craved. The numbness of her gums had eroded to a modest tingling almost an hour earlier. Finally, the combination of sleep deprivation and physical fatigue forced a decision contrary to her desires. Closing her eyes, she accepted her fate—a few more hours with this disgusting little man.

CHAPTER 43
STATISTICS

"Sorry to call so early, Judge. I just got off duty," announced Jim Bob. "One of the boys said someone called last night right before I came on. Said it might've been you."

"Yeah, I called, Jim Bob," admitted Raleigh, making a mental note not to call the Clarke County sheriff's office again until Jim Bob was in the clear. "I was just checking to see if anyone had been around."

"Didn't hear a word last night. Maybe they figured out what we talked about last night by themselves."

Raleigh rubbed his chin, thinking he needed to shave before Virgil arrived.

"Could be. Don't you be worrying unnecessarily about this, Jim Bob. You just stick to your guns and there'll be nowhere for anyone to look. I need to get going. I got an early meeting before church. You and your family coming this morning?"

"Don't think so, Judge. Geraldine took a bad fall yesterday and puffed her face up pretty good. You know how those lady folks are. Prideful and all."

"Pride before the fall."

"Sorry, Judge?" Jim Bob asked.

"Never mind. Now, you go on home and spend some time with your family. Remember, don't panic when they come calling again, and they will. Stick with the story, and nobody'll have anything to worry about."

Raleigh replaced the receiver and sat for a few seconds on the edge of the bed he hadn't shared with his wife for more than ten years. *I've always considered Jim Bob to be pretty smart and dependable. I wonder. He sounds a little more scared than I'd like. I better keep him on a pretty tight leash until this FBI mess is ova with, but I don't want to be calling Harley's office again. No need for Harley Logginfield to go wondering why the county judge of Washington County is so chummy with his deputy.* His thoughts were broken when Viola rapped on his door.

"Judge Pendleton, Sheriff Crawford's here."

"Viola, give Virgil some coffee and offer him some of that banana-nut bread you baked. Tell him I'll be down in a few minutes."

Virgil sat on the front porch, drinking coffee and finishing his second piece of Viola's morning offering. Raleigh limped out the front door in a gray tropical suit, white shirt, and open collar. His tie was draped over his shoulder.

"I swear Viola makes the best damn nut bread in these parts," proclaimed Virgil, rising to greet his host.

"You got that right, Sheriff. How're you this fine Sabbath morning?" Raleigh asked, grasping one arm of the porch swing and seating himself with a slight grimace.

"A little tired. That grandbaby kept us hopping all afternoon and evening. What'd you need to talk about, Raleigh?"

"Virgil, I aim keep about three-quarters of a million of the money that Santos boy was hauling," Raleigh announced.

"You're kidding!" Virgil replied. When Raleigh didn't respond, he asked, "You are kidding, aren't you, Judge?"

For a long minute, Raleigh just sat there.

"Virgil, right after you told me about all that money Lester found, I asked myself, 'What if we could somehow keep a pile of it for the campaign?' I'd be scot-free of my obligations to the party and to Lawrence Rifle. No more need to be shaking down our local constituents, no more shenanigans with the local lawyers. At first, I thought maybe we could keep a couple-a-hundred, which would damn sure help, but as things has worked out, only me, you, and Lester know how much was behind that panel and it ain't been logged into your property log yet. With that young hooligan trying to kill me last night, particularly after me going down there with a pie for him and all, well, I just got to thinking, all we have to do is convince Lester it's the right thing to do and we're set. No one else ever has to know."

With this revelation, it was Virgil who was quiet. Standing, he walked to the banister and looked into the distance. He could see the mirror-like reflection of the lake, but not the house where his deputy was probably sleeping. Or was he being held prisoner?

"Raleigh, we've done some pretty questionable things over the years, from a legal point of view, but this is big time. I don't know, Judge, maybe we'd rather shake down old Jesse Harrington like you talked about a few days ago."

"Hell, Virgil, that's what I'm talking about. Sure, we got plenty a people around here beholding or scared of us, but why shake any more trees during this campaign when we got all the money we need setting right there in my safe? There ain't no one going to come forward and claim it," Raleigh argued.

"Damn, Raleigh, I hadn't even thought about that. What if someone comes looking for their money?"

"Jesus, Sheriff Crawford!" exclaimed Raleigh. "It's not like we recovered a stolen Mercedes Benz. The owner of this money ain't gonna come looking. I thought about that a lot. I saw a special on *Sixty Minutes* awhile back, and these drug dealers figure these kinds of losses into the price of their merchandise. They send out five mules, hoping three of them get through without being arrested. It's all about statistics."

"How about Lester? I don't know if he'll go for it or not."

"You just leave Lester up to me. All I need is a little bait from you," Raleigh proclaimed with a wink.

"Bait?"

When the last chorus of "Bringing In the Sheaves" subsided, the pastor closed the service with a short prayer and dismissal. Raleigh and Lottie had been seated in the family pew, as always, but were accompanied by non-members of the church: a gangly young man, who was vaguely familiar to a few, and a moderately homely young lady. Everyone had naturally assumed the Pendletons were soliciting this young couple for membership and the congregation responded accordingly. Lester had never received more attention in his life. Raleigh simply stood back and allowed the good people of the congregation to help set the trap for the final stage of his plan.

"Lester, after you and that pretty young girl of yours has Sunday lunch ova at the big house with me and the missus, you and me need to take a little walk. I got some things to discuss with you—things you'll want to know about," Raleigh said, intending to heighten the young man's already elevated sense of awe and pride.

Lunch had been mercifully brief for both the Pendletons and the younger couple. It was seldom that Raleigh and his wife dined at the same time or in the same place.

Lester and Belinda returned to the lake house. While he was changing from his only dress suit into more casual attire, the phone rang.

"Lester, this is Judge Pendleton."

"Yes, sir."

"Why don't you kill a few minutes and then drive ova here in about, say, half an hour? That okay with you?"

"Sure, Judge, anything you say."

"Good. I'll see you at two o'clock."

Raleigh clicked the receiver and placed another call.

"Hello," came the female voice on the other end.

"Mrs. Bitterman, how are you this fine Sunday afternoon? This is Raleigh Pendleton. We missed you at church this morning. Is Bobby home?"

The mention of Raleigh's name conjured up the memory of the last time her husband had been with the old county judge and the perfume-impregnated shirt Bobby had dropped on the floor.

"He's mowing the lawn. Just a minute." Her tone was icy. In a more distant voice, Raleigh heard, "Bobby, that Judge Pendleton's on the phone." He heard a door slam.

"Hello," Bobby gasped, his breathing heavy.

"Bobby, what you doing out there in this heat? You could have a stroke, boy." Raleigh's voice was full of life. "Missed you at church this morning."

"We've been going to the First Baptist down at Chastang ever since, well, you remember when I came home—"

"Bobby, I got some good news this morning," Raleigh interrupted, not caring why Bobby and Myrtle Bitterman had changed churches. "The deal's off tonight."

"Why?" Bobby asked numbly.

"No need for a lot of explaining, but I just hated what we was having to do, and I didn't like the possibilities, the statistics. I felt the odds could be against pulling it off. I prayed hard about it this morning at church, and the Lord told me what to do. It just came to me. I called Harley Logginfield and told him enough's enough. We done paid him all he's getting and if he wants to go any further with our little problem, then go ahead. I told him I been keeping records of all the money he's been paid, and he'd have a lot of explaining to do himself if he pursued this matter any further."

"What'd he say?"

"He got madder'n hell at first, but after he thought about it for awhile, he said okay. He's sending Jim Bob ova here in the morning with the pictures. It's ova. We're scot-free, and we called off the deal tonight."

"Oh, my God. Thank the Lord!" Bobby exclaimed and his eyes filled with tears. "Thank the Lord!"

"Thank the Lord, indeed, and it was all His doing. Like I said, it came to me like a lightning bolt while I was praying this morning."

Raleigh heard a muffled sound on the other end of the line.

"Bobby, you okay?"

A few seconds passed and Bobby answered, "Yeah, Judge. I'm okay. I've never felt more relieved in my whole life. Thanks, Judge. Thanks for calling."

Raleigh heard a click at the other end of the line, and he smiled. Dialing a number with which he was becoming more familiar than he cared to, he heard the succulent voice of Vivian Thompson and the same recording as before.

"Leander, call me. I need to talk to you today. Today! You understand?"

Lester's cruiser pulled through the gate to the Pendleton mansion. He immediately saw Raleigh, now in khaki pants and a floral sport shirt, waiting under a tree by the gate. He was fanning himself with a straw fedora. As the vehicle stopped, Raleigh opened the passenger door and climbed in.

"You don't mind if we take a ride, do you, Lester? My knee's acting up this afternoon."

"Sure, Judge, anything you say," Lester replied. "Where you want me to drive?"

"Oh, I got a place you probably heard about, but not many people ever seen. We just refer to it as the lodge. The Lodge of the Brotherhood was the old name. Just turn around and take a left at the gate. It won't take but about fifteen minutes to get there."

"To be honest, Judge, I haven't ever heard of it. What's it for?"

Raleigh ignored the question. "Lester, you know who the last guest to stay ova at the lake house was?"

"No, sir."

"Guess."

"Uh, I don't know. Maybe one of your kids?"

"No, they stay in the big house when they come. The last person to stay there was the governor."

"Governor James?"

"Fob James! Wash your mouth out, boy," Raleigh exclaimed good-naturedly. "There ain't never been no Republican stay at the lake house or no where else a Pendleton ever owned. Now that I think about it, old Fob was a guest during his first term, before he betrayed the party and run on the Republican ticket last time."

"Then, which governor?"

"I mean 'the Governor,' Governor George Wallace," lied Raleigh.

"Oh, my Lord. Governor Wallace slept in the same bed I been sleeping in?"

"Well, the sheets've been changed, of course, but yeah, the very same bed. My daddy built that house when he was judge and I guess every Democratic governor ever since has stayed there at one time or another, except Little Jim Folsom, of course. He wasn't an elected governor though. He succeeded to the position when they convicted Guy Hunt of them ethics violations. Anyhow, I just wanted you to know you're standing in pretty tall cotton, son. Turn in here," Raleigh directed.

Lester drove his cruiser through the first of the three gates. As planned, he didn't see Johnny standing behind a large stand of scrub oak, carbine in hand.

CHAPTER 44

HINTS AND HOPES

Mikey and I had just returned home from church and his favorite Sunday, or anytime for that matter, lunch: a Big Mac, large fries, Dr. Pepper, and apple pie. I had choked down half a chicken breast sandwich and a diet Coke. As I pulled into the driveway, Katie dashed by dressed in a tee shirt, cut-offs—I thought too short—and an Astros baseball cap, resting about thirty degrees off center.

"Bye, Pops," she shouted, waving, but not in my direction.

Looking in the rearview mirror, I observed a red Chrysler Lebaron convertible pulling to the curb.

"Where're you off to, sister?" I shouted while exiting the car.

"Swimming at the club," she replied, continuing her rapid pace.

"I thought you were spending the day with your mother."

"She dropped me off right after you left. Said she needed to work on some paper." Her pace slowed and she stopped.

"You okay with that?" I asked.

"I'm used to it. Besides, Marci, Julie, and I will have more fun at the pool anyway."

I could see an expression in her face I had seen too many times over the past three years.

"Come here for a minute," I responded while Michael ran to the front door. The Martian Invaders were attacking, I assumed.

She walked slowly in my direction, looking over her shoulder at the waiting vehicle.

"Tell you what, when you get through swimming, why don't you come home and we'll catch a movie. Anything on you want to see?"

"Dad, you don't have to—"

"I want to. I've been working pretty long hours the last few weeks, and we haven't had much time together. Let's make it a date, just you and me. Jack can babysit Mikey. We could go to Braum's after and have a banana split or something. Deal?"

By now, she was standing directly in front of me. "If you really want to, sure," she said, placing her arms around my neck and hugging me. "I love you, Daddy. You're the best."

I smiled, hugged her back, and blinked to control the stinging.

"You know what? I believe you're right. Now, you better get going. The boys at the pool are getting restless."

She giggled, kissed my cheek, and rushed toward the car.

Before I could silently swear at my ex-wife, Mikey yelled from the porch, "Hey, Dad, someone's on the phone for you."

Although I heard him clearly, I stood there without responding, watching my fifteen-year-old bouncing toward her friends. My thoughts turned to the Tremonts, and I felt sad.

"Jack, Lawton here," he said when I picked up the phone.

"Lawton, I was just thinking of you. Any word about Janie?"

"No, nothing yet. They're chasing down a lead up in Chatom, but I haven't heard what, if anything, has developed."

"I'm so sorry, Lawton. Is your wife—"

"About the same, but that's not why I called," he interrupted, obviously changing a very painful subject. "Does your company have anything going on over here tonight?"

"Tonight? I don't think so. I've purposely avoided talking to Leander the past couple of days, as you might expect, but I can't imagine anything we'd be doing on a Sunday night. Kenny told me we were way behind on a project up on the industrial corridor. Billy Cudjoe's been spending most of his time up there, but other than that, I don't know. Why?"

"As I told you yesterday, the wiretaps are running and there've been some calls between Pendleton and Leander about something Billy Cudjoe is, or was, doing tonight. You ever heard of a guy named Bobby Bitterman?"

"Bitterman. No, that name doesn't ring a bell. Should it?"

"He's the plant manager of a pulp mill—General Paper Company. Does that mean anything?"

"Yeah, but what was it?" I raked my brain, trying to place the name. "Now I remember. Kenny told me Leander had him code one of the R&P or L&V

bullshit invoices to a job at General Paper. The odd thing was, we didn't have a job there, but Leander told Kenny we were getting one. Does that help?"

"I don't know, maybe. The judge, Bitterman, Leander, and Cudjoe are all somehow mixed up in some deal that's not happening tonight."

"Lawton, you're not making any sense."

"I know. None of this does. There've also been a couple of conversations between Pendleton and a deputy sheriff up in Clarke County—a Jim Bob Davis. Coincidentally, this Davis guy was possibly the last person to have seen Janie."

"What?"

"Yeah. He said he got a call the night she disappeared, and he went to a diner where the bus stops and gave her money to catch a bus home. That's the lead Fred's guys are working on. They're trying to find someone who sold her a ticket—a bus driver, a passenger, anyone who might have seen her after that night. So far, nothing."

"That sounds like good news, Lawton."

"It might be, Jack, but they haven't found that next link yet."

"I'm praying, Lawton. They're going to find her, I just know it."

"Thanks, Jack. I hope you're psychic. One last thing, Pendleton had some kind of deal working last night. He told Leander if it worked out, the deal tonight with Billy Cudjoe could be called off. That's what started this whole series of references to tonight. It's a puzzle. We have a few pieces so far, but none of them fit yet. We'll keep listening, and maybe something will hit."

"Lawton, I appreciate the call. Anything I can do?"

"Just keep praying."

Tina awoke to a foul smell and an annoying disturbance in her pelvic area. Opening her eyes, she blinked twice, hoping it was only a nightmare. It wasn't.

Billy breathed heavily above her face while thrusting his hardened penis in the general vicinity of her vagina, hoping for penetration. In his lustful state, he was oblivious to anything, including the squirming body, now struggling to escape this unwelcome assault.

"Billy, slow down, baby," she pleaded, just before his mouth attacked one of her nipples.

"Ouch! Quit that shit, you pervert!" she screeched, arching her back with all her strength and lifting her knee into his exposed loins.

"Shit!" he screamed, rolling to one side, and then to the floor. He lay there moaning for several seconds.

Now fully aware of her surroundings and in control of her emotions, she slid to the floor and began to comfort him.

"Oh, baby, I'm sorry. Did Tina hurt you bad?"

"Hell, yes!" Billy retorted. "That hurt like shit. What'd you kick me for? Get your ass out of here!"

"I was asleep, Billy baby. I wasn't awake yet. You scared me. I'm sorry, honey. Here, let me fix it."

After five minutes of ecstasy for him, and an eternity of revulsion for her, Tina rose and raced to the small bathroom at the back of the shack. Spitting first, and then vomiting, she purged the fluid from her mouth and stomach. Unaware of the guttural noises, muffled by the thin, hollow-core door, Billy's mind floated in a state of rapture he'd never before experienced.

Partially covered with a stained white bath towel and smoking a cigarette, she returned to the bed and sat down.

"Billy, baby, I'm hungry."

Looking up from the floor, he grinned, exposing the brown triangular stains. "How could you be hungry after a big meal like that?"

"I'm serious, Billy. I need something to eat. Why don't you go over to Sammy's and get us a burger and some fries?"

Billy sat up, pulling his sinewy legs against his chest. "Okay, but it'll cost you."

"How much?"

"Another blow job."

"Now?"

"No, not now, but when I get back. I'll be ready by then."

"On one condition. Will you get me a little more coke?"

"I can't be getting fucked up this afternoon. I got that job I got to do tonight. Remember?" he announced.

"Sure, I remember, but what'll I do while you're gone? A little toot and I won't be so sad and lonesome for you."

"Okay, but remember what you owe me."

"That'll be easy."

"Have they showed up?" snorted Roberto when Manny answered his cell phone.

"Not yet. We've been here since eleven and it's almost two now. Maybe he won't come in today," Manny speculated.

"Has the bar guy heard from either one of them?"

198

"Not since they left here last night. Chances are, she banged him, got paid, and split. She could be on a bus heading back to Florida already."

"The plane just landed in Lauderdale. Charlie's going to the bus station to wait. Nick and Picolo will be in Mobile in about two hours. They have your cell number, and you guys can split up and start covering more territory. Do you know where—"

"Hang on, Roberto. Our guy just showed up."

"That sorry bitch!" Billy barked while Bugger checked the area behind the house. Manuel dialed his phone.

"Shut up, Mr. Cudjoe," Manny ordered. He then spoke into the mouthpiece. "Roberto, the girl's gone."

"I thought he told you she was waiting for the coke?" Roberto asked.

"That's what he said, but she's not here."

"Maybe she just went for a walk or something," Roberto offered hopefully.

"I don't think so. Cudjoe says he had about two grand lying on the table and it's gone. If he's telling the truth, I doubt she'll come back here. I think I believe him."

"Okay, let me think." Roberto walked through the warehouse and puffed on his cigar. "Manny, this girl's pretty sharp. She sets this dumb ass up by sending him off for some blow. He knows she'll be there because she's a cokehead, so he leaves most of his money. You take this guy with you and go to the bus station. Our best shot is she's heading south, and she'll get out of town as fast as possible. Does he have a car?"

Manny placed his hand over the mouthpiece. "You got a car?"

"Pickup," Billy answered. "Out back."

"Hey, Bugger. There a pickup out there?" Manuel yelled.

"Yeah. A beat-up old piece of shit." Bugger answered, returning inside.

"Yeah, Roberto. He has wheels, but she didn't take them."

"Okay. Take this Cudjoe guy with you and get your ass to the bus station."

"Why take him? He's a greaser, Roberto. I think we've gotten all we can from him."

Roberto sighed. "To identify the girl, Manny."

CHAPTER 45

HEROES AND WHORES

"Lester, this here place has been the very heart of Washington County politics for almost a century," Raleigh began as he took his normal position in the rocking recliner by the front window. "Have a seat ova there and make yourself at home."

Lester looked about the structure, selecting a place on the sofa.

"Like I said earlier, not many ever get to see it—only those who've been chosen to take a place in the political structure both here and in the state. Every now and then, we look around the county, searching for young blood— the leaders of tomorrow. That's why we're here today."

While he was sure this was an important moment for him, he couldn't help but feel uncomfortable. Things had moved too fast for Lester over the past three days, and his naivete was showing. Although he felt he should say something, he couldn't.

"Lester, what are your plans for the future?"

He furrowed his brow and looked at the floor. "I guess I haven't thought too much about that, Judge. I want to marry Belinda, of course, but that'll be awhile until I can save up some money. I'd like my own place. My folks are good to live with, real supportive and all, and they like Belinda, but a man just ain't a man until he has his own place. Someday, I thought I might even run for sheriff, after Sheriff Crawford steps down, of course."

"That's what I like to hear out of a young man. Knowing what you want and taking advantage of the opportunities when they arise. Lester, your day has come. By tomorrow afternoon, everyone in the county, probably the state, will know your name. People you don't even know'll be coming up and congratulating you, slapping you on the back, buying you beers, and such. You're going to be a hero, Lester, and I'm gonna make sure it happens. How you feel about that?"

Lester squirmed and swallowed noticeably. "Wow, Judge. I don't know what to think."

"Lester, when I was a young man about your age, my daddy brought me out here and we had a talk, just like the one we're having now. The real world don't run like most folks think. Everyone needs a leader, someone to look up to. Today, you have an opportunity to join a group who folks look up to. But, there're some things I have to tell you that, well, might be hard for you to accept at first, but I have faith in you, boy."

"What kind of things, Judge Pendleton?" he asked.

"Son," Raleigh said in a voice intended to connote a familial connection, "we're holding a press conference in the morning and you'll be the focus of the announcement Sheriff Crawford'll make. We're telling about your cunning in catching a drug dealer, how resourceful you were in finding the dope and the money. But most of all, we'll tell everyone how brave you were when you stepped between me and that hooligan before he killed me. Yes, sir, you'll be the buzz of Washington County, maybe the whole country. We'll take some pictures of you standing in your uniform, the sheriff by your side, and the cocaine and the two hundred thousand will be on a table in front of you. You need to put on—"

"Judge, there's ova nine hundred thousand," Lester corrected, radiating pride.

Raleigh rubbed his chin. "Lester, you know what happens to all that money when the state and federal boys take ova? And I assure you they'll be in the sheriff's office before the last picture's taken."

"I don't know, I guess they put it into evidence or something," Lester replied, his forehead wrinkled.

"That money'll end up being wasted on paying informers and buying nice new equipment for the boys up the line. Hell, most of it won't even make it to Montgomery or Washington. It'll be skimmed off by the damn Republican bureaucrats to line their pockets and fund their activities, and they already get more money than they need from our taxes. We did all the hard work here, and we'll be left with nothing but the bill to bury that Mexican you killed. Does that sound fair?"

"No, sir, it don't," Lester admitted.

"We got lots of needs down here in our poor little county. I'd rather see that money used to help widows that need extra money at Christmas, buy new playground equipment for our public parks, and a whole mess of other things we don't have. Those Republicans what've been running the state have damn near taxed us to death, but the money goes to the rich counties up north of here. Me and the sheriff have prayed about this, and we think it's the only right thing to do. What if you'd been killed when you arrested that drug runner, or he'd killed you when you pushed me aside and put your life on the line? Your family would get a small pittance from the officers' relief fund, but it wouldn't have been enough to even bury you proper like. We can use some of that money to make sure the families of the good men on the force have a little something extra if something bad happens. Lester, me and Virgil think it's our duty to keep most of that money for the county."

Raleigh waited for the young deputy's response. He closely watched his facial expression and body movements. He hoped he wouldn't have to call in Johnny, but he was prepared to if necessary.

Deep in thought, Lester fumbled with his high school ring and stared at the floor. He finally spoke.

"Judge Pendleton, I think you and the sheriff are right. We shouldn't let that money get wasted. That money belongs to Washington County, and it should stay here."

Raleigh grinned. "Me and the sheriff knew we was right about you, Lester. You'll be one of the leaders of the county in the future all right. I didn't want to appear to be trying to influence you with personal gain while you were making your decision, but there's something in this for you. At the press conference, Virgil's going to announce you've been promoted to Under Sheriff. You'll be the youngest one ever to serve Washington County. As a token of our appreciation, we aim to give you a bonus out of the fund—ten thousand dollars. That should be enough for you and your pretty young lady to get that ring you been wanting and a nice down payment on a place of your own. Naturally, with your promotion, you'll be getting a big pay increase."

Lester was speechless. "Ten thousand dollars! Oh, man, I ain't never seen that much money. Thank you, Judge. Thank you so much."

"No, Lester, it's you who should be thanked. Now, no one can ever know about any of this, you understand. No one ever, not even your fiancée-to-be. This little secret will have to go with you to your grave."

"You don't have to worry about me, Judge."

"I knew I could count on you, Under Sheriff Holmboe."

202

Billy looked at his cheap watch and nervously spit in the waste container by the door to the bus station. *Ten o'clock. I got to get out of here.*

"Mr. Santos, could I talk with you for a minute?" he asked, walking toward the tall Cuban who was flipping through his notepad.

"What do you want, Cudjoe?" Manny responded without looking up.

"I have a job to do tonight. I'll get fired or even worse if I don't get it done. That bitch ain't showing up and I got to get going."

Manny continued to turn pages. "That's your problem, gringo. My brother said wait here until she shows, and that's what we're going to do."

"But, I—"

Manuel Santos looked around for anyone watching and slapped Billy hard across the cheek.

"Quit whining or you'll not have to worry about anything ever again. Get it. Now, get back over by that door and keep your eyes open."

As Billy retreated, a cell phone rang and Bugger answered.

"Bugger, she's on her way," Shooter announced.

"How you know?"

"Our man at the Blue Oyster just called. She dropped by his joint, bought a couple of grams, and left in a cab. Said she was going to catch a bus," Shooter explained.

"Where's the bitch been? She jumped the cracker's shack over six hours ago," Bugger asked.

"Said she'd gone to see her old man in some nursing home up north of here."

Before Bugger could respond, a blue-and-white taxi pulled to the curb, twenty feet from where they were standing. Bugger nudged Manny and motioned to the car.

Tina stepped from the cab, retrieving a backpack from the floorboard. Before she could turn around, Manuel placed his meaty hands on her shoulders and twirled her.

"This her, Cudjoe?"

Billy didn't answer but marched toward the young hooker, pulling back a closed fist.

Bugger grabbed his arm, twisting it behind his back. "We're not making a scene here, greaseball. Is this the girl?"

Billy's confirmation was unnecessary. The fear on Tina's face was sufficient. She struggled to free her arms, but Manny's grasp became tighter.

"Settle down, Tina. We won't hurt you unless you do something stupid. All we want is a little information."

"What about me?" Billy exclaimed. "I have to go. I've done what you wanted. Take me back to my house."

"Get your ass out of here, Cudjoe, and don't ever talk about this. We know where you live," threatened Manuel.

"But, I don't have any money. The bitch stole it all!"

Manuel looked at Tina. "You want to buy some coke?"

A minute later, Billy and two hundred dollars were pushed into the back seat of the cab. Before the door slammed behind him, a cell phone rang—a different one. The sound was coming from the backpack. Only Billy recognized the whimsical tune.

"That bitch stole my phone, too!" he shouted as the door closed and the taxi sped to the south.

The sun had been down for almost an hour but a faint glow was still distinguishable above the tops of the pine trees silhouetted against the western sky. Raleigh relaxed in the porch swing, sipped a mint julep, and considered the events of the past twenty-four hours. He was self-absorbed and intoxicated, a dangerous combination for the patriarch of the Pendleton dynasty.

"Slickest shenanigan I ever pulled off," he said aloud, while the crickets chirped and a lone coyote howled in the distance. "That damn fool Lawrence Rifle thought I couldn't get the job done. He doesn't know just how resourceful this old judge can be when the chips are down. Speaking of Lawrence, I think I might give him a call."

He looked at his pocket watch and squinted. "Hell, it's only nine-thirty. That bastard wouldn't hesitate to give me a jingle this time of night."

Rising, he grasped his cane in one hand, retaining a firm grip on the tall glass with the other.

"Evening, Lawrence," he slurred.

"Hello. Hello, Judge," Rifle replied. The uneasiness in his voice was apparent. "Working a bit late, aren't you?"

"Lawrence, what makes you think this is a business call? I could be just a calling an old pal for a friendly little chat or checking on my portfolio."

"I hope so, Raleigh. I hope so."

"Truth is, I have a little surprise for you, Lawrence. I know you told me you didn't need no more money for the campaign and all, when we talked the other day, but I thought maybe you'd like to hear what I've done."

"I'm listening, Raleigh."

"Remember, I told you all along I was working on some projects to raise the money you needed. Well, I wasn't lying. I've been working real hard ever since you first called me in the spring, and I didn't quit when you called a few days ago. Finally, all my efforts paid off. I got five hundred thousand and change in hand right now, and there's some more coming. Now, you sure you don't need no more money?"

"Did you say half a million, Judge?"

"And change," gloated Raleigh, sipping from his drink. "I did get a call from the lieutenant governor a couple of days ago. Offered a whole bunch of favors and such if I could help with his campaign. Now, naturally, I was polite and said all the right things, so as not to burn any bridges, but I do have all this money and—"

"You didn't make any deals, did you?"

"Lawrence, you know me better'n that. I'm a good party man—always looking out for the party's interests. But, you kind of, I don't know how to say it, embarrassed me the other day. Hurt my feelings when you didn't think I could pull my load. Now I don't know where I stand on anything. I've even had some of my precinct captains asking if we're supporting the wrong man in the primary," Raleigh lied, chuckling to himself.

"Judge, I need to think about this. That's a lot of money and we're starting to build up the war chest for the general election. How about I get back to you tomorrow?"

"That'd be just fine, Lawrence. When could I expect your call? I got a press conference in the morning. How about after lunch sometime?"

"I'll call around two. Raleigh, I'm not sure if I should be telling you what I'm getting ready to say but, do you know some Texan named Mitchell, Jack Mitchell?"

"No," Raleigh lied again. "What about him?"

"He owns the company your buddy Leander Rutherford works for. He's the reason I called you off the other day and sent back the money you raised. He's on to Leander stealing from his company and, somehow, you've been implicated."

"What do you mean 'implicated?'"

"I don't have many details and would rather not speculate, but you need to be careful of Leander. This Jack Mitchell's apparently on the verge of dropping a rock on him, and I wouldn't want to see you get hit by mistake. Just a little advice."

"I appreciate your concern, Lawrence, but I don't have nothing to worry about with Leander Rutherford. He's just a cracker I use from time to time— just an errand boy. I don't have no serious dealings with him," Raleigh proclaimed, wishing it were true. "I'll be in my office at two, and while your thinking about things, think about where me and the missus will be sitting come inauguration day."

"I don't have to think about that, Raleigh. You've always been on the podium, right where you belong," Rifle assured him.

Raleigh smiled.

CHAPTER 46
THE PRESS CONFERENCE

A light mist fell on the steps of the Washington County Courthouse Monday morning. Dressed in a white shirt, black slacks, and a clear plastic poncho, an aging man leaned against the flagpole a short distance from one of the handrails. He yawned while reading the morning paper. A young woman in elliptical sunglasses held a black umbrella in one hand and a notepad in the other. She was talking to a lanky teenager with stubble on his face. A commercial-grade camera swung from his neck. A small podium with a built-in speaker rested on the top step and a card table covered by an American Flag was situated to one side. A bulge the size of several stacked shoeboxes formed creases in the patriotic table covering.

Raleigh, Lester, and the judge's niece stood behind one of the heavy glass doors, installed with insurance money after the last tornado destroyed the originals—depositing one in the community swimming pool and the other in Virginia Johnson's vegetable garden a mile and a half away.

"Where the hell are all the press people?" bellowed Raleigh. "And where the hell's Virgil? The press conference was scheduled for nine o'clock, and it's five-'til. Bonnie Mae, didn't you call all the newspapers and radio and TV stations last night like I told you?"

"Yes, Uncle Raleigh. I called all twelve on your list, and they all said they'd send someone over this morning."

"Get on out there and find out who those three waiting out there are."

Bonnie Mae leaned on one of the doors, placing the most recent copy of *The National Enquirer* over her head. She returned a minute later.

"The man works part-time for KRKG down by Chastang, and the other two work for the *Mobile Register*. They didn't seem too happy about being here. Said there was a big story over by the industrial corridor all the senior people were covering."

Before Raleigh could respond, Virgil's Cherokee slid to the curb, his bubble lights flashing. He ran from the vehicle to the glass doors.

"Where've you been, Sheriff?" Raleigh barked.

"I drove like hell all the way over here. They have one helluva fire going on at General Paper. There's fire units from Mobile, Chastang, Grove Hill—damn near every town in south Alabama that has a truck. It's a helluva mess."

Raleigh's face turned ashen.

"Mr. Bitterman, was there anyone working in the mill this morning?" asked one of the television news reporters.

Four microphones were only inches from his face. Bellowing gray smoke in the background gave testimony to the inferno raging only a hundred yards away.

"No, I don't think so. The first shift wasn't due to come on until seven," responded a dazed Bobby Bitterman, clad in blue jeans, work boots, and a pinstriped pajama top.

"Where'd the fire start?" yelled another.

"We're not sure yet. Someone said maybe the pulp kettles."

"What could have caused it?"

"I don't know."

"You sure no one was in there?"

Bobby lifted his hands in front of the cameras, shook his head, and pushed his way through the mob.

"Does the company have insurance? How many people work here? Do you think the company will close the plant?" The questions kept flying until he was inside the administration building and secure behind a locked door.

He leaned against the entry wall, breathing heavily and shaking his head. *The judge said it was called off. He said we didn't have to pay any more. Why did I ever agree to—*

A harsh and persistent knocking interrupted his confusion. Moving to a nearby window, he looked out. A fireman, covered with ashes and his face blackened with soot, stood on the outside steps. Bobby opened the door.

"Are you Mr. Bitterman?" the fireman asked in a hoarse voice, coughing as he spoke.

"Yeah."

"We've found a body, or at least what's left of one."

Bobby collapsed.

Raleigh stood motionless for several seconds, staring at the moisture accumulating on the concrete outside the building. He finally whispered, "Now I have two reasons to have Johnny kill Leander Rutherford."

"Sorry, Judge," Virgil responded from several feet away. "I didn't hear you."

"What about the press conference?" asked Lester, oblivious of the gravity of the sheriff's news.

Raleigh limped about the anteroom, considering his options.

"You want me to go out and tell those reporters we've called it off?" offered Bonnie Mae. "I don't think they'll care."

"No! We called a press conference, and by God, we're having one. Virgil, you got a video camera ova at your office, don't you?" demanded Raleigh.

"Yeah, a pretty fancy one. Confiscated it during a raid ova at the Blue Dragon last summer. Thought it might be helpful sometime—"

"Lester, run ova there and get it and tell the deputy on duty to call in all the patrols. Bring back the best still camera you got, too. Bonnie Mae, go to every office in this building and tell everyone I want them outside in thirty minutes. Call the manager of the A&P and tell him to make an announcement that something important's going on ova at the courthouse. But first, go get them reporters and bring them in and give them some coffee and the donuts I bought this morning. It may not be the way I wanted, but we're having a press conference just the same."

Forty minutes later, eleven confused county workers, three A&P shoppers, four deputies eating donuts, and the three representatives of the media stood outside the building looking up at the podium where Virgil, the judge, and a beaming Lester Holmboe stood. No one noticed a well-groomed young man partially concealed behind an azalea hedge. Following her uncle's whispered commands, Bonnie Mae alternately operated the video and still cameras.

While the event paled in comparison to the gala Raleigh had intended to orchestrate, there were a few moments of genuine fervor among the scant number in attendance. The first was when the flag was ceremoniously removed, exposing five plastic bags of white powder and ten neatly stacked bundles of hundred dollar bills; the second when Virgil, using his limited oratorical skills, depicted the valiant acts of the young deputy. There was only scattered applause, however, when the Sheriff announced Lester's promotion. The deputies, all senior in service and ability, stood in disbelief when the proclamation was made.

CHAPTER 47
LOTS OF PIECES

While she'd been in dozens of tough situations during her twenty-one years, Tina had never felt as insecure and intimidated as she did sitting in the metal armchair across the desk from Roberto Santos. The brief time she had spent in the company of Manuel and Bugger had been unsettling at first, while they waited at the Mobile airport for the Cessna 310 that would carry her to Miami. Although they were obviously men of suspect background, both had been generally pleasant and appropriate given the nature of her business and the seriousness of the investigation they were conducting. She had particularly liked the one who scribbled constantly in a note pad while she described the three hours spent with Julio.

"Tina, I want you to relax and tell me everything you know about what happened to my brother," Roberto said in a soft voice.

"Can I smoke?"

"Certainly. You want some coke? You can have that, too, if it'll help your memory."

"Maybe later," she replied. Her hands shook as she unsuccessfully attempted to touch the match to the tip of the Marlboro.

Roberto leaned over the desk, extending a disposable butane lighter. She grasped his hand to steady hers.

"Like I told your brother," she began, inhaling the cigarette smoke deeply and blowing it toward the ceiling, "I was on my way up the coast to see my father. My car broke down outside Pensacola, and your brother was nice enough to offer me a ride. I only wish I hadn't accepted."

"Why is that? Was he mean to you?" Roberto inquired, attempting to set her at ease.

"Oh, no. He was a complete gentleman. I only said that because, if I hadn't gone with him, he'd probably be here instead of me."

"Okay, go on."

Tina continued to detail every memory she had of that evening, leaving out the part, as she had with Manuel, about the bag of marijuana stems she'd hidden beneath the passenger's seat.

"So the last time you saw my brother, he was lying face down on the highway with his hands cuffed behind him. Is that right?" Roberto confirmed, cracking his knuckles repeatedly as he spoke.

"Yeah. There wasn't any reason for that cop to do that. Julio was being pleasant and respectful to him. Your brother was a real swell guy."

"I know," acknowledged Roberto, looking away. "And this cop shot at you when you ran off?"

"Yeah. I couldn't believe it. Shot at me for leaving a broken tail light!"

"And you think he was a county sheriff or deputy of this, eh, Washington County?"

"That's about all he could be. The roadhouse is about a mile over the Mobile County line. I'm sure I saw the sheriff's badge or emblem on the side of his car."

"So this is everything you know about my brother?"

"I can't think of anything I've left out."

"What about this gringo you were with when Manny found you? What's his story?"

"Just a john. Just a way to get out of Alabama and back to Fort Lauderdale. Greasy son-of-a-bitch. He had some explosives, dynamite I think, and bragged about some big job he was doing last night. Showed me a picture of a naked black girl he said they'd screwed to death—whoever 'they' are. I couldn't wait to get out of there and away from him."

"Maybe you should be more careful in your selection of men."

"In the places I've been, you can't be too choosy or you'll starve to death."

Even through his own anxiety, Roberto felt sorry for this young woman.

"Roberto, Shooter's on the phone," an Hispanic female voice announced from outside the office.

"Shooter, what you got?" Roberto asked, his voice quick.

As Shooter began to talk, Roberto slouched behind the desk, his eyes closed, and he sighed, dropping the phone to the floor.

"What'd he say? How'd he act when you told him about the money?" asked Bugger, who was seated beside a sedated Manuel.

"He didn't say nothing. I don't think he even heard me. When I told him Julio was dead, I think he dropped the phone. Some woman came on the line and said he couldn't talk right now, and she hung up. Too bad," answered Shooter. "How's Manuel doing?"

"Better now. The Xanax calmed him down. It took five pills. What do we do now?" asked Bugger.

"Nothing we can do. We can't go get the body. Whoever shows up for that job will likely get arrested. I guess I could call Calhoun."

"The lawyer?"

"Yeah. He could go request the body and say the family had retained him. I don't think they could arrest a lawyer doing what his client asked. I doubt they'd give it to him, but at least we could find out where it is," Shooter thought aloud. "I'll give Calhoun a call. See what he thinks."

"Glad you could get here so soon, Lawton," Fred Carleton greeted. "You finish the deposition?"

"I could've gone on a while longer, but I got everything I had to get. What do you have?"

"Pieces—a whole bunch of pieces, but if you use your imagination, you can put a part of a picture together."

"You got my attention," Lawton replied, removing his suit coat and rolling up his sleeves.

Fred began, "Okay, let's go step by step. We know money is being routed from Jack Mitchell's company to Raleigh Pendleton, or at least to Chatom. This Findley Ross suggests to Jack that Lawrence Rifle is putting the squeeze on people for money for his campaign. Last night, the tap picks up Pendleton calling Rifle telling him he's got five hundred thousand for him and makes a reference to Rifle turning down his money and sending it back. Rifle asks about Jack and Leander Rutherford and says Jack has the goods on him. Who told him that? Has to be Findley Ross, right?"

"He's about the only one who'd know. So Ross cleaned Rifle up so he wouldn't get caught in a RICO or campaign contribution scam. There goes our shot at Rifle."

"I'm not sure. I listened to the tapes myself, and I'll bet a hundred Rifle takes the money. We'll just have to figure out how. In a minute I want you to listen to the tape of that conversation and see if you think the federal judge would reconsider a tap on Rifle."

"Okay. You got anything else?"

"A lot, but maybe, not so much. You listen and we'll decide. You're a prosecutor and have to deal with facts. I, on the other hand, get to work in a more theoretical world. Remember Pendleton's reference to a big deal he was working on Saturday night—one that would solve all the problems?"

"Yeah."

"And remember the calls to Rutherford, telling him to put Cudjoe on hold for Sunday night? And then Rutherford leaves a message on Cudjoe's cell and then the judge calls both of them and leaves another message to Rutherford, but nothing to Cudjoe?"

"I'm with you so far."

"Then Pendleton calls this Bitterman guy yesterday and tells him the deal's off, and Bitterman breaks down, or that's what the analysts think happened."

"So?"

"Well, listen to what's happened since Friday. A drug smuggler named Julio Santos was arrested Thursday night by a deputy in Washington County. His name was, let's see, Lester Holmboe. Saturday night, this same Holmboe shoots Santos in the county jail, after he allegedly tried to kill the judge with a kitchen knife. Why the hell was the judge down at the jail at nine o'clock on Saturday night? But we'll get back to that. Saturday afternoon, there are two other prisoners in the jail, one remanded without bail, and they're both released. No one's there but Santos and Holmboe. You still with me?"

"You think it was a set-up, but why?"

"Not sure of that, but I have a couple of theories. Let me keep going. It gets better. Last night, or rather about three this morning, there's a big explosion at General Paper Company. It's still burning. They've evacuated the whole industrial corridor."

"No shit?"

"It's been all over the news today."

"I started my depositions at eight, and we worked right through lunch. I haven't seen anything. Anyone hurt?" Lawton inquired.

"They have a John Doe so badly burned they'll have to do dental records and DNA to identify him."

"What does this have to do with the Santos deal?"

Fred ignored the question. "Maybe the judge, Rutherford, and this Cudjoe guy have something to do with the General Paper explosion. Maybe Bitterman, too."

"But the tapes said they were calling off the deal on Sunday," Lawton argued.

"What if Cudjoe didn't get the message? We have record of several calls from Vivian Thompson's house and from Rutherford's phone, attempting to call Cudjoe's cell, but no one ever talks to him."

"What do we know about Cudjoe, I mean, his background?"

"Nothing yet, but you can bet your pension we're working on that right now. I may have something by tonight."

Lawton sat back in a side chair and rubbed his palms together, his mind in overdrive.

"When Jack Mitchell first brought this to me I remember telling him this deal could be pretty twisted. If your theories hold any water, this is the most twisted situation I've ever seen. We've got a judge ordering hits on prisoners, blowing up plants, helping steal money from a business in Mobile, and all for what? It's mind boggling, Fred. You have a theory about the dead guy at the plant?"

"Could be Billy Cudjoe. If the Sunday night theory is true, maybe he got careless and blew himself up. Or, a more devious thought—what if the judge arranged for someone to go with him and whack him after he did whatever he did? Cleaning up the witnesses, so to speak."

"I think you should go see Mr. Bitterman. He could be the key to the plant deal."

"We've already tried, but when he heard about someone dead in the fire, he passed out and is in the hospital with orders no one is to disturb him. They think he had a mild heart attack. I have a man waiting down there now."

"But why would Pendleton want to burn the plant? How would that help him? And Bitterman? He'd be putting his job at risk. How could he benefit?"

"I don't have a theory for that one yet, but I have a theory for killing Santos."

"What?"

"At about six last night, Pendleton called his receptionist, who we believe is a relative, and tells her to call a press conference. He gives her a bunch of names of television stations and newspapers. He doesn't give a reason, so I have one of my men there this morning. Hardly anyone showed up—I guess because of the fire. Anyway, they go on with the ceremony, and it's an announcement of the drug bust Thursday night. They have this table with stacks of cocaine and money, and then the best part. The county sheriff, Virgil Crawford, goes into this ten-minute tribute to Holmboe—every detail of the bust, the killing of Santos, saving the judge's life. The whole thing is like this Lester Holmboe should get the National Medal of Honor or something. They even announced he's been named the new under sheriff, which puts him first in the line of succession."

"So they're a little extravagant with their accolades. So what?"

"Think about it, Lawton. The only people who know how much cocaine and money were confiscated are Lester, the sheriff, the judge, and Santos. Santos is dead, so he can't talk and Lester's the guy who shot him. Most people believe the sheriff's just a puppet for the judge, and Lester just got a promotion over guys who've worked on the force for ten to fifteen years. They said they got two hundred thousand and five kilos of blow. What if there was more? And remember, the judge called the press conference before any of this happened. Sounds like a set up to me."

"What about the property logs? Wouldn't they have logged it in Thursday?" challenged Lawton.

"You bring up another interesting point. The property was logged in Sunday afternoon. Normal procedure, in a bust this big, would have been for the state narcotics boys to have been contacted Thursday night, no later than Friday morning. They found out about it after the press conference today, and they aren't happy campers right now. From what they can determine, the sheriff had this deal on ice for three full days. No attorney filed for a bond, no family members contacted. In fact, we don't know yet where the dead guy's from. They seem to have misplaced his driver's license, but we're working on that. Anyway, let's just assume there was more money or drugs than announced. Odd that the judge suddenly has half a million and change for Mr. Rifle. Now, how this ties to the plant fire, your guess is a good as mine. If we can find this Cudjoe character, and if he's not already on a slab at the morgue, maybe he can fill in some gaps."

Lawton stood, placed his hands in his pockets and paced around the room.

"I'll go to the judge this afternoon for a tap on Rifle. Fred, you need to keep me posted as information comes in. You have a problem with me sharing any of this with Jack Mitchell?"

"No. In fact, I think you should, especially the part about Rifle knowing about him, and now the judge knowing as well. He probably should get over here and kick Rutherford out of his office. No telling what he'll do when the judge tells him the jig's up. You might consider advising him how to proceed legally against Rutherford. We'd rather the judge be left alone for the moment. I want him for all this shit, if my theories are true."

Lawton nodded his agreement. "Fred, I know you're busy as hell, but any word on my case?"

216

"We can't find anyone who saw Janie after the diner. We've made over fifty contacts. No one sold her a ticket. No one, we can find, saw her on a bus going north or south that night or the next day. No one in the immediate area of the diner has seen her. We're going back tomorrow to talk to Deputy Davis again. Maybe we missed something in the first interview."

"Thanks, Fred," Lawton responded, his disappointment evident.

CHAPTER 48
LUCKY LEANDER

Within three hours of the call I'd received from Lawton, I was in a plane on my way to Mobile. Before leaving, I had first scribbled a note to each of the kids, apologizing for leaving so hastily. After making arrangements with Mrs. Larson to stay at the house while I was gone, I placed a call to the Alabama attorney Josh McTiernan had recommended. I gave him a quick overview of the situation and asked that he prepare the initial paperwork for the lawsuit I hoped to file on Tuesday. I then raced home and packed enough clothes for a week; although, I hoped the stay would be shorter. I had grown to hate Alabama.

During the hour and a half flight, I tried to make lists of things I needed to accomplish, but my mind kept drifting back to my conversation with Lawton and the circle of events centering on Raleigh Pendleton. For reasons I can't explain to this day, I kept focusing on one seemingly insignificant detail Lawton had mentioned Sunday morning when he had called, and this particular detail had no apparent bearing on the events of the past weekend. Deputy Jim Bob Davis was the last person to see Jane Tremont, and he and the judge were somehow associated.

The early morning mist had been only a precursor to the storm brewing in the Gulf. By Monday afternoon, a line of thunderstorms began approaching the Alabama coastline. By evening, the rain pelted the ground with sufficient vigor to force low-lying area residents to prepare for evacuation as the creeks and bayous began cresting their banks.

The wipers on Leander's Mercury swished briskly from side-to-side, but the torrents were too much for them. His ability to see the dark roadway was limited to fleeting glimpses as the rain bombarded his windshield. But the difficult driving conditions were secondary to the uneasiness he felt. The judge's voice had been cold when he had ordered him to the lodge at seven that night.

"Leander, don't you ever work?" the judge had scolded, when Vivian had handed him the phone at 3:30 that afternoon.

"All the time, Judge," he had responded defensively. "I worked right through lunch and came ova here for a quick sandwich before I head up to—"

"Bullshit, Leander. I'm so sick and tired of your excuses and lies. Where the hell is Billy Cudjoe? And what the hell happened last night? I thought you said you'd talked to him," Raleigh had barked.

"I ain't seen Billy all day. Judge, I know he didn't go ova there last night. He knew everything was on hold."

"You better find his ass. I want the both of you to be at the lodge at seven sharp tonight, and I don't want no bullshit excuses. Bobby's in the hospital, they say that whole damn plant might burn to the ground, and I want to know what the fuck happened."

So engrossed in reliving the condemnation in the judge's voice, and frustrated by his inability to find Billy, Leander failed to monitor the speed of his vehicle. A small hill preceded a subtle ravine filled with silt-laden runoff from a nearby field. The Mercury plowed into the two feet of water column. Immediately hydroplaning, the front of the car slid to the left while the rear swung quickly to the right.

"Holy shit!" Leander yelled, while his foot pumped the brake pedal and his hands and arms furiously turned the steering wheel to the right.

In an instant, Leander experienced the sensation of traveling backward while he futilely continued to fight with the controls. As the vehicle left the pavement, moving quickly over the inadequate shoulder, a rear tire encountered one of several stumps left by a county road crew. The momentum of the heavy car lifted the trailing side upward, heaving it onto it's top. Inside, Leander's body pitched forward, restrained initially by the seatbelts. He was then rendered unconscious when the airbags inflated, pinning him against the seat as his head whiplashed violently against the headrest.

Within a few seconds, the energy of the crash abated, and the vehicle began a slow drift with the current, occasionally tilting or twisting in response to contact with a tree, a large rock, or the side of the shallow gorge.

Raleigh was well beyond agitated. Contemplating the events of the past twelve hours, he paced the front porch of the lodge like a wounded lion. Johnny leaned casually against the outer wall, sipping from a bottle of Busch. It was now 8:10 and no sign of Leander or Billy.

"It looks like the rain's beginning to stop, Johnny," Raleigh said absently. "Hell, I couldn't even depend on that no account Leander to show up on time to his own execution. What do you think?"

"I don't know, Judge. He could've had some problems getting out here with the rain and all, but my bet is he couldn't find Cudjoe, and he didn't want to come out here without him. If he don't show, you'll hear the dam'dest bunch of excuses you ever heard."

"You think Cudjoe's the corpse they're trying to identify from the fire?"

"If his ability to handle explosives is anything like his performance on anything else I ever knew about, I'd bet a month's pay he blowed himself up," Johnny replied. "Judge, why didn't you let me handle that job? Everything Leander and Cudjoe have touched since I've known them has been screwed up from the get go. They're just a couple of losers. Always have been, always will be."

"Old hindsight's always twenty-twenty," Raleigh lamented. "We'll give them another hour and go on home. I know where Leander lives, and I need to get rid of him quick like. He's become a real liability to me. I can't have him screwing up my position in the party. Damn, that reminds me, Lawrence Rifle never did call me today like he said he would. I was so busy with that special hearing and that smart-ass Mobile lawyer and all, I forgot about him. I'll give that son-of-a-bitch a call tomorrow. He'd better have a damn good reason for not calling or I might have to keep all that—"

He didn't finish the sentence, realizing Johnny wasn't in the loop on everything.

CHAPTER 49
BRINGING JULIO HOME

Long before the sedative should have released its control over his mind, Roberto had awakened, mentally preparing himself for the many tasks at hand. While a complete understanding of the circumstances surrounding Julio's death was his main objective, a logistical problem was first on the list: how to claim the body of his baby brother without leading the drug enforcement agencies to the front steps of Santos Importing. They would get there soon enough.

Before drifting into the drug-induced reprieve, he had called Shooter, asking him to consider a plan for dealing with the dilemma. Recognizing the value of further ingratiating himself to the largest cocaine distributor in the southeast, Shooter had set his street-smart brain in motion and devised a rather simple plan, which had become operational long before Roberto greeted another grief-filled day.

Shooter had retained Johnson Calhoun to determine where Julio's body was being held. Calhoun was the senior partner of Calhoun and Associates, a prominent Mobile law firm with an impressive client list. Most of his fellow members of the Alabama Bar Association respected Calhoun, but considered him a renegade due to his extremely liberal ideals and practices. Having begun his career in the Mobile Legal Aid office, his reputation had grown as he consistently won not-guilty verdicts and mistrials for the guiltiest of criminals. It was through such a representation that he had made the acquaintance of a guilty felon named George M. "Shooter" Pinkston. Although he ran seven hookers and was caught soliciting an undercover detective, Shooter had been acquitted of pandering on a technicality, and Calhoun had represented the pool hall owner and drug dealer ever since.

Lacking the financial resources for a publicly owned morgue, Washington County had for years contracted with the Jefferson-Wilcox Funeral Home in Chatom to provide interim holding services until bodies were either claimed or buried at the county's expense. It had taken Calhoun only one phone call to determine Julio's whereabouts, but the release of the body had been far more problematic.

After hours of bantering with the county attorney, Virgil Crawford, and both the state and federal drug enforcement people, a release had been ordered at a special hearing in front of the local probate judge, Raleigh Pendleton.

"Judge," Calhoun had argued, "there's a plethora of legal precedents for the release of a body to the legal representative of the family."

"But Mr. Calhoun, you've apparently lost sight of the fact that Mr. Santos was in possession of a great deal of money and illegal contraband," Raleigh had countered. "It's my opinion that the people are entitled to know the origin of the confiscated material and a logical place to look would be those closest to the deceased. We wouldn't be here today, wasting my time, if a family member simply came forward to claim the body."

"With due respect to the court, your honor, such an assessment is predicated on the belief that Mr. Santos was guilty of wrong-doing, which is clearly contradictory to the rights guaranteed by the Constitution. Mr. Santos was never charged with anything, according to your own court's records, and doing so now would be a waste of the court's time, laughable in legal circles, and inconsiderate of the family's right to closure."

"I'm afraid, Mr. Calhoun, you're going to have to do better than that to obtain the release you request," Raleigh had replied, yawning as he spoke.

"Then, let me put a different twist on this situation. Please realize what I will say next should in no way to be construed as a threat. It is simply a matter of the facts we have thus far been able to assemble. Mr. Santos was arrested on Thursday. He was held without benefit of legal counsel for almost forty-eight hours before being summarily executed in the county jail. As I said before, no formal charges were ever filed against Mr. Santos, and the drug enforcement agencies were not contacted for over two days after the alleged drug bust was made—clearly an unprecedented and inappropriate action. We feel there could be other irregularities yet to be disclosed or discovered. Without receiving the relief we seek, we will have no choice but to vigorously pursue any such irregularities both legally and with the media. The family of the deceased simply requests that his body be released and, as far as they are concerned, this unfortunate situation will simply go away."

Raleigh had glared at Calhoun for several seconds before making the following statement, which surprised everyone in the courtroom, including the Mobile attorney.

"The court damn sure takes offense at your insinuations, Mr. Calhoun, and I've considered your arguments and find no legal merit. On the other hand, my court's always considered the moral issues of a case and all the victims. While I have no doubt Mr. Santos would've been properly charged, prosecuted, and convicted of numerous felonious acts, if he hadn't attacked me and tried to escape, I'm sympathetic for the personal loss to your client. If they're not involved in this drug running and such, they, too, are victims of Mr. Santos. I'm gonna grant your request for the sake of decency. You got an order prepared for me to sign?"

"I do, your honor," Calhoun responded, successfully hiding his surprise.

After signing the document and having it entered into the court clerk's records, Raleigh motioned Calhoun to the bench.

"You did a good job for your client, Counselor. But don't go thinking you'll ever walk into my courtroom again and walk out a winner. I don't give two shits about your big-time legal reputation. If you ever make the mistake of coming in here and threatening me again, you'll spend thirty days in jail, and it'll be the worst month of you life. Do we have an understanding, Mr. Calhoun?"

Calhoun had simply nodded and smiled, picking up the piece of paper for which he was being well paid to obtain.

Although the receipt of the order had been a major first step, Shooter and Calhoun both knew the job wasn't finished. While the authorities had unexpectedly lost the initial round, it was a certainty the persons actually claiming the body would be questioned and probably arrested on some trumped up charge. After several possible scenarios were considered, they set out to orchestrate a simple sleight-of-hand maneuver, which, if properly executed, should achieve the desired result.

The operation began with a black hearse pulling into the alleyway behind the funeral home. To the surprise and displeasure of the agents waiting to detain and question the driver, Calhoun and one of his legal assistants stepped from the vehicle, opened the cargo doors, and removed an ordinary gray metal casket which rode on a collapsible gurney. Although the helper was asked for credentials by one of the agents waiting inside the establishment, a call to the judge confirmed that client privilege still applied. The body was placed in the casket, returned to the hearse, and driven away by the two lawyers.

The hearse followed a predetermined route from Chatom to Mobile, followed at a distance by two easily identifiable tail vehicles—both dark sedans. Bringing up the rear of the procession was the rented black Suburban driven by Bugger. Manuel rode in the seat beside him.

Shortly after the four vehicles pulled onto Interstate 65 South, the Suburban speeded up, passing the other three vehicles. A few miles later, Calhoun exited on Dauphin Street, apparently heading downtown. As the hearse passed through a residential section immediately west of the city, a right hand turn was negotiated, and then another right into the first available driveway. The waiting Suburban pulled in behind the hearse, following it to the garage behind the two closely spaced houses. Before the trailing vehicles reached the intersection, a second black hearse pulled from the curb, replacing the one obscured by the Suburban. Manny and Bugger grinned as the dark sedans passed by, following the decoy.

By the time the second hearse was stopped on Interstate 10, just before crossing the Florida state line, Julio's body was in the back of the Suburban, heading for a small airport just north of Gulfport, Mississippi. Four hours later, Roberto, three of his men, and Tina met the chartered plane at a small private airstrip. Tootie handed Tina a folded newspaper.

"A big black guy with Manny gave me this to give to Roberto. It's today's Mobile paper. There's a story in there about Julio and the drug bust. He's probably not ready to read it yet but give it to him later. I think he'll want to see it."

Following the hearse toward South Miami, Roberto felt a certain amount of relief to have Julio's body home, but his mind was filled with grief and questions—questions he vowed to have answered. As they pulled through the portico in front of the funeral home, he thought of the last time he'd seen his kid brother and he cried.

CHAPTER 50
CLOSING IN

The phone rang only four times before he answered it, but in his sluggish state, the ringing seemed to have gone on for hours.

"Hello," Bobby Bitterman almost whispered.

"Hey, boss. They say you're going to live," announced Reggie Kendall, the assistant plant manager at General Paper. Reggie had been transferred to the plant three years earlier from a smaller facility in Georgia. He was an up-and-comer in the company, and his current position was just a stepping stone until he got his own plant.

"Yeah, the doc said it wasn't a heart attack after all. Just stress, I guess. Why are you so cheerful?"

"The fire's out, and the damage isn't near as bad as was thought. We'll have to get a new boiler and two kettles, do a little cosmetic work on the pulp house, but we should be up and running in about a month. We're going to have to lay everyone off, but everybody understands, and it looks like it'll all work out."

"Good. What about the body? You sure it wasn't Earnie?"

"I talked to him myself about two hours ago. It scared the shit out of him—said it was a damn big explosion, but he was at the other end of the plant making his rounds. Not so much as a scratch. He did say he got a computer beep on his radio about fifteen minutes before the explosion, but he said he'd been getting some false alarms for the past couple of weeks. He'd reported the problem to maintenance, but they couldn't find any bugs."

"Then, who was it?" Bobby pressed.

"No word yet. Either an intruder who walked in at the wrong time, or someone who was up to no good and got himself blown up, I guess. At any rate, everyone's accounted for except Harvey Greenville, but he went on vacation Friday. He's probably up in the woods at that old cabin of his."

"I didn't remember Harvey on the vacation schedule this month," Bobby replied.

"I didn't either, but I talked to Luke Peterson and Luke told me Harvey said he wouldn't be back for two weeks. Luke said he was planning to run Harvey's crew. I checked in the office, and they had him penciled in, but Harvey didn't confirm it. I guess he forgot."

"Okay, Reggie, anything else I should know about? I think they're letting me out of here in the morning."

"Nothing, other than I got maintenance working through all the electrical systems and the computer ports to make sure nothing shorted. Since we were shut down, there shouldn't be a problem, but it's about all we can do until the arson investigators get out of there."

"They're still there?"

"Yeah. I guess they'll be in and out for a week or more. Told me to keep everyone away from the pulp kettles and the boiler until they've finished."

"So they think it could've been set deliberately?"

"I didn't say that. One of them told me he thought the damage around the ignition point was so bad they'd probably never be able to say for sure one way or the other, but—"

"But what?"

"He said they're taking orders from the FBI right now, and—"

"The FBI? Why would they be involved?" Bobby asked, paranoia taking charge.

"I assumed you knew. Someone said they were at the hospital talking to you."

"I haven't talked to anyone since they brought me here," Bobby announced and a bad feeling came over him. "Reggie, if there's nothing else, I need to pee."

"That's all I got. Sure glad you're getting better. Talk to you later and don't worry about the plant. I'll cover things until you get on your feet."

"Thanks, Reggie."

Bobby closed his eyes, unable to determine if he felt more concern or relief from the conversation he'd just had. Before his mind could ramble too far, there was a soft knock at his door and two young men in business suits walked in.

"Sorry to bother you, Mr. Bitterman, but the nurse said you were awake and—"

"Who are you guys?" Bobby asked, more than a little uncomfortable.

"I'm Special Agent Booker, and this is Special Agent Hawkins. We're with the FBI."

Fred Carleton reclined in Harley Logginfield's chair. Jim Bob was seated himself across the desk.

"Thanks for the use of you office, Sheriff," Fred said as Harley walked toward the door. "I feel like I'm kicking you out."

"No need to apologize, Mr. Carleton. I got plenty to do out front, and the sooner you boys finish up your investigation, the sooner I can get my office back into the business of law enforcement," Harley replied. Looking in the direction of his under sheriff, he said with a steely eye, "Davis, you cooperate with this agent and get this over with. I don't know why in the name of Sam Hill you didn't bring that youngster in that night."

As the door closed, Fred addressed someone whom he now considered a suspect. "That would be a good place to start, Mr. Davis. Why didn't you bring Jane Tremont to the station that night?"

Jim Bob flushed. "Like I said before, I offered to, but she didn't want to come in. She was real upset and—"

"That's my point. If she were real upset, like you say, why would you leave an upset young girl out in the middle of nowhere by herself?"

"I checked on her all night long. She said she was just fine every time I talked to her."

Fred flipped through some pages in a file.

"According to your first interview, there's no mention of you checking back on her. Your story then was, you gave her some money for a bus ticket to Birmingham and she was gone the next morning."

"I guess I forgot the checking back part the first time."

Fred said nothing and stared until Jim Bob looked to the floor. Fred could sense his nervousness. This guy had something to hide.

"Who's Raleigh Pendleton?"

"Who?" Jim Bob blurted.

Fred was silent for a few more uncomfortable seconds. "Raleigh Pendleton. You know him?"

This change in direction confounded Jim Bob. "I...I...eh, that name rings a bell," he replied with a furrowed brow.

Fred said nothing.

"Now, there was this boy ova in Daphne I used to know named Raleigh, eh, but it seems like his last name was Potter or something like that."

"Mr. Davis, let me help you. Raleigh Pendleton's the probate judge in Washington County, about thirty miles from here. Does that help?"

"Oh, Judge Pendleton! Sure, I know him, eh, or I know who he is. I didn't know his name was Raleigh. That's why it threw me," Jim Bob explained, the perspiration now visible on his forehead.

"You getting hot, Mr. Davis?"

"Hot? No, not me. I'm fine...thanks."

"You ever talk to Judge Pendleton?"

Jim Bob squirmed in his chair. "Well, I can't remember if I ever did. Why?"

"How many times did you check on her?" Fred hammered.

"Who?"

"Jane Tremont."

"Oh, her. Let's see, probably four times. Maybe more."

"How much is a bus ticket to Birmingham?"

"To Birmingham? Let's see. I don't know exactly."

"How much money did you give Jane Tremont?"

"Uh... I think about thirty dollars."

"Is that what a ticket to Birmingham costs?"

"Yeah, I guess about that much."

"Are you a wealthy man, Mr. Davis?"

"Wealthy, eh, hell no." He forced a laugh. "You can't get wealthy working for the sheriff." He laughed again and cleared his throat.

Fred stood and walked around the room. Rubbing his chin deliberately, he asked, "Did you kill Jane Tremont, Mr. Davis?"

"Kill her?" Jim Bob gasped. "What're you saying? You think I killed that nigger girl?"

Fred clinched his fist and couldn't remember wanting to hit someone more in his life.

"Mr. Davis, I want you to know that you're our number one suspect in the disappearance of Jane Tremont, and I'm going to bring the entire weight of the FBI against you to prove it. When I leave here in a few minutes, I'm either going to have your confession, or I swear I'll make life so miserable for you that you'll beg me later. By the way, we talked to Judge Pendleton, and he told us you were a good friend of his, went to the same church, and even had a drink together every now and then. Why are you so ashamed of knowing Raleigh Pendleton when he's so proud to know you?"

"You talked to the judge? About me?"

"You want to tell me what happened that night, Jim Bob?" Fred offered in a less threatening voice.

"What night?"

"The night you picked up Jane Tremont and took her somewhere. Maybe where you could have your way with her. She was a pretty young girl, don't you think?" Fred tossed a couple of photos on the desk.

Jim Bob looked away.

"Take a look. Don't you think she was pretty?"

Jim Bob picked up one of the photographs. "Nigger women never appealed to me much."

"Have it your way, Mr. Davis. There's so many holes in your story, we'll have you nailed down in less than a week." While placing the file in his briefcase, Fred had a thought—one he'd not considered until this second. "By the way, you know a Bobby Bitterman?"

The shock on Jim Bob's face would have been noticeable to a blind person.

"We're talking to him right now, and I bet he's selling you out as we speak."

Jim Bob tried to respond, but the words wouldn't form on his lips.

Fred didn't need an answer. There was a connection to all of this. He just needed a few more pieces.

Bobby sat up uncomfortably in the hospital bed. The initial conversation had been friendly and informal. Eugene Booker, an experienced agent of twelve years, decided to change the tone.

"Mr. Bitterman, tell me what you know about a judge named Raleigh Pendleton."

Bobby forced a cough, a telltale sign of nervousness. "I've known the judge for about ten years, I guess. First met him at church. We used to go to the same church."

"When did you last talk to him?"

"Let's see...it's been quite a while."

"How about three days ago?"

"I guess it could've been. Time gets away from me sometimes."

"What'd you talk about?"

"Oh, I don't really remember. Wasn't anything important. He calls every now and then and asks me over to the lodge to play cards and so forth. He was after me last spring to ask the company for a political contribution."

"Did the company make one?"

"No, we've had it pretty tough the last couple of years."

"How'd he take that?"

"Take what?"

"The company turning him down."

"Oh, he was okay with it. Disappointed, naturally, but he understood. Why are you so interested in the judge?" Bobby asked, attempting to appear confused.

"We're interested in anyone who could be associated with the fire set at the plant Monday morning. How about Leander Rutherford or Billy Cudjoe? You know them?"

Bobby reached for a glass of water on the service stand. He had to think.

"Rutherford and Cudjoe. No, I don't think so. Why?"

"Your visitor log shows you gave those two gentlemen a tour of the plant last Friday. Is the log incorrect?"

"Let me think. Yeah, I do remember them now. The judge...I mean, eh, they made an appointment to look at a repair job we were considering going out for bid on. Mr. Rutherford owns a construction company down in Mobile."

"Do you normally walk contractors through the plant? Don't you have a plant engineer or a maintenance manager who'd normally deal with such matters?"

"Sure, but everyone was busy, and I decided to do the tour myself."

"What kind of job?" Eugene Booker continued to apply the pressure.

"What do you mean?"

"You said there was a repair job the company was considering doing. What was it, and where was it in the plant?"

Bobby was now far beyond nervous.

"What's this all about? I don't know why we're playing fifty questions. Do I need a lawyer? Are you accusing me of something?"

Before he could respond, Agent Booker's cell phone rang. "Excuse me a minute."

"Gene, have you talked to Bitterman yet?" Fred Carleton asked.

"We're with Mr. Bitterman right now," the special agent replied.

"How's it going?"

"Hard to say yet. There's something here."

"Have you asked him about the judge, Rutherford, and Cudjoe?"

"Yeah."

"Anything of interest?"

"Not real sure, but I think there's a connection."

"I just finished up in Grove Hill. Ask Bitterman about Jim Bob Davis."

"Say again," Eugene requested, preparing to write down the name of someone with whom he was unfamiliar.

Fred repeated the name and gave his subordinate a brief summary of the interrogation he'd just completed.

"Sounds like there could be a connection. I'll see what happens," Eugene Booker confirmed, and then replaced his cell phone in his breast pocket.

"Sorry, Mr. Bitterman. That was my boss. Where were we?"

"I said, do I need a lawyer?" Bobby, now more composed, answered.

"I can't advise you on that, Mr. Bitterman. Ever heard the name Jane Tremont?"

"No, who's she?"

"I guess you don't read the papers. She's a fifteen-year-old girl who's been missing for about three weeks. Does that ring any bells?"

"No, should it?"

"We don't know yet, but I might be able to answer your question in a few minutes. How about Jim Bob Davis? You know him?"

Turning his head toward the blank wall opposite the agents, Bobby sighed.

CHAPTER 51
PARANOIA

Lawrence Rifle had spent all of Monday morning struggling with the temptation of ignoring Findley Ross's earlier warnings. His mind had been made up, however, when he called the party secretary and was told there would be no additional money available from the general campaign fund until after the primary.

The lieutenant governor had filed for the governor's race in spite of being rejected as the party's candidate for the position, but he had sat quietly while Senator Laughlin and Rifle had spent millions of dollars berating each other while vying for the Democratic electorate's favor. When Senator Laughlin withdrew, as Fin had promised Rifle, the lieutenant governor's staff began to step up their efforts. With a relatively small, but unexpended war chest, they immediately attacked Rifle's limited public service and association with big business, and the ploy seemed to be working. Much of the senator's following had shifted to the lieutenant governor rather than into the Rifle camp. Rifle was now fighting a different campaign with a well-known adversary, and he needed money worse than ever.

He had placed the call at 2:00, as he and the judge had discussed the night before, but he had been advised that an emergency hearing had been set and the judge would be unavailable for an undeterminable period of time. The judge had not called back.

When he finally closed his eyes at midnight, insecurity had crept into his mind. *What if the party leadership has changed candidates, decided to back the lieutenant governor? Was that warning from Findley just some elaborate ruse to deplete my funds? This whole thing doesn't smell right. I better look out for myself from here on out. I still got a good lead statewide, and if I can keep the money coming in, I can beat their new man in spite of them. Then, they'll have to get back in my camp for the general. After I win, I'll deal with those old-line bastards.*

Raleigh's home phone rang at 7:30, Tuesday morning. Having just finished his favorite breakfast of scrambled eggs, fresh side meat, and grits, Raleigh took the call in his study. He poured a jigger of sour mash into his coffee and picked up the phone.

"Judge, Lawrence Rifle here," announced a cheerful voice. "Sorry we missed each other yesterday."

"I thought you were going to call me at two," Raleigh replied curtly.

"I did, Judge. Right at two o'clock, as we agreed. Your girl said you were in court and you'd have to call back later. I waited at the office until about six and then kept my home line open all night."

"That damn niece of mine. Sometimes I don't know where her head is. Sorry, Lawrence, I didn't get a message." The tone in his voice was more congenial.

Rifle exhaled silently. "Judge, is your offer still open?"

Raleigh could sense tension from the other end of the line. "Well, I don't know, Lawrence. After I thought you'd shunned me again, I put a call in to the lieutenant governor."

"What'd he offer?" Rifle asked. He could feel his face beginning to glow.

"Quite a bit. Everything we've discussed ova the past few months and some more," Raleigh lied, testing the water.

"Raleigh, he won't win. He can't beat me. He came into the fight too late, but whatever he offered, I'll match it and then some." His voice was now pleading.

Raleigh sat back in his leather desk chair and smiled like a cat in an aviary. "That's mighty generous, Lawrence. We can discuss the details later. I'll just tell the lieutenant governor I appreciate his offer, but I'm sticking with my old friend Mr. Rifle. How do you want the money sent? The usual channels? Maybe Findley Ross's PAC?"

"No, let's leave Fin out of this. Let's just keep this between you and me. I'll send my brother down there whenever it's convenient for you, and you can give it to him. Five hundred thousand, right?"

"And change."

"Raleigh, I do have one stipulation about this money."

"Oh?"

"You have to assure me that none of it's coming from Leander Rutherford. While I think Fin and the boys in Montgomery are prone to exaggeration, he did convince me that Leander's going to take a fall. Fin went on and on about how straight this Jack Mitchell is. This Mitchell guy could be dangerous to both of us."

"Like I told you, I don't do business with Leander anymore. He's just a lackey. Besides, he may already know something's going down. He missed a meeting yesterday and may've already flew the coop. I only met this Mitchell fellow once, and I think I can handle him if he ever becomes a problem. Now, let's figure out when me and your brother can get together."

Two men in sport shirts and slacks sat in the green Dodge van, furiously making notes. When the line went dead, one looked at the other and high-fives were exchanged.

CHAPTER 52
SALLY'S SEIZURE

Lawton Tremont hung up the phone, rubbing his eyes with open palms. He shook his head, wondering how much more stress he could handle. Before he could sink too far into self-pity, his intercom buzzed.

"Mr. Tremont, a Mr. Mitchell is here to see you. He said he didn't have an appointment."

"That's okay, Brenda. Send him back."

I could tell when I first saw his face that was something wrong.

"Sorry to just drop in. I had some time to kill before I meet my attorney at the courthouse. We're filing the papers against Leander and Miss Vivian this afternoon."

"Good to see you, Jack. Who'd you hire?"

"A guy my Houston attorney recommended. His name's Johnson Calhoun."

"Really?" Lawton smiled, scratching the back of his head.

"You know him? Did I screw up?" I asked, confused by his reaction.

"No, he's probably a good choice." Lawton paused and walked over to his window and looked out. "The more I think about it, he's perfect. Good reputation with a lot of big corporate clients, and he knows his way around the criminal court. Yeah, I think Johnson will be good for your situation. Besides, when criminal charges are filed against Leander, Vivian Thompson, and hopefully, Pendleton, he'll already be representing you and won't be available for any of them."

"That makes me feel better. You okay, Lawton? You don't look good."

"Thanks," he replied with a forced smile.

"Is it Barbara?"

"No, I wish it were. Then I'd know what to do."

I wrestled with the next question. "Is…it isn't Janie, is it?"

He shook his head. "Jack, I only have a few minutes, but I'll share a cup of coffee with you and tell you about another member of my family."

After a trip to the coffee bar, we returned to his office. He closed the door behind us.

"Where to begin?" he said with a sigh. "In 1963, I went off to college. First time I'd ever been out of the state of Alabama. My folks had been killed in a car accident nine years earlier, leaving me and my sister, Sally."

"You've never mentioned a sister, Lawton," I commented.

"I know. Well, my mom's brother and his wife took us in, and they were great to us. Sally was only six at the time, and Aunt Liz was the only mother she ever knew. Uncle Aaron was a sharecropper for the Pendleton family and a good man."

"Raleigh Pendleton's family?"

"The same. Raleigh was quite a bit older than me and used to push me around. You know, bullying, calling me a nigger—that kind of shit. I didn't let it bother me though because that's how it was with black folks in Alabama back in those days. But that's not a part of this story. One night, several weeks after I went off to school, some Klansmen came to the house and killed my aunt and uncle."

I wanted to say something but couldn't. I just sat there and listened.

"We never knew why. Uncle Aaron was the perfect black man for that time. He worked hard, always paid the Pendletons their share, never made any trouble for anyone, but for some reason, they hanged him and shot my aunt. The worst of it was, Sally witnessed the whole thing, I guess."

"They didn't kill her?" I asked and then felt stupid.

"The old house had a root cellar—most of those old places did. Right after we moved in, Sally and I found a crawl space that went out under the living room. It was only about three feet high and a couple of feet wide. I don't think Uncle Aaron even knew it was there. We used to play in there when we were little. It was our own private hideaway. Anyway, when I got the call to come home, no one could find Sally. Everyone assumed the murderers had taken her with them, and she was probably dead. The first thing I did, when I got to the home place, was go look in the crawl space and there she was—almost dead from dehydration, exposure, and shock. Some days I think she'd have been better off if they'd killed her."

236

"My God! What happened? Could she identify anyone?"

"Jack, she hasn't spoken for over thirty-five years. The state put her in a sanitarium, and she just laid in bed, mumbling, occasionally having a seizure. She'd start screaming and crying, 'Please don't be dead. Please don't be dead.' But that's all she's ever said."

"Where is she now?" I asked softly.

"The first thing I did when I signed with the Redskins was go get her. She's lived with us ever since. It was hard at first, especially for Barbara. Sally was a full-time job. You never knew when she'd have a seizure and couldn't do anything for her when she did. But, over time, she's gotten a lot better. The drugs are better now, and she's peaceful most of the time. She looks at magazines, the newspaper, and watches television. I don't know for sure if she comprehends anything, but it keeps her occupied." He swallowed hard and blinked several times. "Janie was devoted to her. From the time she was old enough to talk, she'd sit for hours and talk to Sally, like she was just having a normal conversation. And it worked. Sally never verbally responded, but you could see it in her eyes when Janie would talk to her. She understood. Her eyes would sparkle and—"

By this time, both of us were fighting back tears and neither of us were winning. We sat there for several minutes, saying nothing.

Lawton took a deep breath. "My son called about half an hour ago, right before you came in. Something set Sally off. She hasn't had a seizure in over five years, but she had one, and it wasn't pretty. They're taking her to the hospital. They should be there by now. I was just leaving when you dropped by."

"What the hell are you doing sitting here with me? Can I drive you over there?"

"No, thanks. Like I told you, there's not much you can do when one of these things happens. We got so used to them in the earlier years; we'd just sit by her side and make sure she didn't hurt herself. Anyway, I'd better get going."

"Lawton, I'm sorry I delayed you. If there's anything I can do, all you have to do is ask."

"Thanks, Jack, but there's no need for apologies. I haven't talked about this outside my family in years. It made me feel a little better."

As we walked across the street to the parking lot, a horn honked, and we both turned. Fred Carleton lowered his window and pulled to the curb. The expression on his face was hard to read.

237

"Lawton, I was just coming to your office. Where are you off to?"

"The hospital," he replied.

"Barbara?"

"No, Sally. She's had a seizure."

"I thought she'd been doing better?" Fred responded, obviously aware, to some degree, of the story I'd just heard.

"She has been, but something set her off this morning."

"I'm sorry, Lawton. Get in. I can have you there in five minutes," Fred offered, reaching behind the front seat and retrieving his magnetic bubble light. "If you're up to it, I can give you a quick rundown on where we are. You're welcome to come along, too, Jack."

Lawton and I looked at one another and shrugged.

As the sedan pulled from the curb, we could sense Fred's excitement. "I got a call about fifteen minutes ago. We're damn close to getting Pendleton and Rifle for campaign contribution violations. We just have to intercept the hand-off."

CHAPTER 53
ARRANGEMENTS

Roberto had completed the painful task of making the burial plans for Julio. Tina sat by his side, occasionally touching his arm or patting him on the shoulder when tears would fill his eyes. After leaving the funeral home, they had driven in silence as Roberto gathered himself for the equally heartbreaking task of informing his aging mother of the loss of another son.

Tina sat quietly on the porch outside the upscale nursing home while Roberto went inside. She was relieved to be spared participating in another emotionally draining task. As she waited, her mind turned to her father, and she wondered if he were still alive. He had looked so frail and was suffering so much during her short stay in his room at the nursing home. She prayed he had been spared another excruciating night alone in his bed.

Remembering the newspaper Tootie had provided, it occurred to her that his obituary might be in the paper if he had passed on shortly after her visit. Retreating to Roberto's yellow Hummer, she shuffled through her backpack, extracting the paper. Quickly scanning the index with her finger, she paused at the word "DEATHS."

As she perused the surnames, alphabetically arranged in one-column paragraphs, she was disappointed not to find, "Yokum, Cecil P." Needing a distraction, she turned to the front of the paper where a quarter-page picture of bellowing smoke and fire seemed to leap from the page. "MILL BURNS WHILE COMMUNITY PRAYS," read the headline.

Holy shit! That's right next door to where that perverted asshole my mother married works, she thought. She began reading the text of the story. Flipping the pages to where the story was continued, the words "Arson has not been ruled out" caught her eye.

What was it that creep Billy said? "It'll probably make the papers. It'll for sure make the news."

Dismissing the fire as a coincidence, she continued to scan the headlines for the story in which she was particularly interested. After two quick passes through the four sections, she found it, buried in the middle of section B. It read, "BIG BUST IN CHATOM." Before reading on, she looked at the black-and-white photograph set off beside the article. "Sheriff Virgil Crawford, Judge Raleigh A. Pendleton, and new Under-Sheriff Lester Holmboe display the money and drugs confiscated from the vehicle driven by an unnamed driver (Not pictured)."

She smirked and shook her head. "'Not pictured.' What kind of idiot wrote that?"

While the article was relatively short, she read every word deliberately. *"Five kilos of coke and over two hundred thousand in hundreds."* These guys are big time!

"What are you reading, Tina?" Roberto asked, walking toward the steps.

Tina jumped. "Damn! You scared the shit out of me."

"Sorry, I didn't mean to. What's so interesting?"

Tina looked up and could see the traces of dried tears beneath his chocolate brown eyes.

"Oh, nothing. Just a newspaper Tootie gave me. I thought my old man's obit might be in it."

"Was it?"

"No. I guess he's still hanging on."

"That's good news. Until he quits breathing, he's still got a chance."

"I guess," she sighed. "Roberto, there's an article in here about, well not about, but it refers to Julio. Tootie thought you might want to see it sometime. You want—"

"I don't want to see it," he whispered. "Not yet anyway."

"Okay, I just wanted you to know I have it, whenever you're ready. There's also a big story in here about a fire at a plant up on the industrial canal," she offered as a distraction.

"What's that got to do with anything?"

"Nothing, but I thought it was interesting. You know that guy Billy, the one I was with, you know, earlier?"

"Yeah, the greaser. What about him?"

"He was bragging about a demolition job he had to do Sunday night. He made a big deal about how it would be in the newspapers."

"You think this greaseball blew up some plant? Why would he do that?"
"I don't know. I just thought it was a coincidence."

The seldom-used dead bolt had been engaged immediately after Johnny placed the last of three empty suitcases on the floor and returned to his small office. Even though Raleigh had told Bonnie Mae he was not to be disturbed for any reason, he was taking no chances. After closing all the drapes and clearing the small circular conference table in the corner opposite his desk, he turned the tumblers as quickly as his arthritic fingers would allow. For the next five minutes, he moved bundle after bundle of one-hundred-dollar bills from the safe to the table where it could be counted and separated.

"Five hundred thousand," he said triumphantly, as he neatly positioned another bundle in one of the four suitcases. He had already filled one. "Now, how much change do I want to give Mr. Rifle?"

Looking at the remaining stacks, he limped to his desk, retrieving the stainless letter opener presented to Bull Pendleton by the grand dragon of the Alabama Klan in 1939.

After slicing one side of the tan wrapping paper, Raleigh spread out the smaller stacks; each bound with strips of masking tape encircling fifty one-hundred-dollar bills. He shuffled the edge of one with his thumb.

"I think forty thousand should be sufficient change for my purposes," he declared aloud, although there was no one in the room to hear. He counted out eight of the smaller bundles, tossing them into the open suitcase, closing and locking the lid. "Now, two little ones for Lester, and five for Virgil. That should leave two hundred and fifteen thousand for yours truly."

Flicking his tongue like a bull snake in a research lab, he began counting the remaining larger bundles, placing them in the last empty case. After securing his share in the safe, he shuffled to his desk and extracted a pint bottle of Jack. Time for celebration.

"Uncle Raleigh," Bonnie Mae chirped over the intercom, "you have a call."

"Dammit, I told you I didn't want to be disturbed. Who is it?"

"You probably don't want to take it, but it's Leander Rutherford. Should I—"

Raleigh snatched up the phone. "Leander, you'd better be dead. Where the hell you been?"

"Sorry, Judge. I had a for sure bad wreck coming out to the lodge last night," Leander almost whispered. "I don't remember what I hit, but the next thing I know, I woke up in this hospital bed. It's the Lord's work that I wasn't killed dead."

Raleigh placed the bottle to his lips. "Is this another one of your lamebrain excuses, Leander?"

"No, Judge. Honest to God, I almost got killed. If someone hadn't come along and seen my car, the nurse said I would've drowned in another five minutes."

"How bad you hurt?"

"I got a concussion and a broke wrist. They're still running tests for internal bleeding and such. I don't feel too good, and my head hurts awful. I'm hooked up to all these tubes and wires."

"Where are you? What hospital?"

"Presbyterian, in Mobile."

"Where's Billy Cudjoe?"

"I can't find him, Judge. I sent Vivian down to Bayou le Batre the day I had my wreck, and he wasn't at his place. His old pickup was gone, and he ain't been to the office. He's just disappeared. Wasn't there someone killed in that fire at the pulp mill? Maybe it was him."

"I thought you told him the deal ova there was called off, like I told you to," Raleigh retorted.

"To tell the truth, Judge, I called him fifty times. He never answered his phone. I bet I left twenty messages. Surely he got one of 'em, but I can't say for sure. Maybe his phone was broke or something. He could've gone on and blew the place up. I just don't know, Judge, and that's the gospel truth."

Raleigh sat back at his desk and fumed.

"One good thing, I guess," Leander offered as an afterthought, "we'll still get the job to put the place back together, just like we planned in the first place. Bobby's still on board, ain't he?"

"I haven't talked to Bobby. Somebody said he had a heart attack or something. Leander, you've screwed up your last deal for me. I don't want to have nothing to do with you anymore. Every time I turn around—"

"But what about that leadership position in the party you promised? I've done everything you've asked me to do. Me an' Billy took care of that nigger girl like you wanted. I sent you all that money for Mr. Rifle's campaign. Judge, this ain't fair," Leander pleaded.

The judge took a deep breath and a more rational mind took control of his emotions.

"Leander, you're right, and I'm sorry for what I said. You've been a good friend and a good party man for a long time. We've just had a run of bad luck, that's all. I guess the pressure of the campaign and the things we've had to do to raise the money the party was demanding has made me a little ornery lately."

"Thanks, Judge. Those words make me feel a whole lot better. I'm sorry I couldn't find Billy. I don't know what happened to him. I promise you one thing: when I get out of here, I'll work twice as hard as ever to help you and the party any way I can."

"I know you will, Leander. I know you will. By the way, when are you getting out?"

"The doctor said he wouldn't know for sure until after all the tests come back tomorrow. I'm hoping maybe the day after."

"Okay. You just lay back and take things easy. Don't worry about Billy. If he shows up, we'll find out what he did. If he don't, well, they'll probably figure out he was the one killed in the fire. If that happens, someone'll come calling since he works for you and all. Just deny you know anything about anything. If he's dead, he won't be talking. Another thing, have you talked Jack Mitchell lately?"

"No, come to think of it, I haven't. That's unusual, too. He normally calls every day, but I ain't heard a word from him for some time. Why?"

"No reason. What's the name of his company?"

"You know, Judge. It's Jefferson Construction and—"

"I don't mean ova here, I mean in Houston."

"Oh, Mitchell Environmental," a confused Leander responded.

"Is that the whole name? No Inc. or Company or something."

"I think it's Mitchell Environmental Associates, Inc. Why you so interested in him, Judge?"

"Nothing important. His name came up in a conversation the other day and I couldn't remember. Of course, I only met him that one time at the bar in Mobile. You take care now, Leander. I'll send some flowers or candy or something ova there in the morning."

"That'd be mighty thoughtful, Judge."

CHAPTER 54

SHORT MONEY

Tina strolled around the deep end of the pool, a Corona bottle in one hand and a hand-rolled, fried tortilla in the other. She couldn't remember the last time she'd eaten. Hearing fast moving footsteps from the other side of the pool, she turned to witness two small, dark-skinned boys scampering across the patio followed by an older Hispanic woman—a housekeeper or babysitter, she assumed.

Showered and freshly shaven, Roberto opened a sliding glass door and walked out on the patio. He glanced at the scurrying trio and smiled.

"Slow down, boys. Mama Rosita will have the heart attack," he yelled as they entered the house through another door.

"Yours?" Tina asked, gliding toward the house.

"Yeah, Tomas and Angel. Named after two of my brothers," he explained, crossing himself. "They're twins but not identical. Your beer okay?"

"Yeah, it's fine. Where's your wife?"

"In hell, I hope," he answered casually.

"Not a marriage made in heaven, I take it."

"Hardly. She ran off with some dentist or something about a year ago. She's never even checked on the boys. First class bitch."

"That's too bad."

"Best thing that ever happened to me. She was all nice and sweet until we got married. Then, I couldn't do enough for her, buy her enough. I started to divorce her, but she got pregnant. When the doctor told us it was twins, and boys, I just had to put up with her shit. If I could find the guy she ran off with, I'd kiss him," he said with a smile. "How about you, you been married?"

Tina blushed lightly. "Mr. Santos, women in my profession aren't usually asked to the prom. I'd like to someday, you know, find someone nice, have kids, but that won't be for a long time, I'm afraid. The older lady, who's she?"

"My mother's baby sister. She and her husband stayed in Cuba after Castro and lived there for many years—long after my mother and father escaped to Miami. My uncle died of the cancer about ten years ago, so I brought her to the states. She's an illegal, but no one's ever come looking. She took care of my mother until she became too much for her to handle, so I moved her in here. Worked out well for her, the children, and me. She likes for me to call her Mama. I don't know why, but I don't mind."

Tina was surprised and touched that a drug dealer could talk so affectionately and openly about his life.

"Okay. I feel better after the shower. I didn't ask you, but would you like to clean up?" he inquired while putting ice cubes in a glass from the bar in the gazebo.

"Yeah, I'd like that a lot. I've been in these same clothes for I don't know how long. My wardrobe's pretty limited, but at least my other shorts are clean."

"I have a call or two to make. Why don't you go into the guestroom—it's through the main door and down the hall to the left. I'll have a Cuba Libre ready when you return. You have a place to stay?"

"Mr. Santos, I've never been in Miami in my life, and Manual didn't exactly give me time to make a reservation at the Ritz."

Roberto laughed. "You're right. Stupid question, good answer. Why don't you stay here? The sheets are clean, and Mama's a good cook. There's a whole closet full of clothes across the hall from the guestroom. Pick out anything you want. I don't think my ex-wife will be around anytime soon to collect them."

Thirty minutes and four phone calls later, Tina stepped back onto the patio. Her brown hair touched her shoulders, the borrowed white crepe dress accentuated her green eyes. Instead of fuck-me-pumps, she wore flat, toeless sandals. For the first time since she could remember, she didn't feel like a whore.

"My, my, Miss Tina. You look much different," Roberto exclaimed and meant it.

"Thanks. There were so many dresses to choose from. You sure you don't mind me wearing it?"

"Hell, no. That old bitch never looked so good on her best day. Here's your drink." He extended a tall glass to her, properly proportioned with rum and cola.

"Thanks, Mr. Santos."

"Roberto. Call me Roberto."

"Okay, Roberto. You can call me Mary or Mary Susan. My real name's Mary Susan Yokum."

Roberto nodded. "In that dress, Mary Susan fits a whole lot better than Tina." Then his demeanor changed. "Where is the paper you were reading earlier?"

"In my backpack, in the guest room."

"Would you mind getting it? I think I must read it now."

Mary Susan returned with the Tuesday addition of the *Mobile Register*, handing it to Roberto.

He glanced at the picture on the front page. "That was a big fire, looks like."

He then began flipping the pages.

"Julio's article is on page five of the second section," she offered.

He walked to a grouping of chairs beside a deck table with a green umbrella. Sitting, he tossed all but one section of the paper down beside him. After finding the page he was looking for, he placed it on the table. Mary Susan, who had taken the seat next to him, pointed to the headline. Roberto took a deep breath, exhaled slowly, and began to read. She nervously circled her forefinger around the rim of her glass.

He read the article twice, crossing himself each time he read the words, "the suspect was shot while attacking Judge Pendleton in his cell." Finally, he sat back in his chair, placing his palms together and cupping them over his nose and mouth.

"Roberto, there's something—"

He extended a palm in her direction as if to say, "Please don't say anything right now."

Mary Susan remained silent.

After an uncomfortable two minutes, Roberto picked up his cell phone and dialed a familiar number.

"Manuel, the paper says they recovered only two-hundred-thousand dollars. Where's the rest of the money?"

"How much should there have been, big brother? You said, but I don't remember."

"Almost a million. Why have you not told me this?" Roberto's voice was cold.

"You said you weren't ready to discuss it only half an hour ago. Do you think Shooter could have—"

"Shooter's not stupid. He'd know I'd kill him with my own hands. No, I think the *policia* would be the thieves. If I'm right, Julio wasn't trying to escape. He was killed for the money."

CHAPTER 55

FACT AND SPECULATION

"Okay, let's see what we've got," Fred announced as five other agents seated themselves around the small conference table. "Let's start with the last tapes and work backward."

Special Agent Robert Cagle had been assigned the embezzlement and illegal campaign contribution issues and was the first to report.

"The last conversation between Rutherford and Pendleton seem to corroborate the money going from Jefferson Construction to R&P Materials was intended for Lawrence Rifle's campaign. We already know it was embezzled from the information Mr. Mitchell provided. The Pendleton-Rifle tapes confirm money was sent, but suggest it was returned. We still don't know if a bank or the postal service was involved in either transfer. In my opinion, however, we have enough to go after a warrant for the judge and Leander Rutherford for both embezzlement and illegal campaign contributions right now, and if we can intercept the money transfer discussed in the second Rifle tape, we'll have him, too."

"I agree, Bob, but I want to wait on the transfer before we move. Who's next? How about the Bitterman connection? Gene, what do you have?"

Eugene Booker looked at his notes. "There's not a doubt in my mind that Bitterman is involved with the judge in some way. He even slipped when we interviewed him and implied the judge set up the plant tour for Rutherford and Cudjoe. The tapes infer that the deal being called off was the plant fire at the pulp mill, and Cudjoe apparently didn't get the message. I think if we lean on Bitterman, he'll break and we'll have a co-conspirator to corroborate that the fire was indirectly the judge's work and, hopefully, he'll tell us why they did it. There are some unanswered questions. What was the bit about money being paid to Harley Logginfield? What was it for? And the reference to some pictures being delivered by Jim Bob Davis. I can't find a direct connection to any of that and the fire, but my gut tells me it's all related. When we asked Bitterman about Jim Bob, he went stone silent. He wouldn't talk to us anymore."

"He may not have anything to do with the fire, but this Davis guy's in the middle of something and the judge's calling the shots," Fred speculated. "I have a bad feeling about Jane Tremont. I think Davis knows more about her than he's telling. He's talked to the judge about sticking to his story on two occasions, and I believe he's the link to what happened to her. Rutherford's reference to him and Cudjoe 'taking care of that nig—' I can't say it…that black girl, worries me a lot. I pray to God he wasn't referring to Janie, but everything points in that direction. I just don't know when or what to tell Lawton. I can't find a good scenario to paint with the information we have, but I can't find anything conclusive either. It's all speculation. When do we get the lab reports back on the dead guy at the plant?"

"We should have something by morning," agent Booker responded. "I checked before the meeting and the lab said they were trying to confirm their dental findings with DNA."

Fred nodded. "Good, but there is another area we haven't discussed. I talked to the drug enforcement boys late this afternoon and the name Santos hit one of their hot buttons in Miami. A Roberto Santos has been suspected of being involved in cocaine distribution in south Florida for some time, but they've never been able to pin anything on him. They did some checking, and he has a younger brother named Julio. They haven't confirmed if he's the same Julio Santos as the one shot in the Washington County jail last Saturday night, but it all seems too coincidental. If Santos was carrying more money than the sheriff reported, and this Santos connection hooks up, we could have another charge to consider with Pendleton. Lester Holmboe and Sheriff Crawford could also be implicated. There are so many different angles to this situation, I have trouble keeping everything and everybody in place, but Raleigh Pendleton is right in the middle of all of it."

"I know one thing," Eugene Booker added. "If your speculation about the Santos killing is true and he's the brother of a drug dealer, I wouldn't want to be Pendleton, Crawford, or Holmboe if the brother comes to the same conclusion. We won't have to worry about enough evidence for an indictment against the judge. He'll not live long enough for us to prosecute him. Maybe we should take him into protective custody?"

"If he were a good guy, I'd consider it," Fred responded. "But he's dirty and we know it. He'll just have to take his chances with the Miami boys. Let's just work fast and hope we can beat them to him. Now, let's get to work and nail these suckers, as Lawton would say."

"And you say she's been saying the same thing over and over again ever since this started this morning?" Lawton asked.

"According to Aaron, she woke him up screaming while I was outside working in the flower beds," Barbara answered. "She was crying and gasping for air, clawing at her face—just like she used to do only she was screaming, 'That's him, Aunt Lizzie. That's him, Aunt Lizzie.' She wouldn't stop. They gave her a sedative after we got here, and she went to sleep, but when she woke up, she started up again."

"Do we know what set her off? What was she doing?"

"Aaron said her television was on the *Today* show, and there were magazines and the morning paper all over the floor. It could've been either something she saw on TV or something in one of the articles, or it could've been just something in her mind," Barbara speculated. "Any word today about Janie?"

Lawton pursed his lips and shook his head. "Is Aaron back at the house now?"

"He was pretty shaken up. He hasn't seen one of her fits since he was a little boy. Bad memories, I guess. He left the hospital shortly before you got here."

Lawton reached into his pocket, retrieving his cell phone. He waited quietly while it rang.

"Aaron, you okay, son?" Lawton said when the home phone was answered. He listened.

"If you're up to it, I'd like for you to gather up all the magazines and papers in Aunt Sally's room and bring them to the hospital."

CHAPTER 56
THE ROUNDUP

A lazy sprinkler filled the air with tiny jets of water, creating a kaleidoscope of color as the mid-morning sun refracted each droplet. The oscillating arm positioned on one side of the courthouse lawn transformed the tepid water into a light vapor as it fell on the thick bermuda surface. Two small children, a boy and a girl, laughed as they hurdled through the refreshing spray while a crossbred mutt barked and snapped playfully at their heels.

Lester, oblivious to the activity only yards away, marched over the concrete walkway leading from the steps of the courthouse. His face was flushed, his uniform wet, but not the result of the heat and manmade humidity surrounding him. Excitement consumed his mind, his body responding as if he'd just finished a marathon. Two inch-thick bundles, secured and hidden in the slash pocket of his uniform trousers, felt hot against his upper thigh. He had been summoned to Raleigh's office at 9:30 and awarded the promised bonus for a job well done and a secret never to be divulged.

Filled with himself, he eased his Cherokee into traffic, turning from Main Street onto County Road 423 to continue his morning patrol. After travelling several miles south, he could no longer control his curiosity. Turning off the roadway, he stopped his vehicle and removed the sealed envelope which bore the name and office address of the county probate judge. Using the blade of his pocketknife, he sliced beneath the flap and removed his payoff. He sat motionless for several minutes, thumbing the edges of the bundles and dreaming of the opportunities this kind of wealth represented. The crackling of the radio invaded his reverie. He monitored a routine call for the sheriff, while carefully replacing the two bundles in the envelope. He tossed it in the passenger's seat.

Pulling back onto the highway, he drove to his favorite speed trap located four miles from the Clarke County line. He had sat behind the massive river oak for only a few minutes when a dark vehicle flashed by at over eighty miles per hour. Lester's hands, eyes, and feet simultaneously went into action as the cruiser's powerful engine roared. Flying dust and gravel gave witness to the swiftness of his entry onto the paved surface. The bubble light flashed and the siren wailed while adrenaline began to pulse through every muscle in his body.

The chase lasted an unusually short distance as Lester quickly closed the gap between the speeding vehicles. He saw the brake lights solidly engaged within seconds of his entry into the chase. He smiled self-confidently when the larger vehicle's right turn indicator began to blink and the front tires turned onto the narrow shoulder.

Instinctively reaching for the radio microphone to report the license plate number, he was both surprised and irritated when he realized the numbers and letters were caked with mud, rendering them unidentifiable. Indignantly, he replaced the mike, exited his cruiser, and marched toward the driver's window.

As he approached, both the front and rear windows lowered, providing visual access to the passenger area of the vehicle. There was only one occupant. Moving past the rear of the black Suburban, his stomach muscles tightened when the horn unexpectedly sounded, masking the metallic click of the rear panel door opening.

A large Hispanic man exited the driver's door, apologizing emphatically, "Sorry for honking the horn, *senor*. It was an accident."

"Get your hands above your head!" ordered Lester in his deepest voice. "Your license plate is—"

The blow to the back of his neck was quick and effective. Lester's knees buckled and his body fell to the shoulder. He didn't feel the wetness or sense the contempt when Manuel spit in his face as it sank toward the asphalt surface.

"Good work, Bugger," Manny said, looking up and down the highway.

Bugger was already placing his massive hands under Lester's armpits. Within a few seconds, the body of the under sheriff of Washington County was lying face down in the rear of the Suburban, unconscious, with his handcuffs binding his wrists to a fixed seat brace.

The odor of disinfectant clung to the air while the two women intermittently eyed one another. For Irene Rutherford, an occasional peek toward the other waiting room occupant was quizzical. She had no idea who the other woman was, but her presence unnerved her.

Vivian Thompson, on the other hand, knew Irene well, or at least, she knew who she was. Her glances were more frequent and her emotions toward her perceived adversary ran more in the direction of contempt. They were separated by a wooden-veneer coffee table, cluttered with outdated magazines, tattered coloring books, and a copy of the previous day's *Mobile Register*.

In his drugged state, Leander had advised both of his ladies he was scheduled to be released by noon and had requested transport. Fortunately, for both women, an uncomfortable situation would be avoided as two men in dark business suits accompanied a physician down the hall toward Leander's room.

"Mr. Rutherford, how do we feel this morning?" the young resident asked while scrutinizing his chart.

"I feel great, Doc," Leander replied. "No problems with the tests you run?"

"No, everything looks fine. Now, you'll have to take it easy for the next couple of weeks. No alcohol until you finish your medicine, no physical activity—"

"How about rough sex?" Leander chortled with a wink.

The young physician looked at him curiously. "I'm not sure what you mean by 'rough,' but I'd suggest you take it easy. It would help if you'd quit smoking, too."

Before Leander could respond, there was a sharp knock at the door. Without invitation, the two men in suits entered.

"Everything okay, Dr. Featherstone?" one of them asked.

"He can be released as far as I'm concerned," the young doctor replied.

"Good. Leander Rutherford, I'm Special Agent Cagle with the FBI, and you're under arrest. In accordance with state and federal law, i'm required to read you your rights. You have the right to remain silent. Anything you say…"

During the time the Miranda card was read, and perhaps for the first time in his life, Leander was speechless.

Jim Bob had awoken unusually early that day. Feelings of insecurity had dominated his thoughts since his last interview with the FBI. While he was certain there was little chance of the girl's body being recovered, he was even more certain that Agent Carleton didn't believe his story. Light activity during the graveyard shift had allowed his mind to dwell on Jane Tremont and the likelihood of his being charged with her disappearance. That thought and native ignorance had elevated his emotions to paranoia by 11:00 A.M. His hands were shaking as he rose from his bed and walked down the narrow hallway to the kitchen.

"Jimmy, why're you up so early?" Geraldine asked while she ironed a crease into a pair of his uniform trousers. The swelling in her face was gone but her eye socket and cheek were still discolored with a greenish-yellow hue. "You want some lunch?"

"No, I need a beer," he replied, clad in his white briefs and ribbed undershirt.

"Don't you think it's a little early in the day for that? Let me make you something. How about some cornbread and beans? I cooked a fresh pot last night."

"Dammit, Geraldine, I get so tired of your nagging. If I wanted something to eat, I'd tell you. Now leave me alone and get on with your chores," he snapped, opening the refrigerator door. "Where's the beer? I bought a six-pack yesterday, and it ain't here."

"Jimmy, you drank it all before you went on duty last night," she responded cautiously. "Remember, you said you'd had a bad talk with Harley down at the station, and you were all keyed up."

"The hell I did. I know you been pouring out my beer for a long time." His eyes cut sharply toward her. "If I ever catch you messing with my stuff again, I'll beat your ugly face in for good."

"I told you I'd kill you if you ever touch her again!" Jimbo barked from the screen door leading from the porch to the kitchen.

Jim Bob looked at his son and glared. Before he could respond, the phone rang.

"It's for you, Jimmy," announced Geraldine, looking at Jimbo with a pleading expression. "It's Harley."

Jim Bob snatched the phone from her hand. "Hello!"

"Davis, I want you down here in fifteen minutes," Harley commanded. "I got those two FBI men back in here, and I'm getting tired of this shit. Hell, they're even asking me about some money I supposedly got from that no account judge friend of yours. Now, get down here and get this problem you created over with. You got one more chance before I put you on suspension. Move your ass!"

Jim Bob slammed down the phone.

"Fuck!" he screamed and walked to the bedroom.

When he walked into the sheriff's office dressed in jeans, boots, and a freshly pressed white tee shirt, no one said a word to him. The eyes of the radio dispatcher and two deputies followed him as he marched down the hall toward his boss's office. Three minutes later, he returned, escorted by two men in dark suits. Harley followed, shaking his head. The handcuffs restraining his wrists confirmed that Jim Bob was under arrest.

Johnny loaded the two canvas suitcases in the trunk of Raleigh's Cadillac while the judge opened the driver's side door.

"You sure you don't want me to drive you, Judge?" Johnny asked.

"No, this's something I need to do by myself. Besides, you need to get ready to run that little errand I wanted you to take care of."

"I got plenty of time, Judge. I don't need to leave until this evening," Johnny replied.

"You just get ready and remember what I told you to do."

Johnny shrugged his shoulders as Raleigh backed his car from the parking spot that read "Reserved for Probate Judge."

Twenty-five minutes later, the Cadillac pulled into the gravel parking lot outside of Celia's Café. Raleigh's eyes scanned the area, searching for anything unusual. Everything seemed normal. A red ten-year-old pickup and a light green Lexus were the only other vehicles present. Raleigh had picked 10:30 for this rendezvous, knowing the morning breakfast and coffee crowd should have returned to work, tending to morning chores, and the luncheon customers wouldn't gather for another hour. He wheeled in beside the Lexus.

"Morning, Judge Pendleton. I'm Charles Rifle," announced a tall, slender man in a pair of tan khakis and crimson golf shirt bearing the logo of the University of Alabama. Since Raleigh had never met the younger brother of the gubernatorial hopeful, his attire had been discussed for reasons of security and identification.

"Hell, I wouldn't have insisted on what you're wearing if I knew how much you look like your brother," Raleigh responded. "Let's have a seat. You got a table?"

"No, sir. I just got here a minute or so before you did. How about this table here?" offered the younger Rifle.

Raleigh surveyed the room. A young man with closely cropped sideburns and a red Co-op cap sat on one of the counter stools sipping coffee. His boots were new and his blue button-down shirt was a little too starched, but Raleigh didn't notice such subtle details. Always cautious, however, Raleigh pointed toward the far corner of the establishment.

"Let's take that one ova there. It's my table." He looked through the order-out window separating the counter area from the kitchen and saw a familiar face. "Minnie darling, why don't you bring me a cup of my special and two cups of coffee."

Minnie squinted though the small opening, nodded, and disappeared.

After Raleigh and Charles seated themselves and were served, they talked, keeping their voices only slightly louder than whispers. Five minutes later, they arose and walked toward the door. Raleigh placed a ten-dollar bill on the glass counter by the cash register.

The gravel shifted beneath their feet as they approached their vehicles. Both appraised their surroundings, sensitive to anything unusual or suspicious. Satisfied, Raleigh pushed a button on the remote controller attached to his key ring. Charles Rifle followed suit.

"Now, you tell your brother I may be able to raise a little more. I got one or two more irons in the fire. I'll stay in touch."

"Lawrence wanted me to tell you how much he appreciates your trust, and he won't forget it," Charles Rifle responded.

Raleigh smiled. "I know Lawrence always keeps his promises. He's a good party man, and he'll make a fine governor. Now, there it is, five hundred and forty thousand dollars in cash," the judge proclaimed, pointing toward his open trunk.

Charles lifted the two suitcases and placed them in the truck of his car.

The screeching of rubber on pavement broke the mid-morning silence as two dark sedans slid into the parking lot. Gravel and dust erupted beneath the tires only feet from the bewildered men. Out of the corner of his eye, Raleigh saw movement and heard the door to the café slam as the young man in the red cap rushed in his direction.

Instinctively, Charles turned and began to run away from the dust-filled air toward a dense stand of pine trees only twenty yards away. His legs stopped moving, however, as four men, one carrying a video camera, emerged from beneath the canopy of shade and cover the trees had provided.

Fred Carleton walked past the younger Rifle, knowing his trailing subordinates would detain him.

"Raleigh A. Pendleton, you're under arrest for illegal campaign contributions, RICO violations, embezzlement, arson, murder, and complicity in the kidnapping and possible murder of Jane Tremont. Eugene, read him his rights. I don't have the stomach for it." Normally professional and courteous in such situations, Fred spit each word, his emotions controlling his delivery.

As Special Agent Eugene Booker began reading from the card, Fred retrieved his cell phone and made a call. After completing the short command, he walked to the rear bumper of the Cadillac, removing a voice-activated recorder which had been magnetically attached a few minutes earlier.

Lawrence Rifle sat in his office, reading the text of a speech he would be presenting to the Dothan, Alabama teacher's association that evening. He glanced at his watch. *Charlie should be calling any time now*, he thought.

The light on his intercom button illuminated and he heard the familiar buzz. Picking up the receiver he heard his secretary announce, "Mr. Rifle, there are two gentlemen from the FBI here to see you."

CHAPTER 57
WHO'S WHO

Even though the last smoldering timbers had been extinguished thirty hours earlier, the acrid smell of the destroyed building was still nauseating. The vapors burned his eyes and attacked his nasal passages. This was the second time Bobby Bitterman had viewed the site of the explosion and fire that had devastated his plant two and a half days earlier. Yellow crime scene tape separated him from the hooded figures in protective suits who were probing the ruins. The blue and yellow patches on their backs read "FBI."

Feeling helpless and vulnerable, he turned, proceeding away from the ruins toward the administration building and the office that would never seem the same again. His only respite from the unpleasant reality of his life had occurred that morning when he kissed and hugged his children before they departed with Myrtle in the family station wagon for a visit to her parents in Birmingham. For the next five days, he would be free of her never-ending nagging and sullen disposition.

Before reaching the door of the building, he glanced at his watch, and noted the time; although, time had become an irrelevant dimension for him. After his release from the hospital the evening before, he had lain on the sofa, staring at the television, but his mind had been lost in an abyss filled with dead young black girls and unidentified bodies lying on cold slabs in a morgue. *Surely, if there's a Hell, I'm living in it*, he had thought to himself several times before closing his eyes and drifting into dreams too grisly to remember.

Just as his hand touched the doorknob, he heard the sound of a car's engine pulling through the open gate. Recognizing the face of one of the FBI agents, he sighed, turned his back to the car, and entered the building. A minute later, Eugene Booker and Fred Carleton were seated in his office.

"Mr. Bitterman, I hope you've recovered satisfactorily from your, eh, it wasn't a heart attack, as I understand it," Fred offered in a cordial manner.

"They said it was stress. I don't think they know for sure, but I feel better now," Bobby replied.

"We came by to see if we could tie up some loose ends. You might be interested to know that we arrested Raleigh Pendleton, Leander Rutherford, Jim Bob Davis, and Lawrence Rifle this morning. They'll all be arraigned, probably tomorrow morning, on charges ranging from arson to murder and a lot it between."

Bobby held his breath and stared at the wall directly above Fred. He couldn't make eye contact, but he didn't want his reaction to this news to betray the rush of panic he felt.

"This doesn't seem to surprise you, Mr. Bitterman," Fred pressed.

Refocusing on his interrogator, Bobby asked, "Should it? There's been a shit load of stuff going on around here, and someone has to be blamed. You did say arson and murder, didn't you?"

"Yeah. We believe the fire here in your plant was set on purpose. We believe the person actually striking the match, so to speak, was Billy Cudjoe, and we've issued a warrant for his arrest as well. As of this point in time, we haven't been able to determine his whereabouts."

"I thought someone said he could be the guy who was killed in the fire."

"Who said that, Mr. Bitterman? We've never made public such an allegation or belief. Who did you talk to who suggested the deceased was Mr. Cudjoe?"

Bobby tried to hide his discomfort but failed. His right leg began to fidget, and he shifted uncomfortably in his chair.

"I can't remember, I just thought someone said that. I thought maybe it was you, Agent Booker?"

Eugene Booker maintained a solemn expression and slowly shook his head.

"Which reminds me, Mr. Bitterman, one of the reasons we drove up here was to see if you could help us find the surviving family of one of your employees—a Mr. Harvey Greenville. It was Mr. Greeenville's body that was recovered from the fire."

Bobby made no attempt to hide his shock. "That can't be true. Harvey went on vacation Friday after his shift was over. It can't be Harvey."

"Well, the lab was able to match his dental records. We took a DNA sample from hair in a hairbrush we collected from his home. The DNA matched. There's no doubt the person killed in the fire was Harvey Greenville. I assume you knew him."

Bobby closed his eyes, his chin dropped to his chest, and he sighed. "Harvey worked here longer than I have. He was my first supervisor—gave me my first job here at the plant. He even loaned me some money to help me go to night school. Yeah, I knew Harvey well."

"Good. Then you should be able to help us with his next of kin. We haven't had any luck running down any family members." Fred continued the assault.

"Harvey didn't have any family. His wife died three years ago. They didn't have any children. She could've had a brother or sister, but I never heard her or Harvey talk about any. Harvey had one brother, but he was killed in Korea. He was never married. I don't thing there's any family anywhere."

"That makes sense. Have any idea why Mr. Greenville was at the plant at three o'clock in the morning? If he were going on vacation, as you say, why do you think he'd be at the plant at such an early hour?"

Bobby shrugged.

"Where were you at that time, Mr. Bitterman?"

"Surely you don't think—you couldn't be thinking I had anything to do with Harvey's death. He was like a second father to me. You people are nuts! I think you'd better leave. I'm through answering any questions. If you want anything more from me, you'll have to contact my lawyer," he announced defiantly.

"Okay, who's your lawyer?" Fred asked flatly, pulling a pen and a notepad from his pocket. "You might be interested to know that we believe you were somehow involved with Raleigh Pendleton, Leander Rutherford, and Billy Cudjoe in the explosion that caused the fire here at the plant. If that's true, you're an accomplice in the murder of Harvey Greenville. We also believe you, Pendleton, and Jim Bob Davis were involved in the disappearance of Jane Tremont. We're putting those pieces together, too. One of your buddies will break and fill in the blanks. The first one to flinch will become a state's witness and get a deal, while the rest of you spend the remainder of your lives on death row. Were you being blackmailed, Mr. Bitterman?"

Bobby sat quietly, staring at the floor.

Fred and Eugene stood up.

"Have it your way, Mr. Bitterman. By the way, your company provides life insurance policies for all of its employees. Isn't that correct, Mr. Bitterman?"

Again, Bobby didn't respond.

"It might interest you to know that Harvey Greenville's policy listed you as his sole beneficiary. According to your home office, Mr. Greenville's untimely demise left you with over a hundred thousand dollars. We have tapes suggesting you and Judge Pendleton were trying to raise money. Is that why you had the plant burned? Is that why Harvey Greenville was there at such an odd hour? See how it all looks, Mr. Bitterman? You're the only one around with a clear motive for this whole mess."

"Get the hell out of here!" Bobby screamed. His eyes were wild and his fists clinched as he leaped up from his chair. "Get the fuck out of my office!"

"We're leaving for now, Mr. Bitterman, but you can bet that hundred thousand you just earned that we'll be back, and we'll have a warrant."

Lawton sat on the floor of the private room into which Sally had been moved shortly after dinner. The doctors were satisfied the apex of the seizure had been reached and her vital signs indicated she was back to a more normal level of emotional and physical stability—normal for Sally, given her history.

He had scanned each of the six magazines, but nothing of interest had caught his eye. While he considered this exercise to be futile, it kept his mind from dwelling on his daughter and imagining the worst of situations she might have endured at the hands of men whose hearts were filled with racial hatred.

As he picked up the Tuesday edition of the *Mobile Register*, he heard shuffling and looked up from the floor. The glazed eyes of his sister were open and fixed in his direction, although not directly at him. Standing, he gently caressed the top of her head.

"How's my baby sister feeling?" he whispered.

There was no response, no change in expression, no eye movement—nothing.

"What got you all worked up, Sally girl?" he continued. "Was it something you saw? Was it something on television?"

With the newspaper still in hand, he scooted a molded plastic chair beside her bed and sat down, holding the front page in front of her unresponsive face. He watched her eyes for any change or movement as he flipped from one page to the next.

When he turned to the fifth pages of section B, he saw it. A quick blink, and then another. Lawton quickly tilted his head, his eyes darting from headline to headline. In the lower left-hand corner, a black-and-white photograph caught his attention. The face of Raleigh Pendleton seemed to jump from the page. *We arrested your sorry ass this morning, sucker!*

Without warning, a deep guttural sound, more animal-like than human, began to build in Sally's throat. Her eyes began to blink rapidly and her breathing became labored. Her chest heaved and her body began to writhe between the hospital sheets. Beads of perspiration popped out over her face.

"NO-O-O-O-O!" she screamed.

Lawton looked into the terrified face of his sister.

"What have I done?" he cried out.

"That's him, Aunt Lizzie! That's him, Aunt Lizzie!" Her shrill chant echoed around the room.

"What do you mean, Sally girl?" he pleaded, his eyes frantically searching for the controller that would summon aid from the nurses station.

As quickly as it had started, the screaming stopped and eyes, dead for over thirty-five years, began to focus. He first became aware of the metamorphosis when he felt a soft hand take his. Looking down on a face that had been unresponsive for so long, he saw expression.

"Bubby," she whispered with a weak smile, "where's Janie?"

Lawton began to sob.

CHAPTER 58
THE ARRAIGNMENT

Three men and three attorneys sat behind an oaken table in Courtroom B of the federal courthouse in Mobile. I was in the gallery seated between Lawton and Johnson Calhoun. Lawton and I had met earlier for a quick breakfast and he'd described the awakening of Sally Tremont and the identification she'd made of the murderer of Aaron and Elizabeth Collins. *What a twisted world these people down here live in*, I had thought.

After entering the courtroom that morning and seeing Raleigh Pendleton and his merry men in the custody of the government, I felt a sense of exhilaration and pride. The wheels of justice were beginning to grind against these contemptuous human beings, and I had been the catalyst that had initially tilted the scales; although, somewhat by accident, I must confess.

"All rise," the bailiff chanted in a dull voice as a solid core door behind the witness stand opened. A middle-aged man in a black robe briskly moved behind the wooden framework to a pulpit elevated about five feet above the floor of the courtroom.

"Just like on television," I whispered in Lawton's direction.

"You never been in a courtroom before, Jack?" Lawton responded, also whispering.

"Only during my divorce, but that was more like going to the principal's office."

The judge interrupted. "Please be seated."

The shuffling of chairs and feet slowly abated as the surprisingly young-looking adjudicator opened a file and scanned its contents.

"It appears we have several charges and several defendants to deal with today, so let's get started."

"If it please the court, your honor, may I offer a suggestion which would likely expedite the matters before the court this morning?" announced a silver-haired man seated next to Raleigh.

"Please identify yourself for the record," the judge responded.

"Please let the record show that I am Felton B. Abercrombie, attorney-at-law, representing Judge Raleigh A. Pendleton."

I leaned to my left and whispered to Calhoun, "Is he any good?"

"Hard to say. He's a high-priced gunslinger. I've been up against him several times and been on the same side a couple. One thing for sure, he'll put on one helluva show before it's all over. He's from Birmingham but is licensed to practice in several states. I'll say one thing, there are several guys around I'd rather go up against when we get to the civil actions," Calhoun replied.

"What say you, Mr. Abercrombie?" the judge prodded.

"Naturally, my fellow members of the bar will want their representations made as a matter of record, but I've been authorized to make the following statement on behalf of all the defendants with concurrence of their counsel."

"Very well, let's hear it."

"All of the defendants plead not guilty to any and all charges levied against them by the government. While it would be legally expeditious to move for dismissal of all charges, we recognize that such a motion would be without precedent, and therefore, we will waive such right to said motion until the proper time. We are confident the charges against the defendants are without legal merit; that the charges have been filed as a fishing expedition by an ambitious federal prosecutor whose staff is emotionally and irrationally tied to one of the charges levied; and, lastly, if your honor should determine the charges carry sufficient merit to be further considered, all of the defendants are prominent members of their respective communities and represent no flight risk. We would therefore request that they be released on there own recognizance during the pendancy of these and any continuing proceedings. One final and important point: if your honor will examine all of the charges, we believe you will conclude, as we have, that this court is not the proper venue for any of the charges levied. We will be submitting a motion to have the charges removed to the proper jurisdictions as soon as practicable. Thank you, your honor."

"Would the government like to respond?"

"We would, your honor," answered Charles Schumaker. "First, I will not dignify Mr. Abercrombie's allegation by commenting about my office being emotionally tied or influenced by the charges made. Secondly, the court should be advised that a fourth defendant has been charged in some of the matters before the court this morning, a Mr. Lawrence Rifle, but Mr. Rifle conveniently was taken ill during the night and is, therefore, not present this morning. Thirdly, the court should be advised that there is an outstanding warrant, yet to be served, against one William R. Cudjoe, a known associate and co-conspirator of all of the accused, save Mr. Rifle. Fourth, two of the charges levied are capital charges, and there is sufficient legal precedent in such cases to remand defendants charged in capital cases to the court's custody without bail until all legal proceedings have been judicially determined. Fifth, the court should be advised that these defendants and their activities are the focus of an on-going investigation by the Justice Department and further charges, including additional capital charges, could be forthcoming against some or all of the defendants. Lastly, as to the jurisdictional issue, the government assumes Mr. Abercrombie and the other distinguished officers of the court represented here are familiar with the federal RICO statutes. The government will prove that all the acts of the parties are related and part of an ongoing pattern of illegal actions, which would, by statute, properly place these proceedings under federal jurisdiction. Thank you, your honor."

The courtroom was silent while the judge flipped through his files.

"That was pretty convincing, I thought," I said to Lawton but loud enough for Calhoun to hear.

Calhoun replied first, "Charlie did a good job, but I doubt Judge Black will order them held without bail."

Lawton added, "If I were Davis and Rutherford, I'd demand witness protection status. With what we've got so far, the biggest problem Pendleton has is if one of them cracks and makes a deal. And, I assure you, that dangerous old man knows it. Cudjoe is also on his hit list, Bobby Bitterman as well. If I were any of them, I'd rather take my chances with the legal system than with Raleigh Pendleton."

"Why didn't your boss point that out?" I asked, thinking it a good question.

Both attorneys laughed quietly. Lawton shook his head. Judge Black saved me from my next apparently stupid question.

"Gentlemen, the court has considered all the arguments and orders as follows: all charges will be directed to the Grand Jury which is set to convene in two weeks; no defendant shall be questioned without benefit of counsel;

and bail for each defendant will be set at two hundred and fifty thousand dollars."

A murmur began to build around the courtroom. Several reporters quickly exited. In the midst of all the mumbling, my cell phone rang.

"Who the hell brought a phone into my courtroom," bellowed his honor, Ronald Black.

The room became so quiet that a mouse fart would have sounded like an atomic explosion. I fumbled with the buttons, trying to turn the power off. It rang again, and I could feel the eyes of everyone in the courtroom focus on me.

"Sir—you in the gallery. Stand up!" the judge roared.

After finally killing the power by removing the battery, I stood, red-faced, and looked to the front of the room.

"Identify yourself."

"My name is Jack Mitchell," I mumbled.

"Speak up, sir."

"Jack Mitchell!" I announced a little louder.

"Mr. Mitchell, unless you're blind or can demonstrate you are legally incompetent, you're getting ready to spend some time in our holding facility. Did you not see the sign outside? It clearly says, NO CELL PHONES ALLOWED IN THE COURTROOM! What say you?"

"I…I didn't even know I had it with me, your honor. I thought I'd left it in my car," I stuttered. "I…I'm terribly sorry, sir."

Before the judge could order me caned, Johnson Calhoun came to my rescue.

"Your honor, Mr. Mitchell is my client, and I can assure you he meant no disrespect to the court."

"What's your interest here today, Mr. Calhoun?"

"My client has a vested interest in the outcome of these and the following proceedings. If not for him courageously coming forward several weeks ago, these men standing before you might still be free and unchallenged for the illegal acts with which they have been properly charged. Mr. Mitchell has been financially harmed in a significant way by their activities, and we will file civil actions against three of the defendants at the appropriate time. As for the cell phone, it was merely an oversight, a blunder. I have known Mr. Mitchell for many years and have never known him to be disrespectful in any situation," embellished Calhoun in his eloquent manner. "We beg your honor's forgiveness and leniency."

Federal Judge Ronald Black sat in silence for over a minute. During that time, most of the eyes in the courtroom lost interest in me and began to wander about, save one set. Raleigh Pendleton glared into my eyes with more contempt than I've ever witnessed. I stared defiantly back into his. Standing there, while my fate for the next twenty-four hours was being considered from the bench, I felt rage building inside. Prior to that moment, Judge Raleigh A. Pendleton was just a fat blowhard I'd met a few years back in a bar in Mobile. While I knew he was a bad man, it was during that period of silence and visual confrontation I realized what a dangerous person he truly was.

"Mr. Calhoun," the judge proclaimed, breaking the silence, "the court has decided to grant leniency to your client and not issue a contempt order, as would normally be the case. Please take that damn device away from him and instruct him never to be disrespectful in my court again."

"Thank you, your honor," Calhoun responded.

While bail bondsmen lined up to offer their services to the three defendants, Lawton, Calhoun, and I exited the courtroom.

"Damn, I'm sorry, guys. I really thought I'd left the phone in the car. Thanks for saving me, Johnson."

Again, both attorneys laughed.

"What's so funny? Really, that scared the shit out of me. He was going to put me in jail."

Johnson replied, "Judge Black wouldn't have put you in jail. He's a stickler for controlling his courtroom, but he said all that shit just to make a point with everyone. I'll call him this afternoon or he'll call me at home tonight, and we'll have a good laugh. By the way, who was the call from?"

I shook my head. "Hell, I don't know. I was so busy trying to turn the damn thing off I didn't bother to check the I.D. Let me look."

I returned the battery to the phone and checked for messages.

"Shit, it's my ex-wife," I proclaimed after hearing her recorded voice. I pressed the end button and my eyes grew wild.

"What's wrong, Jack?" Lawton asked, reading the emotion in my face.

"I've got to go…I…I have to get back home. Someone tried to kidnap Michael, and Jackson's in the hospital."

267

CHAPTER 59
BACK TO SHOOTER'S

Manuel watched from the passengers' lounge of Jet-A-Way as the Cessna touched down on the north-south runway at McCarron Field. He absently massaged a swollen knuckle, the cost of the single blow he had delivered to the jaw of Lester Holmboe. While Roberto had been explicit in his instructions that the deputy was not to be harmed, Manny felt he deserved one second of retribution for his fallen brother.

When the Suburban pulled into the alleyway behind Shooter's place of business, Roberto, who had been unusually quiet during the half-hour drive from the airport, asked, "Are we sure the facilities here are adequate for our purposes, Manuel?"

"*Si*, Roberto."

Upon entering Shooter's private domain, Roberto's eyes burned when he first saw the Lester's rigid body, clad only in briefs and sitting in a wooden chair. His wrists were taped to the arm rests and his ankles to the front leg support. Beside him on a small end table were his service revolver and the contents of his pockets, including the two bundles of cash and an envelope. The entire area beneath and around him was covered with a large piece of clear vinyl sheeting.

Like a hyena stalking an injured wildebeest, Roberto slowly circled Lester, his eyes never leaving his prey. Lester could not control the twitching of his muscles. He stared at the floor. Shooter and Bugger stood solemnly behind Shooter's ornate desk, while Manuel, still by the closed door, extracted a pair of pliers from his pocket.

Roberto picked up the one of the bundles of cash, carefully examining the masking tape binding the bills together. He closed his eyes and sighed. He then retrieved the envelope.

"Manuel, this man's face is bruised. *Porque?*"

"I hit him, but only once. It was for Julio," he replied in Spanish, crossing himself.

Roberto pursed his lips and nodded. He made a pronouncement to no one in particular, "If our brother were here, he'd be able to confirm that this money came from Bernardo Lopez Fernandez, our customer in Fort Lauderdale. The tape has his mark on it. See, the small arrow in the corner. Bernardo has always marks his money so there will be no question he paid the amount due. Julio would know this."

Roberto slapped Lester across the face with the stack of bills.

"My brother's life was worth only ten thousand dollars to you, gringo?" Roberto said in a steady voice.

Lester winced and began to stutter. "I…I…I didn't do anything f…for the money. I…I was just…just doing my job. The judge gave me the money as a reward."

"The judge? Who's the judge?" Roberto asked, leaning against the front edge of Shooter's desk. "Is it the judge whose name appears on this envelope?"

"Yes, sir, Judge Pendleton."

"He's the fat man in the picture, *si?* He's the one who gave you the money?"

Lester nodded.

"Why was the judge at the jail when you shot my brother?"

"He brought him some pie."

"A thoughtful man, *si?*"

Lester said nothing.

"Where's the rest of my money?" The pitch in Roberto's voice was beginning to elevate.

Remembering his vow of secrecy, Lester did not answer, looking back to the floor.

"One more time, gringo—where's the rest of my money?"

Lester shook his head. "I…I don't know."

Roberto glanced at Manuel and tilted his head toward Lester. Manuel walked slowly to the wooden chair and grabbed the deputy's left wrist. Centering the jaws of the pliers over the fingernail of one of Lester's pinky-fingers, he began to squeeze until he felt the bone splinter.

"Aghhhhhh!" Lester screeched, twisting his arm back and forth in a vain attempt to extricate his hand from Manuel's grasp.

Manuel looked toward his brother for direction. Roberto simply nodded. The first joint of his ring finger was next. The response was the same.

Roberto spoke. "You have many knuckles. We can do this for the next several hours if you like, gringo. All we want to know is, where's my money and who was involved in the execution of my brother?"

Lester was crying, his left hand shaking violently.

Roberto nodded to Manuel, who grabbed Lester's middle finger, preparing it for the pliers' jaws.

"Don't! P…Please don't! I'll tell y…you anything! Please not again!"

Manuel looked to his brother.

"Just hold him for a second, Manuel," Roberto said in Spanish. Then, reverting to his second language, he addressed Lester, "Where's the money?"

"The judge has it," Lester cried out without hesitation.

"Was Julio killed for the money?"

"I don't know. Probably, but I wasn't in on that. I thought he was trying to escape. I didn't plan on shooting him. I swear to God, I didn't plan on shooting anybody."

"Was the sheriff in on this?" Roberto pressed.

"I don't know. I…I guess he had to be. Me and him and the judge were the only ones who knew about the money."

"You're forgetting my brother, you maggot!" shouted Manuel, twisting Lester's middle finger with all his might. The sound of several small bones cracking was easily heard.

Lester screamed again and passed out.

Casually, Roberto turned to Shooter. "Can you find out where these two pigs live? This sheriff and the judge?"

"Sure, Roberto." He looked toward Bugger and motioned toward the door. Bugger walked out. "The FBI has beaten you to the judge, though."

"Oh?" Roberto responded, his eyebrows lifting.

"It was in the news. He was arrested for a whole bunch of shit along with some dude named Rutherbug, or something like that, and a deputy sheriff up in Grove Hill."

"What kind of charges?"

"I didn't pay a lot of attention, but I can find out. There was something about the plant fire up north over the weekend—some dude was fried. There was something about a girl who was kidnapped or something and some money sent to this cat who's running for governor. They arrested him, too."

Roberto paced about the room. "Interesting. Can you find out more about it?"

"It should be in all the papers in the morning. What I just told you, I saw on the news at noon today."

Lester moaned and his head began to bob.

"You did well, gringo," Roberto announced. "Manuel, give him his clothes. I don't want to look at him anymore."

"But Roberto," Manuel protested in Spanish, "you're not letting this pig go? He killed Julio!"

Roberto responded in English, "He's told us all he knows, of that, I am sure. Why not let him go? He's of no further use to us."

"But brother, he needs to be—"

Roberto raised his index finger and moved it back and forth. "Get his clothes and let him get dressed. I want him out of my sight. *Endela!*"

With his bindings removed and his clothes back on, Lester reached for his possessions on the small table.

"I don't think so, gringo," warned Roberto. "Leave everything there and be happy you're walking out of here with your life."

Lester looked around and saw the three men's eyes fixed on him. Swallowing hard, he asked, "I can just leave? You're not going to kill me?"

Roberto smiled. "Why would we kill you? After all, you were just doing your job, like you said."

Confused, but filled with exhilaration, Lester exclaimed, "Thank you, mister. I'm sorry about your brother. I didn't aim to kill him."

Lester turned and walked toward the door.

Kaboom! The sound of the service revolver echoed around the room.

"Shit!" yelled Manuel, reaching for his weapon.

Lester cried out, his arms flapping as his body was propelled backward by the forward thrust of his leg, his knee mangled by the force of the projectile fired from his service revolver.

Roberto slowly approached the young man, now writhing on the floor. A pool of blood was forming beneath the injured leg, staining the white shag. Roberto turned to Shooter.

"Sorry about the carpet. I'll have it replaced."

Shooter, who was still standing behind his desk, shrugged. "No problem. I was getting tired of it anyway. I was thinking of purple or violet."

Roberto surveyed the room and nodded. "Either one would be nice."

Without any outward emotion, Roberto pointed the pistol toward its owner. Despite his agony, Lester looked up, eyes wild.

"Please mister, don't—"
Roberto Santos fired the remaining five cartridges into the young deputy's chest.

CHAPTER 60
THE GOOD, THE BAD,
AND THE VENGEFUL

I rushed down the corridor of the hospital in search of 318, the semi-private room where Jackson was situated, according to the brusque nurse at the reception station. When I reached it, the door was closed with a sign hanging from the handle, "DO NOT DISTURB. PHYSICIAN IN ROOM." My instincts told me to ignore the printed order and burst in, but I didn't. Taking a deep breath, I looked back down the hallway, my eyes searching for the location of the waiting area.

Retracing my steps, I approached the nurse's station, situated at the intersection of four corridors. No one was there. I looked to my left and saw a black plastic placard extending about ten inches from the ceiling. It read, "VISITOR WAITING."

I walked toward the open door, expecting to find my ex-wife holding court with anyone who'd listen. I was surprised and relieved to see Katie and Michael sitting alone—Katie reading a teen magazine and Michael bombing German positions on his portable computer game.

"Daddy!" my youngest exclaimed as I entered the room. He jumped from his chair and rushed me, throwing his arms around my neck. But for a faint scratch on his cheek, he seemed to be unharmed.

"How's my favorite kung-fu fighter?" I greeted, squeezing him harder than intended, but he didn't seem to mind.

Katie was next. I placed my arms around her, kissing her cheek. She had tears in her eyes.

"You okay, sister?"

She nodded and buried her head in my chest. I swallowed hard. I've never handled my children crying very well.

"Tell me what happened. But first, how's Jackson?"

Katie replied, "He's got a pretty good knot on his head, and his wrist might be broken. They haven't told us yet. I think he'll be all right though." The tears had subsided, and I could sense her relief now that I was there.

"By the way, where's your mother?"

"Guess," Katie answered, with a look of disgust.

I didn't need to. "Is she coming back?"

"She said she'd check with the nurses' station later. She wants you to call her."

"Okay. Now, Mikey, tell me what happened."

"It was pretty scary, but pretty cool, too," he began. "Jackie dropped me off at school this morning, like always when you're gone. Mrs. Lawson made me a sack lunch 'cause we were having wieners and sauerkraut in the cafeteria today."

He paused for me to respond, but I didn't know where he was going, so I just nodded.

"Anyways, I got out of Jackie's pickup and this car pulled up when Jackie drove off. This big man says, 'Hey, boy, your daddy wanted me to talk to you. Come over here.' At first, he kind of scared me, but I thought maybe he was someone from your office, so I went over to his car. He says, 'Get in. I got something for you your daddy wanted me to give you.' I started to walk away 'cause you've always told us not to ever get in a car with a stranger. Then he says, 'I said get in the'…eh…can I say the 'F' word?"

I nodded, feeling the hair standing on the back of my neck.

"Okay. He says 'Get in the fucking car, you little shit!' About that time, I looked up, and Jackie was backing up toward his car."

"Why?" I asked.

"Remember, I told you Mrs. Lawson had made me a sack lunch 'cause we were having wieners—"

"Go on," I interrupted, smiling.

"Anyways, I had left my sack lunch in Jackie's truck, and he was bringing it back to me. Then the neat part. The man gets out of his car and starts coming at me."

"What did he look like, Mikey?" I asked, clinching my fist.

"His face was red 'cause I think he was mad 'cause I didn't get in his car. I started to run, but he jumped and grabbed my legs. We both fell down."

274

"Mikey, slow down a little. What did he look like?"

"I couldn't tell a lot about his face 'cause he had on a big straw hat and dark glasses, you know like that guy in *Cool Hand Luke.* That's kind of what he reminded me of except he was a lot bigger. He had a funny voice, too."

"Funny like what?"

"Like those people in *The Dukes of Hazzard* on TV. You know, he sounded like, 'Now ya'll done jest pissed me off somethin' awful.'" Mikey's voice was low, gravelly and slow.

Although the subject matter was serious, I had to laugh at his delivery and expression. "So this big man had a Southern accent. Right?"

"I guess that's what they call it. Anyways, Jackie jumped out of his truck when he saw the guy tackle me, and before we could get up, Jackie was on top of him, beating him and yelling like crazy. He used the 'F' word a bunch, like 'Leave him alone, you mother—"

I held up my hand. "I can imagine what he said. Go on."

"Then the bad part happened. Jackie was hitting him pretty good, but he was too big for Jackie. He let go of me, threw Jackie off his back, and kicked Jackie in the head. I heard it when he kicked him. He kicked Jackie real hard. Jackie rolled away, but he got right back up and came back at him. He was yelling, 'Run away, Mikey. Get out of here, Mikey.' He was great, Dad."

Once again, I had to swallow hard.

"Then, the man grabbed Jackie by the hand and twisted his arm behind his back real hard. I think I heard a bone crack. Anyways, Jackie didn't cry or anything. He just gritted his teeth and told me to get out of there."

"Did you?"

"Hell, no. I ran over to them and kicked that man right in the balls. I got him good, too, 'cause he let go of Jackie and grabbed himself where it hurts. By then, Mr. Dennison, he was on playground duty this morning, anyways, Mr. Dennison started running toward us, and he was yelling at the man. I guess the man decided he'd better get out of there 'cause he got back in his car, but he said something real silly."

"What was silly, Mikey?"

"He had this mean look on his face and he said, 'Tell your old man to get the hell out of Alabama if he knows what's good for him.' What does that mean, Daddy?"

I stared at the wall across the room and was silent for a few seconds. Finally, I replied, "I think I know what it means, Mikey, but that's not important. What's important is who said it."

"I already told you that. It was the guy me and Jackie had the fight with."

"I know, son, but I want to know who sent him. And when I find out—"

Before I could finish an emotional outburst, a female voice interrupted, "Mr. Mitchell? I'm Doctor Phyllis Humphreys."

Raleigh sat quietly in his office, sipping Jack Daniel's and considering his next move. He'd been released on bail nine hours earlier and had spent most of that time deciding who was most dangerous to him. After considering all the possibilities, he'd determined everyone was: Jim Bob, Bobby Bitterman, Billy Cudjoe, Lawrence Rifle, the state Democratic organization, Leander, and Vivian Thompson, in that order.

While he knew Lawrence Rifle would no doubt blame him for contributing to the candidate's political demise, he felt comfortable with his ability to create enough confusion about the money in the suitcases to skate any real legal liability when the time came. Lawrence was in the investment business, and as far anyone was concerned, that money was nothing more than a personal investment for retirement. After all, Raleigh had legitimately invested money with Lawrence before and had a record of losses to prove it. He'd just claim there was some confusion on the tapes and Lawrence and Charles Rifle damn sure wouldn't contradict him.

As for the party, well, they'd just have to throw their hopes on the lieutenant governor and hope his record didn't kill him in the general election. He had a statewide following and should be a serious candidate with enough money behind him. Raleigh eyed the wooden door, behind which his safe rested. There was over two hundred thousand dollars in there, and he doubted the party would turn him down after wasting so much on Mr. Rifle.

After another two hours and three more drinks, Raleigh was drunk and ready to take on the world. He would meet with Bobby, Jim Bob, and Leander the following evening at the lodge, and they would work out their stories so that no sharp-tongued prosecutor could trip them up. From what Felton Abercrombie had been able to ascertain about the evidence accumulated against them, everything was purely circumstantial and speculative relative to the Tremont girl and the fire. The call from Johnny, received on his new, digitized cell phone a few hours earlier, convinced Raleigh that Mitchell wouldn't make any further trouble for him, now that he had the Texas trashman's attention. If Leander still had unresolved financial issues with the construction company, so what?

The only serious threat remaining, he had determined, was Billy Cudjoe, and he would put Johnny and a couple of investigators on that problem in the morning. *Hell, Cudjoe's probably on a slow boat to China after fucking up that deal so bad,* he rationalized.

All in all, Raleigh felt like he had everything under control until the telephone rang.

"Judge Pendleton, this is Deputy Rinker."

"Who?" Raleigh blustered, the alcohol clouding his focus.

"Deputy Rinker, from the sheriff's office. You know—"

"Oh yeah, Rinker. What can I do for you, boy?"

"Judge, something terrible's happened. Sheriff Crawford and his wife are dead."

"What do you mean 'dead?' I saw Virgil just this morning, and he looked well enough to me. Who'd you say this is?"

"Rinker, Larry Rinker. Judge, I'm out at the sheriff's house right now. I came out here when he didn't come back to the office like he said he would after his missus called. I tried calling but no one answered. I came out here and the place's all tore up. Mrs. Crawford's been mutilated bad and the Sheriff was gut shot with a shotgun, it looks like, and there's a note pinned to his shirt."

"Oh my Lord! What does it say?"

"I got it right here. It says, 'Where is the rest of my money?' It's printed on one of your envelopes. What does that mean, Judge?"

Raleigh was sobering fast, sweat breaking out all over his skin. "Hang on, Rinker!" he ordered, moving as swiftly as his bum knee and half-a-fifth of sour mash would allow. He quickly secured the deadbolt and retrieved a .45 automatic from the bottom drawer of his credenza. "Now, read it to me again."

Rinker did as instructed.

"Who else knows about this?"

"No one, Judge. You're the first person I called. What should I do?"

Raleigh thought for a few seconds. "Call the state troopers, get another deputy on his way out there, and bring that note to me right now! And Rinker, don't say nothing to no one about that note. Where's Under Sheriff Holmboe? He'll be in charge now."

"I don't know where Lester is. No one's seen him since this morning."

The judge sat back in his chair and reached for the whiskey bottle. There was another threat out there he had never considered—the most dangerous threat of all.

"Why did you leave the note on that pig sheriff's chest?" Manny asked as they sat by the pool of the Grand Hotel, south of Fairhope. He drank a Corona while Roberto sipped a Cuba Libre. "It was like a calling card. The authorities could link it to us."

"If the authorities ever see it. If the judge gets his hands on it, it will never surface. It would raise questions he doesn't want to answer. If the FBI retrieves it, then we'll take our chances. The judge will have plenty to deal with either way."

Manuel nodded. "When do we go after the judge?"

"I think we'll wait to see how the government does with the swine. We might even have a little help for them."

"What do you mean help?"

"That greaser bragged to Mary Susan about a bomb he was going to set the night of the plant fire. He also bragged about a dead black girl. Maybe we can figure a way to get that information to the Feds without, I don't know, without exposing ourselves. We got our message across to the judge today, and now we can sit back and watch him squirm. He'll feel like the man overboard with the sharks. He won't know where the attack will come from."

"Who's Mary Susan?"

Roberto smiled as his cell phone rang.

"Hello."

"Roberto, there were agents from the FBI here. They were looking for you and Julio."

"What did you tell them, Anna?"

"I told them I hadn't seen Julio for several days and you were out in the Gulf fishing."

"Did they have a warrant?"

"No. They were nice. They left a card and asked that you contact them upon your return."

"Okay. Thanks for calling, Anna. We'll be home soon."

Roberto sat for a few minutes, contemplating his options.

"What is it, big brother?" Manual asked, sipping his beer.

"The *Federalies* showed up a little quicker than I expected. Get your gear together while I call Tootie. We leave for Miami now. I'll have Shooter monitor the situation with the judge."

CHAPTER 61

THEN THERE WERE THREE

Bobby Bitterman had listened to the outcome of the proceedings against the judge, Leander, and Jim Bob with indifference while watching the local news that evening. The death of Harvey Greenville had left him despondent. Harvey had been like an older brother or a father to him for the last twenty years. While others with more tenure than Bobby had initially resented his movement up the ladder, occasionally giving less than their best to the efficient operation of the plant, Harvey had been his confidante and mentor, on more than one occasion defending Bobby's decisions with the other line supervisors. It had been Harvey who had led the charge to prevent a unionization attempt the year after Bobby had been named plant manager. Yes, Harvey had been a very special friend, and Bobby had participated in his murder.

After picking at a Swanson's pot roast dinner, one of several selections Myrtle had left in the freezer while she and the kids were in Birmingham, he did something he seldom did in his own home. He had a drink. It had taken over fifteen minutes to find the pint bottle of Jim Beam he had hidden in the garage over a year earlier. Myrtle would have maligned him unmercifully had she found the bottle he had placed under a loose piece of paneling behind his workbench.

Sitting on the porch, oblivious to the cacophony of sounds buzzing around the neighborhood, he drank straight from the bottle and began to feel lightheaded. While he had hoped the liquor would dull the sense of guilt and the depression growing like a cancer in his mind, he was experiencing the opposite effect. With every swallow, the despondency grew, and within an hour, he was a man filled with self-loathing.

The first phone call was expected, but less than gratifying—Myrtle calling to remind him to water her rose garden and pick all the vegetables in the plot behind the garage "before those hooligans across the alley steal me blind or the birds peck them to death." While her manner was less abusive than normal, she still ended the conversation by issuing an ironic warning, "Now, don't you go doing something stupid like going over to that Judge Pendleton's for more drinking and philandering. You know he's no good and he always gets you in trouble." Little did she know, contact with Raleigh Pendleton was the last thing he wanted in life.

The second call was even less welcome, but almost prophetic.

"Hey, Bobby, you old polecat," Raleigh had blustered. Even in his liquor-dulled state, Bobby could tell the judge was several drinks ahead of him. "Have the authorities been by to see you yet?"

"Yeah, they think you, Leander, Billy, and I were responsible for the fire and Harvey's death. Judge, I don't understand. You told me the plant fire was off," Bobby lamented. "Why'd you go on with it? You said Harley had agreed we didn't owe him any more money."

"Things don't always go as planned. I don't know why the hell Billy went on with it, but he apparently did and that's that. The important thing is we keep our heads about us and stick together. Have they said anything to you about that negra girl?"

"Yeah," Bobby almost whispered. "This is getting to be more than I can handle, Judge."

"Me, Leander, and Jim Bob are meeting ova at the lodge tomorrow night. Why don't you come ova there and we'll all get things straight?"

"I don't think so, Judge. Myrtle said—"

"Fuck Myrtle! This deal's gotten a little bigger than your being scared of that old war-horse you're married to. Bobby, we could all go to the chair if we don't stick together. We'll be ova at the lodge about six. You'd better be there. Remember, you're the only one whose picture was taken with that dead negra and it was your plant that burned. My attorney thinks it's only a matter of days, maybe hours, before the FBI brings you in like they did the rest of us. You'd better be there tomorrow night, Bobby, or them pictures might show up and this whole mess could be blamed on you and Billy. The rest of us has ourselves to think of."

Bobby tried to swallow, but his mouth and throat were dry. A sip from the bottle seemed only to intensify the constriction of his throat. When the phone rang for the third time, he considered not answering, but a responsible nature forced him to lift the receiver.

"Hello, Mr. Bitterman. This is Senior Special Agent Fred Carleton. I was wondering if you could come to the office in the morning to clear up a couple of matters? We have some photographs we'd like you to see."

"What time?" he responded flatly, picking up the paper and pencil always present on the shelf by the phone in the hallway.

"I ain't going to practice tomorrow, Mom," Jimbo declared while Geraldine methodically turned each piece of the fryer she'd butchered behind the chicken coop an hour earlier. "I may not ever go back. They're calling me names. Me and Hub Armstrong almost got in a fight and he's about the best friend I ever had."

"What kind of names, Jimbo?" Geraldine asked, wiping her brow with her apron, leaving a small dusting of flour on her nose.

"Nigger hater, pervert's son, stuff like that. What the hell did Dad do? What was that trial about this morning?"

Geraldine sighed. "It wasn't a trial, Jimbo. Your father's been falsely accused of something he didn't do. They have a black girl missing and she's the daughter of a federal lawyer down in Mobile. They're just looking for a scapegoat. Your daddy'll be cleared, and this'll all go away."

"How do you know he didn't do it? He's got a mean streak and you know it. Maybe he did what they said. It wouldn't surprise me."

Jim Bob, who had been sitting on the back porch and drinking beer for over an hour, walked into the kitchen.

"So you don't think much of your old man, huh, Jimbo?" he snarled.

Jimbo pursed his lips and looked at the floor.

"You deaf, boy?" he bellowed. "You been listening to them Bible beaters and decided to take up with them against your own flesh and blood?" He walked to the refrigerator and removed two bottles of PBR.

"Jimbo didn't mean nothing," Geraldine pleaded. "The boys were giving him a hard time at school, and—"

"I heard all that shit. You think I'm fucking deaf? Mind your own business, Geraldine. This here's between me and this ungrateful yellow-belly."

"Please, Jimmy, leave the boy alone. You're not the only one affected by your, eh, you and that Raleigh Pendleton's arrest. It's a family matter, and we're all suffering with you. I only pray you're not somehow involved—"

"What're you saying, bitch? You taking sides, too?" Jim Bob placed the bottles on the kitchen table, waving his fist in his wife's direction. "Maybe I need to teach you another lesson."

Without hesitation, Jimbo grabbed one of the bottles, forcefully striking his father just below his ear. "I told you if you ever touched her again, I'd kill you!"

Staggering from a combination of the blow to his jaw and the effects of alcohol, Jim Bob turned and faced his only son. "I guess today's your chance, boy. And you're gonna have to do better than that."

Jim Bob placed his hand around the neck of the remaining bottle, bashing it against the corner of the kitchen counter. It shattered. Foamy liquid and shards of glass exploded over the floor and counter.

"Now, boy, I'm gonna ugly up that pretty face of yours!" Jim Bob threatened.

"No!" screeched Geraldine, jumping between her deranged husband and her son.

As if swatting at a fly, Jim Bob backhanded Geraldine across the face. She fell to the floor, her head bouncing off the linoleum.

"Aaghh!" screamed Jimbo as he lunged toward his father, planting his forehead in his solar plexus and driving his body hard into the corner of the room, just as he had been taught on the gridiron. Jim Bob exhaled, gasping for breath.

Jimbo released his grip and backed away. Watching his father heaving— his hands resting on his knees—he turned to access his mother's injuries. As he leaned down, lifting her shaking body from the floor, he felt a burning sensation between his shoulder blades. Geraldine, now standing, watched in horror as her husband thrust the jagged remains of the bottle into his son's back.

The youngster groaned and reeled to his left, grabbing the edge of the sink for support.

"Oh, God!" he moaned, his arms and legs trembling from the pain spreading over his back and down his spine.

"You're going to kill me, huh?" Jim Bob gloated. "Now look who's gonna kill who. Stand up, boy, I'm gonna finish this thing."

Responding instinctively, Jimbo pushed up against the counter, turning to face his father. So great was his pain and the shock of his injury, he simply stood there, his eyes beginning to glaze.

Even in his rage and intoxication, Jim Bob was mentally paralyzed, watching his once pride-and-joy anguishing from the puncture wound. His bewilderment lasted only a few seconds, however, as the bullet entered his left temple, exiting through the top of his head.

CHAPTER 62
REVELRY AND DESPAIR

"I never expected something like this. Every case has its twists and turns, but this one takes the cake," Fred announced after seating himself in Lawton's office.

"What are you talking about, Fred? You want some coffee?"

"No, thanks, I've been drinking coffee for six hours now. I got the first call at five-thirty this morning." Fred rotated his head several times, attempting to relax a stiff neck. "Our case against Pendleton is falling apart. Jim Bob Davis was killed by his wife last night. She shot him in the head with his own weapon."

"What happened, Fred?"

"Apparently, after the arraignment and the bail being posted, compliments of Raleigh Pendleton I might add, Davis went home after the sheriff suspended him and started drinking. According to the attorney the Battered Women's Shelter hired for her, he's been beating up on her for a long time."

"I assume they'll plead self-defense?"

"That and protecting her son. Davis and his boy, a sixteen-year-old, got into a fight over him beating up on her. Davis stabbed the boy in the back with a broken beer bottle."

"You're kidding!"

"I wish I were. The boy was in surgery for over nine hours. He has a damaged spinal cord. They won't know for awhile if he'll ever walk again. He was apparently a pretty good football player. Anyway, Mrs. Davis found the gun while they were fighting and shot him dead."

"Damn. That leaves Pendleton, Rutherford, Bitterman, and Cudjoe. And, Davis was the only one we can for sure tie to Jane's disappearance," Lawton lamented, his personal disappointment showing.

"Well, that's not exactly right. Bitterman's dead, too." Fred looked at the floor, searching for the right words.

"Tell me again, Felton. I think I was dreaming when I heard what you said." Raleigh was glowing.

Felton Abercrombie shrugged and announced into the telephone for a second time, "I got a call about an hour ago from Dale Donovan, Mr. Davis's attorney. Mr. Davis was killed last night by his wife. Dale was also advised that a Mr. Bitterman, someone under investigation in the two most serious matters with which you are charged, committed suicide last night. I'm not yet sure how Mr. Bitterman fits into all of this, but Donovan said the FBI was less than enthusiastic about his demise. Can you enlighten me, Judge?"

Raleigh opened his desk drawer and withdrew the ever-present bottle. *A celebratory nip.* Clearing his throat to mask the bite of the liquor, he responded, "Mr. Bitterman's the plant manager ova at that General Paper Mill that burned last Sunday night. I guess the stress must've been too much for him. I don't know why the authorities would have thought him important to my case."

"Judge, forgive my directness, but I don't feel you've told me everything. As I understand the situation, assuming I know everything I should, we should file a motion to dismiss the two capital charges. Mr. Davis was the only tie to the missing Tremont girl and he certainly won't be testifying against you or anyone else. Would Mr. Rifle or Mr. Rutherford provide any threat to you relative to this issue?"

"Certainly not," Raleigh responded in as serious a tone as his gleefulness would allow.

"As to the plant fire and the resulting death of Mr. Greenville, I've always thought this charge was the weakest of the lot, absent the testimony of Mr. Cudjoe. He seems to have vanished and until or unless he's found, I doubt the government will want to proceed on this matter without some corroborating testimony. I doubt the U.S. Attorney's office would even object to the motion to dismiss. Would this be why the government seemed so disappointed with Mr. Bitterman's death?"

"How the hell would I know, Felton?" Raleigh answered. "Perhaps he was in cahoots with Cudjoe and they thought Bobby could be broken. But that's pure conjecture."

"If you say so. That leaves us with Mr. Rifle and Mr. Rutherford. I'm afraid they could have enough to get an indictment against you and Mr. Rifle for campaign law violations. We'll just have to play that one by ear. As to Mr. Rutherford, unless they can link him to these other charges, and therefore, by association, or otherwise, link his activities to you, I don't think he's much of problem for you. He's got a slam-dunk embezzlement conviction to deal with and some pretty serious civil liability, but that's really his problem, if I know everything. One more time, Judge, do I know everything?"

"I swear on my honor," Raleigh stated, laughing to himself.

Lawton's palms covered his face, while his shoulders heaved. His mind couldn't accept the finality of what lay before him.

Fred sat across the desk, fidgeting with his wedding ring, not knowing what else to say. The photograph, clipped to the note Bobby Bitterman had written before ending his life, rested in the center of Lawton's desk. The note, speckled with blood, read:

I have tried to live my life in a good Christian way, but I've failed. I am responsible for killing two people over the past month and even though I didn't mean to, they are dead just the same.

Bobby, Jr. and Karen Ann, try to remember me as a loving father, not for the final acts I have committed.

Myrtle, I'll even miss you and pray you'll forgive my wickedness.

To the family of Jane Tremont, please forgive me. I never intended to hurt your daughter.

To Harvey Greenville, I can only say I would never have hurt you on purpose.

To the men who also sinned with me, I hope you will see the wickedness of your ways and confess your transgressions.

Finally, I pray to Almighty God that you'll have mercy on my soul and forgive all my sins.

Robert David Bitterman

CHAPTER 63
WHO, WHEN, AND WHERE?

After hearing the news about Jim Bob and Bobby, Leander had unsuccessfully tried to reach the judge several times, feeling his efforts were being purposely avoided. He had spent the first night and the morning following his release from custody holed up at Miss Vivian's house. Unexpectedly, after breakfast that morning, she announced her intentions to sell the house and move to Louisiana. She had conjured up a story about an ailing aunt in need of her care. In reality, she recognized that the Leander Rutherford gravy train had been derailed and it was time to move on to greener pastures. A call to an old boyfriend, a Louisiana legislator with whom she had shared a bed several times in the past, confirmed his divorce had been finalized. She could hear the lust in his voice when she told him she was available for relocation.

No longer welcome in the love nest Jefferson Construction had financed, and with the office keys he possessed no longer capable of opening a door, he was forced to slither back home, hopeful his wife of forty years would still accept him. As Findley Ross had professed many times, the women of the South are both resilient and willing to accept the frailties of their men folk, and Mrs. Rutherford was no exception. She may have even set a new standard for turning the other cheek.

With nothing else to do, no "amazingly incredible deal" to work on, no other sheep readily available to fleece, Leander resigned himself to waiting for the criminal indictment that was sure to come. He prayed some district judge would apply leniency to an old political wannabe. He only hoped Raleigh wouldn't consider him too great a risk and end his life prematurely, as had occurred with two of his fellow conspirators. And, God only knew what the judge had done with Billy Cudjoe.

Three distinguished-looking men sat in the elegant surroundings of the University Club in Birmingham. All more powerful than a casual observer would imagine, they sipped their dry martinis while deliberately perusing hardbound menus. A slender young man in black slacks, vest, and bow tie approached and the tallest of the three closed his menu, eyeing the empty chair and place setting to his right.

"Looks like Mr. Rifle's running late. Why don't we go on and order? He can catch up. Likely he'll not have much of an appetite after we've talked anyway," suggested Findley Ross.

The other two nodded. The young man made his way around the table, scribbling the orders with precise strokes of his pen. Before the last selection was noted, there was a shuffle of approaching feet. Breathing heavily, Lawrence Rifle rushed across the wooden floor while removing his raincoat.

"Sorry, gentlemen," he offered. "Damn thunderstorm kept us from landing for over half an hour."

"Not at all, Lawrence," Fin responded. "We were just ordering, but we'll wait, now that you're here. Young man, would you please take this gentleman's raincoat and bring him something to drink? A martini perhaps, Lawrence?"

"Fine."

The candidate shook hands around the table and seated himself.

"Good to see you, Lawrence. How goes your legal situation?" Fin inquired.

"Good, very good. That's why I asked you gentlemen to meet with me. I think I have everything worked out. The judge and I have talked twice and both he and his attorney think this whole mess could go away in a matter of weeks."

"That's good news for you personally, Lawrence, but the damage's been done already—the horse's out of the barn, so to speak," drummed one of the other men, Southern twang filling his inflection.

"This campaign isn't over yet. I can still beat the lieutenant governor in the primary and you know I have a better chance in the general," Rifle proclaimed.

"Had, Lawrence, you had a better chance. It's not enough that you ignored Fin's warnings about Raleigh Pendleton, but now he's been accused of murder, embezzlement, and I don't know what else. No matter what we do, the lieutenant governor won't have to spend a nickel getting all the press he wants. You and the judge are big news, and there's nothing we can do about it," added the other.

"Dammit, I'm the best candidate you got! We can't give up so easy. Surely there's something we can—"

"Lawrence, as much as I hate to say it, you need to face reality. The race is over for you. You cooked your goose, and there's nothing left to give up. We've even heard rumors that the money Raleigh gave your brother was drug money. If that gets out, well, it doesn't take a genius. Lawrence, you need to go on back home, run your business, and hope you can avoid time in a federal correctional facility. I'm afraid your days of public service are over for good. You'll never be able to rid yourself of Raleigh Pendleton and the shit that follows him around." Findley's statement, although direct, was characteristically well stated and accurate. "One last piece of advice. If I were you, I'd watch my backside. If things don't go well for you and the judge, well, two of the men implicated in the judge's activities are already dead."

Rifle stared blankly at the tablecloth, his expression hard to read. Finally, he spoke. "Gentlemen, I guess I have to accept reality, as you said. I'll officially withdraw from the race in the morning. As for my physical well being, Judge Pendleton's the one who should keep an eye over his shoulder. If you'll excuse me, I think I'll return home. I have some planning to do."

As Fin walked across the street to the parking lot, his cell phone rang. He looked at the faceplate. Although the number was vaguely familiar, he couldn't place it.

"Hello," he answered, while pushing a button, activating his door locks.

"Fin, Jack Mitchell here," I announced.

"Jack, how you been? From what I hear, you sure stirred up a hornet's nest down South. You aim to get your money back?"

"That's a secondary issue at this point, Fin. Can you talk for a few minutes?"

"Sure, all the time you need. I got about three hours to kill while I drive back home."

"Good, but it won't take that long. Fin, I'm calling you from a hospital in Houston," I proclaimed, pausing to evaluate his reaction.

"You sick, Jack?" His inflection seemed genuine.

"No, but one of my kids has been hurt."

"How'd it happen, Jack? Is it serious?"

"He'll be all right, but that's only part of what I'm concerned about. Fin, you remember when I called you about Raleigh Pendleton?"

"Sure, I remember."

"You were very candid about your position in the party down there and the candidacy of Mr. Rifle. You basically told me your loyalties were tied to the party and you wouldn't be able to help me if in so doing it jeopardized the election, or words to that effect."

"Yeah, that's an accurate paraphrase of what I said. Where are you going with this, Jack?" he asked, his voice filled with what sounded like genuine confusion.

"How far would the party go to protect your investment in your candidate?"

"Jack, I must admit, I don't have a clue what you're asking me. Mr. Rifle's pretty well crapped in his own mess kit. There's nothing left for the party to protect. Now, what's this all about?"

"Fin, someone from Alabama tried to kidnap one of my kids."

"Good Lord, Jack. That's awful. When did it happen? Is he or she okay?"

Good catch on the gender, Fin. You either don't have any idea of what happened or you're very good, I thought before answering.

"He's fine, but it scared the hell out of him and got his brother a broken arm and a minor concussion. I guess what I'm asking is, how far would the people in your party go to intimidate me into calling off the dogs?"

Fin laughed. "Now I see where you're going. Did the party send some goon over to Texas to send you a message? The answer is no, Jack, no way. We've done some pretty creative things over the years to put our man in office, but we haven't yet stooped to Mafioso tactics."

"I'm not trying to be abrasive, Fin, but I just thought I'd ask before I start going down the list. If I've offended you, I'm sorry, but put yourself in my shoes."

"I'm not offended, but your conclusion's a little off the wall."

"How about Lawrence Rifle? Is he capable of—"

Ross interrupted. "Jack, I just finished a meeting with Mr. Rifle. He knows who screwed up his chances for the governor's mansion, and it wasn't you. Why ask about him?"

"Fin, he mentioned my name in a conversation with Raleigh Pendleton. He warned him about me by name. Hell, I've never met the man. This conversation took place right after I called you the last time. Draw your own conclusions."

"I don't have to. I told him about you shortly after we talked. I told him you were a straight arrow and you'd get the judge if he was involved in any funny business with Leander Rutherford. Jack, I told him to stay away from Raleigh. I even made him send back the money the judge had already sent him. As far as I'm concerned, I was doing you a favor. If he took the heat off the judge for money, maybe he and Leander would quit raiding your bank account. I hope you put the sorry son-of-a- bitch away for the rest of his life. The judge has a whole lot more to fear from Rifle or the party than you do. I'd bet another four years of a Republican in the governor's mansion that the bullshit with your kids was courtesy of Raleigh. You told the authorities about this yet?"

"Not yet."

Lawton walked slowly around the swing set he'd bought for Janie on her sixth birthday. His eyelids were swollen pockets of flesh, stinging from the hour he'd spent trying to console his wife after he'd delivered the final blow. Although he had spared her the photograph, Bobby Bitterman's suicide note had left no doubt that their only daughter would never graduate from college as Fred had predicted during the early days of the investigation. The sedative had finally done its work and Barbara fallen into a mercifully needed sleep.

Slumping into one of the slings, he gazed at the ruts made by small feet pushing and dragging, the laughter of innocent childhood echoing in his ears. For the first time since the nightmare had begun, he allowed his mind to focus on the one emotion he had fought so diligently to bury in the deepest recesses of his mind—revenge.

Closing his eyes, the distorted face of Raleigh Pendleton, ablaze within an inferno of satanic proportion, provided a momentary feeling of contentment. During his years as a prosecutor, he had often looked into the faces of the survivors of crime. He had always felt compassion, recognized their desire for vengeance, but his was the way of the legal system, and within his discipline there was no place for vigilantism. Now, he, Barbara, and Aaron were those survivors and no longer insulated from the desire for revenge by the objectivity of emotional distance.

He didn't know how long he had sat there, the rage and frustration building in his mind, when the idea wove its way into his consciousness. The more he considered the possibilities, the more energized he became. While it would not bring his precious daughter back and while it would not soften the misery his beloved wife would never get beyond, it would serve justice in a

291

way foreign to him until this moment. As the idea continued to take shape—the details and irony merging together like a well-written ballad—rationalization became the lubricant that guiltlessly slid the pieces into place.

The legal system would never convict Raleigh Pendleton of the most heinous of his crimes. The testimony of a victim, emotionally deranged for over thirty-five years, would never stand up against the expert witnesses Felton Abercrombie would assemble, and the murders of Aaron and Lizzie Collins would also remain unanswered. The words of a suicide note, written by a mind possessed with self-absolution, would relegate the legal system to accept the confession as the final nail in a massive coffin only partially filled.

Yes, the decision was made. Only time and opportunity were left to uncertainty.

After the legal realities of the report from Felton Abercrombie sank in, Raleigh decided to take a drive and enjoy a renewed feeling of freedom. Using his favorite oaken cane, he lumbered down the backstairs of the courthouse, unusually aware of the fragrant smell of jasmine and the light cloud cover providing relief from the scorching rays of the August sun. Pausing on the bottom step, he heard the laughter of the local children as they jumped haphazardly through the spray on the front lawn. *This is indeed a cheerful day*, he thought, proceeding to his parking space.

"Judge Pendleton," he heard from behind him. It was the familiar drawl of his clerk.

"Whatcha need, Johnny?" he responded, tuning to face the doorway. "I aim be out for awhile."

"I just got a call from the state troopers' office. They found Lester's car in a ravine ova in Clarke County. Said it was covered up with brush and so forth, but some stray dogs was hanging around there and someone called the dog catcher."

"Stray dogs?" Raleigh repeated, wiping his forehead with his pocket-handkerchief, confusion showing on his pink face.

"Yeah, there was something in the back end that smelled real bad and them dogs was about to scratch all the paint off trying to get in. Know what it was?"

"Johnny, you know I don't like playing kid games. What was it?"

"Lester's head. There was a hundred dollar bill stuck in his mouth."

Roberto replaced his cell phone in his shirt pocket.

"Manuel, is that everything from the truck?" he called out as he walked down the driveway of the white wooden frame house where he and his brothers had been raised.

"That's it, big brother. Who was on the phone?" asked Manuel, sipping root beer from a can.

"Shooter. A bunch of shit has happened since we left Mobile yesterday and none of it's good."

"*Porque?*"

"Two of the men involved with the swine are now dead. Mr. Calhoun told Shooter he thought the pig would beat the wrap on the two murders and the fire unless that greaser Cudjoe gets caught, assuming he's still alive. Maybe we were too hasty in dealing with the sheriff and the pig who shot Julio," Roberto conceded, crossing himself, as did Manuel. "We know for a fact that the judge ordered the hit on our brother and stole our money."

"Yeah, but we talked about that. There was no way we could have proven what the two cops told us without exposing our business and ourselves. Besides, they would've never told the same story without persuasion. Do we go after the judge now, Roberto?"

"Soon, but I want to think about it. I need to know more about him, his habits, his secrets. You sure we got all the stuff out of the warehouse? The *Federalies* will come back."

"Yeah, every last kilo, deposit slip, and the ledger. You think they'll be safer here at the old house?"

"For the time being. We must change our way of doing business. This whole affair has brought the attention of the authorities to our doorstep. If only Julio hadn't made the run. Everything would have…and the swine…" Emotionally charged, Roberto couldn't finish the either sentence.

CHAPTER 64

ASHES TO ASHES, DUST...

I received the call from Lawton on Saturday morning. After bringing Jackson home from the hospital the evening before, everything in my household was returning to normal by Mitchell family standards. Uncharacteristically, my ex-wife had agreed to stay with the kids for a few days while I traveled to Alabama to attend a memorial service for Jane Tremont on Monday and began the task of putting my business there back in order. There were still outstanding legal matters involving Leander and Vivian and, of course, the still ominous threat of a retaliatory event.

Perhaps exercising more caution than necessary, although where my children's safety is concerned, unnecessary is a term I cannot define, I obtained the services of a reputable security company recommended by Josh McTiernan. We had all met on Sunday evening, my ex included, and outlined the security procedures that would be in place until I was satisfied the threat was no longer present. I had no idea how long that might take, given the tangled web of crimes centering on Chatom, Alabama.

Lawton had offered to pick me up at the airport, but I declined, wishing not to be an additional burden to an already overburdened soul, and needing independent transportation to carry out my other plans and business requirements. I arrived at his house at 9:00 Monday morning. The services were set for 10:30.

"Glad you could come," he greeted, dressed in a black suit, white shirt, and a particularly flamboyant Tabasco tie. He noticed my eyes being drawn to it.

"It was Janie's favorite. She picked it out one day while we were in the mall shopping."

I nodded my approval and hugged him sympathetically. He returned the gesture and I could feel the trembling of a body overwrought with sadness.

"We've been praying for you guys," I whispered.

"I know," he replied. "Come on in. Barbara wants to see you. By the way, Fred asked if you could spend a little time with him this afternoon."

I swallowed hard and accompanied him into the den. Looking around, I acknowledged Fred Carleton, standing by a pretty, slightly overweight lady of his approximate age. I assumed she was his wife. The only other familiar face was that of his boss, Charles Shumacher.

The next ten minutes were spent in quiet conversation with a courageous and surprisingly composed Barbara Tremont. We mostly made small talk while she held a copy of the most recent photograph of her only daughter, dressed in the pink suit she had worn to Easter services two months before her disappearance. Hopefully, this would be the way she would always remember her baby, since Lawton had spared her the photograph stapled to the suicide note.

The service was mercifully brief, but not a dry eye walked from the doors of the First Baptist Church that morning. There was a simple wooden casket, covered with yellow roses, resting beneath the pulpit from which the pastor had executed the last rites. During most of the ceremony, I couldn't take my eyes off of the ordinary looking rectangular box. It was eerie to me, and I am sure it was for many others—an empty casket—only a symbol meant to represent the closure that would likely never come for the Tremont family.

Raleigh and Lottie Pendleton sat near the middle of the small chapel where the last rites were being spoken over the concealed body of Jim Bob Davis. Four pews in front of him sat the family of the deceased. Only Geraldine and Jim Bob's mother were weeping. His daughter, Sissy, and other more distant relatives separated them. The nature of Jim Bob's death had placed a strain on the once pleasant relationship between the two women. Jimbo sat in a wheelchair at the end of the pew. A white strap restrained his head, his neck immobilized by a brace.

Across the middle aisle and one row closer to the front sat Sheriff Harley Logginfield and two Clarke County deputies, all dressed in their uniforms. Raleigh noticed several times during the service that Harley seemed disinterested in the ceremony, his eyes constantly surveying the mourners.

When not gawking, he often whispered to one of his subordinates. At one point, Raleigh was fairly certain the sheriff was asleep.

As the people walked from the church, Raleigh made his way to Harley.

"It's been awhile, Sheriff," the judge announced, extending his hand.

Harley stared at him with a perplexed expression and nodded, ignoring the judge's physical gesture of greeting. He turned and took a step in the opposite direction.

"Something stuck in your craw, Harley?" Raleigh asked in a menacing tone. He was not accustomed to being publicly shunned.

The sheriff stopped and turned toward the unwelcome voice. "Not really, Judge. I just don't have much use for the likes of you. I've got an officer lying in a casket in there, a nice local family, I've known for years, torn apart for the rest of their lives, and I've been questioned about money you and that plant manager down at General Paper supposedly paid to me, which I don't know nothing about. The boys at my office tell me you and Jim Bob had been talking pretty regular before him being arrested. What were you and Jim Bob up to?" His expression was serious and his delivery filled with contempt. "Jim Bob was a good boy until he got mixed up with you."

Raleigh took a step back, a defensive reaction to the unexpected attack. "You don't have no call to be talking to me that way, Sheriff. You don't know how powerful my influence is around here, and in Montgomery."

"I don't give two shits about you and your political cronies. I've won six elections and never got a dime of help from the party. I ain't beholding to anyone up there at the capitol. If Jim Bob hadn't got hooked up with you and all that good old buddy nonsense, he'd have learned you don't have to play by those rules to get yourself elected. You only need to be honest and work your ass off campaigning, and then, do your job if you win. Now, if you don't mind, I don't have any more time for the likes of you," he scoffed, turning and walking toward the group gathered around Jimbo.

Red-faced and filled with anger, Raleigh shuffled to his wife, briskly grabbing her by the arm.

"Come on, we don't have nothing more to do here. We need to get back to Chatom for Virgil and Mary Belle's services this afternoon. I got to give a eulogy and I want to look at my notes. "

Johnny stood by the Cadillac, opening the rear door for his boss and his missus as they approached. Neither the judge nor his clerk noticed the young man in a dark suit who snapped several pictures of Raleigh's subordinate as he walked to the driver's door.

"Ashes to ashes, dust to dust," proclaimed the minister as the final words droned over Bobby Bitterman's coffin before it was lowered into the vault.

Myrtle and her two children sat in the row of folding chairs reserved for the immediate family. Her mother, two sisters and their husbands were lined up to her right. To her left were Bobby's only brother and his aged father. A walker rested by his side.

After the procession of well wishers had paraded through the tent, Bobby's brother politely ushered his sister-in-law to the shade of a magnolia tree where they could talk privately.

"Sorry I couldn't get here any earlier so we could talk before the services. Dad wasn't sure he could make the trip, and I had to rent a van so he'd have enough room. He's not in very good health and this thing with Bobby has, well, I don't know if he'll get past it. Myrtle, what the hell happened with Bobby? Last Easter, when I was down here, he was so upbeat, so happy. What caused this change in him? He wasn't the type to do something like this."

This was not an easy conversation for Dean Bitterman. While he and Bobby had tried to stay close, Myrtle had shunned Dean after he'd been convicted of involuntary manslaughter and sentenced to five years in the Georgia state prison for killing a man in a bar fight. He was twenty-three years old at the time, and life had been difficult for him ever since his release ten years earlier.

In her normally curt manner, Myrtle replied, "I was surprised you even came at all. You've never been the reliable type, Dean. But since you ask, I'll tell you what happened to your dear brother. Whoring, drinking, and carousing with that no good judge over in Chatom. The times he went over to that lodge and the shenanigans that went on. It is the black hole of sin and Bobby became a sinner. His conscience finally couldn't take it anymore. You haven't been around to watch him change, but ever since he hooked up with that judge, he became a different man. Lord only knows how many times I've told him…"

The diatribe went on for over five minutes. Dean listened politely, hoping something she might say would provide the answers he, and, more particularly, his father needed.

When she finally paused to take a breath, he tried to summarize the important points she had made—a difficult task with so much chaff to weed out.

"So you think he somehow got involved with this judge, eh, Pendleton, and this man was putting him under pressure to do something he didn't want to do. Do you know what it was? And you said this judge has been arrested by the FBI and was charged with murder and something to do with the plant fire at Bobby's plant?"

"Yes, that was certainly going on, and I think the FBI must've been talking to Bobby, too. They came to see me after he blew his brains out," she said with no apparent feelings of remorse.

Dean closed his eyes and shuddered. *I'd have killed myself years ago if I had to live with this bitch,* he thought.

"Well, I appreciate the information. Dad and I won't be coming over to the house. I think we'll drive on back to Atlanta. Tell the children we'll be praying for them." *If anyone ever needed praying for, it's those kids. Bobby, why didn't you think of them?*

The priest performed the ritualistic Catholic service in Spanish as requested by Roberto's mother. Mary Susan sat beside the oldest son and was eyed suspiciously by the aging matron of the family. After all, she was barely half his age and Mother Santos was almost sure Roberto's first wife had worn the same navy dress to the funerals of Tomas and Miguel Angel; although, she admitted to herself, *Not nearly so well.*

The large cathedral had been filled to capacity, partly out of respect for the family's patriarch, but largely because Julio had been a popular young man in the neighborhood. Roberto had been particularly aware of the four Caucasians in dark suits and sunglasses who were not members of the large Cuban community represented at the service. He was certain they were agents and he expected to meet one or more of them soon. But such concerns were of minimal consequence. His mind was far more consumed with a judge in Chatom, Alabama.

The memorial service for Lester was sparsely attended. There were so many that day and his parents had purposely set the time to coincide with the services for the sheriff and his wife. The Holmboes were simple, quiet people and were only concerned with the proper burial of their son, notwithstanding the fact that only part of his anatomy had been found. His gruesome death and the rash of circumstances centering in their part of the county had caused them to commit to radical changes in life. Perhaps the most practical and enlightened of all the people grieving in Alabama that day, they had listed their home with a local realtor and planned to leave this God-forsaken part of the state, never to return, as soon as their personal affairs could be cleaned up.

CHAPTER 65

THE MEETINGS

After leaving the services, I drove to the office. I had placed Kenny temporarily in charge of my business interests in Alabama the day after Johnson Calhoun had filed the lawsuits against Leander and Vivian. Both Lawton and Fred were less than enthusiastic about Kenny's elevated status, but I decided I had no choice, short of moving to Mobile—a thought too nauseating to consider. While searching for an empty space for my rental, I noticed a van parked in front of the office door. It bore Georgia plates and an Enterprise sticker on the rear window.

Entering, I acknowledged Virginia Turner, the temp we had made a permanent employee on Kenny's recommendation. Two men, both unfamiliar to me, were sitting in the waiting room. There was a walker beside the frail, older gentleman. After picking up my telephone messages, I looked at them and smiled.

"Mr. Mitchell, these two gentlemen are waiting to see you."

Before Virginia could continue, the younger one, a nice-looking man in his early forties, I judged, stood and approached me.

"Mr. Mitchell, I'm Dean Bitterman," he announced, extending his hand. He was dressed in a cheap black suit, a wrinkled white shirt, and a clip-on tie. His callused hands and weathered skin suggested he spent most of his time in overalls and work boots. Turning his body to the older man, he continued the introductions. "This is my father, Tom Bitterman." The elderly gentleman nodded his head in my direction.

"Nice to meet you. Would you be related to the plant manager at General Paper?" I guessed, not knowing what else to say. I was less than comfortable with this unexpected visit.

"Yes, sir," Dean answered solemnly. "I'm his younger brother and Dad's his, eh, well, his dad."

"What can I do for you? I'm sorry for your loss," I offered; although, I hadn't yet decided what the world had lost when Bobby Bitterman killed himself.

"Thanks. Could I have just a few minutes of your time?" asked the stranger. "It shouldn't take long and could be important to us."

"Sure," I answered. "Come on into our conference room."

"Dad'll just wait out here, if that's all right?"

I looked at the older man and nodded. "Would you care for something to drink, Mr. Bitterman?"

He simply waved his palm.

"Virginia, you keep Mr. Bitterman company, and if he needs anything—" I didn't finish.

"What can I do for you…Dean, was it?"

"Yes, sir," he acknowledged. "Dad and I came down here for the funeral. We live outside Atlanta. Dad's in pretty bad health and we left right after the burial service. We're the only family Bobby had on our side, and, well, we don't get along too good with his wife and her family."

"Sorry to hear that. Family can be pretty important at times like these."

"I know, but if you knew Myrtle, that's Bobby's wife, you'd understand."

I nodded; although, I couldn't imagine what any of this had to do with me.

"But you're not interested in all that. What I wanted to ask you about is a judge up north of here named Raleigh Pendleton."

The question caught me off-guard. "I, eh, met Judge Pendleton a few years back. Why do you ask?"

"I've been trying to figure out why my brother killed himself. Did you ever meet Bobby?"

I shook my head.

"I talked to Myrtle, and she's convinced the judge was somehow responsible for his, I don't know what to call it, his change in personality. Bobby was always a rock. I was always the fuck-up in our family, pardon my language, but my brother wouldn't have ever killed himself without something being terrible wrong, and maybe he didn't kill himself at all. Maybe he had some help. I got a list of names I've made, talking to different people, and your name was mentioned as being involved with a man named Rutherford and a Billy Cudjoe."

I cringed at the thought of my name being tied to Leander and Billy, but unfortunately, there was an association I couldn't deny.

"Both of them used to work for me, but they don't any longer." Obviously, there was more I could say, but I had no idea where this man was heading and felt it wise to limit my comments until I knew our destination.

"Well, folks have told me this Rutherford was tied in with the judge somehow, and I thought maybe you were, too." His tone and demeanor were very direct, almost accusatory.

I wanted to stand and end the conversation immediately, but felt in so doing I would validate his conclusion. Instead, I tried to change direction.

"Dean, are you aware that Judge Pendleton, Leander Rutherford and Billy Cudjoe face serious legal problems?"

"Yes, sir, I heard something about that."

"Have you been told that I'll likely be a witness against them in those proceedings?"

"No, sir, I haven't been told that. I guess, then, you aren't close to them?"

"No, Dean, I'm anything but close to them. Are you aware that Billy Cudjoe is the prime suspect in the plant fire?"

"I heard that rumor. Someone said he either lit out or was killed in the explosion, and they haven't found his body or nothing yet."

"Those are both possibilities, but I hope he's still alive."

"Why? If he burned the plant, and killed Bobby's friend, I hope he's dead and burning in Hell."

"I understand your feelings, but he might be the best chance we have of tying Raleigh Pendleton into several matters, including your brother's suicide. Now that you understand my relationship with these men, maybe we should start this conversation over."

Dean sat quietly for a few seconds. "I guess I came in here kinda out of turn. I just assumed that—. Well, I guess I jumped the wrong way. Sorry, I didn't mean to be—"

"No need to apologize, Dean. I've not personally experienced what you and your father are going through, but I'm close to some people who are trying to deal with a similar situation. I can imagine how tough it is. Your dad doesn't look well. How's he dealing with this?"

I could almost feel the stinging in the man's eyes as he blinked several times, looking at the floor.

"Dad may not make it through this, Mr. Mitchell. His health was failing before, but now, I don't know." He rubbed his eyes with his thumb and fingers. A single tear escaped his attempt to conceal them.

I sat quietly for a few seconds, allowing this obviously proud man the opportunity to regain himself.

"Dean, my name is Jack. I'd be more comfortable if you'd call me that. What are you trying to do?"

"I'm not sure. I guess I'm trying to find someone to blame for Bobby." His voice cracked.

"What else have you found out?"

He took a deep breath. "His wife thinks this lodge he used to go to sometimes was, I don't know, she thinks it somehow had something to do with the change in Bobby. But she's a crazy old bitch, and I don't know how much her opinion matters."

"Lodge? What lodge?"

"There's this place out in the woods, on some land up by the river, owned by this Judge Pendleton. I hadn't ever heard about it until Myrtle mentioned it. I asked a couple of old friends of mine about it after the funeral and one of them went up there once. He said it's a place where this judge has political meetings, stag parties, and things like that. I was told it used to be where the Klan met."

"The Ku Klux Klan?"

"Yeah. They used to be pretty active up in Washington County in the old days. Someone said the Pendletons were the big shits in the Klan up there."

"Really. Do you know where the place is?"

"Generally. It's pretty hard to get to, I was told. There's several locked gates, only one road, and, like I said, it borders the river. I guess Myrtle caught Bobby carousing with some whores up there."

"Caught him? How'd she find it? Did she get in?"

"I don't think she actually caught him. I talked to him one time awhile back, and he said Myrtle had left him over him having some perfume or something on his clothes. He said he'd been out with some boys one night, and there were some women around, but he didn't do anything. I told him to say he did and maybe that old war-horse would divorce him. That would've been the best thing ever happened to Bobby."

"If you find out the judge was in some way involved in your brother's...eh...death, what do you intend to do?"

"Kill him."

After sending the two gentlemen from Georgia on their way, I spent an hour with Kenny getting caught up on the company's activities. As had been the case since purchasing Jefferson Construction and carving out Delta Disposal as a separate company, the construction activities were losing money and the environmental business was doing well. After assessing the assets held by Jefferson, I instructed Kenny to start talking to used equipment dealers and determining how much additional time and work would be required to close out the remaining construction jobs. I was finally on my way to withdrawing from construction, a long overdue objective frustrated by Leander for over two years.

The only other relevant topic Kenny and I discussed was a city councilman in a neighboring town, where one of our landfills was located, attempting to shake us down for a thousand dollars to "expedite and insure" the approval of a required city permit we renewed annually. As was normally the case, he had asked for the money in a paper bag. I made a note of the man's name and decided I would simply turn it over to Fred at my meeting later that day.

As I drove to Fred's office, I recounted the number of times such bribes had been solicited during the time I'd done business in Alabama. I concluded there had been over seven such attempts, not counting the ones I had not heard about and Leander had likely paid.

I arrived at Fred's office at 4:00 and waited in the reception area for several minutes. During that time, I checked in at home and received the typical admonishments from my ex-wife on subjects ranging from Mikey's dental care to the freshness of the lettuce in the refrigerator. I simply listened and patronized her. My only real interest was confirming that everyone was safe and there'd been no unusual occurrences.

"Sorry to keep you, Jack," Fred offered as he rushed through the outer entrance, picking up his telephone slips. "Had an interview with Myrtle Bitterman, Bobby Bitterman's widow. Man, she's a talker."

"So I've heard," I responded, following Fred down the hallway to his office. I thought it coincidental that both of us had visited with Bittermans that day.

After removing our suit jackets, we settled in Fred's office while he scanned his messages. As if an afterthought, he announced, "Charlie Schumaker will be joining us any time now. He wants to go over all the charges pending against Pendleton, et al. How are you doing? That service was rough, wasn't it?" Fred seemed to be juggling several different thoughts at one time.

"I can't believe how well Lawton and Barbara are holding up. I don't know what I'd be doing right now if one of mine were missing and assumed dead."

Fred looked up from his desk. "Jack, there's no assuming about it. Didn't Lawton tell you about the photograph?"

"Yeah, but is that proof? I mean absolute proof?"

"We had it analyzed in Washington. The experts think it's conclusive. Speaking of photographs, look at this one," he directed, handing me a candid pose of a rather imposing Caucasian in a cowboy hat and western suit, wearing dark glasses. "Ever seen him before?"

I shook my head. "I don't recognize him. Who is he?"

"Could be the guy who hassled your kids over in Houston. Name's John Docker. He works for Pendleton. His official title is clerk, but he's been known to be more involved in the judge's affairs than his job description suggests. It's just an educated guess at this point, but how would you feel if we had your boys look at it?"

"Sure, why not?" I responded.

"You have a computer at home? A pretty good one?"

"Yeah. Both boys are hooked on the damn thing. I get it upgraded about every six months. Why?"

"We could send the photo via the internet and get an initial response. What's your e-mail address at home?"

I wrote it on the back of one of my cards.

"I'll get it on the way. Why don't you call home and put them on alert?"

I nodded, not looking forward to talking to Myrtle Bitterman's clone again. Fortunately, Mikey answered the phone and I told him to be on the lookout for the photograph. Not knowing how he would react to the process, I was amused when he responded, "Cool!"

While waiting for Lawton's boss to join us and for Mikey's email response, I asked Fred a question. "You know about some place the judge owns up in the woods called the lodge?"

Before he could answer, a familiar voice offered from the doorway, "I know a little about it. Why?"

We both looked up in surprise.

"Lawton, what are you doing here?" Fred asked. "You should be at home with Barbara and—"

Lawton interrupted. "Barbara has more company right now than she needs, and I got tired of entertaining. I remembered you boys were meeting, so I slipped out. Barbara encouraged it. Now, why are you asking about the lodge, Jack?"

I detailed my meeting with Dean Bitterman.

"Sounds like I need to have one of my boys visit with him," Fred announced. "All we need is an amateur running around asking questions, getting the folks nervous. With what's gone on up to now, he'll either get himself killed, or run all the rats back into the gutter. He needs to get on back to Georgia and let the system work. Now, what about this lodge, Lawton? I've never heard about it either."

"It used to be called the Brotherhood Lodge. An old sharecropper who worked for the Pendleton family built it. Word was that it used to be the main meeting place for the Klan around here." Lawton explained.

"Why are we just now discussing this?" Fred asked. "It could be something we should investigate."

Before anyone could respond, Charles Schumaker entered the room. "Lawton, why aren't you at home with your family?"

Lawton provided the same explanation as before.

"Okay, but you, in particular, aren't going to like what I've got to tell everyone. I just finished meeting with Judge Black and Felton Abercrombie in the judge's chambers. We're not going to get a grand jury investigation for any of the charges. Mr. Abercrombie filed motions to dismiss and the judge went along, and I didn't object. We'll have to start all over after what's happened over the last few days. I want these guys, but I want a slam-dunk when we refile. The judge commented that he felt there was sufficient evidence to charge Rutherford with embezzlement, but that would have to be filed in Mobile County since it's a state issue. Naturally, we'll turn our information over to the district attorney and I suspect he'll prosecute. I wouldn't be a bit surprised if Mr. Abercrombie isn't holding a press conference as we speak."

The room became very quiet.

Roberto replaced the receiver in the cradle. He stared numbly at the television and the image of an almond-complected man, sitting behind the news desk at one of the local Hispanic television stations. While the reporter's lips were moving, the room was silent. Roberto had muted the TV when Shooter had called five minutes earlier.

Several minutes passed as Roberto sat quietly, unaware of anything but the frustrating information he had received from his Mobile customer. His muscles tensed as soft fingers touched the back of his neck. He then relaxed as Mary Susan began gently massaging tight muscles.

"I must go back to Mobile," he announced.

"Why? What's happened?" she asked.

"The pig has beaten the rap. They're not going to charge him. Shooter just got a call from the lawyer Calhoun. Where is Manuel?"

"He went to pick up some fresh fruit at the store. I'm making dinner, and I wanted to make you a fruit salad."

"I'd rather have a steak sandwich and some fries."

"You eat too much fried food. You need something healthier. I've made some fresh tortillas and salsa, and we have goat cheese."

"You made tortillas?"

"Your mother helped me. She's very nice."

"I think she likes you," he responded, turning and kissing her softly on the lips. "Why don't you go buy some new clothes? You don't have to wear the bitch's hand-me-downs."

"A waste of money. There are dozens of perfectly good dresses, pantsuits, sweaters—everything anyone would ever want. A lot of them still have price tags. She had a lot of clothes. Why didn't she take them?"

Roberto laughed. "I think she was afraid I would kill her if I ever saw her again. The truth is, I would have given her everything she wanted and a fist full of money just to get her out of this house. She was a witch."

They both looked up as the front door slammed.

"I got it, Mary. I got everything on the list," declared Manuel.

"In here, Manny," shouted Roberto. "We have more work to do."

CHAPTER 66
UP JUMPED THE DEVIL

Raleigh had spent the last four days dealing with a crowded docket placed on hold for the week he'd taken off to enjoy his victory in the judge's chambers. His closer friends had wanted to throw the party the day after Felton Abercrombie's press conference, but Raleigh had insisted on waiting a few days to let things get back to normal. There was still the need to polish the story he and Lawrence Rifle would embrace relative to the botched money transfer, Leander was still a potential threat, and then, there was Billy Cudjoe.

The offer of a quarter-of-a-million dollars waiting for Leander, after an abbreviated stay in the state prison, and the promise of the party leadership position in Mobile had sealed the old fool's lips. Rifle and Raleigh needed one another, and although the ex-candidate held the judge responsible for ruining his political career, Rifle agreed to hold firm to the investment story the judge had conjured up. Except for the mystery of Billy, and the judge's yet-to-be defined role in the lieutenant governor's race for the governor's mansion, Raleigh was content and at peace with life.

He and Johnny arrived at the Chatom Community Center at 5:30. The judge exited the front seat, retrieving the finished oak walking stick he only used at campaign rallies and for other special occasions. More than fifty cars, pickups, and county vehicles were already assembled in the asphalt parking lot. A twenty-foot red-white-and-blue campaign banner was draped over the door, while helium-filled balloons bobbed from any location a string could be attached. A sign painted in block letters was stapled to the overhead doorframe. It read WELCOME HOME JUDGE—FREE AT LAST.

Donald Crawford, Virgil's oldest son, was the first to greet Raleigh as he entered the small building. Donald placed a large tumbler of Jack Daniel's in his new mentor's hand and then hugged him, slapping him repeatedly on the back. Raleigh had orchestrated Donald's appointment to serve out the remainder of his dead father's term.

The din of the other attendees momentarily subsided and someone in the crowd shouted, "Let's hear it for the judge. Hip, hip, hooray! Hip, hip, hooray!" The throng joined in for several salutations and then the piano started playing, "For he's a jolly good fellow, for he's a jolly good fellow," and the group joined in, singing the chorus several times.

Raleigh made his way toward a small podium, shaking hands with everyone in his path. When he reached the stage, he turned to the crowd, lifted his tumbler, and slugged down the last third of the drink the acting sheriff had provided. A cheer went up and fists filled with beer bottles and plastic cups were lifted into the air. He motioned Johnny over to him.

"Johnny, why don't you fill this back up and I'll say a few words to these nice people. Make one for yourself. This here's a night for celebration."

Johnny nodded and retrieved a bottle and a plastic cup from the makeshift bar erected in the far corner of the room. Spirits were normally forbidden inside the community center, but this was a special occasion. Everyone in authority was in attendance and sharing in the celebration.

As the uproar subsided, Raleigh took a sip from his revitalized container, adjusted the unnecessary microphone, and began to speak.

"Friends and neighbors of Washington County, I want to thank each and every one of you for being here this evening to celebrate the honesty and fairness of a judicial system that works. Our legal system has its flaws, however. Me and my fellow innocent co-defendants was falsely accused, humiliated in front of our families and friends, and caused to be subjected to the racial bias of a federal system that resents and doesn't understand the people of the South."

People clapped politely while Raleigh again sipped from his glass.

"We're an honest, God-fearing society down here, and just because our customs and values are different from the Yankees that has controlled the government since Jefferson Davis' time, they still take any opportunity to try and stomp out the last strongholds of the Southern way. But our founding fathers created a constitution that protects our citizens, and praise God Almighty, I stood up to their tyranny, and stand here tonight a free man."

A few more rounds of "Hip, hip, hooray" broke out. The judge raised his palms and the chanting began to settle.

"Now, I've taken up enough of your time. We're all here to have some fun, and not spend all night listening to a broke-down old judge. It would only be appropriate, however, to recognize the loss of some of our most loyal and bravest neighbors. Let's all bow our heads for a moment of silence for Sheriff Virgil Crawford, his wonderful wife, Mary Belle, and that brave young man that saved my life, Under Sheriff Lester Holmboe."

For a few seconds, the room was quiet. After what he thought was a proper period of time, Raleigh broke the silence.

"Now, I want to thank all of you for your prayers through my time of tribulation and for you standing behind me when things looked so dark. God bless all of you, and God bless Dixie!"

The chords of the old Wurlitzer upright were struck again, and a familiar tune began to fill the community center as everyone sang, "Oh, I wish I was in the land of cotton, old times there are not forgotten, look away, look away, look away, Dixie land."

As the judge exited the stage, shaking hands and cajoling at anything spoken to him, a young boy in a dirty tee shirt and jeans tugged on Johnny's sleeve. The large man looked down menacingly. The youngster handed him a plain, sealed envelope and scampered out the door. Johnny eyed the envelope, which had Raleigh's name typed in bold letters on the front. In the corner, it read "URGENT."

The hum of the powerful engine was faint inside the plush interior of the luxury automobile. Johnny blinked repeatedly, attempting to ward off the effects of too much liquor. Raleigh made no such effort. He squeezed a fifth of Jack Daniel's between his thighs, occasionally taking a sip and mentally reliving his victory in the federal courthouse and the revelry of the party.

"Judge, you haven't told me why we're driving out here. Have anything to do with the envelope I gave you?" Johnny asked before exiting the vehicle and unlocking the first of the three gates.

"Yeah, there was a note. He wants money and says he'll go away," the judge replied loud enough for his driver to hear from outside the car. "Leave the gates unlocked so he can get in."

Johnny did as instructed and returned to the car.

"Billy Cudjoe's finally showed up. I guess he survived the fire. Don't see no reason why I can't read this to you. You're up to your ass in most everything anyway. Me and you have to stick together, Johnny."

Raleigh pulled his reading glasses from his lapel pocket and switched on the courtesy light. He squinted at the plain piece of typing paper containing pasted words cut out of magazines. He chuckled to himself. *It has to be Cudjoe all right. No one else'd be simple enough to waste time cutting out all these pieces. Like I'd ever show this to anyone.*

"Let's see. Johnny, slow down a bit. This old road's rougher'n a cob. I can't keep my eyes focused for all this jostling about."

Johnny complied.

"Okay, here goes."

Judge,

Glad every thing went good for you. I been laying low, but I got to get out of the country for good. I need money—a lot of it. Meet me at lodge after party. Bring $150,000. I left a letter with a friend. If I don't call by midnight, he'll send it to the cops. Remember, I know where she is and a lot more. No tricks. Be there by 10:00.

B.C.

"We aim to kill him?" Johnny asked flatly.

"Probably, but I need to see if he's bluffing about the letter he's given someone. Could be Leander. He knows everything Billy knows and he needs money real bad. I think I can trick an answer out of that idiot. Yeah, I imagine we'll kill him and then deal with Leander sooner than later."

"What the hell is that?" blurted Johnny as he turned off the ignition and stepped from the vehicle now parked in front of the lodge.

A second door slammed and the robust figure of the judge hobbled to the back of the car. He eyed the distant scene suspiciously.

"Is that a motor running down there at the barn?" Raleigh's thick tongue garbled some of the words.

"I think so. I think I can see someone standing down by the back of the old barn. You figure Billy beat us here? How'd he get through the gates?" Johnny wondered aloud. "Where's his truck?"

"Who's down there?" Raleigh yelled, his voice echoing through the pines. Even in his stupor, he could make out a silhouette walking slowly in front of an unknown source of light. Drunken eyes blinked, as the saw motor revved. "Johnny, let's get down there and get this ova with. Get that suitcase out of the trunk."

They began to stagger in the direction of the light and running motor, moving with all the speed their impaired condition would allow. Johnny stumbled when his foot failed to negotiate an exposed root. He got up and hurriedly caught up with his boss, who hadn't noticed his clerk's tumble. Their pace slowed as they moved into the dull circle of light created by a butane lantern. Instinctively, they huddled closer together and began to creep as if they were stalking an animal.

The report of the revolver was deafening as dirt kicked up between Raleigh's left foot and Johnny's right.

"Shit!" screamed Johnny, as he jumped away from the flying dust, gravel, and pine straw. The suitcase fell to the ground. "What the hell was that for?"

Both men froze. A dark stain began to radiate downward from Raleigh's crotch.

"Gentlemen, I've been waiting for this moment," a calm voice announced.

He stepped from the shadows of the barn into the dull glow of the lantern. A bandana masked his face from the bridge of his nose to the top button of tan coveralls. A blue cap covered his head. His extended right hand held a thirty-eight, its barrel still smoking from the discharged round.

"Now, Billy, we don't want no trouble here tonight!" uttered Raleigh, his hands rising slowly without a command to do so. "We ain't up to nothing what would hurt you. I brought the money, just like you said."

"I see you've brought a suitcase. Where's the note I sent?"

Reaching into his breast pocket, Raleigh's trembling hand produced the letter.

"Throw it over by the suitcase—envelope, too."

Raleigh hesitated and then complied.

"Now, I want to visit with you gentlemen for a minute. To insure there's no need for the gun, I want both of you to sit on the ground," he ordered, his voice muffled by the bandana.

"You ain't Billy Cudjoe," Raleigh offered, his mind becoming more lucid. He glanced toward Johnny who was slowly distancing himself from the light.

The second bullet tore into a dust-covered cowboy boot. Johnny screamed.

"I said sit down," the stranger commanded, his voice still even, unemotional. He walked slowly toward Raleigh, pointing the barrel of the revolver at the judge's nose. "Don't make me use this again."

Raleigh could smell the freshly spent powder. His eyes became wild, staring into the dark barrel of the weapon. His bad knee collapsed and his

312

body fell heavily to the ground near where Johnny was rolling in the dirt, unsuccessfully attempting to remove the smoking boot from his foot. He was alternately crying and cursing.

The masked man threw two pieces of heavy twine into Raleigh's lap and instructed him to tie Johnny's feet together. Remembering the consequence of hesitation, Raleigh roughly grabbed his clerk's injured foot. Johnny screamed and reflexively kicked with the other leg, striking Raleigh squarely in the mouth. The judge fell backward, blood covering his gums and teeth.

With Raleigh preoccupied with his own injuries, the intruder turned his attention to Johnny. A swift kick to the side of the clerk's head dazed him. Placing the revolver in his coverall pocket, the stranger tied the larger man's hands behind his back. He made a slipknot with a piece of the twine, cautiously flipped the loop over the injured foot, and secured the other in much the way a calf's legs are wrapped by a team-roper.

By the time Johnny had regained consciousness, Raleigh had been forced to tie his own feet together, roll onto his stomach, and lie motionless while his hands were bound firmly behind him.

The masked man walked back and forth in front of the two injured men for several seconds without saying a word. Terrified eyes were glued to their tormentor.

"I have only three questions for you, Judge, and if you answer honestly, and I believe you, we can call it a night and go home. If you lie to me, however, the end of this evening will be most unpleasant, I assure you."

"Wh…What do you want?" Pendleton stuttered.

"What did you do with the girl's body?"

"What girl?" the judge replied.

Boom! Another round kicked up dust not six inches from Raleigh's leg.

"Don't trifle with me."

Raleigh looked toward the ground, his mind searching for an answer that would satisfy.

"Leander and Billy took the body away. I'm not sure where they put it."

Their inquisitor paused for a few seconds, waving the revolver from one of the restrained men to the other. "We'll come back to that one in a minute."

"Were you blackmailing Bobby Bitterman? Is that why he killed himself? Did he have anything to do with Jane's death?"

"Whose death?" Raleigh asked, honestly confused.

For the first time, the masked man showed the emotion swelling inside him.

"You killed her and didn't even know her name?" he roared, slapping Raleigh with the gun barrel.

"Shit!" Raleigh screeched. "Johnny was the one who killed her, but he told me Bobby did it. I was just trying to raise some money for the election. Nobody was supposed to get hurt. Cudjoe blew up the plant, but we told him not to." Pain and fear were in control of the judge's rambling. The desire for self-preservation drove him to confess more than he had planned.

"Did Jim Bob Davis take her that night?"

"Yeah. It was all his idea. He asked me to have a party here at the lodge, and he showed up with this negra girl. I didn't have no part in it. I didn't even know she was here until they killed her and told me about it. I was a victim, just like that poor girl." Raleigh pleaded.

"Too many contradictions, Judge. One final question, and be careful with your answer. Did you kill Julio Santos for the money?"

"Lester did it. It was in the paper." The judge was crying.

"But you set it up, didn't you? That's where you got the money for Rifle, wasn't it?" He leaned forward, his eyes glaring into Raleigh's blood and sweat covered face. "Don't lie about this, Judge. You're perilously close to making me angry."

Defeated, but hopeful an honest answer might save him, he answered, "Yeah, I set it up, but it was drug money, dirty money earned by corrupting our children."

The stranger nodded and stepped toward Johnny, now lying on his side and sobbing.

"Well, Johnny, it seems the judge sold you out. So you killed her?"

Johnny didn't respond.

Grabbing the bindings securing his legs, Johnny was dragged face down across the dirt to the carrier that once fed raw logs into the band saw. The stranger gripped the block and tackle hovering above the apparatus, and attached Johnny's belt to the hook at the end of the chain. He began the slow task of lifting a squirming body above the conveyor. The weight of Johnny's torso was disproportionately balanced. His head hung lower than his feet.

"Johnny, was it like the judge said? Did you kill her? Was it yours and Jim Bob's idea?"

Johnny desperately twisted and squirmed, his eyes glaring at the band saw.

"No, it was all the judge's idea. He was trying to get money from Bobby for the campaign. Bobby wasn't playing ball, so the judge and Jim Bob set up the girl. Me and Jim Bob only did like we was told. I swear I'm telling the truth!"

"You know what, Johnny, I believe you are."

Reversing the direction of the chain, he began to lower the dangling body to the conveyor.

"What you doing, you crazy son of a bitch?" screamed Johnny. "Who the hell are you?"

Turning like a recoiling spring, he placed his nose six inches from Johnny's contorted face. His eyes burned with the intensity of a welding rod touching steel. Removing the bandana, he exclaimed with far greater passion than he'd portrayed during the preceding twenty minutes, "Look at my face, you pervert! It's the last face you'll ever see. It's the face of death! It is the face of retribution!"

Johnny's eyes bulged.

The bandana was forced into the clerk's mouth. Johnny jerked and twisted with even greater effort than before. His back arched and his nostrils flared as he struggled for air.

With Johnny writhing helplessly above the conveyor, the man turned. Looking Raleigh in the eyes, he proclaimed almost indifferently, "You boys will never kill anyone again and while you watch this, I want you to think hard about where the body is hidden. It's your only hope."

Raleigh began speaking gibberish and rolling in the dirt as his fate became apparent. His panic intensified as he heard the drive motor rev higher and higher until the band was moving at maximum speed. His eyes bulged as he watched his clerk's feet severed at the arches. The struggling body was then dropped onto the carrier and pushed slowly, while the rotating band moved with only intermittent hesitation up one leg, through the pelvic bone and sternum, stopping just below the chin. As life drained from Johnny's body, the clutch was disengaged.

"There are many ways justice can be served, Judge. Now, where's the body?"

There was no answer. The judge lay face down in the dirt and pine needles, the foul smell of human waste rising from his body. Reaching down, he touched Raleigh's neck, searching for the pulse of a beating heart. He could feel nothing. He rolled him over and looked into a face claimed by fear, more fear than his aging heart could withstand. Raleigh Pendleton was dead.

"I want to know where her body is, you son of a bitch!"

He squatted beside the old demon and sighed. He studied the judge's face and considered the possibilities. Disappointed, but relieved it was over—justice had finally been served—he considered how this unexpected change of circumstance might appear to investigating officers.

He removed the revolver from his pocket, placed the handle in the judge's hand, and, applying pressure to a lifeless forefinger, fired one shot harmlessly into the air. Cutting the bindings and placing them in his coveralls, he dragged Raleigh's body to the carrier, allowing it to slump over the conveyer. Retrieving the suitcase and most of the items he'd brought with him, he walked into the darkness.

CHAPTER 67
WHO DONE IT?

It has been two months since Raleigh Pendleton and Johnny Docker's bodies were discovered. Due to the remoteness of the lodge and the relatively few remaining who knew of its existence, it took over four days for someone to consider it as a place to look for the missing men. Not that the scene required the effects of a thunderstorm and the scavenging of wildlife to be horrific, these elements only amplified the shock experienced by the two Washington County deputies who had been dispatched for a cursory look around the premises. From a criminologist's point of view, the effects of time had significantly limited the reliability of the physical evidence present at the crime scene, although no one in my circle seemed to care much.

We had agreed to meet for a drink in the bar of the River View Hotel—the place where we had launched this odyssey only months earlier.

"So you got your deal closed?" Lawton inquired as I joined him at the table. He already had a gin and tonic in front of him.

"It's a done deal. The money was wired to my bank account in Houston about an hour ago. You're now speaking to someone who no longer does business in this great state of yours."

He laughed. "It ain't my state, Bubba, as the local folk might put it. Barbara and I listed the house yesterday. I've been transferred back to Washington."

"That sounds like good news to me. Is it?" I asked, turning my attention to the waitress who had just approached. "Dewar's and water, please."

"Yeah, I think it is," he sighed. "Alabama's been home to me most of my life, but I think it'll be good for Barbara to get away from here—away from the little things that are a constant reminder."

"How's she doing? And how about you?" I asked while acknowledging the waitress as she placed my drink on a cocktail napkin.

"She has her good days and her bad days. The good ones are getting better and more often, and Sally keeps her busy. Imagine trying to catch up on half a lifetime. She asks a hundred questions a day. As for me, I only wish we could find her body. They did find the clothes she was wearing the night she disappeared. They were stuck behind a crate in that old barn. At least we have that. They've dug up most of the area around the lodge, but they haven't found anything."

He was rambling, absently repeating information he knew I already possessed. I just sat, listened, and felt his pain.

"I've taken a rather spiritualistic position on her leaving us at such an early age. I think God has a purpose for all of us, but we don't have a clue what it is. I guess when our mission's over, it's time to go home. I suppose Janie completed hers and she's in a better place. I just have to be grateful for the time I got to spend with her."

"That's pretty much what I believe, too," I responded. "How about a toast to Miss Janie Tremont?"

We clinked our glasses, took a sip, and sat quietly for a few seconds.

His tone changed when he added, "Maybe her purpose on earth was to expose Raleigh Pendleton for what he was, and create the opportunity for Satan to recall his damned soul!"

I didn't respond directly to this flash of emotion.

"Speaking of the judge, any news about the Pendleton and Docker situation?"

"Nothing of importance. Fact is, I don't think anyone's spending much time on it. It'll be a cold case in another few months, if it isn't already. I just wish they'd find Cudjoe, but I don't think anyone really cares but me."

"What do you mean by that?"

"As I said before, her body could provide the closure our family needs. Rutherford knows where she is but he won't talk. It would implicate him in her murder. As it is, he's facing five to ten on your embezzlement charges, and he'll probably be out in a year or two. The system isn't perfect."

"Like I told you the first time we met on the airplane, I've never had reason to trust the system and, with everything that's happened over here, my feelings haven't changed much."

"I hear you, brother," he lamented.

"Let's have another toast. This one's to whoever by-passed the system and provided final justice for Raleigh Pendleton." I watched Lawton's body language, something we had discussed the first time we met. His reaction was transparent, almost practiced.

"Sure, why not?"

"Let's put a name on that toast. To Mr. Santos, Dean Bitterman, Findley Ross and the boys, Lawrence Rifle, Billy Cudjoe, or," I paused for effect, "Lawton Tremont."

"Hear, hear," he responded, raising his glass without a blink.

"Lawton, did you do it?"

He looked at me for several seconds, the strain of the past few months showing in his face.

"You know, that's the third time I've been asked that. First Barbara, then Fred, and now, you. You'd probably like to hear me admit it, and in certain respects, I wish I could. Lord knows, I thought about it a lot—even schemed up a plan in my mind. But the truth is, I didn't. I confess, if someone hadn't killed them, sooner or later, I would have. I don't think I could ever rest until Raleigh Pendleton paid for what he did to my little girl, as well as to his other victims. It's fortunate for my family that someone else took care of it, because I would have turned myself in, and Barbara would have had to live out her days alone. No, Jack, it wasn't me, but I'm grateful to whomever it was."

I got on the plane that evening, content in the knowledge I would never have to make the trip again, except to testify against Leander. I had sold my Alabama properties to one of my competitors for two million dollars, or about half their economic value. While I could have held out a little longer and made a better return, I was just happy to be free of a system I despised with all my heart. I also felt satisfied in the belief that Lawton and Barbara would have a happier life someplace else, although they would never be free from a calling to return. While Janie's body wasn't in the wooden box we buried that day, the memory of her was. For the rest of their lives, they would feel drawn back to that headstone and forced relive those horrendous months over and over again.

As the plane lifted off, I closed my eyes, remembering my conversation with Lawton and his reaction to my not so subtle accusation. We both knew Fred Carleton and Charlie Schumaker considered Lawton the most motivated to see Raleigh and Johnny dead. Had the evidence conclusively pointed to him, they would have wanted to look the other way, but they, like Lawton, believe in the system and would have pursued justice, although not with the vigor typically employed. Fortunately for everyone, the evidence pointed everywhere and nowhere.

I feel certain the Santos brothers would have taken advantage of an opportunity to avenge the judge's role in the execution of Julio, but it would have taken time. They were the prime suspects in the murders of Lester, Virgil, and his wife and they were being investigated by both the federal and state drug enforcement agencies. Every move they made was being carefully watched. I'm convinced they are capable of the savage manner in which Johnny had died, and likewise believe they would have employed the same methodology on Raleigh had his heart not done their work for them. Why they wouldn't have completed the butchery in order to dehumanize his body would have been left to speculation.

After my two visits with Dean Bitterman, I was convinced he was very capable of seeking vengeance for his brother's suicide and the resulting death of his father. Dean appeared to me to be a good person, but not the brightest star in the universe. I doubt he would have been able to pull it off, and if he had, he would almost certainly have been caught and lived the balance of his life in prison or died at the hands of the Alabama penal system.

When I considered all the other victims of Raleigh Pendleton, I methodically eliminated each of them for various reasons. Jimbo and Geraldine Davis were better off with Jim Bob resting in the cemetery. Findley Ross and the good ol' boys got what they wanted—the lieutenant governor won the governor's mansion and they were back in power. Lawrence Rifle probably lacked sufficient motive. He was a businessman and would eventually realize his paranoia and greed had ultimately led to his political demise. Leander Rutherford? Well, Leander is Leander. The judge was his only hope of obtaining the one thing in life that mattered to him—a position of importance in the party. That hope died with Raleigh. So whom does that leave?

I have always considered myself a good man, not a perfect man. I've tried to live a moral, principled life, and believe I've been reasonably successful in that endeavor. Likewise, I knew Lawton was just as principled. He had spent most of his adulthood fighting within a system he believed in and wanted desperately to work. The evening Charlie Schumaker announced that Raleigh had won, I saw in Lawton's eyes the defeat and betrayal he felt. I knew it would only be a matter of time before he could no longer contain his need for justice. Vigilantism would win out, and one of the few true believers in the system would be lost forever. Such men have to be saved.

At first, the thought of murdering them was only a fantasy—final justice outside a system that often protects the worst of society's offenders. But the fantasy continued to haunt me. I wrestled with the idea for days before conscience gave way to reality. I have been accused of being deliberate in my thinking—an accusation to which I must plead guilty. As I considered the possibilities of inaction against the judge, every possible scenario was unacceptable to me. Yes, I was the masked stranger, Janie's avenger, the protector of my children, and the savior of Lawton Tremont.

Perhaps you're shocked—the Boy Scout, the straight arrow? No, that couldn't be. But it is.

You might recall, I didn't ask Johnny if he was the man who attacked Michael and Jackson on the schoolyard that morning. I already knew the answer. The boys had identified him from the photograph Fred forwarded via the internet. From the moment his identity had been confirmed, I knew something had to be done. I would give the system its opportunity, and if it failed, as it too often does, I would insure that nothing like that could ever happen again.

The seed had been planted when Dean Bitterman mentioned the lodge, its remoteness, and its legacy of racial hatred. I visited with Dean by telephone a few days after the charges against Raleigh had been dismissed, and he provided more specific information about the lodge and its location. A trip to the Washington county clerk's office supplied a list of all Pendleton land adjoining the Mobile River. Only two parcels met the description and I got lucky on the first try. An inflatable boat and a seldom-used county road on the opposite side of the river allowed access for an exploratory trip to the more likely of the two pieces of property.

Dressed for a day of fishing, I navigated across the river to a spot I judged to be Pendleton land. I pulled the light craft up the bank, hiding it beneath some saplings I cut with the utility knife my father gave me when I was ten. I dodged my way through the dense underbrush for almost an hour until a clearing opened up before me. There it was: the Lodge of the Brotherhood.

I remember standing beneath the canopy of those magnificent pines, imagining the worst of what had likely taken place there for almost a century. Just being there stirred emotions I never knew existed within me. As I walked around the structure, I could feel the presence and passion of racism, and it revolted me. The ghosts of a suppressed people seemed to ooze from the ground. I wanted to run away from that place and forget it existed.

I instinctively began to distance myself from the building. As I backed away, keeping my eyes focused on the structure, I bumped into something hard, something solid. I heard a metallic clink.

Turning, my eyes fixed on the saw and I was immediately transported back to that first day I met Lawton on the airplane and the stories he told me of his youth. I remembered an aging uncle and his nephew cutting raw logs on an old band saw, building a barn in which to cure the green boards. I remembered that Lawton was the one who knew about the lodge that day in Fred's office and wondered, *Is this all just a coincidence?* It was as if someone were whispering to me, and at that moment, I decided this was the place and this derelict device would be the instrument that would bond irony with justice.

The old motor was encrusted beneath flaky layers of ruddy brown—the metallic liver spots of age, weather, and disuse. I retrieved a length of brittle rope from the barn and wrapped it around the starter wheel. I held my breath as I pulled, hoping the internal mechanism had withstood the effects of time with less deterioration. It cranked. It wasn't frozen. Within fifteen minutes I had assessed the parts needed to revive this relic. I was certain I could do it.

My second trip to the lodge, the following day, was less exploratory. Familiarity with the terrain shortened the journey to less than twenty minutes. It took only two hours to bring the saw back to life. The engine sputtered at first, but with a minor carburetor adjustment, began to purr as smoothly as the day some work-hardened lumberman first pulled the starter rope half a century before.

The rest of the task was simple: a coat of grease to the moving parts of the block and tackle and conveyor, and a way to lure Raleigh to this location at the appropriate time. The night of the "freedom celebration" seemed perfect and the bait was self-evident—Raleigh needed to eliminate his most eminent threat, Billy Cudjoe.

As the time of execution grew closer and I waited in the shadows of the old barn, I surveyed my surroundings and considered the morbidity of what I was preparing to do. Twice I considered abandoning my plan and retreating to the boat, but I maintained my focus, not totally sure why. Even as I watched the lights of the vehicle bouncing haphazardly up the road, I emotionally wrestled with myself, uncertain if I could complete this task for which I had diligently prepared.

My resolve was cemented when he first stepped into the glow of the lantern. Before he could see me, I looked into his eyes and remembered him glaring at me in the courtroom the morning of the hearing. I could still feel the icy stare, the danger he represented. For just a moment, before making my presence known, I thought of my children, of Janie Tremont, of Aaron and Lizzie Collins, and the numerous faceless victims of his viciousness.

The rest of the story—you already know.

EPILOGUE

A year has passed since I exited Alabama forever. I no longer obsess on the memories of my time and actions there. I'm no longer in the environmental business, having sold my remaining Texas and Louisiana businesses within six months of divesting Delta Disposal. Retirement has been a welcome respite from the day-to-day grind of business. I still tinker with small engines in my garage, I started coaching Mikey's little league team three months ago, and I have even taken up golf, not sure if it's worth the time and effort.

I go to church most Sundays and continue to ask forgiveness for that night in Alabama when I ended the lives of two immoral souls. I'm not particularly proud of my actions, but, as you might imagine, I've spent hours rationalizing why I did what I did. On those occasions when guilt creeps into my mind, I only have to think of Michael, Katie, Jackson, and the Tremonts, and the guilt melts away for awhile. I know I'll have to answer for my actions when I depart this world, but I continue to pray, and believe my prayers will be answered.

Billy Cudjoe hasn't surfaced yet, and I doubt he ever will. It's my belief his body was atomized in the blast at the plant, but we'll likely never know for sure.

Contrary to Raleigh's promise of a light sentence, Leander's past finally caught up with him. The district judge who heard his case was from a once prominent banking family in Mobile. It seems when Leander's "construction empire" imploded, it left in its wake a banking institution mortally wounded financially. The judge's family had been forced to sell virtually everything they owned to keep the bank afloat, but it ultimately failed anyway.

You might ask, "Wouldn't the judge have a conflict of interest in hearing a case involving a man who'd taken his inheritance from him?" The answer is simple: this is South Alabama.

Leander received the most aggressive sentence the law would allow. With the multiple acts of fraud and embezzlement the state was able to document, he was given six ten-year sentences. Unless he outlives normal mortality rates by a substantial amount, he'll likely die behind the walls of Alabama State Prison, the bitch of someone named Bubba.

I talk with Lawton or Barbara one or two times a month, and they are doing well given the burden of loss they will always carry with them. Sally is making remarkable progress following her awakening. Lawton told me she would obtain her high school diploma in another year and is even talking of going to college.

The kids and I took a trip to Washington during spring break last March and the Tremonts acted as our tour guides. We had a wonderful time. I couldn't help but notice the attention Barbara focused on Katie. It made me both happy and sad at the same time.

I talked with Lawton last week, and he told me he had received an unexpected, yet, appreciated letter from Grambling State University, his alma mater. The letter advised that an anonymous donation in the amount of one hundred and fifty thousand dollars had been made to the university in the name of Jane Tremont. He asked if I knew anything about it. Naturally, I said no, and acted just as surprised as he was.

My most recent correspondence from Lawton came today. It was a plain envelope with no return address. The postmark was from Washington, D.C. It contained only a single sheet of white typing paper. Each word of the brief message had been cut from a magazine and pasted in sequence, similar to the note I sent to Raleigh Pendleton. It read:

Thanks for everything. L.T.

I wonder how long he's known.

Printed in the United States
22757LVS00004B/166

9 781413 735406